HORSE & PONY STORIES

EDITED BY
JANET BARBER

Sundial

contents

THE FORTY
POUND PONY

K. M. Peyton

Ruth cycled slowly up the driveway that led to McNair's. She wished it was longer than it was, for she was dry-mouthed with nervousness. The great moment had arrived, but perversely she felt no joy: she was too frightened. It meant so much, and she knew so little. Reading her old-fashioned horse-books by the light of a torch most of the night before had done nothing to help. Her head reeled with the fatal diseases of the horse, imperceptible to the inexperienced eye; with the vices that meant doom: from bolting to wind-sucking. She had read about dealers who filed their horses' teeth to pass them off as youngsters, and dealers who injected their horses with sedatives when prospective buyers were trying them out. 'No foot, no horse', was an adage to remember, and, from the feet up, the possible blemishes were legion: curbs, splints, spavins, thoroughpins, windgalls and sidebones on the legs alone. Expressive words with ominous meanings floated through her brain: stargazer, daisy-cutter, herring-gutted, Roman-nosed, ewe-necked, cow-hocked . . . She pressed down on the pedals, standing up, as the gravel bogged her tyres. 'I don't know anything,' she thought in a panic.

But now she was in a yard, meticulously tidy, surrounded with loose-boxes, like a photograph captioned 'A desirable layout'. The loose-boxes were new and smart, with concrete forecourts. At one side was a wooden chalet labelled 'Office'; beyond, behind the stableyard, the roof of a large modern house stuck up. Ruth put her bike against the nearest wall, where it looked very untidy, and went to the door marked 'Office'. Before she got there a man came round a corner from the direction of the house, and Ruth stopped short, feeling like a burglar. Mr McNair, she thought. He was what Ted would have called very hacking-jacket. He said, 'Can I help you?'

Ruth took a deep breath. 'I want to buy a pony.' Her voice sounded very peculiar.

McNair looked at her carefully. He was smart, almost dapper, in a tweed jacket and well-pressed trousers. His expression was non-committal, his eyes shrewd. He had grey hair and hard, working hands.

'For yourself?'

'Yes.'

'About thirteen hands? Thirteen-two perhaps. How well do you ride?'

'I can't really.'

He smiled. 'That's honest. Mostly they say, "Oh, I can ride," as if the question is an insult. About ten per cent of them can, after a fashion.'

Ruth felt better. If he appreciated honesty, he must be honest with her, surely?

'What do you want it for?' McNair asked. 'Wembley? Or just to keep the grass down at home?'

'Oh, the grass,' Ruth said hastily. Mr McNair was smiling, but she didn't notice. She was beginning to think that Mr McNair's ponies might cost more than forty pounds. Everything was so new and expensive, from Mr McNair's trousers to the first shining bolt that he was pulling back on loose-box 12. There was no rust at Mr McNair's, no chipped paint, no dirty straw blowing in the evening breeze. Only perfection. Ruth remembered Peter, holding Toadhill Flax on a quivering rein, while he dropped the string. Perfection. 'This isn't my sort of place,' Ruth thought, and in her imagination she saw a stableyard, slightly untidy, with dipping tiled roofs and pigeons, and loose-boxes converted from the old carriage-horse stalls, with cobbles, and cats, and a faithful head looking over the half-door . . . the sort in books. She swallowed desperately.

'Pennyroyal,' Mr McNair said. 'Nice sort. Six years old.'

Pennyroyal was a dark liver chestnut with no white on him, save a small star. He had a kind eye, and he gave a friendly knucker. Ruth, trying to hold back, loved him immediately, and felt doom descending. She just looked, speechless.

Mr McNair smiled again. He ran his hand down the hard muscle of the pony's neck, patted his shoulder, and came out into the yard again.

'I don't tell my customers that my horses are what they're not,' he said. 'I don't tell them they're marvellous. They're not marvellous. I just buy horses I like myself.' He was leading the way to loose-box 7. 'I'm hard to please. I've been buying horses for thirty years now. And for every horse I've bought, I'd say I've looked at twenty.'

None of her horse-books had described to Ruth a dealer like Mr McNair. She was lost, and she knew it. She was far too frightened now to say that she wanted a pony that only cost forty pounds. She looked into loose-box 7, and saw a grey mare, dappled like a Victorian rocking-horse, with black legs and eyes blue-black

like best coal. To Ruth she was perfect, utterly desirable, from the
bold glance of her lovely eyes to the tip of her frosty tail.

'Sixpence,' said Mr McNair.

Ruth, in her nervous state, almost jumped out of her skin.
'*Sixpence?*'

'Her name,' said Mr McNair gently. 'The price is somewhat
more.'

'Oh!' Ruth went scarlet with horror at her idiocy.

'She's Welsh mountain. I've got her papers in the office. A bit
on the small side for you probably. Not now, of course, but in a
year or two she would be. Attractive pony, though.'

'Oh, she's lovely!' Ruth's voice was full of misery.

'Most of the ponies are in the field. I'll get Peter and we'll go
and see them.'

They left Sixpence and walked down the row of loose-boxes to
a gate which led to the house behind and, presumably, the field.
Ruth glimpsed aristocratic heads, honest hunter heads, and the
flashy gold beauty of Toadhill Flax. She paused. Mr McNair said,
'He takes some holding, that one. I wouldn't offer him to a young
girl. I'd lose my reputation.'

They went through the gate, which led down between the new
house and a newly planted orchard, to another gate at the bottom.
As they passed the house, McNair turned his head and bawled,
'Peter!' By the time they got to the bottom Peter McNair was
coming down behind them, a couple of halters in his hand. He
joined them, leaning on the gate, and nodded to Ruth, but said
nothing.

There were about ten ponies in the field, which was large,
stretching away to a line of elms on the top of a rise. Some of them
raised their heads and looked towards the gate; two walked towards
them in a hopeful fashion; one looked, gave a shrill whinny, and
galloped away. Against the ridge of the hill, the gallop looked
splendid, wild and free, and Ruth watched admiringly.

McNair said, 'Damned animal!'

The pony was a bright bay, not bold in the way of Toadhill Flax, but with an airy, fine action. It seemed to float over the grass. Its gallop set off two or three of the others, but none of them was in earnest like the bay. They wheeled round a few times and went back to grazing. The bay stopped when it was on the horizon, and stood with its head up, watching.

'We made a mistake, turning her out in this field,' Mr McNair said to Ruth. 'Woodlark, a Dartmoor, T.B. cross. But wild as they come. There's a lot of work there, to make anything of that one. Peter, fetch Sandalwood first.'

Ruth watched Peter walk away across the field, feeling guilty to be causing all this trouble, when she knew now, with a deep-down, horrid certainty, that none of Mr McNair's ponies cost as little as forty pounds. Half of her longed to enjoy this feast of ponies; the other half trembled with fear at the thought of telling Mr McNair of her paltry savings. Even when buying things like toothpaste, she did not like to cause the assistant any trouble. She always took the first one she saw, even if she did not like the taste, rather than ask the person to go to any trouble looking. And now here she was, having all this time and trouble spent on her by the exalted McNairs, and it would be to no avail. In silence she watched Peter approach a group of three ponies, talking to them quietly. One came up to him, nuzzling his pockets, but he walked on to a bay that was still grazing, and offered it something out of his pocket. It came up and he haltered it, and one of the other ponies came up, pushing in for a titbit. There was a squeal of jealousy and a great show of teeth and laid-back ears, but Peter disentangled his pony with quiet tact and brought it back to the gate. It was a stocky bay gelding with a thick black mane and tail, a homely pony. Ruth could see him nicely in her back garden, a dependable sort who would go calmly past a dustcart and stop when she fell off. He was not as handsome as the others, but she could love him easily. He looked at her with humble, patient eyes.

'A good beginner's sort,' said Mr McNair. 'Nothing spectacular, but foolproof. Eight years old.'

'Oh, he's lovely,' Ruth said despairingly.

'Ginny, I think,' McNair said to Peter. 'Then I think that's the lot, at the moment.'

Peter went away and came back with a dark bay mare with a mealy nose and a lot of wild mane. Ruth leaned on the gate, clenching her sticky hands over the top bar, as if she were being tortured. The two ponies stood, heads up, utterly desirable in every way, and she looked at them as if she knew what she was looking for, feeling only this terrible despair, and not able to utter a word of sense. McNair went on talking, but Ruth did not take in what he said. It was no use. They let the ponies go and walked back up to the yard. McNair said, 'Those are the ones that are suitable, just now. In a week or two I may have something else to offer you. We have new ponies in nearly every week.'

Ruth knew it was her turn to say something. They were back in the tidy yard. Peter stood just behind his father, saying nothing, and there was a pointed silence. Mr McNair looked at Ruth. Gathering up all her courage, and feeling herself going scarlet, she said, 'What—what is the price of—of—' All the ponies' names completely eluded her. The only one she could remember was Toadhill Flax. '—of—them?'

'I could let the bay go for a hundred and twenty. And Ginny, perhaps. The others . . . Pennyroyal, say, a hundred and fifty. He's quite a useful jumper, and is good in gymkhana events. The Welsh mare the same: she's a little winner, and you could get some good foals out of her later.'

Her worst fears confirmed, Ruth felt her scarlet fade, and the cold despair take its place. All her instincts had been right. Not only twice but three times as much as her miserable forty pounds . . .

She said, 'I shall have to ask my father.'

At that moment a large car drove into the yard and Mr McNair said to Peter, 'Here's Matthews,' and to Ruth, 'Excuse me a moment.' He hurried over to the car and Ruth, grateful to Matthews, whoever he was, was left standing with the silent Peter. Her tumbled emotions no longer disturbed her. It was all useless.

She looked down at her feet and mumbled, 'Thank you. I'll go now.'

Politely, still saying nothing, Peter followed her across the yard to where her shabby bicycle was propped against the wall. They passed McNair and his visitor, talking hard on the steps of the office, and McNair called out to Peter as he passed, 'Stay around, Peter. We'll get a saddle on that Woodlark tonight if it's the last thing we do.'

'All right,' Peter said, without any expression.

Ruth picked up her bike. 'Thank you,' she said again, awkwardly. 'Good-bye.'

'I'll come down to the gate. It's supposed to be shut.'

Ruth would rather have shaken off Peter's unforthcoming company, but was obliged to walk on with him down the drive. It then occurred to her that she would never have such an opportunity again to seek advice. At least to Peter she could admit her forty pounds, if not face to face with Mr McNair.

'Doesn't your father ever have anything cheaper?' she asked him. 'I haven't got that much money.'

'Well—no. Not unless it's very small. There's never anything under eighty.'

'I've only got forty,' Ruth muttered.

'Forty?' Peter's voice was doubtful. 'You'd only get a young pony for forty, an unbroken pony. Or some old crock.'

'A young pony? Like Woodlark, you mean?'

'Oh, heavens, you don't want a pony like Woodlark! She's not worth anything at all. You want a quiet one. Mr Marks, at Ramsey Heath, has young ponies quite cheap, sometimes. You ought to go and see him.'

'Mr Marks?' Ruth fastened on the name, with a great uplifting of her spirits. 'You mean he might have one for forty?'

'He might. A two-year-old. He buys them at the sales, for a sort of hobby. If you get one with a quiet temperament, you ought to be able to manage all right. He lives at Bramhall, the farm on the right past the pub.'

In that instant, Ruth's world was transformed. She turned to Peter with an eager, shining face. 'I shall go and see him. Thank you for telling me. Oh, thank you!'

Peter looked quite surprised. He smiled, which made him look much more human. Ruth noticed that he had freckles, and was quite ordinary, on the ground. She pushed her bike through the gate and he shut it behind her.

'Thank you very much!' she said again, fervently. As she pedalled away down the road, she thought, 'He thinks I'm barmy. But I don't care!' And she started to sing, free-wheeling down the hill.

The next evening she pedalled to Bramhall, and found herself jerking down a rutted lane, with high out-of-control hedges on either side and ditches full of stinging-nettles. Bramhall was a collection of ramshackle old buildings, dung-heaps and picking hens, hemmed in with elms full of cawing rooks. It looked to Ruth far more like a forty-pound place than McNair's, and she liked it instinctively. She liked the faded rose-red of the stable bricks and the thatch with grass growing out of it, and the sour smell of an early elderberry. She was full of hope. She left her bicycle by the gate, where it looked quite smart, and went into the yard. A youngish man was just shutting three cows into a cowshed. He turned round and looked at her with a cheerful grin.

'I'm looking for Mr Marks, about buying a pony,' she said.

'I'm Marks,' said the man.

He was not frightening at all, and Ruth was able to say quite easily, 'I want a pony, but I only have forty pounds. Peter McNair said you might have one.'

'Oh, you've been to McNair's, have you? I'll bet Mr McNair didn't offer you one for under a hundred, eh?'

'No, he didn't.'

'Smart place, McNair's.'

'Yes, very.'

'Somebody has to pay for it.'

'Yes.'

Mr Marks led the way down to the ponies' field.

'Let's see what we've got, then, eh? It's for you, is it?'

'Yes.'

'He told you they're only partly broken? You can catch them, and halter them and handle them, but they're only youngsters. Two-year-olds. I got this lot from Beaulieu—the New Forest sales. I got a dozen, last September, but I've sold most of them. There's four left now. They're down in the bottom field. We'll go along. Just a moment.'

He went into a shed and fetched a sieve of oats and a halter, and then led the way down a rutted track between more massive rampant hedges. It was a dull day, and Ruth had a sense of the earth, fed on damp, overwhelming Mr Marks's property with its swaggering growth. The verges were lush with forward grass, the budding branches tossed over their heads with an uncultivated abandon. The gate to the ponies' field was set deep in rampant hawthorn, with gnarled Constable oaks on either side; the field was not very large, and sloped down to a stream and a thick wood full of crows. Ruth was enchanted with the old-fashionedness of it; the lovely scorn of modern clearance, the encouragement of crows and vermin-sheltering hedges. Later, she could see, it would be all knee-high buttercups and cow-parsley, like a Victorian painting. 'There will be a pony here for me,' she thought. 'It is a "me" place. Not like McNair's.' A little shiver of excitement ran through her.

Mr Marks gave a shout and a whistle, and the four ponies converged upon the gate. They were all rough and muddy and, after McNair's, definitely of a half-price breed. Except for one. Ruth's eyes went past the thick-legged grey, the wall-eyed skewbald and the nondescript black, and rested on the pony that held back from the others. 'That is for me,' she thought.

It was, in fact, nothing special in its looks: a gelding of an unusual bay-roan colour, like a bright bay that had been left out in the frost. His legs were black and his head was dark, with a small crescent of white between the eyes; the forelock was black and the mane grew whiter as it went down towards the withers where the frosty mantle seemed to have fallen most thickly. The stocky quarters were almost pure bay, and the thick tail black. 'Circus pony,' Ruth could almost hear Ted say. But the pony had a look, a presence, a way of standing which made the other three ponies look like cab-horses. He did not come up, but stood behind, head up, watching Ruth.

'Oh, I like that one,' Ruth said.

Mr Marks gave a grin and said, 'You watch him.'

He started to give each of the other three ponies a handful of oats out of the sieve, and immediately the little bay roan came up, shouldering the black and the skewbald roughly out of the way. His eyes, large and lively, showed no white, only his ears went back with greed and he plunged eagerly for Mr Marks's hand. The other ponies moved over for him, making jealous faces. Ruth had seen his cocky walk, the firm planting of his round, rather shaggy feet: it was jaunty, sure.

'He's the boss around here,' said Marks, smiling. 'You're our fly boy, eh? Our smart one? That's what we call him, Fly. He's fly all right.'

'Oh.' Ruth was dubious now. What was fly, as an adjective? As a noun, and a name, it was horrid. As a description, it was rather worrying. Did Fly qualify, she wondered, for Peter McNair's stipulation: a quiet temperament?

'Is he—is he all right? I mean, quiet?'

Mr Marks pursed his lips. 'Well now, if you're looking for a real quiet one, I'd take the skewbald. Or the black. You can do anything with those two.'

Ruth looked at the skewbald, and the black. But beside Fly they were nothing ponies. They were nice, because they were ponies; they had gentle, interested faces. But they hadn't got the— the—Ruth groped for a word and could not find it—the *thing* that Fly had. Fly was a character.

'But Fly—he's quiet?' She had to persist.

'He's got no vices. Wouldn't kick or bite you. But he's got more spirit than the others. I reckon he'll be a more lively ride, when you get a saddle on him. I'll be honest with you, you see. If it's really quietness you're looking for, you should have the skewbald or the black.'

But Ruth could no longer consider the skewbald or the black. She knew already that it was going to be Fly. She only wanted Marks to tell her that he wasn't actually bad.

'Is he forty pounds?'

'Well, yes, I suppose so. If you want him that bad. I was asking fifty really. He's a three-year-old, this one. He's ready to be ridden. But I haven't the time to school him myself. It takes too much patience for me. And my kid's too little yet to ride.'

Ruth, having found that Fly, by the nod of her head, could be hers, was suddenly petrified. She stared at him. She looked for all the things in the books, the faults with the strange names, and deficiencies of conformation, the signs of vice, and the indications of dire disease. And Fly stared back at her, four-square on his black hairy legs, and she could see nothing that the books mentioned, only the pony of her heart, as perfect as Shakespeare's bit in all the anthologies, out of 'Venus and Adonis'. 'Oh, I must be sensible!' she thought to herself. And Fly was looking at her boldly as if it was she who had the faults, knock-knees and rickets and pigeon-toes: it was a straight look, with a glint in it. It was not a look to make her feel sensible. It quenched her fright and her doubts.

'Oh, please, I would like him,' she said to Mr Marks. 'I've only got forty pounds.'

'Well then, we'll call it a deal,' said Mr Marks comfortably. He did not strike Ruth as a worrier. 'He's a good pony. The vet's seen 'em all and can't find anything wrong, so you'll be all right there.'

Was it that easy, after all? Ruth could hear her heart thudding, as if it had grown into two. She gripped the top bar of the gate, looking at Fly. She saw him going round the Hunter Trials course at Brierley Hill, and herself sitting easily in the saddle, confident, easy . . . He had bold, wide nostrils, and was wide between the forelegs. But he wasn't common.

'Is—is he New Forest?' she asked Mr Marks.

'He hasn't any papers,' Marks said. 'But he came from the forest. I'll bring him down your place, if you like—I know a man with a truck. Save you walking along the road. Where do you live?'

'Wychwood. On the new estate.'

They started walking back to the farmyard. Ruth was in a daze. 'I'll have to get my money cashed. It's in National Savings.'

'Tomorrow do you?'

'Oh, yes. But I won't have the money by then. At least, not all of it. I can give you some.'

'No hurry. I'm not worried. What house is it?'

'South View.'

'About six, then.'

'Yes, thank you very much.'

Ruth found she was cycling home. Her head was filled with the image of Fly, standing there with his legs planted out so firmly, the wind in his tail. She thought, 'Fly is a horrid name, if you think of fly like the thing that makes spots over the windows and sits on cream-cakes in the summer. But if you think of Fly as in flying, up in the sky, it is a lovely name. He will be that sort of Fly. Fly. Fly-by-Night.' Ruth was pleased with Fly-by-Night. 'He can be Fly, short for Fly-by-Night. In the Hunter Trials he can be down in the catalogue as Fly-by-Night.' Ruth was cycling through the village and up the concrete road of Sunnyside Estate, her eyes seeing nothing.

'I've bought a pony,' she said to her father, who was having his supper.

He looked up. 'Really bought it?'

'Well, I've got to get the money out. But the man doesn't seem to mind about waiting for it. He's bringing the pony tomorrow.'

'*Tomorrow?*' Mrs Hollis spun round from the sink.

'Yes.'

'Oh, Ruth, surely—' Even her father looked rather annoyed. Her mother was speechless, gesticulating out of the kitchen window. 'Where on earth—?'

Ruth, feeling rather cold, looked out of the kitchen window and remembered that the back-garden, or field, was full of bricks. There was wire-mesh between it and the adjoining two gardens, but nothing round the sides of the house and at the bottom, save a hedge full of holes. She looked at it forlornly, thinking of the lush spring bounty of Mr Marks's field. Fly would surely find life here a little different.

'Oh, I'll have it all right by tomorrow,' she said.

Her assumption that a fence would grow out of the ground before the following evening made her parents exchange despairing glances. Fortunately at this moment Ted came in with his friend from work, Ron. Ron, like Ted, was seventeen, tall, skinny, and amiable, with a beloved motor bike.

'We're going to work on Ron's camshaft tonight,' Ted said happily.

'I think,' said Mr Hollis, 'that you're going to build a fence.'

A vast cattle-truck, trailing small clots of dung, laboured up the slight incline to 'South View' and parked incongruously outside.

The driver leaned out of the cab and yelled towards the house, 'Six cows for Hollis!'

Ruth ran blindly down the drive and into the road. 'It's my pony! The pony from Mr Marks?'

'That's right, miss,' said the driver, grinning. He let down the back ramp with a crash and shower of straw, and from the depths of the big lorry Fly's dark eyes stared at Ruth, wild and shining.

'I'll get him, miss. He's a bit scared like.' The man went into the lorry and united Fly's halter. Fly charged for the daylight, his hoofs drumming the wooden floor, pulling the driver with him.

'Hey, hey, steady on, my bold fellow!'

He crashed down the ramp, skidded on the concrete, and pulled up, quivering, nostrils wide, held sharply by the rope halter. A quiet one, Ruth remembered, was what she should have had. No animal that she had ever seen, she thought at that moment, looked less quiet than Fly.

THE OLD
GREY MARE

J. Frank Dobie

A half-century back, Dr J. O. Dyer of Galveston was pursuing an unsleeping passion for the lore of early days. Some of it he wrote down. Along in the '70s he heard the following story, which in his last years—and that was a long time ago, too—he transmitted to me. It was, according to Doctor Dyer, told by a woman who as a girl came with German colonists to settle in Texas, about the year 1848.

They were moving up the Guadalupe River in wagons. Gretchen's family, at the end of the train, had a gentle old grey mare that followed their wagon without rope or halter, stopping every once in a while to grab a mouthful of particularly lush grass. She was stupid and lazy and her ears flopped, but she was faithful.

She carried two big sacks of corn meal so arranged that they made a kind of platform.

The wagon was running over with such things as German settlers carried—beds and bedding, pots and pans, mugs and plates, a heavy chest of drawers, a sauerkraut keg, and a great many children. Gretchen, eight or nine years old, was the liveliest of these. One day she asked her father to let her ride the old grey mare. He could see no harm in this; in fact, her absence might lessen the constant hubbub. So he lifted Gretchen up on the platform of corn meal sacks and tied her there with a rope in such a way that she would be comfortable but could not fall off. The old mare hardly batted an eye, and with Gretchen on her back continued as usual to walk and pick grass along behind the wagon.

That afternoon at a gully the tyre of a wagon wheel fell away from the felloes, shrunken by dry weather, and several spokes were broken. When the halt was made for repairs, Gretchen was asleep, firmly tied on her pillion of corn meal. She did not know when the old grey mare grazed out of sight down a draw. Her father was busy with the wheel; her mother, like the old woman who lived in a shoe, had so many children that she did not know what to do; and so neither of them noticed. It was only after the wagon was repaired and the other children were counted into it and the train started on, that little Gretchen was missed. Then the old grey mare could not be found. None of the German men, so new to the frontier, could follow her tracks in the maze of mustang tracks they now discovered. They struck camp to search. Night came and no little Gretchen; the next day came and passed and no little Gretchen. Then on the morning of the third day the old mare brought her in, and this is the explanation the little girl gave.

After dozing she knew not how long, she awoke with a start. The lazy old mare had come to life and was lumbering along in a gallop after a neighing, pacing white horse with cream-coloured mane and tail. She tried to stop the old mare, but she had neither bridle nor halter. She tried to jump off, but she was tied on and the knots of the rope were beyond her reach.

The old mare continued to walk behind the wagon.

After the old mare had trotted and galloped until nearly sun-down, the white horse all the time pacing ahead 'like a rocking chair', they came to a large bunch of mares. They came out full of curiosity to greet their new sister, and they were very cordial in their greeting.

The wild mares seemed not to notice little Gretchen at all. They were so cordial in their nosings of the old grey mare that soon their muzzles were touching the meal sacks. Probably the sacking was salty. Some of the meal had sifted through. The mares tasted it. No matter if it was the first taste of corn they had ever had, they liked it.

They began to nip at the meal sacks so eagerly that they nipped Gretchen's bare legs. She screeched. She expected to be chewed up right away, even if the mares meant no harm. But at her cry the Pacing White Stallion was with one bound beside her. He was as considerate as he was intelligent. He drove the wild mares off. Then he chewed in two the ropes that bound Gretchen. Next he took her gently by the collar of her dress, very much as a cat takes one of her kittens, and set her down upon the ground.

It was about dark now and the coyotes were beginning to howl. Little Gretchen howled too, but there was no danger. After a while she made a kind of nest in some tall fragrant grass near a Spanish oak and, having cried a while, fell asleep.

When she awoke, the sun was high and not a horse was in sight. She was hungry. She went down to a waterhole that she saw close by and drank water for breakfast. She had heard that a person lost away out in the wilds had better stay in one place until he 'found himself' or until someone found him. She had no hope of finding herself; she wished her papa would come. She remained near the waterhole.

Noon came and still no horse or person appeared within sight. Gretchen was hungrier than ever. It was late spring, and she gathered some of the red agrito berries (called also wild currants) growing near, but the thorny leaves pricked her fingers so severely that she quit before she had eaten enough to satisfy her hunger.

Evening fell and she was still alone. She gathered some sheep sorrel down in the bottom of the draw and drank more water. Darkness came, the stars came out, the coyotes set up their lonely howling. Little Gretchen lay down in her nest again and again cried herself to sleep.

When she awoke the next morning, there standing over her, sound asleep, ears flopped down and lower lip hanging shapeless like a bag of curd, was the old grey mare. Gretchen was as glad as the redbird singing over her head. She jumped up and ran to the mare and tried to get on her. But the old mare was too tall. Then Gretchen grasped her by the mane and tried to lead her to a log that lay near at hand. If she could get the old mare beside it, she could use it as a stepping block. But the stupid old mare would not budge. After vainly pulling, coaxing, and jumping about for a long time, Gretchen began to wail.

She was leaning against the shoulder of the old mare sobbing when she heard swift hoofbeats, rhythmic and racking. She looked up and saw the beautiful White Steed. The sunshine was on his whiteness. He came arching his neck and pacing with all the fire of a mustang emperor, but there was something about him that prevented Gretchen from being in the least frightened. On the contrary, she stretched her arms towards him and gave a childish 'oh' of welcome. He paced right up to where she stood, gently grasped the collar of her dress at the scruff of her neck in his teeth and lifted her upon the mare. Then he must have told the old grey mare to go home. At least she went—went with Gretchen but no corn meal.

Home was the camp by the gully where the wagon had broken down. Gretchen's parents were so happy at having her restored that they did not mind the loss of the meal.

In after years she told the story many, many times. If her children and grandchildren seemed doubtful of the facts, she would in a pet pull down her cotton stockings and show the small, faint scars on her legs where the wild mares had nipped her. Then the children would have to believe.

MY FRIEND FLICKA

Mary O'Hara

R eport cards for the second semester were sent out soon after
school closed in mid-June.

Kennie's was a shock to the whole family.

'If I could have a colt all for my own,' said Kennie, 'I might do
better.'

Rob McLaughlin glared at his son. 'Just as a matter of curiosity,'
he said, 'how do you go about it to get *a zero* in an examination?
Forty in arithmetic; seventeen in history! But a *zero*? Just as one
man to another, what goes on in your head? I would really like
to know.'

'Yes; tell us how you do it, Ken,' chirped Howard.

'Eat your breakfast, Howard,' snapped his mother.

Kennie's blond head bent over his plate until his face was almost hidden. He cheeks burned.

McLaughlin finished his coffee and pushed his chair back. 'You'll do an hour a day on your lessons all through the summer.'

Nell McLaughlin saw Kennie wince as if something had actually hurt him.

Lessons and study in the summertime, when the long winter was just over and there weren't hours enough in the day for all the things he wanted to do!

Kennie took things hard. His eyes turned to the wide-open window with a look almost of despair.

The hill opposite the house, covered with arrow-straight jack pines, was sharply etched in the thin air of the eight-thousand-foot altitude. Where it fell away, vivid green grass ran up to meet it; and over range and upland poured the strong Wyoming sunlight that stung everything into burning colour. A big jack rabbit sat under one of the pines, waving his long ears back and forth.

Ken had to look at his plate and blink back tears before he could turn to his father and say carelessly, 'Can I help you in the corral with the horses this morning, Dad?'

'You'll do your study every morning before you do anything else.' And McLaughlin's scarred boots and heavy spurs clattered across the kitchen floor. 'I'm disgusted with you. Come, Howard.'

Howard strode after his father, nobly refraining from looking at Kennie.

'Help me with the dishes, Kennie,' said Nell McLaughlin as she rose, tied on a big apron, and began to clear the table.

Kennie looked at her in despair. She poured steaming water into the dishpan and sent him for the soap powder.

'If I could have a colt,' he muttered again.

'Now get busy with that dish towel, Ken. It's eight o'clock. You can study till nine and then go up to the corral. They'll still be there.'

At supper that night, Kennie said, 'But Dad, Howard had a colt all of his own when he was only eight. And he trained it and schooled it all himself; and now he's eleven and Highboy is three, and he's riding him. I'm nine now, and even if you give me a colt now, I couldn't catch up to Howard because I couldn't ride it till it was a three-year-old and then I'd be twelve.'

Nell laughed. 'Nothing wrong with that arithmetic.'

But Rob said, 'Howard never gets less than seventy-five average at school; and hasn't disgraced himself and his family by getting more demerits than any other boy in his class.'

Kennie didn't answer. He couldn't figure it out. He tried hard, he spent hours poring over his books. That was supposed to get you good marks, but it never did. Everyone said he was bright, why was it that when he studied he didn't learn? He had a vague feeling that perhaps he looked out the window too much; or looked through the walls to see clouds and sky and hills, and wonder what was happening out there. Sometimes it wasn't even a wonder, but just a pleasant drifting feeling of nothing at all, as if nothing mattered, as if there was always plenty of time, as if the lessons would get done of themselves. And then the bell would ring and study period was over.

If he had a colt—

When the boys had gone to bed that night Nell McLaughlin sat down with her overflowing mending basket and glanced at her husband.

He was at his desk as usual, working on account books and inventories.

Nell threaded a darning needle and thought, 'It's either that whacking big bill from the vet for the mare that died, or the last half of the tax bill.'

It didn't seem just the auspicious moment to plead Kennie's cause. But then, these days, there was always a line between Rob's eyes and a harsh note in his voice.

'Rob,' she began.

He flung down his pencil and turned around.

'Damn that law!' he exclaimed.

'What law?'

'The state law that puts high taxes on pedigreed stock. I'll have to do as the rest of 'em do—drop the papers.'

'Drop the papers! But you'll never get decent prices if you don't have registered horses.'

'I don't get decent prices now.'

'But you will someday, if you don't drop the papers.'

'Maybe.' He bent again over the desk.

Rob, thought Nell, was a lot like Kennie himself. He set his heart. Oh, how stubbornly he set his heart on just some one thing he wanted above everything else. He had set his heart on horses and ranching way back when he had been a crack rider at West Point; and he had resigned and thrown away his army career just for the horses. Well, he'd got what he wanted—

She drew a deep breath, snipped her thread, laid down the sock and again looked across at her husband as she unrolled another length of darning cotton.

To get what you want is one thing, she was thinking. The three-thousand-acre ranch and the hundred head of horses. But to make it pay—for a dozen or more years they had been trying to make it pay. People said ranching hadn't paid since the beef barons ran their herds on public land; people said the only prosperous ranchers in Wyoming were the dude ranchers; people said—

But suddenly she gave her head a little rebellious, gallant shake. Rob would always be fighting and struggling against something, like Kennie; perhaps like herself too. Even those first years when there was no water piped into the house, when every day brought a new difficulty or danger, how she had loved it! How she still loved it!

She ran the darning ball into the toe of a sock, Kennie's sock. The length of it gave her a shock. She suddenly realised that the boys were growing up fast, and now Kennie—Kennie and the colt—

After a while she said, 'Give Kennie a colt, Rob.'

'He doesn't deserve it.' The answer was short. Rob pushed away his papers and took out his pipe.

'Howard's too far ahead of him; older and bigger and quicker and his wits about him, and—'

'Ken doesn't half try; doesn't stick at anything.'

She put down her sewing. 'He's crazy for a colt of his own. He hasn't had another idea in his head since you gave Highboy to Howard.'

'I don't believe in bribing children to do their duty.'

'Not a bribe.' She hesitated.

'No? What would you call it?'

She tried to think it out. 'I just have the feeling Ken isn't going to pull anything off, and—' her eyes sought Rob's 'it's time he did. It isn't the school marks alone, but I just don't want things to go on any longer with Ken never coming out at the right end of anything.'

'I'm beginning to think he's just dumb.'

'He's not dumb. Maybe a little thing like this—if he had a colt of his own, trained him, rode him—'

Rob interrupted. 'But it isn't a little thing, nor an easy thing to break and school a colt the way Howard has schooled Highboy. I'm not going to have a good horse spoiled by Ken's careless ways. He goes wool-gathering. He never knows what he's doing.'

'But he'd *love* a colt of his own, Rob. If he could do it, it might make a big difference in him.'

'*If* he could do it! But that's a big if.'

At breakfast next morning Kennie's father said to him, 'When you've done your study come out to the barn. I'm going in the car up to section twenty-one this morning to look over the brood mares. You can go with me.'

'Can I go too, Dad?' cried Howard.

McLaughlin frowned at Howard. 'You turned Highboy out last evening with dirty legs.'

Howard wriggled. 'I groomed him—'

'Yes, down to his knees.'

'He kicks.'

'And whose fault is that? You don't get on his back again until I see his legs clean.'

The two boys eyed each other, Kennie secretly triumphant and Howard chagrined. McLaughlin turned at the door, 'And, Ken, a week from today I'll give you a colt. Between now and then you can decide what one you want.'

Kennie shot out of his chair and stared at his father. 'A—a— spring colt, Dad, or a yearling?'

McLaughlin was somewhat taken aback, but his wife concealed a smile. If Kennie got a yearling colt, he would be even up with Howard.

'A yearling colt, your father means, Ken,' she said smoothly.

Kennie found himself the most important personage on the ranch. Prestige lifted his head, gave him an inch more of height and a bold stare, and made him feel different all the way through. Even Gus and Tim Murphy, the ranch hands, were more interested in Kennie's choice of a colt than anything else.

Howard was fidgety with suspense. 'Who'll you pick, Ken? Say —pick Doughboy, why don't you? Then when he grows up he'll be sort of twins with mine, in his name, anyway. Doughboy, Highboy, see?'

The boys were sitting on the worn wooden step of the door which led from the tack room into the corral, busy with rags and polish, shining their bridles.

Ken looked at his brother with scorn. Doughboy would never have half of Highboy's speed.

'Lassie, then,' suggested Howard. 'She's black as ink, like mine. And she'll be fast—'

'Dad says Lassie'll never go over fifteen hands.'

Nell McLaughlin saw the change in Kennie and her hopes rose. He went to his books in the morning with determination and really studied. A new alertness took the place of the day-dreaming. Examples in arithmetic were neatly written out and, as she passed his door before breakfast, she often heard the monotonous drone of his voice as he read his American history aloud.

Each night, when he kissed her, he flung his arms around her and held her fiercely for a moment, then, with a winsome and blissful smile into her eyes, turned away to bed.

He spent days inspecting the different bands of horses and colts. He sat for hours on the corral fence, very important, chewing straws. He rode off on one of the ponies for half the day, wandering through the mile-square pastures that ran down towards the Colorado border.

And when the week was up, he announced his decision. 'I'll take that yearling filly of Rocket's. The sorrel with the cream tail and mane.'

His father looked at him in surprise. 'The one that got tangled in the barbed wire? that's never been named?'

In a second all Kennie's new pride was gone. He hung his head defensively. 'Yes.'

'You've made a bad choice, son. You couldn't have picked a worse.'

'She's fast, Dad. And Rocket's fast—'

'It's the worst line of horses I've got. There's never one amongst them with real sense. The mares are hellions and the stallions outlaws; they're untamable.'

'I'll tame her.'

Rob guffawed. 'Not I, nor anyone, has ever been able to really tame any one of them.'

Kennie's chest heaved.

'Better change your mind, Ken. You want a horse that'll be a real friend to you, don't you?'

'Yes—' Kennie's voice was unsteady.

'Well, you'll never make a friend of that filly. She's all cut up and scarred up already with tearing through barbed wire after that bitch of a mother of hers. Mark my words, no fence'll hold 'em—'

'I know,' said Kennie, still more faintly.

'Change your mind?' asked Howard briskly.

'No.'

32

Rob was grim and put out. He couldn't go back on his word. The boy had to have a reasonable amount of help in breaking and taming the filly, and he could envisage precious hours, whole days, wasted in the struggle.

Nell McLaughlin despaired. Once again Ken seemed to have taken the wrong turn and was back where he had begun; stoical, silent, defensive.

But there was a difference that only Ken could know. The way he felt about his colt. The way his heart sang. The pride and joy that filled him so full that sometimes he hung his head so they wouldn't see it shining out of his eyes.

He had known from the very first that he would choose that particular yearling because he was in love with her.

The year before, he had been out working with Gus, the big Swedish ranch hand, on the irrigation ditch, when they had noticed Rocket standing in a gully on the hillside, quiet for once, and eyeing them cautiously.

'Ay bet she got a colt,' said Gus, and they walked carefully up the draw. Rocket gave a wild snort, thrust her feet out, shook her head wickedly, then fled away. And as they reached the spot, they saw standing there the wavering, pinkish colt, barely able to keep its feet. It gave a little squeak and started after its mother on crooked, wobbling legs.

'Yee whiz! Luk at de little *flicka*!' said Gus.

'What does *flicka* mean, Gus?'

'Swedish for little gurl, Ken—'

Ken announced at supper, 'You said she'd never been named. I've named her. Her name is Flicka.'

The first thing to do was to get her in. She was running with a band of yearlings on the saddleback, cut with ravines and gullies, on section twenty.

They all went out after her, Ken, as owner, on old Rob Roy, the wisest horse on the ranch.

Ken was entranced to watch Flicka when the wild band of

33

youngsters discovered that they were being pursued and took off across the mountain. Footing made no difference to her. She floated across the ravines, always two lengths ahead of the others. Her pink mane and tail whipped in the wind. Her long delicate legs had only to aim, it seemed, at a particular spot, for her to reach it and sail on. She seemed to Ken a fairy horse.

He sat motionless, just watching and holding Rob Roy in, when his father thundered past on Sultan and shouted, 'Well, what's the matter? Why didn't you turn 'em?'

Kennie woke up and galloped after.

Rob Roy brought in the whole band. The corral gates were closed, and an hour was spent shunting the ponies in and out through the chutes, until Flicka was left alone in the small round corral in which the baby colts were branded. Gus drove the others away, out the gate, and up the saddleback.

But Flicka did not intend to be left. She hurled herself against the poles which walled the corral. She tried to jump them. They were seven feet high. She caught her front feet over the top rung, clung, scrambled, while Kennie held his breath for fear the slender legs would be caught between the bars and snapped. Her hold broke, she fell over backwards, rolled, screamed, tore around the corral. Kennie had a sick feeling in the pit of his stomach and his father looked disgusted.

One of the bars broke. She hurled herself again. Another went. She saw the opening and as neatly as a dog crawls through a fence, inserted her head and forefeet, scrambled through and fled away, bleeding in a dozen places.

As Gus was coming back, just about to close the gate to the upper range, the sorrel whipped through it, sailed across the road and ditch with her inimitable floating leap, and went up the side of the saddleback like a jack rabbit.

From way up the mountain, Gus heard excited whinnies, as she joined the band he had just driven up, and the last he saw of them they were strung out along the crest running like deer.

'Yee whiz!' said Gus, and stood motionless and staring until the ponies had disappeared over the ridge. Then he closed the gate, remounted Rob Roy, and rode back to the corral.

Rob McLaughlin gave Kennie one more chance to change his mind. 'Last chance, son. Better pick a horse that you have some hope of riding one day. I'd have got rid of this whole line of stock if they weren't so damned fast that I've had the fool idea that someday there might turn out one gentle one in the lot—and I'd have a race horse. But there's never been one so far, and it's not going to be Flicka.'

'It's not going to be Flicka,' chanted Howard.

'Perhaps she *might* be gentled,' said Kennie; and Nell, watching, saw that although his lips quivered, there was fanatical determination in his eye.

'Ken,' said Rob, 'it's up to you. If you say you want her, we'll get her. But she wouldn't be the first of that line to die rather than give in. They're beautiful and they're fast, but let me tell you this, young man, they're *loco*!'

Kennie flinched under his father's direct glance.

'If I go after her again, I'll not give up whatever comes, understand what I mean by that?'

'Yes.'

'What do you say?'

'I want her.'

They brought her in again. They had better luck this time. She jumped over the Dutch half door of the stable and crashed inside. The men slammed the upper half of the door shut and she was caught.

The rest of the band was driven away, and Kennie stood outside of the stable, listening to the wild hoofs beating, the screams, the crashes. His Flicka inside there! He was drenched with perspiration.

'We'll leave her to think it over,' said Rob, when dinnertime came. 'Afterwards, we'll go up and feed and water her.'

But when they went up afterwards there was no Flicka in the barn. One of the windows, higher than the mangers, was broken

The window opened into a pasture an eighth of a mile square, fenced in barbed wire six feet high. Near the stable stood a wagon load of hay. When they went around the back of the stable to see where Flicka had hidden herself, they found her between the stable and the hay wagon, eating.

At their approach she leaped away, then headed east across the pasture.

'If she's like her mother,' said Rob, 'she'll go right through the wire.'

'Ay bet she'll go over,' said Gus. 'She yumps like a deer.'

'No horse can jump that,' said McLaughlin.

Kennie said nothing because he could not speak. It was, perhaps, the most terrible moment of his life. He watched Flicka racing towards the eastern wire.

A few yards from it, she swerved, turned and raced diagonally south.

'It turned her! It turned her!' cried Kennie, almost sobbing. It was the first sign of hope for Flicka. 'Oh, Dad! She has got sense. She has! She has!'

Flicka turned again as she met the southern boundary of the pasture; again at the northern; she avoided the barn. Without abating anything of her whirlwind speed, following a precise, accurate calculation and turning each time on a dime, she investigated every possibility. Then, seeing that there was no hope, she raced south toward the range where she had spent her life, gathered herself, and shot into the air.

Each of the three men watching had the impulse to cover his eyes, and Kennie gave a sort of howl of despair.

Twenty yards of fence came down with her as she hurled herself through. Caught on the upper strands, she turned a complete somersault, landing on her back, her four legs dragging the wires down on top of her, and tangling herself in them beyond hope of escape.

'Damn the wire!' cursed McLaughlin. 'If I could afford decent fences—'

Kennie followed the men miserably as they walked to the filly. They stood in a circle watching, while she kicked and fought and thrashed until the wire was tightly wound and knotted about her, cutting, piercing and tearing great three-cornered pieces of flesh and hide. At last she was unconscious, streams of blood running on her golden coat.

With the wire cutter which Gus always carried in the hip pocket of his overalls, he cut all the wire away, and they drew her into the pasture, repaired the fence, placed hay, a box of oats and a tub of water near her, and called it a day.

'I don't think she'll pull out of it,' said McLaughlin.

Next morning Kennie was up at five, doing his lessons. At six he went out to Flicka.

She had not moved. Food and water were untouched. She was no longer bleeding, but the wounds were swollen and caked over.

Kennie got a bucket of fresh water and poured it over her mouth. Then he leaped away, for Flicka came to life, scrambled up, got her balance, and stood swaying.

Kennie went a few feet away and sat down to watch her. When he went in to breakfast, she had drunk deeply of the water and was mouthing the oats.

There began then a sort of recovery. She ate, drank, limped about the pasture; stood for hours with hanging head and weakly splayed out legs, under the clump of cottonwood trees. The swollen wounds scabbed and began to heal.

Kennie lived in the pasture too. He followed her around, he talked to her. He too lay snoozing or sat under the cottonwoods; and often, coaxing her with hand outstretched, he walked very quietly toward her. But she would not let him come near her.

Often she stood with her head at the south fence, looking off to the mountain. It made the tears come to Kennie's eyes to see the way she longed to get away.

Still Rob said she wouldn't pull out of it. There was no use putting a halter on her. She had no strength.

One morning, as Ken came out of the house, Gus met him and said, 'De filly's down.'

Kennie ran to the pasture, Howard close behind him. The right hind leg which had been badly swollen at the knee joint had opened in a festering wound, and Flicka lay flat and motionless, with staring eyes.

'Don't you wish now you'd chosen Doughboy?' asked Howard.

'Go away!' shouted Ken.

Howard stood watching while Kennie sat down on the ground and took Flicka's head on his lap. Though she was conscious and moved a little, she did not struggle nor seem frightened. Tears rolled down Kennie's cheeks as he talked to her and petted her. After a few moments, Howard walked away.

'Mother, what do you do for an infection when it's a horse?' asked Kennie.

'Just what you'd do if it was a person. Wet dressings. I'll help you, Ken. We mustn't let those wounds close or scab over until they're clean. I'll make a poultice for that hind leg, and help you put it on. Now that she'll let us get close to her, we can help her a lot.'

'The thing to do is see that she eats,' said Rob. 'Keep up her strength.'

But he himself would not go near her. 'She won't pull out of it,' he said. 'I don't want to see her or think about her.'

Kennie and his mother nursed the filly. The big poultice was bandaged on the hind leg. It drew out much poisoned matter and Flicka felt better and was able to stand again.

She watched for Kennie now, and followed him like a dog, hopping on three legs, holding up the right hind leg with its huge knob of a bandage in comical fashion.

'Dad, Flicka's my friend now; she likes me,' said Ken.

His father looked at him. 'I'm glad of that, son. It's a fine thing to have a horse for a friend.'

Kennie found a nicer place for her. In the lower pasture the

She kicked and fought and thrashed.

brook ran over cool stones. There was a grassy bank, the size of a corral, almost on a level with the water. Here she could lie softly, eat grass, drink fresh running water. From the grass, a twenty-foot hill sloped up, crested with overhanging trees. She was enclosed, as it were, in a green, open-air nursery.

Kennie carried her oats morning and evening. She would watch for him to come, eyes and ears pointed to the hill. And one evening Ken, still some distance off, came to a stop and a wide grin spread over his face. He had heard her nicker. She had caught sight of him coming and was calling to him!

He placed the box of oats under her nose and she ate while he stood beside her, his hand smoothing the satin-soft skin under her mane. It had a nap as deep as plush. He played with her long, cream-coloured tresses; arranged her forlock neatly between her eyes. She was a bit dish-faced, like an Arab, with eyes set far apart. He lightly groomed and brushed her while she stood turning her head to him whichever way he went.

He spoiled her. Soon she would not step to the stream to drink but he must hold a bucket for her. And she would drink, then lift her dripping muzzle, rest it on the shoulder of his blue chambray shirt, her golden eyes dreaming off into the distance; then daintily dip her mouth and drink again.

When she turned her head to the south, and pricked her ears, and stood tense and listening, Ken knew she heard the other colts galloping on the upland.

'You'll go back there someday, Flicka,' he whispered. 'You'll be three and I'll be eleven. You'll be so strong you won't know I'm on your back, and we'll fly like the wind. We'll stand on the very top where we can look over the whole world, and smell the snow from the Neversummer Range. Maybe we'll see antelope—'

This was the happiest month of Kennie's life.

With the morning, Flicka always had new strength and would hop three-legged up the hill to stand broadside to the early sun, as horses love to do.

The moment Ken woke, he'd go to the window, and see her

there; and when he was dressed and at his table studying, he sat so that he could raise his head and see Flicka.

After breakfast, she would be waiting for him and the box of oats at the gate; and for Nell McLaughlin with fresh bandages and buckets of disinfectant; and all three would go together to the brook, Flicka hopping along ahead of them.

But Bob McLaughlin would not look at her.

One day all the wounds were swollen again. Presently they opened, one by one; and Kennie and his mother made more poultices.

Still the little filly climbed the hill in the early morning and ran about on three legs. Then she began to go down in flesh and almost overnight wasted away to nothing. Every rib showed; the glossy hide was dull and brittle, and was pulled over the skeleton as if she was a dead horse.

Gus said, 'It's de fever. It burns up her flesh. If you could stop de fever she might get vell.'

McLaughlin was standing in his window one morning and saw the little skeleton hopping about three-legged in the sunshine, and he said, 'That's the end. I won't have a thing like that on my place.'

Kennie had to understand that Flicka had not been getting well all this time; she had been slowly dying.

'She still eats her oats,' he said mechanically.

They were all sorry for Ken. Nell McLaughlin stopped disinfecting and dressing the wounds. 'It's no use, Ken,' she said gently, 'you know Flicka's going to die, don't you?'

'Yes, Mother.'

Ken stopped eating. Howard said, 'Ken doesn't eat anything any more. Don't he have to eat his dinner, Mother?'

But Nell answered, 'Leave him alone.'

Because the shooting of wounded animals is all in the day's work on the western plains, and sickening to everyone, Rob's voice, when he gave the order to have Flicka shot, was as flat as if he had been telling Gus to kill a chicken for dinner.

'Here's the Marlin, Gus. Pick out a time when Ken's not around and put the filly out of her misery.'

Gus took the rifle. '*Ja*, Boss—'

Ever since Ken had known that Flicka was to be shot, he had kept his eye on the rack which held the firearms. His father allowed no firearms in the bunkhouse. The gun rack was in the dining room of the ranch house; and, going through it to the kitchen three times a day for meals, Ken's eye scanned the weapons to make sure that they were all there.

That night they were not all there. The Marlin rifle was missing.

When Kennie saw that, he stopped walking. He felt dizzy. He kept staring at the gun rack, telling himself that it surely was there —he counted again and again—he couldn't see clearly—

Then he felt an arm across his shoulders and heard his father's voice.

'I know, son. Some things are awful hard to take. We just have to take 'em. I have to, too.'

Kennie got hold of his father's hand and held on. It helped steady him.

Finally he looked up. Rob looked down and smiled at him and gave him a little shake and squeeze. Ken managed a smile too.

'All right now?'

'All right, Dad.'

They walked in to supper together.

Ken even ate a little. But Nell looked thoughtfully at the ashen colour of his face; and at the little pulse that was beating in the side of his neck.

After supper he carried Flicka her oats, but he had to coax her and she would only eat a little. She stood with her head hanging, but when he stroked it and talked to her, she pressed her face into his chest and was content. He could feel the burning heat of her body. It didn't seem possible that anything so thin could be alive.

Presently Kennie saw Gus come into the pasture carrying the Marlin. When he saw Ken, he changed his direction and sauntered along as if he was out to shoot some cottontails.

Ken ran to him. 'When are you going to do it, Gus?'

'Ay was goin' down soon now, before it got dark—'

'Gus, don't do it tonight. Wait till morning. Just one more night, Gus.'

'Vell, in de morning den, but it got to be done, Ken. Yer fader gives de order.'

'I know. I won't say anything more.'

An hour after the family had gone to bed, Ken got up and put on his clothes. It was a warm moonlit night. He ran down to the brook, calling softly, 'Flicka! Flicka!'

But Flicka did not answer with a little nicker; and she was not in the nursery, nor hopping about the pasture. Ken hunted for an hour.

At last he found her down the creek, lying in the water. Her head had been on the bank, but as she lay there, the current of the stream had sucked and pulled at her, and she had had no strength to resist; and little by little her head had slipped down until when Ken got there only the muzzle was resting on the bank, and the body and legs were swinging in the stream.

Kennie slid into the water, sitting on the bank, and he hauled at her head. But she was heavy and the current dragged like a weight; and he began to sob because he had not strength to draw her out.

Then he found a leverage for his heels against some rocks in the bed of the stream, and he braced himself against these, and pulled with all his might; and her head came up onto his knees, and he held it cradled in his arms.

He was glad that she had died of her own accord, in the cool water, under the moon, instead of being shot by Gus. Then, putting his face close to hers, and looking searchingly into her eyes, he saw that she was alive and looking back at him.

And then he burst out crying, and hugged her, and said, 'Oh, my little Flicka, my little Flicka.'

The long night passed.

The moon slid slowly across the heavens.

The water rippled over Kennie's legs, and over Flicka's body. And gradually the heat and fever went out of her. And the cool running water washed and washed her wounds.

When Gus went down in the morning with the rifle, they hadn't moved. There they were, Kennie sitting in water over his thighs and hips, with Flicka's head in his arms.

Gus seized Flicka by the head, and hauled her out on the grassy bank, and then, seeing that Kennie couldn't move, cold and stiff and half-paralysed as he was, lifted him in his arms and carried him to the house.

'Gus,' said Ken through chattering teeth, 'don't shoot her, Gus.'

'It ain't fur me to say, Ken. You know dat.'

'But the fever's left her, Gus.'

'Ay wait a little, Ken—'

Rob McLaughlin drove to Laramie to get the doctor, for Ken was in violent chills that would not stop. His mother had him in bed wrapped in hot blankets when they got back.

He looked at his father imploringly as the doctor shook down the thermometer.

'She might get well now, Dad. The fever's left her. It went out of her when the moon went down.'

'All right, son. Don't worry. Gus'll feed her, morning and night as long as she's—'

'As long as I can't do it,' finished Kennie happily.

The doctor put the thermometer in his mouth and told him to keep it shut.

All day Gus went about his work, thinking of Flicka. He had not been back to look at her. He had been given no more orders. If she was alive, the order to shoot her was still in effect. But Kennie was ill, McLaughlin making his second trip to town taking the doctor home, and would not be back till long after dark.

After their supper in the bunkhouse, Gus and Tim walked down to the brook.

They did not speak as they approached the filly, lying stretched out flat on the grassy bank, but their eyes were straining at her to see if she was dead or alive.

She raised her head as they reached her.

'By the powers!' exclaimed Tim, 'there she is!'

She dropped her head, raised it again, and moved her legs and became tense as if struggling to rise. But to do so she must use her right hind leg to brace herself against the earth. That was the damaged leg, and at the first bit of pressure with it, she gave up and fell back.

'We'll swing her on the other side,' said Tim. 'Then she can help herself.'

'*Ja—*'

Standing behind her, they leaned over, grabbed hold of her left legs, front and back, and gently hauled her over. Flicka was as lax and willing as a puppy. But the moment she found herself lying on her right side, she began to scramble, braced herself with her good left leg and tried to rise.

'Yee whiz!' said Gus. 'She got plenty strength yet.'

'Hi!' cheered Tim. 'She's up!'

But Flicka waved, slid down again, and lay flat. This time she gave notice that she would not try again by heaving a deep sigh and closing her eyes.

Gus took his pipe out of his mouth and thought it over. Orders or no orders, he would try to save the filly. Ken had gone too far to be let down.

'Ay'm goin' to rig a blanket sling fur her, Tim, and get her on her feet and keep her up.'

There was bright moonlight to work by. They brought down the posthole digger and set two aspen poles deep into the ground either side of the filly, then with ropes attached to the blanket, hoisted her by a pulley.

Not at all disconcerted, she rested comfortably in the blanket under her belly, touched her feet on the ground, and reached for the bucket of water Gus held for her.

Kennie was sick a long time. He nearly died. But Flicka picked up. Every day Gus passed the word to Nell, who carried it to Ken. 'She's cleaning up her oats.' 'She's out of the sling.' 'She bears a little weight on the bad leg.'

Tim declared it was a real miracle. They argued about it, eating their supper.

'Na,' said Gus. 'It was de cold water, washin' de fever outa her. And more dan dot—it was Ken—you tink it don't count? All night dot boy sits dere, and says, "Hold on, Flicka, Ay'm here wid you. Ay'm standin' by, two of us togedder"—'

Tim stared at Gus without answering, while he thought it over. In the silence, a coyote yapped far off on the plains; and the wind made a rushing sound high up in the jack pines on the hill.

Gus filled his pipe.

'Sure,' said Tim finally. 'Sure, that's it.'

Then came the day when Rob McLaughlin stood smiling at the foot of Kennie's bed and said, 'Listen! Hear your friend?'

Ken listened and heard Flicka's high, eager whinney.

'She don't spend much time by the brook any more. She's up at the gate of the corral half the time, nickering for you.'

'For me!'

Rob wrapped a blanket around the boy and carried him out to the corral gate.

Kennie gazed at Flicka. There was a look of marvelling in his eyes. He felt as if he had been living in a world where everything was dreadful and hurting but awfully real; and *this* couldn't be real; this was all soft and happy, nothing to struggle over or worry about or fight for any more. Even his father was proud of him! He could feel it in the way Rob's big arms held him. It was all like a dream and far away. He couldn't, yet, get close to anything.

But Flicka—Flicka—alive, well, pressing up to him, recognizing him, nickering—

Kennie put out a hand—weak and white—and laid it on her face. His thin little fingers straightened her forelock the way he used to do, while Rob looked at the two with a strange expression about his mouth, and a glow in his eyes that was not often there.

'She's still poor, Dad, but she's on four legs now.'

'She's picking up.'

Ken turned his face up, suddenly remembering. 'Dad! She did get gentled, didn't she?'

'Gentle—as—a kitten—'

They put a cot down by the brook for Ken, and boy and filly got well together.

THE GIPSIES' PONY

James Herriot

As I stopped my car by the group of gipsies I felt I was looking at something which should have been captured by a camera. The grass verge was wide on this loop of the road and there were five of them squatting round the fire; it seemed like the mother and father and three little girls. They sat very still, regarding me blankly through the drifting smoke while a few big snowflakes floated across the scene and settled lazily on the tangled hair of the children. Some unreal quality in the wild tableau kept me motionless in my seat, staring through the glass, forgetful of the reason for my being here. I wound down the window and spoke to the man.

'Are you Mr Myatt? I believe you have a sick pony.' The man

nodded. 'Aye, that's right. He's over here.' It was a strange accent with no trace of Yorkshire in it. He got up from the fire, a thin, dark-skinned unshaven little figure, and came over to the car holding out something in his hand. It was a ten shilling note and I recognized it as a gesture of good faith.

The gipsies who occasionally wandered into Darrowby were always regarded with a certain amount of suspicion. They came, unlike the Myatts, mainly in the summer to camp down by the river and sell their horses and we had been caught out once or twice before. A lot of them seemed to be called Smith and it wasn't uncommon to go back on the second day to find that the patient and owner had gone. In fact Siegfried had shouted to me as I left the house this morning: 'Get the brass if you can.' But he needn't have worried—Mr Myatt was on the up and up.

I got out of the car and followed him over the grass, past the shabby, ornate caravan and the lurcher dog tied to the wheel to where a few horses and ponies were tethered. My patient was easy to find; a handsome piebald of about thirteen hands with good, clean legs and a look of class about him. But he was in a sorry state. While the other animals moved around on their tethers, watching us with interest, the piebald stood as though carved from stone.

Even from a distance I could tell what was wrong with him. Only acute laminitis could produce that crouching posture and as I moved nearer I could see that all four feet were probably affected because the pony had his hind feet right under his body in a desperate attempt to take his full weight on his heels.

I pushed my thermometer into the rectum. 'Has he been getting any extra food, Mr Myatt?'

'Aye, he getten into a bag of oats last night.' The little man showed me the big, half empty sack in the back of the caravan. It was difficult to understand him but he managed to convey that the pony had broken loose and gorged himself on the oats. And he had given him a dose of castor oil—he called it 'casta ile.'

The thermometer read 104 and the pulse was rapid and bounding. I passed my hand over the smooth, trembling hooves, feeling the abnormal heat, then I looked at the taut face, the dilated nostrils and terrified eyes. Anybody who has had an infection under a finger-nail can have an inkling of the agony a horse goes through when the sensitive laminae of the foot are inflamed and throbbing against the unyielding wall of the hoof.

'Can you get him to move?' I asked.

The man caught hold of the head collar and pulled, but the pony refused to budge.

I took the other side of the collar. 'Come on, it's always better if they can get moving.'

We pulled together and Mrs Myatt slapped the pony's rump. He took a couple of stumbling steps but it was as though the ground was red hot and he groaned as his feet came down. Within seconds he was crouching again with his weight on his heels.

'It seems he just won't have it.' I turned and went back to the car. I'd have to do what I could to give him relief and the first thing was to get rid of as much as possible of that bellyful of oats. I fished out the bottle of arecoline and gave an injection into the muscle of the neck, then I showed the little man how to tie cloths round the hooves so that he could keep soaking them with cold water.

Afterwards I stood back and looked again at the pony. He was salivating freely from the arecoline and he had cocked his tail and evacuated his bowel; but his pain was undiminished and it would stay like that until the tremendous inflammation subsided—if it ever did. I had seen cases like this where serum had started to ooze from the coronet; that usually meant shedding of the hooves—even death.

As I turned over the gloomy thoughts the three little girls went up to the pony. The biggest put her arms round his neck and laid her cheek against his shoulder while the others stroked the shivering flanks. There were no tears, no change in the blank expressions, but it was easy to see that that pony really meant something to them.

Before leaving I handed over a bottle of tincture of aconite mixture. 'Get a dose of this down him every four hours, Mr Myatt,

All five gipsies pulled at the halter.

and be sure to keep putting cold water on the feet. I'll come and see him in the morning.'

I closed the car door and looked through the window again at the slow-rising smoke, the drifting snowflakes and the three children with their ragged dresses and uncombed hair still stroking the pony.

'Well you got the brass, James,' Siegfried said at lunch, carelessly stuffing the ten shilling note into a bulging pocket. 'What was the trouble?'

'Worst case of laminitis I've ever seen. Couldn't move the pony at all and he's going through hell. I've done the usual things but I'm pretty sure they aren't going to be enough.'

'Not a very bright prognosis, then?'

'Really black. Even if he gets over the acute stage he'll have deformed feet, I'd like to bet. Grooved hooves, dropped soles, the lot. And he's a grand little animal, lovely piebald. I wish to God there was something else I could do.'

Siegried sawed two thick slices off the cold mutton and dropped them on my plate. He looked thoughtfully at me for a moment. 'You've been a little distrait since you came back. These are rotten jobs, I know, but it's no good worrying.'

'Ach, I'm not worrying, exactly, but I can't get it off my mind. Maybe it's those people—the Myatts. They were something new to me. Right out of the world. And three raggedy little girls absolutely crazy about that pony. They aren't going to like it at all.'

As Siegfried chewed his mutton I could see the old glint coming into his eyes; it showed when the talk had anything to do with horses. I knew he wouldn't push in but he was waiting for me to make the first move. I made it.

'I wish you'd come along and have a look with me. Maybe there's something you could suggest. Do you think there could be?'

Siegfried put down his knife and fork and stared in front of him for a few seconds, then he turned to me. 'You know, James, there just might be. Quite obviously this is a right pig of a case and the ordinary remedies aren't going to do any good. We have to pull something out of the bag and I've got an idea. There's just one thing.' He gave me a crooked smile. 'You may not like it.'

'Don't bother about me,' I said. 'You're the horseman. If you can help this pony I don't care what you do.'

'Right, eat up then and we'll go into action together.' We finished our meal and he led me through to the instrument room. I was surprised when he opened the cupboard where old Mr Grant's instruments were kept. It was a kind of museum.

When Siegfried had bought the practice from the old vet who had worked on into his eighties these instruments had come with it and they lay there in rows, unused but undisturbed. It would have been logical to throw them out, but maybe Siegfried felt the same way about them as I did. The polished wooden boxes of shining, odd-shaped scalpels, the enema pumps and douches with their perished rubber and brass fittings, the seaton needles, the ancient firing irons—they were a silent testament to sixty years of struggle. I often used to open that cupboard door and try to picture the old man wrestling with the same problems as I had, travelling the same narrow roads as I did. He had done it absolutely on his own and for sixty years. I was only starting but I knew a little about the triumphs and disasters, the wondering and worrying, the hopes and disappointments—and the hard labour. Anyway, Mr Grant was dead and gone, taking with him all the skills and knowledge I was doggedly trying to accumulate.

Siegfried reached to the back of the cupboard and pulled out a long flat box. He blew the dust from the leather covering and gingerly unfastened the clasp. Inside, a fleam, glittering on its bed of frayed velvet, lay by the side of a round, polished blood-stick.

I looked at my employer in astonishment. 'You're going to bleed him, then?'

'Yes, my boy, I'm going to take you back to the Middle Ages.' He looked at my startled face and put a hand on my arm. 'But don't start beating me over the head with all the scientific arguments against blood-letting. I've no strong views either way.'

'But have you ever done it? I've never seen you use this outfit.'

'I've done it. And I've seen some funny things after it, too.' Siegfried turned away as if he wanted no more discussion. He cleaned the fleam thoroughly and dropped it into the sterilizer. His face was expressionless as he stood listening to the hiss of the boiling water.

The gipsies were again hunched over the fire when we got there and Mr Myatt, sensing that reinforcements had arrived, scrambled to his feet and held out another ten shilling note.

Siegfried waved it away. 'Let's see how we get on, Mr Myatt,' he grunted. He strode across the grass to where the pony still trembled in his agonized crouch. There was no improvement; in fact the eyes stared more wildly and I could hear little groans as the piebald carefully eased himself from foot to foot.

Siegried spoke softly without looking at me, 'Poor beggar. You weren't exaggerating, James. Bring that box from the car, will you?'

When I came back he was tying a choke rope round the base of the pony's neck. 'Pull it up tight,' he said. As the jugular rose up tense and turgid in its furrow he quickly clipped and disinfected a small area and inserted a plaque of local anaesthetic. Finally he opened the old leather-covered box and extracted the fleam, wrapped in sterile lint.

Everything seemed to start happening then. Siegfried placed the little blade of the fleam against the bulging vein and without hesitation gave it a confident smack with the stick. Immediately an alarming cascade of blood spouted from the hole and began to form a dark lake on the grass. Mr Myatt gasped and the little girls set up a sudden chatter. I could understand how they felt. In fact I was wondering how long the pony could stand this tremendous outflow without dropping down.

It didn't seem to be coming out fast enough for Siegfried, however, because he produced another stick from his pocket, thrust it into the pony's mouth and began to work the jaws. And as the animal champed, the blood gushed more fiercely.

When at least a gallon had come away Siegfried seemed satisfied. 'Slacken the rope, James,' he cried, then rapidly closed the wound on the neck with a pin suture. Next he trotted over the grass and looked over a gate in the roadside wall. 'Thought so,' he shouted. 'There's a little beck in that field. We've got to get him over to it. Come on, lend a hand everybody!'

He was clearly enjoying himself and his presence was having its usual effect. The Myatts were spurred suddenly into action and began to run around aimlessly, bumping into each other. I was gripped by a sudden tension and preparedness and even the pony seemed to be taking an interest in his surroundings for the first time.

All five of the gipsies pulled at the halter, Siegfried and I looped our arms behind the pony's thighs, everybody gave encouraging shouts and at last he began to move forward. It was a painful process but he kept going—through the gate and across the field to where the shallow stream wandered among its rushes. There were no banks to speak of and it was easy to push him out into the middle. As he stood there with the icy water rippling round his inflamed hooves I fancied I could read in his eyes a faint dawning of an idea that things were looking up at last.

'Now he must stand in there for an hour,' Siegfried said. 'And then you'll have to make him walk round the field. Then another hour in the beck. As he gets better you can give him more and more exercise but he must come back to the beck. There's a lot of work for somebody here, so who's going to do it?'

The three little girls came shyly round him and looked up, wide-eyed, into his face. Siegfried laughed. 'You three want the job, do you? Right, I'll tell you just what to do.'

He pulled out the bag of peppermint drops which was ever-present among his widely-varied pocket luggage and I settled myself for a long wait. I had seen him in action with the children on the farms and when that bag of sweets came out, everything stopped. It was the one time Siegfried was never in a hurry.

The little girls each solemnly took a sweet, then Siegfried

55

squatted on his heels and began to address them like a professor with his class. They soon began to thaw and put a word in for themselves. The smallest launched into a barely intelligible account of the remarkable things the pony had done when he was a foal and Siegfried listened intently, nodding his head gravely now and then. There was all the time in the world.

His words obviously went home because, over the next few days whenever I passed the gipsy camp I could see the three wild little figures either grouped around the pony in the beck or dragging him round the field on a long halter shank. I didn't need to butt in—I could see he was improving all the time.

It was about a week later than I saw the Myatts on their way out of Darrowby, the red caravan rocking across the market place with Mr Myatt up front wearing a black velvet cap, his wife by his side. Tethered to various parts of the caravan the family of horses clopped along and right at the rear was the piebald, a bit stiff perhaps, but going very well. He'd be all right.

The little girls were looking out of the back door and as they spotted me I waved. They looked back at me unsmilingly until they had almost turned the corner into Hallgate, then one of them shyly lifted her hand. The others followed suit and my last sight was of them waving eagerly back.

I strolled into the Drovers and took a thoughtful half pint into a corner. Siegfried had done the trick there all right but I was wondering what to make of it because in veterinary practice it is difficult to draw definite conclusions even after spectacular results. Was it my imagination or did that pony seem to feel relief almost immediately after the blood-letting? Would we ever have got him moving without it? Was it really the right thing in these cases to bash a hole in the jugular and release about a bucketful of the precious fluid? I still don't have the answers because I never dared try it for myself.

HOLLYWOOD HORSES

Anthony Amaral

When Marilyn Monroe was starting her career, she was warned about the scene-stealing appeal of a male star she was to work with in a western movie.

'It's not him that worries me,' she is said to have answered. 'It's those hammy horses.'

It is true that movie horses are hams. After years of making movies and going on personal-appearance tours, they have learned to react to public attention, sensing that they must parade, show off, and play the role of a star.

Actors and actresses admit that animals often steal scenes. When a handsome horse fills half the screen, it is difficult to concentrate on the actors. For instance, if television's Fury limps and nickers pathetically with a leg injury, audiences tend to remember it longer than they remember the name of the actor who cared for Fury's wound.

Since the horse is the animal most used in Hollywood and is in virtually all pictures except modern dramas, he is classified, like a human actor, in categories according to function: extras, stunt-horses, specialty actors, and stars. More than half of the one thousand horses stabled around Hollywood for movie work are extras. They carry the posse for westerns and troopers for cavalry pictures, pull wagons and buggies, and lend atmosphere to certain scenes. They are all colours and sizes and their one shared characteristic is that they are gentle. Frequently, the human extras playing possemen or cavalrymen have never ridden before and their horses must be thoroughly reliable and not buck off amateur riders.

Stunthorses are more special; they are trained to fall on com-mand, leap cliffs, and gallop steadily alongside a train or stage-coach while their riders leap from the saddle and onto the moving vehicle.

Next in the hierarchy come the specialty horses. These have a particular routine or even a natural deformity which may be asked for in a script. Nellie, an old mare, was a character player with a deformity that got her jobs in about forty movies. She had a sway back and played low comedy roles with zany comedians like the Three Stooges.

Little John is a highly rated specialty performer and might be remembered as the bucking horse in *The Big Country*. But he is no ordinary bucking horse. This Appaloosa was specially trained to rear up and then kick out his hind legs in a comic combination of jumping and bucking. Gregory Peck's attempt to ride Little John was the humorous highlight of *The Big Country*. Little John is an accomplished jumper as well, and follows the horse-show circuit regularly when he is not working in films.

Probably the specialty horse best known to Hollywood stars and the public was Steel. He never played solo roles, but carried

John Wayne in *The Conqueror*, Robert Taylor in *Westward the Women*, Joel McCrea in *Buffalo Bill*, and Randolph Scott in his many westerns. Steel was a favourite mount of actors in westerns because of his beautiful chestnut colour, white blaze face marking, and long flaxen mane and tail. Steel's movies were made between 1940 and 1950, after which he was retired. It is a tribute to his beauty and easy manageability that no other horse since has been so great a favourite with male movie stars as he was.

Finally, there are the star horses who, no less than human actors, have exceptional personality, beauty, and talent. Star horses, while selected mostly for their adaptability to movie work, are also well-bred. Television's Flicka is an Arabian, the oldest and purest breed of horse. Fury and most other star horses are American Saddlebreds, a breed originating in America during the plantation days in the South, and popular with horse trainers in Hollywood because of its beauty, size, and intelligence.

But even a fine pedigree will not gain a horse top acting roles unless it can face the rigours and the strange-looking apparatus of movie making. A star horse must have a quiet and sensible temperament. Highly sensitive horses that become nervous and edgy from the noises, equipment, and people surrounding a movie set will not qualify.

One beautiful black stallion was groomed for stardom only to disappoint his trainer when he could not adjust to the cameras, rolling reflectors, and sound booms. Consequently, the horse disqualified himself from the movie business. Now he is used by actors who have to learn to ride for a movie role.

Beauty is another requirement—one of the most important. A star horse must be well-formed, have expressive eyes, a zestful spirit, and good colour. Black is a favourite, and also the rich chestnut hues, which photograph well in Technicolor. White horses have always been a special attraction in Hollywood. In the older movie days the 'good guys' in the westerns rode white horses and wore white hats as symbols of goodness and purity; the badmen rode dark-coloured horses and wore black hats. And, of course, the wild, white stallion movie is almost as old as motion pictures.

But none of these assets is of much use to a horse if he doesn't have intelligence. In fact, Harold Melniker (AHA Hollywood Office director) believes that star movie horses are all of above average intelligence. Movie horses must perform by trained responses. Because the trainer does not restrain the horse with a halter or bridle, obedience is the essential quality.

It has been estimated that only one horse in five hundred has the potential qualities of a star horse. Fat Jones, who until his recent death owned the largest stable of movie horses, commented, 'I look at a thousand horses to buy maybe ten, and only four or five of them ever make it in pictures.'

Trainers and stable owners, like Hollywood's talent scouts, are always watching and searching for an outstanding animal that might become a star like Fury or Black Diamond. Some horses qualify for a movie or two, only to fail eventually through boredom with the routine. A horse that shows interest and spirit, role after role, is rare indeed. It is not surprising, therefore, that there have been only a few top horse stars in the history of movies. But these particular horses have been in the business fifteen or twenty years and have appeared in hundreds of films.

Whenever trainers, stable owners, and wranglers (horse-handlers) reminisce and discuss the merits of the star horses—and whatever their arguments may be—they all agree that the greatest movie horse was Rex. The older generation will remember Rex as the daring hero of many silent epics and also a few talkie films.

Hollywood publicity men, who have a tendency to exaggerate about Hollywood and the stars, were for once correct when they tagged Rex King of the Wild Horses. He was wild—an independent thinker and actor—and rarely allowed himself to be governed by cues from the handler off-camera. When it was time for Rex to act, cameras would be grinding away before he was released from his halter, because he would do pretty much what he pleased, and all

The 'good guys' rode white horses and wore white hats.

the cameraman could hope for were a few shots that could be edited into a plausible sequence.

Fred Jackman, a cameraman-director on the early Rex movies, called Rex mean and undependable. Training, he added, was almost impossible and the only way Rex could be made to perform was to fool him. When Jackman wanted Rex to show alertness and leave hurriedly in a certain direction, Jackman would have another stallion held at a distant point. Rex would immediately race for the other stallion to 'bite its head off'. But on the screen, Rex would be seen appearing at the hero's side. Actually, Rex had a double named Brownie who appeared in all scenes showing Rex with people. Rex himself couldn't be trusted with the actors.

Others labelled Rex ornery, arrogant, and warped. One wonders why the studios tolerated a horse with such a bad reputation. The answer is simple: Rex was a superbly natural wild horse. A black Morgan stallion, he was unmanageable from birth. Left in a pasture at a state reform school near Golden, Colorado, according to one story, Rex killed one of the students who tried to work him.

When the Hal Roach Studios were searching for a horse to play in *Black Cyclone*, Rex was chosen because he would need the least training to play a wild horse.

For the first half of *Black Cyclone*, Rex was left virtually wild. Somehow the film seemed more like a documentary about a wild horse than a Hollywood production. The picture, a silent movie, grossed the studio $350,000 (a considerable amount in the 1920s); Rex had cost $150. The picture was so popular that movie stories with similar themes were written for Rex to play. *Wild Beauty*, *Plunging Hooves*, *Stormy*, *King of Wild Horses*, *Black Stallion*, and serials made Rex the first horse to star in his own pictures.

Rex was not so popular on the set, however. An eye-witness remembers an occasion when Rex threw an actor twenty feet and then commenced to tear off his clothes with his teeth.

Eugene Forde, who directed the first version of *Smoky* in 1933, said, 'Rex had a tremendous personality. He was a vicious horse and dangerous to work with. I stayed away from him . . .' Forde went on to explain that one scene showed Rex charging a cowboy, knocking him down, and trampling him to death. 'First of all,' commented Forde, 'it took a lot of talking to get a stuntman who was willing to work the scene with the horse. During the filming, two women fainted when Rex charged and knocked over the cowboy. They were certain Rex had killed him. Some of this footage was finally cut from the film because the studio believed audiences would be certain that the cowboy had actually been killed. It was just too real!'

Rex stayed in the movies for nearly fifteen years. He finally retired on the ranch of his owner, Lee Doyle, at Flagstaff, Arizona, where some of his films had been made. A few of Rex's pictures are seen on television, and the trainers and wranglers around Hollywood enjoy seeing the horse working again. They respected Rex, remembering him as the horse that could never be trusted but was still the king.

If Rex was undisputedly king, then Misty was the prince of movie horses. Misty is dead, but, like Rex, is still talked about more than any living horse star. For almost twenty-five years Misty worked in movies—playing the villain.

A sleek, almost black Thoroughbred stallion, Misty's career in motion pictures started by accident. Mist-A-Shot was his registered name, and while being hauled to a race track in the early 1930s, he developed a leg ailment. Misty was left to rest at the Jones stable. A veterinarian diagnosed the ailment as a bowed tendon, which meant that Misty would never be able to put out the burst of speed needed for a race horse. Jones liked the horse's looks and bought Misty as a possible movie candidate. Misty became a star and was known in Hollywood circles as the John Barrymore of movie horses.

Misty played in about seventy pictures. He was best known for his roles as a fighting stallion. 'No horse,' said Jones, 'could snake out his neck, show his teeth, and fight like Misty. You knew he meant business when he was cued to fight. But he was gentle; a real gentleman.'

Trainer Les Hilton worked Misty in some of his pictures. Hilton feels that Misty's most unusual attribute was his ability to take direction even when working with a herd of horses. When stallions are around mares, they instinctively direct all their attention towards them. Yet Hilton could call Misty from the herd—which even Hilton admits was more an indication of how fine a horse Misty naturally was than of the quality of his training. Probably not one stallion in a hundred would respond as Misty did coming to the sound of Hilton's voice, or searching him out, much like a dog. This rapport between Misty and Hilton was once used in a scene which showed Misty running around a ranch yard looking for a small boy. Hilton would hide in a barrel and call Misty, and the horse would race to the barrel, poking it with his muzzle. Then Hilton would hide in a wagon and call the horse, and again Misty would run to the spot. On the screen this sequence of searching and running gave the impression that Misty was looking for the boy in likely hiding places.

Misty received great public recognition when he played the role of Banner in Mary O'Hara's eloquent horse stories, *My Friend Flicka* and *Thunderhead, Son of Flicka*. Misty was in his prime during these films and actually stole the show from the lead horses, Flicka and Thunderhead. When horse films are shown, many young people write to the studios for pictures of the horses. Twentieth Century-Fox Studios had more requests for Misty as Banner than for Flicka and Thunderhead combined. The films were in Technicolor, and Misty, with his glossy dark coat and wonderful animation, made the requests for his picture understandable.

One of Misty's last roles was for the epic western *Duel in the Sun*, with Gregory Peck. Scenes called for Peck to fight hand to hoof, so to speak, with a cantankerous stallion in a corral. Since Peck did not use a double for the entire sequence, Misty, who could act vicious and still be gentle, was transported to the location site around Tucson, Arizona, for the fight sequence. Misty was so manageable that only one day was required to film the scene.

A few months later, Misty began to fail. Age rapidly slowed the noble stallion to an arthritic and helpless condition. The order to put Misty to sleep was a difficult one for Fat Jones to give. They had been together for a quarter of a century and on the day that Jones gave his order, he locked himself in his office and did not come out the entire day. Wranglers around the stable say that no other horse of the hundreds that Jones owned ever captured his heart as Misty did.

As Misty's career drew to an end, another black stallion, Black Diamond—also owned by the Jones stable—was groomed for the sort of role Misty had made famous. Black Diamond is a very tall American Saddle-bred. He played major roles in *The Track of the Cat*, *Red Canyon*, *Flame of Araby*, *Black Horse Canyon*, and *The Reward*, and appeared in dozens of other movies in minor parts during the twenty years he was in the picture business.

If one horse had to be named as the most popular with the public, the choice between Mr Ed of television, Fury, and Roy Rogers's Trigger would be difficult. These three horses have what Hollywood calls a public image, meaning that they are known and recognized for specific roles. Since Mr Ed is more of a comedian and Trigger a co-star, Fury is probably the most prominent as a star. Now about fifteen years old, Fury has been a star performer most of his life. His gross earnings are far above $500,000 and he is second only to Lassie as a great money earner in Hollywood's animal kingdom.

Ralph McCutcheon, who owns and trained Fury, found the black stallion on a farm in Missouri when he was eighteen months old. His real name was Highland Dale and he had completed his basic dramatic training when Twentieth Century-Fox announced they were casting horses for *Black Beauty*. Black horses are in abundance in Hollywood and many were considered for the part. But Fury was selected for the title role. Although the picture was not very popular, Fury established himself as a reliable and capable performer.

He played a number of 'bit' parts, whenever a black horse was

needed for a picture. Then MGM announced they were to film
Gypsy Colt, a poignant story about a girl and her almost human
horse. Fury was selected for the part.

Reading the script, McCutcheon was slightly disturbed by the
number of tricks written into the script for the horse to perform.
Fury knew some of them but had to learn many more. MGM
allowed McCutcheon three months to prepare him. Fortunately,
Fury is an intelligent horse and learned the acting routines with
speed. He had to open doors with his mouth, run to the schoolhouse to pick up his young owner, poke his head into windows,
and let himself be chased down a road by motorcyclists.

The picture received good reviews and MGM stepped up the
publicity—Fury had become a star. A number of important roles
were added to his list of credits. He played a wild Nevada stallion
in *Wild Is the Wind*, with Anthony Quinn and Anna Magnani.
Because he is gentle, he was used as Elizabeth Taylor's horse in the
picture *Giant*, in which his most important scene was set in the
early morning on the Texas plains. Just after dawn, Fury was seen
limping towards the ranch. A medium shot of the horse showed
his bridle broken and hanging over his head; blood on his flanks
revealed he had been spurred viciously. After limping to the ranch
house, Fury stood there, on three legs, and whinnied softly. This
was Fury's closing scene in *Giant*, and he stole the acting honours
from the human stars.

Fury's fame grew larger in the role that made his name familiar
to many—the television series *Fury*. The series ran over five years
and made Fury the most publicized horse in films. There are story-
books about Fury, puzzles, comic strips, and Fury hobby horses.
His fan mail is as extensive as Trigger's and Champion's was in
their heyday.

Fury amassed a number of acting awards from the American
Humane Association: an award of excellence for *Outlaw Stallion*
(1955), the PATSY award for *Gypsy Colt* (1956), and second-place
awards for *Giant* (1957), and *Wild Is the Wind* (1958). He received
similar awards for his television work.

Star movie horses have doubles and stand-ins just as human stars do. The studio prefers not to risk the star horse in wild running scenes or falling stunts. Obviously, if anything happened to the star horse, the production would have to stop until a replacement was trained. Studios worry about their star horses, and justifiably so. Making movies costs thousands of dollars a day and unscheduled delays in shooting add enormously to the cost of a production.

Dice, a pinto stallion, highly trained in movie techniques and tricks, once ran outside the studio in a fit of temperament and was hit by a car. Fortunately the accident wasn't serious. But, because Dice's double was not so highly trained and could not replace him, the studio had to shoot around the scenes that involved Dice. In the meantime, a casual mention of the accident in the newspapers immediately brought hundreds of get-well cards, telegrams, and even flowers from Dice's fans.

During the 1948 filming of Will James's *Smoky*, the double was only scheduled for use in a falling scene. However, just at the end of filming, Smoky caught cold from location shooting in the mountains of southern Utah. Every time the director was ready to shoot the last scene Smoky would start to cough into the camera. Finally Smoky was replaced. To the surprise of the director, letters arrived asking what had happened to the real Smoky. The audience had discovered the switch in spite of the horses' close likeness. The giveaway, to the sharp eye, was Smoky's 'fox ears', which curled at the tips. The double had straight ears.

Another switch, although not detected by the public, still gave jitters to the studio filming *Tonka* on location in Oregon. The studio had selected a chestnut gelding to play the title role of a horse that survived Custer's Last Stand. Tonka worked well for about half of the picture and then, like a temperamental human star, literally walked off the set. He just refused to work! Probably he simply lost interest. After a hurried conference, the trainer flew back to Hollywood, borrowed television's Flicka and flew her to Oregon. Make-up men duplicated Tonka's white markings so successfully that Flicka looked exactly like the gelding. The picture was finished with Flicka playing the title role. Needless to say, the temperamental gelding never played a leading role again, and his actions show why a quiet temperament and reliability are so important in a star horse.

Doubles do all the rough-and-tumble routines. Trigger, for example, does tricks and looks pretty for close-up shots. But a double carries Roy Rogers in the galloping scenes. Solid-colour horses are easy to match for doubles; pinto horses are practically impossible because no two are exactly alike. Dice's double, for instance, is easily detected on the screen.

The stand-in is the untrained member of the star horse's company, but an important one. Between takes, when lights are being adjusted and the camera exposure checked, the stand-in takes the lead position on the set. If the star horse had to stand through the lengthy preparations for shooting a scene he would be nervous and fidgety by the time the director was ready to shoot. In this way, the star horse is brought onto the set fresh and willing to concentrate on his cues.

When a film relates the complete story of a horse's life, as in *Smoky* and *Thunderhead, Son of Flicka*, many animals of the same colour and markings are needed to show the age progression. In all, eight different horses played the part of Thunderhead—one each for newborn foal, yearling, two-year-old, and finally mature horse; the other four were doubles and stand-ins.

Starring horses have a small staff of humans who cater to their personal and movie needs: a groom, to clean and feed the horse in a private stall with all the attentions befitting a star; a veterinarian, who is hired for the duration of shooting on location; and a make-up man, who, oddly enough, spends more time with the horse than do any of his handlers. Manes and tails constantly have to be combed, brushed, and trimmed. White horses must have their noses powdered to hide the tiny black hairs that would be considerably magnified on the screen. For close-up shots, the horse's eyes have to be treated with mascara to hide wrinkle blemishes. Black horses lose their strong colour after weeks of shooting in bright sun, and walnut juice is used to darken the areas faded by the sun.

Special make-up problems also arise. Starring horse Country Gentleman, who played in *Smoky*, had to appear neglected by his cruel owner. To make Country Gentlemen thinner, make-up men painted shadows on his haunches so that his bones seemed to protrude. Grey lines were drawn around the eyes to make them appear dull and droopy. Finally, after not being groomed for two days, the transformation from a spirited stallion to ill-treated wagon horse was complete.

There are other luxuries. Ever since Tom Mix gave his horse Tony a special trailer, all star horses have travelled in private trailers—plush accommodations painted in bright colours with the horse's name in large letters on the outside, and with a padded interior so that the horse won't chafe his legs. Hollywood publicity men have turned this into a status symbol, but the trailers are necessary to protect the horses on long trips.

After years of the special attentions of the movie business, star horses develop definite screen personalities that become well known to the studios and the public. Consequently, movie fans can quickly tell that the black horse they see in a film is the same one they recall from another. People may not know the horses' names, but a look in their eye, or the way they hold their head, becomes a trademark. In fact, it is often the personality of a horse (aside from his dramatic ability) that carries him to the heights of popularity. Above all, however, he must have acting talent, and not just a repertoire of tricks to be performed with the trainer standing less than two feet away. Movie horses are often on camera alone, and the extent of their ability to perform and to obey cues from long distance is one of the major qualities that makes a horse a valued performer.

THE HAUNTED HUNT

R. J. Richardson

The smoking-room of the Haycester and County Club looked cheerful enough in the firelight which was slowly getting the better of the dreary winter's day, and the white-haired man lay back in his chair, and, stretching out his slight, neatly-gaitered legs to the blaze, pulled thoughtfully at his cigar.

'As you all probably know,' he said at length, Anthony Nunn took the hounds close on fifty years ago, and hunted them himself for eleven seasons until his death.'

He paused with a grim, short laugh.

'"*Until*," did I say? Well, be that as it may, it is thirty-nine years since Anthony Nunn met with his death, and the Haycester lost the keenest huntsman that ever cheered a hound. The man was born to hunt hounds, he lived to hunt hounds, he died hunting hounds—and then came that ghastly day which I can never recall without a shudder.

'He was too keen; he thought of nothing but the hounds from year's end to year's end. In fact, whether he was always so, or whether it grew upon him, there is not a shadow of doubt that at the last he was a monomaniac on the subject of fox-hunting.

'He always killed a May fox; and there were strange tales about his having been seen cub-hunting by himself with a couple of hounds in out-of-the-way parts of the country before the end of June. Of course he always denied it, and said that he was merely exercising the hounds; but, knowing the man, I can well believe that rumour, for once, was no liar. It was just the sort of thing he would do. Indeed, as he himself said, only lack of sufficient means prevented him from hunting seven days a week.

'He was very far from being an ideal Master of Hounds. He never considered the field in the least; and time and time again he slipped out of cover without so much as a touch on the horn, leaving the entire field, and sometimes even the whips, too, behind. It was not selfishness; only that in the hunting field he was practically a hound himself.

'Many considered him bloodthirsty; and certainly he would go to extraordinary lengths to kill his fox, often digging him out of what had seemed the most impregnable places at all hours of the night. The more trouble a fox gave him, the more bent on killing him he became; and if he and his hounds were baffled he used to get beside himself with rage. With him, hunting was not a sport, it was an obsession.

'Fortunately the fox supply in the Haycester country has always been exceptionally good, and fortunately they take a good deal of killing; he would have well-nigh exhausted most countries in a very short time. As it was the show of foxes in some of the more open parts was low for several years after Nunn's régime.

'He was no society man. He cut an awkward little figure on foot, with his bandy legs and wizened, scowling face like a monkey's. He was a bachelor, and lived by himself in the huntsman's cottage at the kennels, acting as his own kennel-huntsman. He never entertained, and rarely went out anywhere. Away from the hounds he was impossible, curt and morose almost to rudeness; but the Haycester people forgave him all his faults for the sake of the sport he showed.

'The way Anthony Nunn hunted hounds was Fine Art: to watch and listen to him was the most exquisite pleasure I have ever enjoyed. He had a voice like a bell, and the cleverness of the fox himself. I verily believe that people preferred the bad-scenting days to the good in his time, it was such a delight to watch him help hounds. The sheer inspiration of some of his casts was enough to take away one's breath.

'With the hounds he was on the best of terms, and going to cover or returning home used to talk to them as if they were human beings, keeping up a continual prattle, after this style: "Shall we find a fox in Coney Rough, my lads, think ye? Old Challenger there thinks not. Didn't find there last time, says Challenger.—And which of you boys is going to cut out old Marksman today? You, Primate? Primate thinks he'll have a try.—Well, Sympathy, are you going to let us hear your voice today, Sympathy? You and I will have to part if you don't find your voice, you know, Sympathy"—and so on, addressing not a word to any of the field; and even in answer to a question only growling a monosyllable over his shoulder. To ride over hounds would have been as much as one's life was worth. I once saw him thrash a man, whose horse had kicked a hound, till he had to be dragged off him. Although he looked such a shrivelled up little fellow, Nunn could box like Nat Langham and hit like a kicking horse.

'There was one hound in particular that was the apple of his eye; an ugly hare-pied brute called Marksman, in his eighth season and still running to head when Nunn's death took place. This hound was so savage that none of the men at the kennels dared handle him, but with Nunn he was as gentle as a lamb. He was a wonderful working hound with a curious deep voice, and a marvel at holding a cold line. We used to say that Nunn's "For-ard to Marksman!" was as good as a view-hallo, and that the two were sufficient to account for any fox. Anthony Nunn and the Haycester Marksman were renowned all over England.

'I have dwelt somewhat on Nunn's peculiarities because, to my mind, when it is realized what manner of man he was, the experiences which I am about to relate become so much more credible. Looking back with a calm mind, the whole thing seems to me in perfect accord.

'I have told you how the killing of his fox was the be-all and end-all with him, how he looked upon the hunted fox as his natural and most deadly enemy, and how he would rage if Reynard managed to save his brush. To lose a fox affected him like a mortal insult, and he would brood over it until he was satisfied that he had brought the offender to book.

'That last fox was a typical instance. Twelve days before Nunn's death the hounds met at Yewbarrow Mill, then as now in the Monday country. We found a fox in Canonby Whin, and he broke close to where I was standing. He was good to know, that fox, and I could have sworn to him again among hundreds: a great raking, grey dog-fox, with most of his brush missing. Details of the run are immaterial; it is enough to tell you that after a clinker of eighty minutes we lost him the other side of Hareham, and, try as he might, Anthony Nunn with all his craft was beaten. Of course it upset him as usual, and he took hounds home there and then.

'No one acquainted with Nunn's idiosyncrasies was surprised when the following Monday's meet was changed from Wingley to Yewbarrow Mill. Again we found the big grey fox in Canonby Whin; and he gave us an even better run than before: by Hareham, Owlands Banks, and Buckfield; over Priestland Park and Shepley Down; past Hindholt to Windleby, where, after two hours and thirty minutes, we lost him again. This time Nunn's fury was a sight to behold. He raved and cursed, and screamed out, *"I'll kill that—bobtail if I have to jump the gates of Hell to do it!"* He tried forward and back, round and round, every place that could possibly hold a fox. Long after the last remnant of the field had gone home he was at it, until pitch darkness forced him to give it up.

'Eccentric as we thought him, no one was prepared for his next move. The next day messengers and telegrams were flying about the country to say that Wednesday's meet was abandoned, and that hounds would meet next on Friday at Yewbarrow Mill *at 9 a.m.* The telegrams bore the cryptic addition, "*Cub-hunting*".

'Naturally the people, especially those on the Wednesday and Friday sides, were furious, and the weight of their wrath fell on the Secretary, a mild person, very much in awe of Nunn, who could throw no light on the enigma. Many indignation meetings were held, and feeling ran so high that the Mastership of the Haycester Hounds would certainly have become vacant at the end of the season, even had the event not been precipitated as it was.

'Under the circumstances a very small field turned out at Yewbarrow Mill on the Friday. There were not half a dozen of us, besides the remarkable cavalcade that arrived with hounds. Nunn had with him not only the whippers-in and second horsemen, but every man and boy in any way connected with the kennels; all his own and the hunt servants' horses were out, ridden by stablemen, feeders, and what not; and he had brought every hound that had a leg to stand on: dogs and bitches, forty-seven couple in all.

'Nunn himself looked as if he had been out of bed for a week; and we heard afterwards that, having spent all the preceding days in destroying every earth and stopping every place where the fox could get in between Canonby Whin and Ridgeweather Hill, he had been out with the earthstopper the night before the meet, had gone carefully over all his work again to make sure that it was intact, and had then returned to Canonby Whin, watched the grey fox out, and made all safe behind him.

'He never even stopped his horse at the meet, ignored our salutations, and went straight on to cover.

'When we got to the Whin he turned round and addressed us; and then we understood the meaning of the strange telegram and of his miscellaneous following. "Get all round it," he said, "and hold him up like a cub." I think it had dawned upon all of us by this time that the man was insane, so, thinking it best to humour him, we spread ourselves out round the Whin.

'However, you know what a wild, straggling place it is, even now; and we were not nearly numerous enough to invest every corner of it, especially with a bold, enterprising customer like the grey fox inside. And sure enough, hounds were barely in when he broke at the far end and went away like a greyhound.

'Nunn came tearing out to the holloa, black in the face with passion, and blowing the gone-away note as if he would burst his lips. The forty-seven couple swept out like a great breaking wave and opened on the line with a crash of music that I have never heard the like of. I could hear old Marksman throwing his tongue like an organ above them all, and Nunn's beautiful voice blaspheming and cheering them on.

'I can shut my eyes and think I see him now, with his eyes glaring out of his ape face with madness. Driving his horse along and "forrarding" to the hounds, he never seemed to realize that there was a bank just in front of him, and was within two strides of it when he awoke to his danger. He tried to collect his horse, but the impetus was too great; the horse went into it like a shot from a gun, turned a complete somersault, and came down on the other side with a thud that could have been heard fields away. When we got over, there were two things to be done at once: to send for a gun to finish the horse, and the whips after the hounds to stop them if possible. One look at Nunn as we turned him over was enough. The full weight of the horse must have come on his head with tremendous force, smashing his skull and driving his face into the ground.

'It was the middle of January when Nunn was killed; and a fortnight after the funeral we hunted again, the first whip carrying the horn, under a temporary committee, for a couple of months.

'Next season Furlong, from the Burstover, took the mastership, bringing his own whips and engaging a professional huntsman.

This huntsman was one of the slow, "try-back", family-coachman sort, and although, thanks to a succession of good-scenting days in the early part of the season, we had fair sport, the proceedings seemed very dull after Nunn's brilliance.

'Furlong brought a few hounds of his own, but took over the greater part of Nunn's pack, and even these seemed affected by the changed spirit of things. Old Marksman in particular was not the same animal; from being the oracle of the pack he became a mute, listless shirker; so markedly so that Furlong talked of putting him down, and the huntsman remarked with a grin, "So this is the famous Marksman!"

'The hounds had not been in Canonby Whin at all that season until one day late in December, nearly a year after Nunn's death, when they met at the "Black Bull", which, as you know, is a very few miles from there. There was no scent in the morning, and we had done nothing but potter about until we came to the Whin in the afternoon. There I got on to my second horse, a brown, five-year-old thoroughbred called Pride of Tyrone, which I had bought out of Ireland for a longer price than I could really afford, but which I confidently expected him to recover with interest as a steeplechaser: I even cherished golden dreams of future Grand Nationals. My young horse was rather a handful in a crowd, so I went on to the whip at the far end of the cover.

'We had not long to wait before there was a whimper; and half a minute later, there, stealing away, was my old acquaintance the big, grey, bobtailed fox. Away he went on his familiar line; and I, with the thoughtlessness of youth, and in the excitement of getting well away with hounds, never reckoned that I was riding at the very part of the bank which had been fatal to Anthony Nunn. I was coming nicely at it, when suddenly Pride of Tyrone swerved, crossed his legs, and fell, shooting me out of the saddle. Quite unhurt, I picked myself up at once. Pride of Tyrone was already on his feet some yards away, drenched with sweat and plunging back towards the Whin. As I started to go after him, he circled round at a canter and went at the bank exactly as if he had been ridden at it. I was too late to intercept him, and he popped on and off like a bird, and strode away over the rise of the next field.

'I remember noticing as he went past me that the reins had somehow got caught on the saddle.

'By this time the field were galloping by me, some going over the bank as the shortest way, others following the huntsman through a gap a hundred yards or more to the right.

'Running across the next field and climbing on to the next bank for a better view, I could see the hounds fairly racing, and close up with them, served by his great speed, was the runaway Pride of Tyrone; a widening space between him and the rapidly tailing field.

'Pursuit on foot and in riding boots was out of the question, and as there was no probability of any one stopping him my anxiety was great lest he should manage to injure himself.

'I was at my wits' end what to do until it occurred to me that my first horse might still be within hail. I ran back as fast as I could across the two fields and on to the road at the top of the Whin, where I came upon a group of second horsemen just turning away from watching the disappearing hounds, and among them was my man. Fortunately we had done nothing to speak of before I changed on to Pride of Tyrone, so the horse was quite fresh, and I galloped down the line in pursuit of the fugitive.

'Hounds and Pride of Tyrone and all were out of sight and earshot by this time, but the tracks of the horses led straight away over the line the grey fox knew so well. It was not long before I began to meet people coming back, thrown out by falling or beaten by the pace, among them the first whip with his horse badly staked. But of Pride of Tyrone there was not a sign, and the tale of casualties did not tend to lessen my uneasiness on his account.

'The tracks became fewer and fewer, and at length between Humbleby Farm and Buckfield I encountered a man leading his horse back. From him I learnt that the pace, terrific for the first few miles, had slackened to a slow hunting run, when he, alone of all the field anywhere within sight of the hounds, had come to grief. He said that when he last saw the hounds they were running straight ahead, more slowly now, but in full cry; and right up alongside them, moving like a machine, as though he revelled in the game, was my embryo racehorse.

'Wasting no time, I followed Pride of Tyrone's trail. For the greater part of the way it was plain enough, and I was able to travel at a good pace; but in places, especially on the Downs and higher-lying grasslands, it was only with the greatest difficulty that I could find anything to guide me at all.

'The tracks went straight over Priestland Park and Shepley Down to just below Hindholt, where the fox had evidently been headed and had swung left-handed along Kelton Bottom. I saw the tracks of the hounds in the soft ground there, and knew that Pride of Tyrone was still with them.

'Coming up by Checkley on to the high land again the line lay to the right over Anyman's Down to Cockover Wood, where the hoofprints were a puzzle that took me some time to unravel. From what I could make of it, Pride of Tyrone had galloped into the wood, had turned back half-way down the ride, had walked and trotted back, standing still more than once, and had broken into a gallop again before leaving the wood by the way he had entered it, going away in the direction of Swingstone.

'In another hour or so it would be too dark to see any tracks at all, and as I seemed to be no nearer to Pride of Tyrone than when I started, my chance of catching him before nightfall appeared remote in the extreme; but I was determined to persevere while I could, and kept plodding along on the trail.

'From Swingstone it led right on by High Firs and Kyte Common, as straight as a die past Ridgeweather Hill, and on to the Teal Valley. Sinking the valley, I followed it on through Frogbere plantations and across the water-meadows straight to the Teal.

'"Surely," I thought, "the water would stop him." But no; I saw the marks where he had taken off. "What a horse!" The Teal at that point was thirty feet across.

'I knew the horse I was riding could not jump it, so going round by the bridge, quarter of a mile higher up towards the village, I came along the opposite bank till I found the tracks again. As the valley was already in twilight this was no easy matter, but I struck them at length and discovered that Pride of Tyrone had landed with a yard to spare, and gone straight on without hesitating.

'By this time my mount had had quite enough of it, and as I had more and more difficulty every minute in tracking my way along, I came to the conclusion that further pursuit was hopeless, and was just turning my horse's head in the direction of home when the sound of a hoof on a road caught my ear.

'I rode quickly towards the sound, and, sitting on his horse in the lane which leads up out of the valley by the edge of Baron's Wood, came upon the new huntsman listening intently with his hand behind his ear. Though how he, who never jumped a stick if he could help it, and almost a stranger in the country, had managed to get so far, I could not imagine. Certainly he had a marvellous knack of picking his way about by lanes and gates, and this was the only direction in which I ever knew him to exhibit the least intelligence.

' "Hark!" he said, when he caught sight of me, "Hark! they're in there," and pointed up to where Baron's Wood, lying along the top of the valley side, loomed against the sunset sky. I stopped my horse and listened, but the bellringers were practising in Frogbere Church, and the sound, echoing from both sides of the valley, lent itself to any construction the imagination liked to put upon it.

' "They're in there," said the huntsman, "I heard them before the bells began. And there's someone hunting them!"

'Someone hunting them! At this piece of information the notion flashed across me that I had come all this way on a wild-goose chase. What more likely than that someone had nicked in with them, probably when the fox had swung out to Checkley and back to Cockover Wood? And had I read aright the riddle of the returning tracks in Cockover Wood? I was convinced that I had been following a single line of tracks and that those belonged to Pride of Tyrone. "But," I said to myself, "I am not a Red Indian, and it is quite possible that I have made a mistake somewhere in spite of all my care.'' After all, was it probable that any horse, least of all a young one who had that season seen hounds for the first time, would, of his own free will and riderless, stick to them all through a run like that, jumping everything as it came and the Teal as well? The more I reasoned on it the more absurd did the idea seem to me.

'As we sat there straining our ears, a labourer came down the lane from the direction of the wood. "The Hounds?" he said in answer to our questions. "Yes, they've been up there hunting about in the big wood this half-hour. Yes, there's someone with them, I heard him. No, I didn't see him; I saw some of the dogs; and there's a horse that's lost his master."

'We rode up the lane and turned into the wood. "Now," said the huntsman, "we shall see who is meddling with my hounds."

'We had gone some way along the main ride before we heard the hounds running towards us from the left. They came nearer and nearer, and presently burst out of the undergrowth about eighty yards ahead of us, turned sharp left-handed, and went straight up the ride in full cry. Just as they passed a branch ride leading from the left, an object dashed out of it and followed in their wake. It was Pride of Tyrone in full career.

'Both our horses were dead beat, so, bucket along as we might, we could not keep the hounds in view, and the cry was getting fainter and fainter when the huntsman's horse behind me came down with a squelch and a clatter. I never even stopped—I am afraid I set more value on Pride of Tyrone—but sent my horse along for all he was worth to the end of the wood. There I found that the hounds had crossed the road into Oxlow Wood, Pride of Tyrone with them.

'As you know, Oxlow Wood is an irregular crescent in shape, with only one ride through it lengthways, and a horse can therefore only get in or out at the ends, or horns, of the crescent. It was just the same in those days; so, having made sure that Pride of Tyrone had entered, I cut across to the far end, thinking to intercept him.

There were no tracks leading out of the wood, and the chances were against his turning back, so I awaited developments.

'The sun was just setting blood-red. The sky in the west was like a sheet of flame. Not a breath of wind stirred the woods, and behind them the mist was creeping out of the Teal Valley. The bells of Frogbere Church were still faintly audible, mingling with the intermittent cry of hounds, which, now on one side of the wood, now on the other, was gradually coming towards me.

'At length the cry ceased altogether, and then from the wood came a sound that made my spine crawl.

'It was a voice. A voice that never had a like: the voice of *Anthony Nunn*!

'"*Yeu-eup!*" it went, "*Try for-ard!*"

'With the cold sweat dripping off me I sat there paralysed; and the beautiful voice came on:

'"*Eu, Marksman!—Yooi, my lads!—Yooi, wind him!*" Nearer and nearer it came, ringing and echoing through the wood like a bell. And still I sat there. My limbs were lead and my brain was numb, and I sat there waiting, for what unspeakable apparition I had no conception.

'Louder and louder it grew: "*Yeu-eup!—Push him up!—Youi, lads!—Yeu, try in there!*"

'Then from the wood there crept the dim form of the grey bobtailed fox. With one foot raised he stood listening a moment, and stole away towards the sunset.

'In cover a hound spoke, then another: a deep note like an otter hound.

'The voice cheered him till the air throbbed. "*Huic!—Huic!—Huic! to Marksman!—Ho-o-o-o-ick!*"

'The old hound crashed through the brushwood, alert and eager – the Marksman of yore. Throwing that sonorous tongue of his, with his nose on the line he drove along. Scoring to cry the hounds poured out. And then, every muscle on my body literally twitching, I heard the voice close at hand, and an approaching horse.

'It seemed hours that I stared with aching eyes that I dared not blink at the end of the ride where the Thing must appear.

'What I saw burnt into my brain.

'Out of the wood came—Pride of Tyrone!

'Pride of Tyrone, white with lather, eyes wild and nostrils distended. The bit was pressing on his mouth; the reins extended stiffly back from the bit to empty air above the withers. They were held in a grasp, and they were held by—*nothing*!

'And from the empty air above the saddle, from on a level with my own head, pealed and cheered that clarion voice.

'Pride of Tyrone passed close by me: I could have touched him. And as he passed a sense of unutterable, nameless horror and doom swept over me. And the voice blared like a trumpet right in my ear: "*For-ard. Awa-ay!*"

'Blind with terror, I drove the spurs into my horse and rode for my life.

'My recollection of the journey home is a blurred jumble of furious galloping and weary leading of a foundered horse.

'Next morning I went to the kennels. I found the huntsman, scared and shaken, big with news. After the fall his horse was dead lame, and as he could not hear a sound of the hounds he went home. It was after nine o'clock when he got to the kennels; the whips were already there, having collected four and a half couple of lost hounds—all new hounds of Furlong's. Of the rest of the eighteen couple taken out in the morning there was not a trace.

'He got his supper and went to bed; and had been asleep some time when he was aroused by a violent knocking at the door, which continued until his hand was on the latch to open it. He looked out. In the yard, which was as light as day with brilliant moonlight, stood six couple of hounds. Not a sign of anything else. He was about to call out, when such a feeling of utter horror came over him as he had no words to describe. Something was hurled past his head into the house. And out of nothing, right in his face rang yells and shrieks of unearthly laughter.

'How he even managed to bang the door to, and how long he

The horse went down the bank like a shot from a gun.

crouched there sick with fright, he had no idea. He left the six couple outside to shift for themselves till daylight.

'He showed me the object thrown through the door. Still lying where it had fallen was the mangled, wolfish mask of a great dog-fox, and crammed into the mouth were the four pads and a grey fragment of a brush.

'During the next few days tidings came in.

'Pride of Tyrone was found, stiff and dead, in a lonely by-road within five miles of the kennels.

'Singly and in twos and threes the rest of the hounds came back, led, in carts, and limping home alone on weary bleeding feet.

'By the end of the week there was only one hound unaccounted for. Then we had the story of the doctor at Stoatswold, in the heart of the Oaklands country.

'Driving home late on the night of the run, he heard hounds killing a fox on the moor above the village, and someone whooping and whooping till the whole countryside resounded.

'The doctor said it was gruesome and turned him cold. The villagers heard it, broad awake, and shivered in their beds.'

MARENGO AND COPENHAGEN

Stella A. Walker

MARENGO — NAPOLEON'S CHARGER

Napoleon's spectacular successes on the field of battle were due, almost entirely, to the brilliant way in which he used his cavalry. He once wrote: 'Cavalry charges are equally effective at the beginning, in the middle and at the end of a battle'; but in fact his usual custom was to keep a cavalry force as a strong reserve to assure victory and to use it finally for the vigorous pursuit and annihilation of the enemy. In 1806 his cavalry numbered 65,000, but he later raised it to 100,000 with officers, men and horses carefully selected.

It is not surprising, therefore, to find that Napoleon himself was mounted on excellent chargers, all of them Arabs or Barbs, and nearly always grey or cream in colour. These horses were specially schooled at the Imperial Stud Farm at St Cloud. They were trained to remain steady and alert under gunfire, and to become easy-gaited for the long, weary marches of distant campaigns. To be one of Napoleon's chargers was a dangerous privilege, as he is supposed to have had eighteen horses killed under him in battle.

The most famous of these chargers was Marengo, a light grey or white Arab stallion imported from Egypt as a six-year-old in 1799 after the Battle of Aboukir. It is thought he was probably descended from the renowned El Naseri stud. The Emperor rode the horse at Marengo, and was wounded by cannon-shot which carried away a piece of his left boot. The engagement was saved from defeat only by the initiative of General Kellerman, who ordered a cavalry charge at the crucial moment, turning near disaster into brilliant victory. Napoleon was so impressed by the courage, speed and vitality of his new charger under fire, that he named him after the victorious battle.

Marengo stood only 14.1 hands high, but no horse was so long or so closely associated with Napoleon. This little Arab carried him at Austerlitz, Jena and Wagram. He survived the ill-fated Russian expedition of 1812, when it is said he stumbled on the icy roads and unhorsed his imperial rider. This mishap was regarded by the superstitious as an omen of the misfortunes that befell the brave and devoted French army, thousands of whom perished from famine and the bitter cold in the retreat from Moscow.

Marengo was not, apparently, among the horses sent to share the Emperor's exile in the Isle of Elba. The imperial stables suffered little change under the new régime and he was kept in his usual surroundings until Napoleon's re-entry into France.

The Emperor then took his old favourite to Waterloo, though Marengo at that date was twenty-two years old. The final and culminating defeat there was largely due to the failure of the newly re-organized French cavalry which lacked its former unity and co-ordination, and was thus unable to break through the British squares of mounted soldiers.

On the eve of the battle the Emperor's horses were stabled at La Ferme du Caillou. Three chargers were installed there, Désirée, Marie and Marengo, and it was the little Arab that carried Napoleon through the early part of the battle. According to one report he was slightly wounded in the left hip, his eighth wound in action. Later in the day Napoleon rode Marie and was hotly pursued by the English and Prussian cavalry. As he galloped by La Ferme du Caillou he stopped to change the tired Marie for a fresh horse. There was no time to saddle Marengo, and only an instant to take the first horse that stood ready, before the Emperor dashed away at full speed for Charleroi, where he picked up a carriage, and, travelling without pause, reached Paris in three days. Marengo, left in the stables at the farm, was captured by the British.

He was brought to England by Lord Petre, and there was some idea that he should be exhibited publicly as Napoleon's charger, but he was purchased by General J. J. Angerstein of the Grenadier Guards, who hoped to breed racehorses from him. He stood at New Barnes near Ely, and was well cared for and petted. He was advertised, in spite of his age, as late as 1820 at a fee of ten guineas, but his progeny achieved no success on the turf, which perhaps is not remarkable, as one contemporary description admits he was of bad conformation and ill-tempered, and, of course, his small size was not conducive to the production of racing stock. On the other hand, a different authority pronounces him faultless with all the finest eastern characteristics.

He died in 1831 at the great age of thirty-eight years, and his skeleton is preserved in the museum of the Royal United Services Institution. One of his hooves was made into a snuffbox and presented by General Angerstein to brother officers of the Brigade of Guards at St James's Palace.

There has been considerable controversy whether Marengo was a Barb or an Arabian, and whether he was light grey and only white in old age. The evidence is conflicting on both points, but in the many paintings of him he is depicted with the points and conformation of the typical Arab, and both artists Vernet and Meissonier show him as a white horse. In the familiar picture painted by James Ward, RA, in 1824, Marengo also appears as pure white, but as the horse was over thirty years old at the time it provides no real evidence.

COPENHAGEN – THE IRON DUKE'S CHARGER

Copenhagen, the famous charger of the Duke of Wellington, was almost as renowned as the Iron Duke himself. Contemporary diaries and letters are full of references to this stallion and anecdotes abound of his amazing stamina and personality.

Copenhagen's dam was Lady Catherine, the mare that carried General Grosvenor at the siege of Copenhagen. She embarked for England in foal to Meteor, second in the Derby of 1786, himself the son of the famous Eclipse; and in 1808 produced the bright chestnut foal that was named Copenhagen, after the campaign. Though he is referred to as a thoroughbred, he was not actually eligible for the General Stud Book as his grand-dam was a half-bred hunter mare. However, as he was well endowed with speed and good looks, General Grosvenor had him trained for the turf, but in his thirteen races in public he won only a match at Newmarket and a sweepstake at Huntingdon.

The Duke of Wellington bought him in 1812 from Sir Charles Stewart in Spain, where he was being used as a charger, and from that date he never changed hands again. The Duke rode him throughout the Peninsular Campaign and is supposed to have hunted him with the sixteen couple of hounds he brought over from England.

On active service the two were inseparable, and the spectacle of the stern, taciturn Duke galloping from one vantage point to another soon became a familiar and much-loved sight with the troops. Copenhagen's speed and agility made him an ideal ride, and the sudden dashing appearance of Wellington on his hand-

Napoleon named him after the victorious battle at Marengo.

some chestnut at the crucial moment steadied many a wavering division and snatched victory when defeat was imminent.

The endurance of Copenhagen at the time of the Battle of Waterloo was tested to the utmost limits. On the day previous to the conflict, Wellington rode Copenhagen nearly sixty miles on visits to the headquarters of the Prussian troops and also to conferences with his own generals. The Duke wrote: 'On June 17th before 10 o'clock I got on Copenhagen's back – so much to do that neither he nor I were still for many minutes together. I never drew bit and he never had a morsel in his mouth till 8 p.m. The poor beast I myself saw stabled and fed in the village of Waterloo.'

Seven hours later, at 3 a.m., Wellington rose and wrote important letters. As soon as it was light he mounted Copenhagen and rode him throughout the entire battle, a period in all of over seventeen hours. Undeterred by cannon shot, rainstorms and the devastating cavalry charges of General Ney, Wellington on Copenhagen calmly directed operations, reconnoitring and galloping from one viewpoint to another. The Duke personally launched the Household Cavalry against the French with the words, 'Now, gentlemen, for the honour of the Household Cavalry!' At the enemy's capture of La Haye Sainte he took command of the Brunswickers and saved the day. The Duke and his chestnut horse, both oblivious of danger, were everywhere. The final phase of the battle lasted from 7.30 p.m. until dark. Night had fallen when Wellington met Blucher at the farm La Belle Alliance, and the two men embraced each other in the hour of victory in the presence of the troops.

Wearily the Duke and Copenhagen returned to the village of Waterloo across the field of battle, where 45,000 dead and wounded lay in an area of three square miles. As Wellington and his charger picked their way along the muddy road in the bright moonlight, wounded men recognized the pair and roused from their pain and delirium to cheer the two as they passed. But the Duke was sunk in deep depression, worn out by sheer physical fatigue and devastated with grief at the appalling losses his victory had entailed. At last he reached his quarters and stiffly slid from the saddle, but

Copenhagen, perhaps feeling that the hour of triumph merited some display of spirit, lashed out and only by inches missed killing his master.

The next day, when the Duke and Copenhagen were in Brussels, the horse once more kicked up his heels as his rider dismounted, and this time he broke loose and galloped half through the city before recapture. An animal of such indefatigable energy and verve deserves his place in the records of England's great victory against Napoleon.

In the years of peace that followed Copenhagen lived at the Duke's seat at Strathfield Saye. Both he and Wellington were much flattered and admired by the fair sex; and the Duke gave to a favoured few the privilege of a ride on Copenhagen, which proved, in some cases, an uncertain pleasure for the lady. Frances Lady Shelley writes in 1815 in her diary: 'I dined at three o'clock in order to ride with the Duke, who offered to mount me on Copenhagen. A charming ride of two hours. But I found Copenhagen the most difficult horse to sit of any I have ever ridden. If the Duke had not been there, I should have been frightened. He said, "I believe you think the glory greater than the pleasure in riding him!" '

Lady Georgiana Lennox also found him a trying mount: as always, at the sight of troops, he neighed loudly. When she was riding him he greeted in this way a bunch of soldiers who shouted at her: 'Take care of that 'ere horse, he kicks out; we knew him well Spain.'

In later years he sired several good foals for the Duke. Mrs Arbuthnot, Wellington's great friend and confidante, relates how on 16 July 1826 she was taken to see a fine foal by Copenhagen 'which was the most beautiful creature I ever saw'.

For the last ten years of his life Copenhagen was not ridden, and he became accidentally blinded in one eye. The Duke's devotion to the horse never lessened, and when Copenhagen died in February 1836, he was buried with military honours at Strathfield Saye, where a headstone marks his grave, with this inscription:

> *God's humble instrument, though meaner clay,*
> *Should share the glory of that glorious day.*

There was universal grief at the passing of the famous old charger, which R. E. Egerton Warburton voiced in a poem entitled 'Epitaph'.

> *With years o'er burdened, sunk the battle steed;*
> *War's funeral honours to his dust decreed;*
> *A foal when Cathcart overpower'd the Dane,*
> *And Gambier's fleet despoil'd the northern main,*
> *'Twas his to tread the Belgian field, and bear*
> *A mightier chief to prouder triumphs there.*
> *Let Strathfield Saye to wondering patriots tell*
> *How Wellesley wept when Copenhagen fell.*

Years later, in extreme old age, the Duke would still talk of his famous horse and relate endless stories of his fire and energy. He is recorded as saying: 'There may be faster horses, no doubt many handsomer, but for bottom and endurance I never saw his fellow.'

In London, opposite Apsley House, there is a fine bronze statute by Sir Joseph Edward Boehm of Wellington on Copenhagen. The most successful portrait is that by James Ward, which was painted as a companion picture to Napoleon on Marengo.

CARROT FOR A CHESTNUT

Dick Francis

Chick stood and sweated with the carrot in his hand. His head seemed to be floating and he couldn't feel his feet on the ground, and the pulse thudded massively in his ear. A clammy green pain shivered in his gut.

Treachery was making him sick.

The time: fifty minutes before sunrise. The morning: cold. The raw swirling wind was clearing its throat for a fiercer blow, and a heavy layer of nimbo-stratus was fighting every inch of the way against the hint of light. In the neat box stalls round the stable yard the dozing horses struck a random hoof against a wooden wall, rattled a chain, sneezed hay dust out of a moist black nostril.

Chick was late. Two hours late. He'd been told to give the carrot to the lanky chestnut at four o'clock in the morning, but at four o'clock in the morning it had been pouring with rain – hard, slanting rain that soaked a man to the skin in one minute flat, and Chick had reckoned it would be too difficult explaining away a soaking at four o'clock in the morning. Chick had reckoned it would be better to wait until the rain stopped, it couldn't make any difference. Four o'clock, six o'clock, what the hell. Chick always knew better than anyone else.

Chick was a thin, disgruntled nineteen-year-old who always felt the world owed him more than he got. He had been a bad-tempered, argumentative child and an aggressively rebellious adolescent. The resulting snarling habit of mind was precisely what was now hindering his success as an adult. Not that Chick would have agreed, of course. Chick never agreed with anyone if he could help it. Always knew better, did Chick.

He was unprepared for the severity of the physical symptoms of fear. His usual attitude toward any form of authority was scorn (and authority had not so far actually belted him one across his sulky mouth). Horses had never scared him because he had been born to the saddle and had grown up mastering everything on four legs with contemptuous ease. He believed in his heart that no one could really ride better than he could. He was wrong.

He looked apprehensively over his shoulder, and the shifting pain in his stomach sharply intensified. That simply couldn't happen, he thought wildly. He'd heard about people getting sick with fear. He hadn't believed it. It couldn't happen. Now, all of a sudden, he feared it could. He tightened all his muscles desperately, and the spasm slowly passed. It left fresh sweat standing out all over his skin and no saliva in his mouth.

The house was dark. Upstairs, behind the black open window with the pale curtain flapping in the spartan air, slept Arthur Morrison, trainer of the forty-three racehorses in the stables below. Morrison habitually slept lightly. His ears were sharper than half a dozen guard dogs', his stable hands said.

Chick forced himself to turn his head away, to walk in view of that window, to take the ten exposed steps down to the chestnut's stall.

If the guvernor woke up and saw him . . . Gawd, he thought furiously, he hadn't expected it to be like this. Just a lousy walk down the yard to give a carrot to the gangly chestnut. Guilt and fear and treachery. They bypassed his sneering mind and erupted through his nerves instead.

He couldn't see anything wrong with the carrot. It hadn't been cut in half and hollowed out and packed with drugs and tied together again. He'd tried pulling the thick end out like a plug, and that hadn't worked either. The carrot just looked like any old carrot, any old carriot you'd watch your ma chop up to put in a stew. Any old carrot you'd give to any old horse. Not a very young, succulent carrot or a very aged carrot, knotted and woody. Just any old ordinary *carrot*.

But strangers didn't proposition you to give any old carrot to one special horse in the middle of the night. They didn't give you more than you earned in half a year when you said you'd do it. Any old carrot didn't come wrapped carefully alone in a polythene bag inside an empty cheesecracker packet, given to you by a stranger in a car park after dark in a town six miles from the stables. You didn't give any old carrot in the middle of the night to a chestnut who was due to start favourite in a high-class steeplechase eleven hours later.

Chick was getting dizzy with holding his breath by the time he'd completed the ten tiptoed steps to the chestnut's stall. Trying not to cough, not to groan, not to let out the strangling tension in a sob, he curled his sweating fingers around the bolt and began the job of easing it out, inch by frightening inch, from its socket.

By day he slammed the bolts open and shut with a smart practised flick. His body shook in the darkness with the strain of moving by fractions.

The bolt came free with the tiniest of grating noises, and the top half of the split door swung slowly outward. No squeaks from the hinges, only the whisper of metal on metal. Chick drew in a long breath like a painful, trickling, smothered gasp and let it out between his clenched teeth. His stomach lurched again, threateningly. He took another quick, appalled grip on himself and thrust his arm in a panic through the dark, open space.

Inside the stall, the chestnut was asleep, dozing on his feet. The changing swirl of air from the opening door moved the sensitive hairs around his muzzle and raised his mental state from semi-consciousness to inquisitiveness. He could also smell the carrot. He could also smell the man: smell the fear in the man's sweat.

'Come on,' Chick whispered desperately. 'Come on, then, boy.'

The horse moved his nose around towards the carrot and finally, reluctantly, his feet. He took it indifferently from the man's trembling palm, whiffling it in with his black mobile lips, scrunching it languidly with large rotations of jaw. When he had swallowed all the pulped-up bits he poked his muzzle forward for more. But there was no more, just the lighter square of sky darkening again as the door swung shut, just the faint sounds of the bolt going back, just the fading smell of the man and the passing taste of carrot. Presently he forgot about it and turned slowly round again so that his hindquarters were toward the door, because he usually stood that way, and after a minute or two he blinked slowly, rested his near hind leg lazily on the point of the hoof and lapsed back into twilight mindlessness.

Down in his stomach the liquid narcotic compound with which the carrot had been injected to saturation gradually filtered out of the digesting carrot cells and began to be absorbed into the bloodstream. The process was slow and progressive. And it had started two hours late.

Arthur Morrison stood in his stable yard watching his men load the chestnut into the motor horse box that was to take him to the races. He was eyeing the proceedings with an expression that was critical from habit and bore little relation to the satisfaction in his mind. The chestnut was the best horse in his stable: a frequent winner, popular with the public, a source of prestige as well as revenue. The big steeplechase at Cheltenham had been tailor-made for him from the day its conditions had been published, and Morrison was adept at producing a horse in peak condition for a particular race. No one seriously considered that the chestnut would be beaten. The newspapers had tipped it to a man and the bookmakers were fighting shy at 6-4 on. Morrison allowed himself a glimmer of warmth in the eyes and a twitch of smile to the lips as the men clipped shut the heavy doors of the horse van and drove it out of the yard.

These physical signs were unusual. The face he normally wore was a compound of concentration and disapproval in roughly equal proportions. Both qualities contributed considerably to his success as a racehorse trainer and to his unpopularity as a person, a fact Morrison himself was well aware of. He didn't in the least care that almost no one liked him. He valued success and respect much more highly than love and held in incredulous contempt all those who did not.

Across the yard Chick was watching the horse van drive away, his usual scowl in place. Morrison frowned irritably. The boy was a pest, he thought. Always grousing, always impertinent, always trying to scrounge up more money. Morrison didn't believe in boys having life made too easy: a little hardship was good for the soul. Where Morrison and Chick radically differed was the point at which each thought hardship began.

Chick spotted the frown and watched Morrison fearfully, his guilt pressing on him like a rock. He couldn't know, he thought frantically. He couldn't even suspect there was anything wrong with the horse or he wouldn't have let him go off to the races. The horse had looked all right, too. Absolutely his normal self. Perhaps there had been nothing wrong with the carrot. . . . Perhaps it had been the wrong carrot, even. . . . Chick glanced around uneasily and knew very well he was fooling himself. The horse might look all right but he wasn't.

Arthur Morrison saddled up his horse at the races, and Chick watched him from ten nervous paces away, trying to hide in the eager crowd that pushed forward for a close view of the favourite. There was a larger admiring crowd outside the chestnut's saddling stall than for any of the other seven runners, and the bookmakers had shortened their odds. Behind Morrison's concentrated expression an itch of worry was growing insistent. He pulled the girth tight and adjusted the buckles automatically, acknowledging to himself that his former satisfaction had changed to anxiety. The horse was not himself. There were no lively stamping feet, no playful nips from the teeth, no response to the crowd; this was a horse that usually played to the public like a film star. He couldn't be feeling well, and if he wasn't feeling well he wouldn't win. Morrison tightened his mouth. If the horse were not well enough to win, he would prefer him not to run at all. To be beaten at odds-on would be a disgrace. A defeat on too large a scale. A loss of face. Particularly as Morrison's own eldest son Toddy was to be the jockey. The newspapers would tear them both to pieces.

Morrison came to a decision and sent for the vet.

The rules of jump racing in England stated quite clearly that if a horse had been declared a runner in a race, only the say-so of a veterinarian was sufficient grounds for withdrawing him during the last three-quarters of an hour before post time. The Cheltenham racecourse veterinarian came and looked at the chestnut and, after consulting with Morrison, led it off to a more private stall and took its temperature.

'His temperature's quite normal,' the veterinarian assured Morrison.

'I don't like the look of him.'

'I can't find anything wrong.'

'He's not well,' Morrison insisted.

The veterinarian pursed his lips and shook his head. There was nothing obviously wrong with the horse, and he knew he would be in trouble himself if he allowed Morrison to withdraw so hot a favourite on such slender grounds. Not only that, this was the third application for withdrawal he'd had to consider that afternoon. He had refused both the others, and the chestnut was certainly in no worse a state.

'He'll have to run,' the veterinarian said positively, making up his mind.

Morrison was furious and went raging off to find a steward, who came and looked at the chestnut and listened to the vet and confirmed that the horse would have to run whether Morrison liked it or not. Unless, that was, Morrison cared to involve the horse's absent owner in paying a heavy fine?

With the face of granite Morrison resaddled the chestnut, and a stable lad led him out into the parade ring, where most of the waiting public cheered and a few wiser ones looked closely and hurried off to hedge their bets.

With a shiver of dismay, Chick saw the horse reappear and for the first time regretted what he'd done. That stupid vet, he thought violently. He can't see what's under his bloody nose, he couldn't see a barn at ten paces. Anything that happened from then on was the vet's fault, Chick thought. The vet's responsibility, absolutely. The man was a criminal menace, letting a horse run in a steeplechase with dope coming out of its eyeballs.

Toddy Morrison had joined his father in the parade ring and together they were watching with worried expressions as the chestnut plodded lethargically around the oval walking track. Toddy was a strong, stock professional jockey in his late 20s with an infectious grin and a generous view of life that represented a direct rejection of his father's. He had inherited the same strength of mind but had used it to leave home at 18 to ride races for other trainers, and had only consented to ride for his father when he could dictate his own terms. Arthur Morrison, in consequence, respected him deeply. Between them they had won a lot of races.

Chick didn't actually dislike Toddy Morrison, even though, as he saw it, Toddy stood in his way. Occasionally Arthur let Chick ride a race if Toddy had something better or couldn't make the weight. Chick had to share these scraps from Toddy's table with two or three other lads in the yard who were, though he didn't believe it, as good as he was in the saddle. But though the envy curdled around inside him and the snide remarks came out sharp and sour as vinegar, he had never actually come to hate Toddy. There was something about Toddy that you couldn't hate, however good the reason. Chick hadn't given a thought to the fact that it would be Toddy who would have to deal with the effects of the carrot. He had seen no further than his own pocket. He wished now that it had been some other jockey. Anyone but Toddy.

The conviction suddenly crystallized in Chick's mind as he looked at Toddy and Morrison standing there worried in the parade ring that he had never believed the chestnut would actually start in the race. The stranger, Chick said to himself, had distinctly told him the horse would be too sick to start. I wouldn't have done it, else, Chick thought virtuously. I wouldn't have done it. It's bloody dangerous, riding a doped steeplechaser. I wouldn't have done that to Toddy. It's not my fault he's going to ride a doped steeplechaser, it's that vet's fault for not seeing. It's that stranger's fault, he told me distinctly the horse wouldn't be fit to start. . .

Chick remembered with an unpleasant jerk that he'd been two hours late with the carrot. Maybe if he'd been on time the drug would have come out more and the vet would have seen. . .

Chick jettisoned this unbearable theory instantly on the grounds that no one can tell how seriously any particular horse will react to a drug or how quickly it will work, and he repeated to himself the comforting self-delusion that the stranger had promised him the horse wouldn't ever start – though the stranger had not in fact said any such thing. The stranger, who was at the races, was entirely satisfied with the way things were going and was on the point of making a great deal of money.

The bell rang for the jockeys to mount. Chick clenched his hands in his pockets and tried not to visualize what could happen to a rider going over jumps at thirty miles an hour on a doped horse. Chick's body began playing him tricks again: he could feel the sweat trickling down his back and the pulse had come back in his ears.

Supposing he told them, he thought. Supposing he just ran out there into the ring and told Toddy not to ride the horse, it hadn't a chance of jumping properly, it was certain to fall, it could kill him bloody easily because its reactions would be all shot to bits.

Supposing he did. The way they'd look at him. His imagination blew a fuse and blanked out on that picture because such a blast of contempt didn't fit in with his overgrown self-esteem. He could not, could *not* face the fury they would feel. And it might not end there. Even if he told them and saved Toddy's life, they might tell the police. He wouldn't put it past them. And he could end up in the dock. Even in jail. They weren't going to do that to him, not to *him*. He wasn't going to give them the chance. He should have been paid more. Paid more because he was worth more. If he'd been paid more, he wouldn't have needed to take the stranger's money. Arthur Morrison had only himself to blame.

Toddy would have to risk it. After all, the horse didn't look too bad, and the vet had passed it, hadn't he, and maybe the carrot being two hours late was all to the good and it wouldn't have done its work properly yet, and in fact it was really thanks to Chick if it hadn't; only thanks to him that the drug was two hours late and that nothing much would happen, really, anyway. Nothing much would happen. Maybe the chestnut wouldn't actually *win*, but Toddy would come through all right. Of course he would.

The jockeys swung up into their saddles, Toddy among them. He saw Chick in the crowd, watching, and sketched an acknowledging wave. The urge to tell and the fear of telling tore Chick apart like the Chinese trees.

Toddy gathered up the reins and clicked his tongue and steered the chestnut indecisively out on to the track. He was disappointed that the horse wasn't feeling well but not in the least apprehensive. It hadn't occurred to him, or to Arthur Morrison, that the horse might be doped. He cantered down to the post standing in his stirrups, replanning his tactics mentally now that he couldn't rely on reserves in his mount. It would be a difficult race now to win. Pity.

Chick watched him go. He hadn't come to his decision, to tell or not to tell. The moment simply passed him by. When Toddy had gone he unstuck his leaden feet and plodded off to the stands to watch the race, and in every corner of his mind little self-justifications sprang up like nettles. A feeling of shame tried to creep in round the edges, but he kicked it out smartly. They should have paid him more. It was their fault, not his.

He thought about the wad of notes the stranger had given him with the carrot. Money in advance. The stranger had trusted him, which was more than most people seemed to. He'd locked himself into the bathroom and counted the notes, counted them twice, and they were all there, £300 just as the stranger had promised. He had never had so much money all at once in his life before. . . Perhaps he never would again, he thought. And if he'd told Arthur Morrison and Toddy about the dope, he would have to give up that money, give up the money and more. . .

Finding somewhere to hide the money had given him difficulty. Three hundred used £1 notes had turned out to be quite bulky, and he didn't want to risk his ma poking around among his things, like she did, and coming across them. He'd solved the problem temporarily by rolling them up and putting them in a brightly coloured round tin which once held toffees but which he used for years for storing brushes and polish for cleaning his shoes. He had covered the money with a duster and jammed the brushes back on the shelf in his bedroom where it always stood. He thought he would probably have to find somewhere safer, in the end. And he'd have to be careful how he spent the money—there would be too many questions asked if he just went out and bought a car. He'd always wanted a car . . . and now he had the money for one . . . and he still couldn't get the car. It wasn't fair. Not fair at all. If they'd paid him more. . . Enough for a car. . .

Up on the well-positioned area of stands set aside for trainers and jockeys, a small man with hot dark eyes put his hand on Chick's arm and spoke to him, though it was several seconds before Chick started to listen.

'. . . I see you are here, and you're free, will you ride it?'

'What?' said Chick vaguely.

'My horse in the Novice Hurdle,' said the little man impatiently. 'Of course, if you don't want to. . .'

'Didn't say that,' Chick mumbled. 'Ask the guvnor. If he says I can, well, I can.'

The small trainer walked across the stand to where Arthur Morrison was watching the chestnut intently through the race glasses and asked the same question he'd put to Chick.

'Chick? Yes, he can ride it for you, if you want him.' Morrison gave the other trainer two full seconds of his attention and glued himself back on to his race glasses.

'My jockey was hurt in a fall in the first race,' explained the small man. 'There are so many runners in the Novice Hurdle that there's a shortage of jockeys. I just saw that boy of yours, so I asked him on the spur of the moment, see?'

'Yes, yes,' said Morrison, ninety per cent uninterested. 'He's moderately capable, but don't expect too much of him.' There was no spring in the chestnut's stride. Morrison wondered in depression if he was sickening for the cough.

'My horse won't win. Just out for experience you might say.'

'Yes. Well, fix it with Chick.' Several other stables had the coughing epidemic, Morrison thought. The chestnut couldn't have picked a worse day to catch it.

Chick, who would normally have welcomed the offer of a ride with condescending complacency, was so preoccupied that the small trainer regretted having asked him. Chick's whole attention was riveted on the chestnut, who seemed to be lining up satisfactorily at the starting tape. Nothing wrong, Chick assured himself. Everything was going to be all right. Of course it was. Stupid getting into such a state.

The start was down the track to the left, with two fences to be jumped before the horses came past the stands and swung away again on the left-hand circuit. As it was a jumping race, they were using tapes instead of stalls, and as there was no draw either,

Toddy had lined up against the inside rails, ready to take the shortest way home.

Down in the bookmakers' enclosure they were offering more generous odds now and some had gone boldly to evens. The chestnut had cantered past them in his way to the start looking not his brightest and best. The bookmakers in consequence were feeling more hopeful. They had expected a bad day, but if the chestnut lost, they would profit. One of them would profit terrifically—just as he would lose terrifically if the chestnut won.

Alexander McGrant (Est. 1898), real name Harry Buskins, had done this sort of thing once or twice before. He spread out his fingers and looked at them admiringly. Not a tremble in sight. And there was always a risk in these things that the boy he'd bribed would get cold feet at the last minute and not go through with the job. Always a gamble, it was. But this time, this boy, he was pretty sure of. You couldn't go wrong if you sorted out a vain little so-and-so with a big grudge. Knockovers, that sort were. Every single time.

Harry Buskins was a shrewd middle-aged East End Londoner for whom there had never been any clear demarcation between right and wrong and a man who thought that if you could rig a nice little swindle now and then, well, why not? The turnover tax was killing betting . . . you had to make a quick buck where you could . . . and there was nothing quite so sure or quick as raking in the dough on a red-hot favourite and knowing for certain that you weren't going to have to pay out.

Down at the post the starter put his hand on the lever and the tapes went up with a rush. Toddy kicked his chestnut smartly in the ribs. From his aerie on top of the stand the commentator moved smartly into his spiel, 'They're off, and the first to show is the grey. . .' Arthur Morrison and Chick watched with hearts thumping from different sorts of anxiety, and Harry Buskins shut his eyes and prayed.

Toddy drove forward at once into the first three, the chestnut beneath him galloping strongly, pulling at the bit, thudding his hooves into the ground. He seemed to be going well enough, Toddy thought. Strong. Like a train.

The first fence lay only one hundred yards ahead now, coming nearer. With a practised eye Toddy measured the distance, knew the chestnut's stride would meet it right, collected himself for the spring and gave the horse the signal to take off. There was no response. Nothing. The chestnut made no attempt to bunch his muscles, no attempt to gather himself on to his haunches, no attempt to waver or slow down or take any avoiding action whatsoever. For one incredulous second Toddy knew he was facing complete and imminent disaster.

The chestnut galloped straight into the three-foot-thick, chest-high solid birch fence with an impact that brought a groan of horror from the stands. He turned a somersault over the fence with a flurry of thrashing legs, threw Toddy off in front of him and fell down on top and rolled over him.

Chick felt as if the world were turning grey. The colours drained out of everything and he was halfway to fainting. Oh God, he thought. Oh God. *Toddy*.

The chestnut scrambled to his feet and galloped away. He followed the other horses toward the second fence, stretching out into a relentless stride, into a full-fledged thundering racing pace.

He hit the second fence as straight and hard as the first. The crowd gasped and cried out. Again the somersault, the spread-eagled legs, the crashing fall, the instant recovery. The chestnut surged up again and galloped on.

He came up past the stands, moving inexorably, the stirrups swinging out from the empty saddle, flecks of foam flying back now from his mouth, great dark patches of sweat staining his flanks. Where the track curved round to the left, the chestnut raced straight on. Straight on across the curve, to crash into the rail around the outside of the track. He took the solid timber across the chest and broke it in two. Again he fell in a thrashing heap and again he rocketed to his feet. But this time not to gallop away. This time he took three painful limping steps and stood still.

Back at the fence Toddy lay on the ground with first-aid men bending over him anxiously. Arthur Morrison ran down from the stands towards the track and didn't know which way to turn first, to his son or his horse. Chick's legs gave way and he sagged down in a daze onto the concrete steps. And down in the bookmakers' enclosure Harry Buskins's first reaction of delight was soured by wondering whether, if Toddy Morrison were badly injured, that stupid boy Chick would be scared enough to keep his big mouth shut.

Arthur Morrison turned towards his son. Toddy had been knocked unconscious by the fall and had had all the breath squeezed out of him by the chestnut's weight, but by the time his father was within 100 yards he was beginning to come round. As soon as Arthur saw the supine figure move, he turned brusquely round and hurried off towards the horse: it would never do to show Toddy the concern he felt. Toddy would not respect him for it, he thought.

The chestnut stood patiently by the smashed rail, only dimly aware of the dull discomfort in the foreleg that wouldn't take his weight. Arthur Morrison and the veterinarian arrived beside him at the same time, and Arthur Morrison glared at the vet.

'You said he was fit to run. The owner is going to hit the roof when he hears about it.' Morrison tried to keep a grip on a growing internal fury at the injustice of fate. The chestnut wasn't just any horse—it was the best he'd ever trained, had hoisted him higher up the stakes-won list than he was ever likely to go again.

'Well, he seemed all right,' said the vet defensively.

'I want a dope test done,' Morrison said truculently.

'He's broken his shoulder. He'll have to be put down.'

'I know. I've got eyes. All the same, I want a dope test first. Just being ill wouldn't have made him act like that.'

The veterinarian reluctantly agreed to take a blood sample, and after that he fitted the bolt into the humane killer and shot it into the chestnut's drug-crazed brain. The best horse in Arthur Morrison's stable became only a name in the record books. The digested carrot was dragged away with the carcass but its damage was by no means spent.

It took Chick fifteen minutes to realize that it was Toddy who was alive and the horse that was dead, during which time he felt physically ill and mentally pulverized. It had seemed so small a thing, in the beginning, to give a carrot to the chestnut. He hadn't thought of it affecting him much. He'd never dreamed anything like that could make you really sick.

Once he found that Toddy had broken no bones, had recovered consciousness and would be on his feet in an hour or two, the bulk of his physical symptoms receded. When the small trainer appeared at his elbow to remind him sharply that he should be inside changing into colours to ride in the Novice Hurdle race, he felt fit enough to go and do it, though he wished in a way that he hadn't said he would.

In the changing room he forgot to tell his valet he needed a lightweight saddle and that the trainer had asked for a breast girth. He forgot to tie the stock round his neck and would have gone out to ride with the ends flapping. He forgot to take his watch off. His valet pointed everything and thought that the jockey looked drunk.

The novice hurdler Chick was to ride wouldn't have finished within a mile of the chestnut if he'd started the day before. Young, green, sketchily schooled, he hadn't even the virtue of a gold streak waiting to be mined: this was one destined to run in the ruck until the owner tired of trying. Chick hadn't bothered to find out. He'd been much too preoccupied to look in the form book, where a consistent row of noughts might have made him cautious. As it was, he mounted the horse without attention and didn't listen to the riding orders the small trainer insistently gave him. As usual, he thought he knew better. Play it off the cuff, he thought scrappily. Play it off the cuff. How could he listen to fussy little instructions with all that he had on his mind?

On his way out from the weighing room he passed Arthur Morrison, who cast an inattentive eye over his racing colours and said, 'Oh yes . . . well, don't make too much of a mess of it. . .'

Morrison was still thinking about the difference the chestnut's death was going to make to his fortunes and he didn't notice the spasm of irritation that twisted Chick's petulant face.

There he goes, Chick thought. That's typical. *Typical*. Never thinks I can do a bloody thing. If he'd given me more chances . . . and more money . . . I wouldn't have given . . . Well, I wouldn't have. He cantered down to the post, concentrating on resenting that remark, 'don't make too much of a mess of it,' because it made him feel justified, obscurely, for having done what he'd done. The abyss of remorse opening beneath him was too painful. He clutched at every lie to keep himself out.

Harry Buskins had noticed that Chick had an unexpected mount in the Novice Hurdle and concluded that he himself was safe, the boy wasn't going to crack. All the same, he had shut his bag over its swollen takings and left his pitch for the day and gone home, explaining to his colleagues that he didn't feel well. And in truth he didn't. He couldn't get out of his mind the sight of the chestnut charging at those fences as if he couldn't see. Blind, the horse had been. A great racer who knew he was on a racetrack starting a race. Didn't understand there was anything wrong with him. Galloped because he was asked to gallop, because he knew it was the right place for it. A great horse, with a great racing heart.

Harry Buskins mopped the sweat off his forehead. They were bound to have tested the horse for dope, he thought, after something like that. None of the others he'd done in the past had reacted that way. Maybe he'd got the dose wrong or the timing wrong. You never knew how individual horses would be affected. Doping was always a bit unpredictable.

He poured himself half a tumbler of whisky with fingers that were shaking after all, and when he felt calmer he decided that if he got away with it this time he would be satisfied with the clean-up he'd made, and he wouldn't fool around with any more carrots. He just wouldn't risk it again.

Chick lined up at the starting post in the centre of the field, even though the trainer had advised him to start on the outside to give the inexperienced horse an easy passage over the first few hurdles. Chick didn't remember this instruction because he hadn't listened, and even if he had listened he would have done the same, driven by his habitual compulsion to disagree. He was thinking about Toddy lining up on this spot an hour ago, not knowing that his horse wouldn't see the jumps. Chick hadn't known dope could make a horse blind. How could anyone expect that? It didn't make sense. Perhaps it was just that the dope had confused the chestnut so much that although its eyes saw the fence, the message didn't get through that he was supposed to jump over it. The chestnut couldn't have been really blind.

Chick sweated at the thought and forgot to check that the girths were still tight after cantering down to the post. His mind was still on the inward horror when the starter let the tapes up, so that he was caught unawares and flat-footed and got away slowly. The small trainee on the stand clicked his mouth in annoyance, and Arthur Morrison raised his eyes to heaven.

The first hurdle lay side-by-side with the first fence, and all the way to it Chick was illogically scared that his horse wouldn't rise to it. He spent the attention he should have given to setting his horse right in desperately trying to convince himself that no one could have given it a carrot. He couldn't be riding a doped horse himself . . . it wouldn't be fair. Why wouldn't it be fair? Because . . . because. . .

The hurdler scrambled over the jump, knocked himself hard on the timber frame, and landed almost at a standstill. The small trainer began to curse.

Chick tightened one loose rein and the other, and the hurdler swung to and fro in wavering indecision. He needed to be ridden with care and confidence and to be taught balance and rhythm. He needed to be set right before the jumps and to be quickly collected afterwards. He lacked experience, he lacked judgment and he badly needed a jockey who could contribute both.

Chick could have made a reasonable job of it if he'd been trying. Instead, with nausea and mental exhaustion draining what skill he had out of his muscles, he was busy proving that he'd never be much good.

At the second fence he saw in his mind's eye the chestnut somersaulting through the air, and going round the bend his gaze wavered across to the broken rail and the scuffed-up patches of turf in front of it. The chestnut had died there. Everyone in the stable would be poorer for it. He had killed the chestnut, there was no avoiding it any more, he'd killed it with that carrot as surely as if he'd shot the bolt himself. Chick sobbed suddenly, and his eyes filled with tears.

He didn't see the next two hurdles. They passed beneath him in a flying blurr. He stayed on his horse by instinct, and the tears ran down and were swept away as they trickled under the edge of his jockey's goggles.

The green hurdler was frightened and rudderless. Another jump lay close ahead, and the horses in front went clattering through it, knocking one section half over and leaving it there at an angle. The hurdler waited until the last minute for help or instructions from the man on his back and then in a muddled way dived for the leaning section, which looked lower to him and easier to jump than the other end.

From the stands it was clear to both the small trainer and Arthur Morrison that Chick had made no attempt to keep straight or to tell the horse when to take off. It landed with its forefeet tangled up in the sloping hurdle and catapulted Chick off over its head.

The instinct of self-preservation which should have made Chick curl into a rolling ball wasn't working. He fell through the air flat and straight, and his last thought before he hit was that that stupid little sod of a trainer hadn't schooled his horse properly. The animal hadn't a clue how to jump.

He woke up a long time later in a high bed in a small room. There was a dim light burning somewhere. He could feel no pain. He could feel nothing at all. His mind seemed to be floating in his head and his head was floating in space.

After a long time he began to believe that he was dead. He took the thought calmly and was proud of himself for his calm. A long time after that he began to realize that he wasn't dead. There was some sort of casing round his head, holding it cushioned. He couldn't move.

He blinked his eyes consciously and licked his lips to make sure that they at least were working. He couldn't think what had happened. His thoughts were a confused but peaceful fog.

Finally he remembered the carrot, and the whole complicated agony washed back into his consciousness. He cried out in protest and tried to move, to get up and away, to escape the impossible, unbearable guilt. People heard his voice and came into the room and stood around him. He looked at them uncomprehendingly. They were dressed in white.

'You're all right, now,' they said. 'Don't worry, young man, you're going to be all right.'

'I can't move,' he protested.

'You will,' they said soothingly.

'I can't feel . . . anything. I can't feel my feet.' The panic rose suddenly in his voice. 'I can't feel my hands. I can't . . . move . . . my hands.' He was shouting, frightened, his eyes wide and stretched.

'Don't worry,' they said. 'You will in time. You're going to be all right. You're going to be all right.'

He didn't believe them, and they pumped a sedative into his arm to quiet him. He couldn't feel the prick of the needle. He heard himself screaming because he could feel no pain.

When he woke up again he knew for certain that he'd broken his neck.

After four days Arthur Morrison came to see him, bringing six new-laid eggs and a bottle of fresh orange juice. He stood looking down at the immobile body with the plaster cast round its shoulders and head.

'Well, Chick,' he said awkwardly. 'It's not as bad as it could have been, eh?'

Chick said rudely, 'I'm glad you think so.'

'They say your spinal cord isn't severed, it's just crushed. They say in a year or so you'll get a lot of movement back. And they say you'll begin to feel things any day now.'

'They say,' said Chick sneeringly. 'I don't believe them.'

'You'll have to, in time,' said Morrison impatiently.

Chick didn't answer, and Arthur Morrison cast uncomfortably around in his mind for something to say to pass away the minutes until he could decently leave. He couldn't visit the boy and just stand there in silence. He had to say *something*. So he began to talk about what was uppermost in his mind.

'We had the result of the dope test this morning. Did you know we had the chestnut tested? Well, you know we had to have it put down anyway. The results came this morning. They were positive. . . . *Positive*. The chestnut was full of some sort of narcotic drug, some long name. The owner is kicking up hell about it and so is the insurance company. They're trying to say it's my fault. My security arrangements aren't tight enough. It's ridiculous. And all this on top of losing the horse itself, losing that really great horse. I questioned everyone in the stable this morning as soon as I knew about the dope, but of course no one knew anything. God, if I knew who did it I'd strangle him myself.' His voice shook with the fury which had been consuming him all day.

It occurred to him at this point that Chick being Chick, he would be exclusively concerned with his own state and wouldn't care a damn for anyone else's troubles. Arthur Morrison sighed deeply. Chick did have his own troubles now, right enough. He couldn't be expected to care all that much about the chestnut. And he was looking very weak, very pale.

The doctor who checked on Chick's condition ten times a day came quietly into the small room and shook hands with Morrison.

'He's doing well,' he said. 'Getting on splendidly.'

'Nuts,' Chick said.

The doctor twisted his lips. He didn't say he had found Chick the worst-tempered patient in the hospital. He said, 'Of course, it's

It landed with its forefeet tangled up and catapulted Chick over its head.

hard on him. But it could have been worse. It'll take time, he'll need to learn everything again, you see. It'll take time.'

'Like a bloody baby,' Chick said violently.

Arthur Morrison thought, a baby again. Well, perhaps second time around they could make a better job of him.

'He's lucky he's got good parents to look after him once he goes home,' the doctor said.

Chick thought of his mother, forever chopping up carrots to put in the stew. He'd have to eat them. His throat closed convulsively. He knew he couldn't.

And then there was the money, rolled up in the shoe-cleaning tin on the shelf in his bedroom. He would be able to see the tin all the time when he was lying in his own bed. He would never be able to forget. Never. And there was always the danger his ma would look inside it. He couldn't face going home. He couldn't face it. And he knew he would have to. He had no choice. He wished he were dead.

Arthur Morrison sighed heavily and shouldered his new burden with his accustomed strength of mind. 'Yes, he can come home to his mother and me as soon as he's well enough. He'll always have us to rely on.'

Chick Morrison winced with despair and shut his eyes. His father tried to stifle a surge of irritation, and the doctor thought the boy an ungrateful little beast.

THE PONY'S
SIXTH SENSE

Eric Squires

Working down a coal mine is a sweaty, dirty and extremely dangerous business. Not that the risk of death hangs over the miners all the time, but the possibility is there from various sources, both known and unexpected. Injury, too, is always at hand and ready to strike in one form or another.

The air is stale and hot for the most part, but never staler or hotter than in the headings—those one-way-in and one-way-out passages with special ventilating systems of their own. In the whole of my district, all the way in from the main haulage, we breathed air which was fanned through 2ft-diameter canvas tubes suspended from the props or steel spikes driven into a crevice in the rock sides. The mechanism was driven by compressed air which was taken to the fan via a stout rubber hose. The principle was that the air driven into the heading via the fan and tubes would be driven out again along the roads by its own pressure, but the movement was always sluggish.

Between six and seven hours of constant, hard sweating was the norm and, because the ponies always worked much harder than the men or boys, they sweated even more profusely. The entire surface of their skin would glisten with globules of perspiration which, where the harness touched the skin and moved upon it, turned into foam. The amount of fluid that a pit pony lost during a shift never ceased to amaze me. No other animal on the earth ever worked so hard, but where the sweat came from was always a puzzle.

The animals stank to high heaven, if that was at all possible since they were nearer to hell, both physically and mentally. That horsey stink and the foam was always a test as to how much a driver thought about his pony. I thought nothing of the smell, it was a part of me and Ben my pit pony and we shared the ups and downs, the abuse and compliments, we also shared our sweat.

The smell caused by a pony's hard exertions, however, often led to Ben having to take a beating. At times I would be ordered to assist with jobs in some other part of the pit and the men would then have to do their own driving. Apart from the smell, Tubguts hated having to touch the pony's skin and find his hand wet with foam and sweat. Ben was accordingly made to suffer, but I always avenged him on returning from other work.

On the junction where the drift heading turned off from the end of the pass-by, there was an extra fan which picked up the air from the main line and fanned it into the heading. It was this fan which gave me the idea of revenge, after Tubguts had beaten Ben on one occasion during my absence. Tubguts was the name I gave a fat and cruel miner Ben and I worked for

The shift had been a bad one up to that time, with me returning to find Ben hacking at the prop bark with his teeth, a sure sign of distress. 'That bloody Tubguts!' I remember exclaiming, 'what can I do to stop him hitting Ben?'

Ben was as regular as clockwork in his habits, with the evacuation of his bowels and bladder. He always carried this out at the junction during snap-time, after he had drunk his fill of the tepid water from the barrel and eaten the handful or so of oats from his wooden bin. That day, as Ben raised his tail to carry out his waste removal, the idea came to me. Quick as flash, before he had begun to empty his bladder, I stepped smartly to the extra fan and unhooked it from its suspension point on the junction girder. Another unhooking farther along the canvas tube and I was able to lower the fan to the ground—just as Ben pushed his hind legs backwards to empty his bladder. That awful stench was drawn into the fan and pushed forward into the drift heading. The very thought of the men's discomfort curled me up on the ground with laughter. So great was my enjoyment that I only just managed to get the fan suspended again before Tubguts came raging out of the heading, 'Get that blasted manure heap away from the fan . . .'

I obeyed and apologized, playing the innocent in order to avert any suspicion of intentional fouling of the air. Tubguts never did suspect anything and I was content in the knowledge that I was avenging Ben.

It was on that same junction I learned that, despite man's mining knowledge and expertise in underground engineering, he is puny in comparison with natural phenomena.

Every snap-time, after drinking from his barrel at the far end of the pass-by, Ben would return in the darkness to the junction for his rewards. To eat my bread and dripping, I always sat with my back against the same huge prop, in a depression padded with brattish sheet—a thick type of hessian that was used for air curtains where air doors were not practicable.

We had a routine, Ben and I, and I always made certain that the work was well in hand so as to extend the snap-time by an extra ten minutes or so. Without fail—and I loved this action of his so much that it never failed to thrill me—he would use his soft lips to lift off my beret. Gently he would take it, toss his head up and down then drop the beret at my feet. I could not take any praise for teaching him this because, according to Ted, Ben had done this with his previous driver.

What Ben was doing was asking for his bread and jam. Like the Shetland in the pit fields, he preferred the tarty plum jam to the sweeter flavours. I would tease him by replacing my cap, but, with a shake of his head as though to admonish me, Ben would once again take it off and drop it at my feet. No matter how many times I replaced the beret he would take it off and obviously enjoyed asserting his right to the tit-bits which he knew would eventually follow. Finally, as if saying, 'Look here, mate, I've had enough of this,' he would nudge my snap-tin. That was when I would take out one of his two slices of bread and jam and feed them to him in four pieces.

After eating the tit-bits, he would again remove the beret; this time he was asking for his jelly babies. These I kept in my pocket and, although they were always soft and mushy with the heat from my body, he relished them with a great show. Four was his ration and it was impossible to fool him with less. He would then raise his head and grin—at least, I called it a grin and still prefer to think it was—he shook his head with his lips drawn back and a low rumble coming from deep in his throat. This always prompted me to say, 'And thank you, Ben, for being such a great pony.'

I often tried him with bread and dripping, but this caused him to react strongly, sending him back a pace or two, as if he were disgusted with the greasy remains of an animal being offered to him. When the apples were ripe on the trees, I used to go scrumping for them to feed to Ben. If I held an apple in my palm and offered it to him whole, he would shake his head until I held it firmly for him to bite at. Even if it were a small one, he would bite at it without even touching my fingers. What a strange creature he was. But should Tubguts come towards the heading at that moment, Ben would take the whole apple very quickly and move around behind me. Ben was no fool.

The stableman had offered me one piece of information which I came very close to ignoring. 'Always take notice of Ben's instincts, not only Ben, but any other pony you may be working with,' he warned me. 'The pit pony knows more than the miner and if you follow his instincts he could well save your life.' How true those words were; but for Ben's inner something I most certainly would not be relating the story now.

The incident occurred during snap-time, when Ben should have come to me for his tit-bits, but on this occasion he remained ten or more yards away, and adamantly refused to come nearer despite all my cajoling.

I looked around for Tubguts, knowing that Ben would always keep well away from that man, but I saw no one; the junction and entrance to the drift were empty. 'Come on, Ben,' I called, 'Tubguts isn't here to hurt you.'

Ben shook his head and backed off a pace or two. He had not been hurt and I could see no reason whatsoever for his behaviour. To encourage him, I took his sandwiches from the paper in the snap-tin, and holding the bread and jam near my mouth I said, 'Look, Ben, this is your grub and I'm going to eat it.'

Holding my lamp high for him to see what I was doing, I took a bite and this brought a reaction from him. He whinnied loudly and moved around in a rapid, prancing circle, before facing me again. I laughed and said loudly, 'They'll have you in the bloody circus before long, mate.'

On previous occasions when I had pretended to eat his sandwiches as he approached me after drinking, he had come running like a child about to be robbed of a treat. Now, when I took another bite, he backed off, then darted forward to within five or six yards of me before spinning and moving quickly away again, the paces taking him away being far quicker than those which had brought him close. He was acting like a dog asking its master to follow.

Suddenly, as he turned to face me again, he screamed, much as he had done when he went after Tubguts in the drift heading, though this time it did not have the same angry note; it was higher pitched and stretched, a sound that I later learned was motivated by terror.

I recall the icy shiver that went through me, something I had never experienced before, and I came slowly to my feet. This move brought a stronger reaction from Ben; once again with rapid movements, he ran forward before digging his hooves in, then turned to retreat and prance and paw the ground. Once again he screamed and I knew then that he wanted me to follow him. In a flash I felt an invisible link between us, a telepathic communication as if he were screaming down the phone for me to go to him.

I did, dropping my snap-tin, snatching up my lamp instinctively and racing towards him as though all hell was on my tail. The moment I started running there was a vicious crack above the junction, with thunderous rollings and boomings coming from above. The junction collapsed with a roar that shook the ground and gave me strength to run harder. One girder did not simply fall, it was sprung down and towards the pass-by with the immense weight which had caused the collapse; the end of that girder grazed the heel of my clog and overbalanced me.

Terror speared through me, bringing me to my feet again and sending me staggering after Ben. Hundreds of tons of hard grey rock crashed down on the place where the junction had been, mangling my snap-tin and dudley into flat pieces of useless metal. Had I been still seated with my back to that prop I would have been crushed to a bloody pulp.

I was far from being a mining expert but, on reaching the far end of the pass-by, I hesitated about leaving its comparative safety. The pass-by was strongly girdered because of its width, but the road beyond which led off to the main haulage was ungirdered. I knew that when a fall occurs it causes a shift in the weight above, resulting in further falls some distance away from the original one. Such a weight shift might be supported by the pass-by, but not by the area which was not girdered.

I did not have long to think about this, however, because Ben, who was standing fairly quietly beside me, backed round behind and nudged me forward with his nose; and he nudged hard. He voiced his fear, too, not with such a loud squeal as before, but I heeded his new warning quickly.

I snatched at his lead rope, intending to jerk him after me, but he was already pushing and nudging me towards the main haulage. I ran and he ran, and not until I had put some 50yd between the pass-by and myself did I ease off. Everything was quiet now, but the dust was thick and choking. Suddenly, there came the roaring and crashing of another fall. It transpired later that it occurred exactly at the end of the pass-by, beyond the girdered section and right in front of where Ben and I had been standing while I was undecided.

That second fall made up my mind for me and, with the lamp little more than useless in the heavy dust, I hurried off towards the main haulage. Ben did not hurry until I jerked him into speed, and here again he was demonstrating his occult sense. He knew that no more falls would occur, but I did not.

The man working on the main junction telephoned the box hole, the office at the pit bottom, and the wheels of rescue began to whir. The four men trapped behind those two falls were lucky; the headings were unaffected by the weight shift. Except for small isolated falls, they had not been in immediate danger.

The reaction to what had happened did not set in until the man on the main junction had taken over; then my legs turned to fluid and I collapsed trembling with delayed shock. Ben stood by me, constantly nuzzling my face and making that deep rumbling in his throat. He was the consoler. He knew the effect the incident had had on me and was showing his concern.

I like to think that when he placed his own life in jeopardy by trying to warn me of the disaster, Ben was reciprocating the deep love and affection I had always shown him. He could have run at any time but he did not.

How did Ben know that the junction was about to collapse? There had been none of the customary signs which herald a fall. Normally, bitting occurs, that is, small bits of stone are dislodged from the roof as the weight shifts to a particular area. Sometimes there are crackings and rumblings; on rare occasions a prop will crack or a girder shift, but this time there had been no warning at all. So how did Ben know?

He knew by the same instinct which warns human beings when things are not well, that there is a threat somewhere to their safety. In most people this instinctive sense is only developed to a minor degree, but there are others who are extremely sensitive in this respect and who possess a more acute extra-sensory perception. In animals, this ESP factor is much more highly developed in some species.

The pit pony's occult sense is something that has to be experienced to be believed, as also is his intelligent application of what he feels in relation to his alien environment. It is curious, though, that such awareness should be so highly developed in a pony of Ben's age, six years; normally it is found in older ponies of ten years of age or more.

The headings were soon working full blast again, the falls cleared and the junction re-set, but there was a difference. Something disturbed Ben, upsetting his normal, mental balance; yet there was nothing I could put my finger on specifically.

I thought at first that the two roof falls had caused me to be over cautious and that my fear was being transmitted to Ben and unsettling him. This was suggested by Ted and, being young and impressionable, I believed this to be true. Ted had as much control over Ben as I did, and when he put it to the test by driving the pony he discovered that Ben was more or less as he used to be. 'See,' said Ted. 'He works all right for me. It's you, lad. You're too tense, too frightened of something else happening. Ben can sense it; your fear is causing him fear. Once you get down to accepting roof falls as part of pit life, you'll lose your fear and Ben will lose his too.'

I believed this because Ted was an authority on pit ponies and he knew mining; he knew me and thought a great deal of Ben because he had worked with him and known him longer than I had. But there was something which a thousand Teds could not explain.

Ben worked harder and was more controllable in the forward heading; he was less so when we were in the pass-by, but in the drift heading he was jumpy and sometimes hard to keep under control. It was there that the trouble was. I sensed it and hated the stomach-tingling fears I experienced before going down; and when I did so this tingling became a clutching. There was something in the drift heading that was frightening Ben and me.

I began to act like a young lad lost in a dark and eerie wood, glancing behind me and jumping at the slightest sound; but, as bad as I was, Ben was worse. He took to wandering out of the heading when I took my eyes off him and, whereas he would normally back up to the full tub, then halt when the limber pin clacked on the tub, now he had to be coaxed back. Worse was the fact that he showed an intense dislike of both the men in the heading, but Tubguts seemed to disturb him most.

Whenever Tubguts approached, regardless of his current mood, Ben would circle around and position himself behind me. The sound of the fat man's voice was like a sharp thorn jabbing into Ben's hide. The pony would jump with startled suddenness when Tubguts gave one of his furious yells because something had gone wrong.

The most curious thing was the way Ben used to push his muzzle into my hand when Tubguts was around. Like a dog presenting its ears for a scratching session, Ben would not cease nuzzling until I had rubbed the underside of his jaw and generally fondled him. Ben was obviously frightened of Tubguts, more frightened than I was, as was borne out when the pony began taking the full tubs up that steep drift at a greater speed than normal. On many occasions he hauled the tub out at a near gallop, ending up in the pass-by with trembling limbs and searching for my hand as though his life depended upon it. His most significant act, though, was to refuse to go on to the coal face and this was something Tubguts could do nothing about.

If only I had known then what I know now. If only I had paid attention to Ben's new whims and traits. If only I had remembered to take notice of Ben's instincts at all times and act accordingly. He had saved my life, but how was I to know that his present behaviour was a plea for me to save his?

One morning I had been instructed to assist the rope runner with his job. This lad was also a pony driver, but he worked his animal in conjunction with a stationary compressed-air engine, which had been set in the side of my main road where it met the main haulage junction. The engine was a large, two-drummed type with $\frac{1}{2}$in steel rope coiled around each drum. The rope from one drum was used to keep my headings working, and the other for another set of workings.

The system was for the pony driver to attach the rope to the coupling on the rear tub of a run of ten tubs, then hitch his pony to the front tub and haul both tubs and rope on to my pass-by, with the engine driver allowing the drum to turn over and pay out the rope. At the pass-by, the rope-running lad would switch the rope to the coupling at the front of my run of full tubs; then, by pressing together two galvanized wires, which were suspended from steel pegs driven into the rock side of the road, he would cause a bell to give two rings at the engine. The engine driver would then apply compressed air to the engine cylinders and haul in the rope and the full tubs, the rope runner following with his pony.

That morning I was detailed to work the rope on that district until it was clear of full tubs and stocked up with empty tubs, then to return to the headings and carry on with my own work.

I shall never forget the way Ben acted when I made to leave him. The noise he made was a cross between his usual throat rumble and a whinny, as he laid the near side of his head against my chest after pushing his nose into my hand.

'What is it, Ben?' As though my voice increased his anxiety, he repeated the sound, then pushed me along the road and made to follow. 'Sorry, Ben, but you've got to stay here.'

He refused to come nearer despite all my cajoling.

He would not stay near his water barrel and I had to tie him to a prop with his lead rope. Ben visibly sagged. His proud bearing became like that of a tired old nag ready for the knacker's yard and he turned away from me, as though saying, 'Go if you must.'

At the time I thought he had accepted the inevitability of being left behind, but there was that same old niggle at my stomach, making me want to stay with him. But I had my orders and, after stroking and fondling him a little longer, I gave him his jelly babies and left.

It took me the best part of three hours to clear the other district before I was free to return to Ben. Perhaps it was the very close relationship that I had built up with him that caused me to suspect something, but during that first hour I was as tight and twanging as a fiddle string, and this feeling became worse the longer I remained there.

When I was eventually allowed to return to my own headings, it was with relief and hurried steps. When I reached my own main road, I met up with the deputy. It felt strange for him to say, 'Hello, lad.' He walked on in front without another word, his yard stick cracking against the side occasionally as though he were angry.

Not until we reached the pass-by did he say anything positive. Turning and facing me, he said, in an unusually quiet voice, 'You'd better stay on the pass-by until the stableman has put Ben down. Then you can walk off and bring back whichever pony is given to you!'

'Eh?' was all I could say as the cold, cold shiver swept through me.

'Are you bloody deaf?' he snapped, obviously in a bad mood. 'You can't do any good in the heading, so stay here till the stableman's finished, then go back to the stables with him. You can't work without a pony, can you?'

My throat was dry, my legs trembling and my heart steam-hammering with the terrible effects of what I suspected. My voice could have been only just audible as I repeated, 'Eh?'

He pushed his face close to mine. 'You can't drive a crippled pony, can you? And you can't drive a dead one when the stable-man's put him down, can you?'

'Ben . . . Ben!' I yelled. 'My pony. What's happened to him?'

I made to run towards the heading, but the deputy grabbed my arm, spun me around and pinned me against a nearby full tub. 'Didn't you know Ben had been hurt?'

My brain and mind froze solid. It was hot in the pass-by, but I was as cold as ice. Tears flooded to my eyes as I tried to break away from the deputy. I automatically knew at that moment that Ben was in the drift heading. The deputy dropped his stick and lamp and held on to me much tighter, his voice deeply sympathetic but very wisely firm. 'Ben's been crushed against the coal face by a full runner, his back has been broken and his ribs caved in . . . he'll have to be put down.'

With a sudden desperate effort, I broke free. Every ounce of speed and strength was powered into my legs as I skidded into the heading and started the headlong descent. The deputy was hard on my heels, shouting at me to stop; but there was no chance of me stopping—not with Ben lying badly injured. I could visualize his crushed body, that beautiful, powerful body reduced to a mangled mess by a full tub of coal crushing him against the face.

I wondered if Ben was still standing with the full tub supporting him, or whether he would be lying on the ground with his eyes closed.

Ten yards or so from the face I could see the lights and hear the men's voices. Despite my headlong flight into the heading to be with Ben, I was actually dreading the thought of seeing him hurt. If I paused to think, I would be grabbed by the deputy and prevented from seeing Ben. If I went on, I might be stopped by the two men or confronted by a sight I did not really want to see.

I ran on to the coal face. From behind a full tub on my right, I could hear the men's voices. Tubguts was saying to his mate, '. . . awkward swine lately and we might get a better pony now we're rid of him.'

Those words spoke volumes to me when I was able to think about them later, but, for the moment, I forgot them and looked down on Ben. The poor, unfortunate crippled animal was lying on his off flank, breathing very shallowly and rapidly; his back was towards me with his head thrown back at an extremely awkward angle. I knelt beside his head, half afraid to touch him in case I caused him hurt. His eyes were wide open and he looked at me, giving a very slight rumble which was choked off.

'Get away from that pony,' snarled Tubguts, who had come up behind me without me hearing him.

I jerked to my feet, my lamp swinging menacingly from my right hand. There was no necessity to issue the warning for Tubguts to stay away from me; my stance, silence and the lamp told him what was in my mind. I was sobbing with tears flowing freely as he backed off. I dropped to my knees again and stroked Ben's nose. He closed his eyes whilst trying to speak to me again, but failing, and I broke down completely.

A hand descended gently on my shoulder and the deputy said, 'Come on, son, there's nothing you can do and these things happen, you know.'

I made no reply and unbuckled Ben's bridle gently, sliding it off his head and laying it aside, all the while trying to prevent my tears from falling upon the pony's head as I stammered soothing words to him.

The deputy tried to lift me up. 'You can't stay here, son, the stableman will be here soon to put him . . .' He checked himself and said no more.

'Why isn't Ben moving?' I asked, rather stupidly.

'Because he can't, he's hurt too bad.'

'But he must be feeling a lot of pain and he isn't making a sound,' I protested.

'They don't,' explained the deputy. 'I've seen it all before, they just lie there. I don't think they feel pain like you and me would.'

He pulled at me gently again and I resisted. 'Please let me stay till the stableman comes.'

'All right then. You leave here as soon as he arrives, right?' The deputy turned to the men. 'What happened?'

'The full tub ran back from the pass-by,' said Tubguts. 'We'd come back for the second tub when that one came roaring down.'

'What about the jack-catch?'

'I pulled the tub over it,' the fat man said defensively.

'Then how did the tub come back?' the deputy asked. 'Once over the catch it should stay there.'

'The catch must have stuck, you know, came back up part of the way and didn't get a proper bite.' Tubguts was far too glib and quick with his answers.

When the time came for Ben to be put down, I went to the pass-by and checked the jack-catch. It was free; there were no stones preventing it from working, the spindle was greased and nothing I did could make it stick. The deputy hummed and haahhed over my suggestion that Tubguts had purposely killed Ben because the pony had become somewhat unmanageable. I told him Ben had once attacked him when he had struck the animal, but I was on my own, with no real evidence. Even my disclosure of what I had overhead Tubguts say—'. . . awkward swine lately and we might get a better pony now we're rid of him'—had no effect on the deputy. But those words and the way in which they were said were all I wanted to know.

The men in the forward heading had not hauled any full tubs off since Ben had been hurt, as there was no other pony to use. Yet the points onto the pass-by were set for the forward heading; had a tub run back from the jack-catch as Tubguts had said, they would have had to be set for the drift heading. A tub running back from the pass-by under those circumstances would have naturally run on into the forward heading.

Tubguts and his mate did haul the tub off, but not onto the pass-by. It was hauled to the top of the drift, the pony being taken back to the face and left standing while the full tub was released. The two men had murdered Ben.

I had heard of sick and ailing ponies being killed by the men in order to have a fitter and younger animal allocated to them. I also knew that the pony drivers often assisted in this slaughter, but I was never to hear of the death of a pony because it was disliked, particularly a young and powerful animal like Ben.

When Ben had been put down, I refused to stay and work in the heading and the deputy knew why. As it would in any case have been shift ending by the time I could have got back from the stables with another pony, he let things go. Another driver was sent to the headings the next day, while I was given a different job elsewhere in the pit.

THE LITTLE HORSES

Shirley Marler

My interest in horses started when I was six years old, but my interest in miniature or Falabella horses was aroused only in 1965 by an article I read in a Sunday newspaper with fascinating photographs. I felt, having seen and read the article, that I must import some of these tiny horses. I was very lucky because at the time we were fortunate in having some friends living in Buenos Aires who were experts on horses, so I was able to write to them and ask them to select a stallion and three mares. In the meantime I started to find out something about the midget horses that roam the pampas on Señor Julio Falabella's ranch in the province of Buenos Aires. I then found out that Señor Falabella's family had been breeding these horses for about forty years. They started off by breeding from a tiny thoroughbred, Shetland blood being used occasionally to bring the size down. I have not yet mentioned their size—they are all under seven hands (25in–30in). Señor Falabella has them running wild on his ranch and does not feed them, worm them, or bring them in to foal; in fact they are very hardy indeed. Señor Falabella has broken them in to ride and also to drive, and says that once you have their confidence they are very easy to handle, a point I was to find quite correct later on. These horses have been exported all over the world, particularly to North America: in fact Mrs Jackie Kennedy has some and we were lucky in that our friends in the Argentine selected Mrs Kennedy's horses, so we knew we would get good stock which is all important.

Anxiously I awaited news from the Argentine. At last the letter came. My friend had visited the Falabella Farm and had seen three horses he thought I would like. They all resembled horses, but in miniature, were under seven hands and of three different colours; and all were of good type, sound and healthy-looking. The stallion was bay with black spots, one mare was very dark grey with black spots, and the other mare skewbald.

It was suggested that it would be a good idea to bring the horses back to Buenos Aires and feed them and fatten them up for their long journey by boat to England, and also that it would be a good idea to have them used to handling a bit before travel as none of them had ever been handled; he also promised to send me photographs just as soon as he could.

How excited I was at the prospect of having some Falabellas of my own here on our farm, but in fact another four months were to elapse before the horses arrived.

All the transport had to be arranged and we had to make sure that the horses did not go on a ship which called at a port in any country which was infected by African Horse Sickness, otherwise the horses would not be allowed to land in England; this, however, was quite easily arranged.

The photographs arrived in due course, and how sweet the

Falabellas looked. They had all been clipped out and wore special pale blue rugs with dark blue bindings, with special head collars, and they had even been plaited up for the photograph. I hoped they would not be too cold without their coats on the long voyage.

Another letter arrived to let me know which ship the horses had been sent on, so I hurriedly rang up the shipping line to see when they were to be expected at London docks.

At last the great day arrived and I ordered a horse-box to go and collect the three Falabellas from the docks. So on a sunny October afternoon in 1964 three minute horses were unloaded in Weston Underwood (still complete with rugs and head-collars!). They had travelled very well, the box-driver told me; they had been shipped in wooden crates, which had been strapped to the deck of the ship, and when they had been released from the crates they did not even appear particularly stiff.

Our two small children were delighted with them and began to feed them with bowls of oats which they seemed to enjoy; but they enjoyed themselves far more when we turned them out in their small paddock, and they could gallop about and stretch their legs after six weeks of confinement in their crates.

I let them out in the paddock for twenty-four hours only, and then penned them up in a small corral with a shed at one end so that we could start to make friends with them, and also feed them up as they were a bit thin after their journey, and as they had been clipped we did not want them to catch cold.

I soon began to realize that all the horses had—as all horses have—very different characters; the stallion was very proud and kept his mares in order, and would stand no nonsense, so we christened him Perky. The little black mare was very shy and timid but so attractive—a real miniature thoroughbred—we called her Blackbird. The skewbald was not as attractive in looks but such a character and much less timid than Blackbird. Food was most important to her and we soon had her running up to us as soon as we appeared, quite happily eating out of our hands, while Blackbird was very much more cautious. We called her Mrs Skew. I found that if you knelt down the horses were far less timid; obviously a huge two-legged creature towering above them was very frightening.

A few weeks after the Falabellas arrived an Australian company rang me saying that they had two mini mares which had been part of a consignment to a client in Australia; they had broken their journey from the Argentine in England, and then, according to regulations, had to spend six months in this country. During that time they had been found not to be in foal, and the company's client had refused to have the mares as he had stipulated that the mares must be in foal before they left the Argentine, and he did not want barren mares, so the company wondered if I would like to buy the two. Of course I jumped at the opportunity to acquire two more mini horses. The mares were on a farm in Sussex and the company suggested that I went down to see if they were to my liking.

How amused we were to see the two little mares with long coats —unlike ours which had been clipped—and oh, what luck! the two mares were not the same colour as ours; one was chestnut with a flaxen mane and tail, and the other piebald. The chestnut was called Lucy and the other Mrs Pie. They were very quiet and obviously quite at home being handled and led about. The lady who was looking after them thought they were about three or four. We decided to buy the pair of them.

We wondered what Perky would think of his two new wives; he seemed delighted with them when we put them in the corral, but Lucy was very greedy and bad-tempered, so we decided that she and Mrs Pie, with their good thick winter coats, would be quite all right in the paddock, where there was a shelter, and as they were a good deal fatter than the others, a bit of hay in cold weather was really all they needed; we also thought that if we got them too fat it would not be a good thing when it came to trying to get them in foal. They soon settled down very well in their new home.

We suddenly had a surprise telephone call from the BBC, who had heard of the arrival of our Falabella horses and wondered if

Our two small children were delighted with them.

they could come to Weston Underwood and film the horses together with my husband, myself and our two children, for a children's programme. We said we should be delighted for them to do so and would they like to arrange a date to come down. A date was soon fixed and the children especially were very excited about becoming television 'stars'. We wondered how the horses would take to cameras, etc. The arrangements were that my husband and I were to lead two of the horses out of the shed and down the length of the corral with the children and the other minis following behind. We decided that Mrs Skew and Perky would be best for this, and then we were asked, would it be possible to put one of the children on one of the horses! I said I would try anything once, and James (aged three) said he was quite willing to try. I thought that Mrs Skew would be best for this; I knew that none of them had been broken but Mrs Skew was the quietest of all the Falabellas. The thing was to keep James on Mrs Skew just long enough to get the shot, and also not to have anyone in the picture holding him on but to have someone near enough so that if he did slip he could be caught before he fell—all rather difficult—but Mrs Skew was sweet and she walked along with James on her back as though she had been giving children riders all her life—when, in fact, eight months before she had never been touched by a human being!

After the filming had been done at Weston Underwood we were told that my husband and I and two of the Falabellas would be required at the television centre in Bristol for a studio appearance —and could we arrange it? This was not difficult as my husband and I could go down to Bristol the night before, and the Falabellas we had decided to take would go down and back in the day by horse-box. We decided that Mrs Skew obviously must go, and as my husband had led Perky about for the filming at Weston Underwood Perky was a must too.

We all arrived at the studio on the morning of the appointed day; I was very nervous at so many lights and cameras and monitor sets. Luckily we did not have any lines to learn. Johnny Morris and

Keith Shackleton asked us questions about the Falabellas and we just answered them; we were to have three rehearsals and then the fourth time the film proper would be shot. Perky and Mrs Skew had been brushed and their manes and tails well combed out, and the white parts on Mrs Skew had been french-chalked to make her look whiter. They both behaved very well, perhaps the heat of the lights made them both rather sleepy, certainly they seemed more relaxed than we were, though actually after three rehearsals one began to feel more at home and less nervous. It was an exciting though exhausting day and none of us were sorry to get to bed that night.

Since the television the Falabellas' life has been somewhat mundane; we hoped last summer that one of the mares would produce a foal, but no such luck, but then we saw them all covered by Perky during May, so we knew we would have to wait another year. Both the last two winters they have survived very well on plenty of hay. Last winter, as it was so mild, they just had hay on the coldest nights and no concentrates at all. They grew good long coats each winter, and shed them to very fine thoroughbred coats with no hair on the heels at all during the summer.

After the New Year it was evident that the three mares were certainly in foal, so we began to get excited as no Falabella had ever foaled in England, or in fact in Europe. Their largeness was made more evident when Mrs Pie, whom I sold, came back to visit Perky in late March, and she had a very neat figure, in comparison. Our girl groom left for a few weeks on April 10th to go to Nice and Rome with the British Team, helping to drive one of the boxes; she was disappointed, as she felt sure one of the Falabellas would foal or burst before she left! Early on the morning of 14 April I went out to check the mares and Mrs Skew was lying down in pain. I rushed indoors and phoned the vet: he was out within ten minutes; the foal was coming head first and worst of all was dead. Oh, what a disappointment! Eventually my husband and our vet managed to foal her.

What a shame! A beautiful colt foal, skewbald like his mother and weighing 32lb. Mrs Skew was then filled up with anti-tetanus injections, penicillin, etc., and within a few hours was on her feet again, quite happily munching away at some hay and gobbling up her bran mash as though nothing had happened: and after a week we were able to turn her out with Mrs Pie and Perky. Luckily she was not torn or hurt in any way, and we can only hope and pray she will get in foal again later this summer and have better luck next year.

In the early morning of April 21, however, Lucy produced a lovely chestnut colt foal. He really is adorable and looks very much like Lucy. He is now two weeks old and is doing very well indeed. The following Sunday morning Blackbird produced a skewbald colt, a lovely little thing with a bit more bone and substance than Lucy's son; he is also doing very well.

Mrs Skew and Blackbird have already been covered again, so let's hope they are in foal.

So that is my Falabella story up to date. It has been very fascinating and interesting for us and I hope for you too.

THE GYMKHANA

Enid Bagnold

Velvet Brown, the butcher's daughter, wins a horse in a raffle. 'A mad piebald gelding' and quite a handful for a fourteen year old. Then she is left five horses in an eccentric old man's will. Velvet and the other Brown children decide to enter the local gymkhana.

Mi raised thirty shilling for the gymkhana. He borrowed it from his girl for Velvet's sake. That is to say he treated love worse than he treated adventure.

'Your girl,' said Velvet, frowning in thought. 'Which girl? Didn't know you had a girl.'

'Nor I had. Met her at the dance last night,' said Mi. 'Pleased as Punch, she was. Lent me the money too.' So Mi behaved badly, and Velvet knew it. But neither she nor Mi cared when they set their minds firm.

On the day of the gymkhana, about mid-morning, it grew suddenly very hot and the rain came down in sheets. Inside the living-room, polishing the bits, it was like the tropics. The girls' faces were wet. Rain came down outside on full leaves, making a rattle and a sopping sound. Everything dripped. The windows streamed. The glass was like glycerine.

'Oh, Lord,' said Mally, 'oh dear, oh damn!'

'We've only two mackintoshes. Velvet's has stuck to the wall in the hot cupboard. Won't it rain itself out?'

'The grass'll be slippery. What about their shoes being roughed?'

'We've no money,' said Velvet, 'for roughing.'

'If Mi had a file . . .' said Mally.

'A file's no good. You want nails in.'

'I'm sweating,' said Edwina, 'can't we have a window open?'

She opened the yard window and the rain came crackling in over the cactus.

'Hot as pit in here!' said Mi, coming in from the yard, and taking off his dripping coat. 'The yard's swimming.'

'Will they put it off?'

'The gymkhana? No, it'll be over soon. It's a water-spout. There's a great light coming up the way the wind's coming from. Your ma going to serve dinner early?'

'Yes, at twelve,' said Edwina. 'We better clear now. Put the bridles and things in the bedroom. Better father doesn't see too much of it!'

'He knows, doesn't he?' said Meredith.

'Yes, he knows, but he doesn't want to think too much about it.'

At dinner they had sardines instead of pudding. Mrs Brown always served sardines for staying power. Dan had dropped them into her mouth from the boat as she crossed the Channel.

Donald considered his on his plate.

'I'll take your spines out, Donald,' said Meredith.

'I eat my spines,' said Donald.

'No you don't, Donald. Not the big spine. The little bones but not the big one in the middle. Look how it comes out!'

'I eat my spines I say,' said Donald firmly with rising colour, and held her knife-hand by the wrist.

'But look . . . they come out lovely!' said Merry, fishing with the fork. The spine of the slit sardine dangled in the air and was laid on the edge of the plate. Quick as lightning Donald popped it into his mouth with his fingers and looked at her dangerously.

'I crunch up my spines, I like them,' he said.

'Leave him alone,' said mother.

'D'you eat your tails too?' said Merry vexedly.

'I eat my tails and my spines,' said Donald, and the discussion was finished.

At one the rain stopped and the sun shone. The grass was smouldering with light. The gutters ran long after the rain had stopped.

'Keep up on the hog,' said Velvet, as the horses moved along. 'We don't want 'em splashed. Gutters are all boggy.' They were well on the way to the gymkhana, held in the football field at Pendean.

'We look better in our mackintoshes!' called Mally. 'I'm glad it rained.'

'I'm steamy,' said Edwina. 'Merry, you can wear mine.'

'I'm all right. I don't want it, thank you, Edwina.'

But Edwina was struggling out of her mackintosh. 'You'll look better. You're all untidy. . . Put it on!'

'I don't want it!'

'You're a bully, 'Dwina,' said Mally. 'You jus' want to get rid of it an' not sweat.'

They turned up a chalk road between a cutting and in a few minutes they could see below them the gathering of horse-vans in the corner of Pendean field, the secretary's flagged tent, white-painted jumps dotting the course, and a stream of horses and ponies drawing along the road below.

The soaking land was spread below them, and the flat road of the valley shone like a steel knife. Getting off their horses they led them down the chalk path between blackberry bushes, and in ten minutes of slithering descent they were at the gates of the gym-khana field.

'Competitors' passes,' murmured Edwina and showed their pasteboard tickets.

They picked out a free tree in the field and established themselves.

'Here's someone's programme!' said Mally. 'Squashed and lost. Sixpence saved!'

They crowded round to read it.

After endless waiting the band arrived. Then the local broadcaster rattled up, mounted on its ancient Ford, and settling into its position against the ropes, began to shout in bleak, mechanical tones . . . 'Event Number One! Event Number One! Competitors in the Collecting Ring, please . . . PLEASE.'

Instantly the field was galvanized. Children and ponies appeared from behind trees and hedges and tents. Mally mounted George and rode towards the ring.

In five minutes it was over and Mally was back again. George had had no idea of bending. Nor Mally either. They had broken three poles on the way up and were disqualified.

'We haven't practised!' said Mally, trying to carry it off.

But Velvet, busy saddling Mrs James, made no reply.

'Here's Jacob!' said Edwina suddenly. Jacob sprang lightly against Mrs James's flank and grinned. 'Mi must be here.'

'Event Number Two!' shouted the Voice, and Velvet mounted, and made for the Collecting Ring. Seeing Pendean Lucy waiting at the gate for the first heat, she thrust up beside her. The bar fell and Velvet, Lucy, and three others, two boys and a fat little girl, were let out to the potato posts.

'You know what to do?' shouted the Starter, his flag under his arm. 'Leave the posts on your right! Take the furthest potato first! . . .'

Velvet tried to take it in but the trembling of Mrs James distracted her attention. Mrs James had broken already into a sweat of hysteria that had turned her grey coat steel-blue.

They were lined up, the flag fell, and Mrs James made a start of such violence that Velvet could not pull her up at the fifth post.

Six strides were lost before they could turn. Lucy was cantering down the posts with her potato and Velvet heard the jingle of the bucket as the potato fell neatly into it. The heat was over, and Mrs James, too big, too wild, too excited, too convinced that she was once again playing polo, was left three potatoes behind when the winner had drawn up beside the Starter. Pendean Lucy won the first heat.

'Five shillings gone . . .' muttered Velvet with humiliation as she trotted slowly back to the tree. Mi was there standing beside Sir Pericles.

'Five shillings gone, Mi,' said Velvet aloud to him.

'It's a gamble,' said Mi. 'Keep yer head. Afternoon's young.'

'Jumping . . .' said Mally. 'It's the jumping now. Which you jumping first?'

'Sir Pericles.'

The blazing sun had dried up the burnt grass and the afternoon shone like a diamond as Velvet sat on Sir Pericles in the Collecting Ring. Mi wormed his way between the crowds against the rope. Lucy came on her roan pony, but the pony refused the Gate. Twice and three times, and she trotted back disqualified. A schoolboy in a school cap quartered in purple and white rode out. His almost tailless pony jumped a clear round. Jacob wriggled with excitement between Mi's legs.

'Number Sixteen!' called the Broadcaster.

Sixteen was Lucy's elder sister, a fat girl in a bright blue shirt.

'Blasted girl!' said Mi under his breath, as the blue shirt cleared the first and second jumps. His heart was in his mouth, but he spat whistlingly and joyfully between his teeth as the pony landed astride the wall, and scrambled over in a panic, heaving the wall upon its side.

It seemed they would call every number in the world except Velvet's.

'Break her nerve, waiting!' grumbled Mi. He could see her cotton hair bobbing as she sat.

A small girl came, with pigtails. A little shriek burst from her throat each time her chestnut pony rose at a jump. The plaits flew up and down, the pony jumped like a bird. A clear round.

'Hell!' said Mi. 'Two clear rounds.'

'Number Fifteen!'

Out came Velvet from the black gap between the crowds. Sir Pericles arched his neck, strained on his martingale, and his long eyes shone. He flirted his feet in his delicious doll's canter and came tittupping down over the grass. Velvet in her cotton frock stood slightly in the stirrups, holding him short—then sat down and shortened her reins still more. Mi's stomach ran to soup.

'Got her stirrups in her armpits . . .' sighed Mi approvingly.

There was nothing mean, nothing poor about Sir Pericles. He looked gay as he raced at the first jump.

'Too fast, too fast!' said Mi, praying with his soul.

The horse was over safely and had his eyes fastened on the next jump.

'Haul 'im in, haul 'im in!' begged Mi of the empty air. 'He'll rocket along . . .' He saw Velvet's hands creep further up the reins, and her body straighten itself a little. The horse's pace decreased. It was the double jump, the In-and-Out. Sir Pericles went over it with his little hop—one landing and one take-off. Mi saw Velvet glance behind—but nothing fell. And the Gate. The Gate was twelve paces ahead.

He cleared the Gate with one of his best jumps, an arc in the air, with inches to spare.

'He'll do the wall,' said Mi with relief.

He did the wall, but a lathe fell at the stile. Half a fault. She was out of it then. Mi yawned with fatigue. He had held his breath. His lungs were dry. Jacob was gone from between his legs. He looked round.

'Bitches . . .' he murmured vaguely, then turned again to the ropes to wait for the piebald.

There were no more clear rounds till the piebald came, and when it came a murmur went up from the villagers who stood in the crowd.

'Jumping *that* animal!' said a voice.

'Why that's the one she won at the raffle!'

The piebald strode flashing into the sun. He paused, stood still, and gazed round him. Velvet's knees held him steadily, and she sat behind his raised neck without urging him on.

'I don't expect anything . . .' she whispered. 'Do what you can. Keep steady. You're all right.'

'You next,' said a man at the bar of the Collecting Ring. 'You waiting for anything?'

'I'm going,' said Velvet quietly. 'He just wants to look round.'

Mi saw them come down the grass, the piebald trotting with a sort of hesitation.

'He's in two minds whether he'll bolt,' thought Mi.

'Showy horse . . .' said a spectator.

'Butcher's girl . . .' said another. 'The youngest. Got a seat, an't she?'

The piebald's best eye was towards the crowd, his white eye to the centre of the field.

The trot broke hesitatingly into a canter, but the horse had no concentration in him. He looked childishly from side to side, hardly glancing at the jump ahead.

'He'll refuse,' said Mally, who had arrived at Mi's side. But Mi made no answer.

Sir Pericles had jumped like a trained horse. The piebald's jumping was a joke. Arrived at the jump in another two paces, he appeared to be astonished, planted his forelegs for a second, looked down, trembled, then leapt the little bush and rail with all four legs stiff in the air together. Dropping his hindquarters badly he came down on the rail and broke it in two.

'Two faults,' said Mi.

'Only two for breaking that?'

'Hind feet. Only two.'

Again the piebald trotted, flashing, his grass-fed belly rounded, and his shoulders working under the peculiar colour of his hide.

'Why don't she canter 'im?' said a voice.

Mi turned on the voice. 'First time he's seen anything but his own grazing. It's a miracle if she gets him round.'

'The In-and-Out'll finish him,' said Mally under her breath.

The piebald jumped willingly into the In-and-Out then paused, and remained inside.

A shout of laughter went up from the crowd.

'Oh . . . poor Velvet . . .' murmured Malvolia, agonized.

The piebald attempted to graze, as though he were in a sheep pen, and again the crowd laughed.

'She's handling him gentle,' said Mi. 'She's trying to keep him thinking he's a winner. She's backin' him, see . . . I don't believe he's ever backed a pace before.' The piebald had backed two paces till his quarters lay against the first jump of the In-and-Out. With a light heart he responded to his rider, and with a spring he was out again and cantering on.

'Do they count that as a fault?'

'I don't know,' said Mi. 'Watch out . . . now . . . It's the Gate.'

The piebald broke the gate. He would have liked a stout, stone wall, but this flimsy thing that stood up before him puzzled him and he did his goat jump, all four legs in the air at once, and landed back upon the lathes and broke them.

'That horse is breaking up the field,' said a voice.

Mi glared. 'He's knocked his hock,' said Mi, 'that'll learn him.' For the piebald limped a pace or two. It learnt him. Unlettered as he was he had no thought of refusing. He saw the friendly wall ahead, and taking it to be enduring flint he went for it with a glare of interest, ears pricked and eyes bright. The wall was three foot six. He leapt five. For a second it seemed to the crowd as though the horse had nothing to do with the wall but was away up in the air. A little cheer went up and hands clapped in a burst.

'Don't she ride him!' said the voice. 'It's that Velvet girl. The ugly one.'

'What, that kid with the teeth?'

'That's who it is.'

Mi knew that Mally's beauty stood beside him and he resented it. He half turned his shoulder on her. While Velvet sat the piebald he thought her the loveliest thing on earth. Like Dan, his father, he hardly saw the faces of women.

'Hullo, she's missed the stile!'

'Did he refuse?' asked Mi, keenly.

'I don't think she saw it,' said Mally. 'She simply rode on.'

The judge waved his stick and called to a Starter. Velvet cantered, glowing, radiant, to the exit gate. The man who held the exit spoke to her and pointed. Velvet looked behind her, paused, then shook her head.

'Not coming . . .' shouted the man to the Steward.

After a brief pause.

'The last Competitor,' announced the Broadcaster, 'did not complete the round.'

'Why ever didn't she?' said Mally, as she and Mi left the rope to fight their way round to the tree. They scrambled out from the crowd and ran.

Velvet was standing looking at the piebald as though bemused. Merry, her face happy with pride, was holding the horses.

'Marvellous, Velvet, to get him round!' said Mally, coming up. 'Why didn't you jump the last jump?'

Velvet turned and looked, and Mi could see how her face was shining.

'I thought I'd better not,' she said gently.

'Why?'

'He did the wall so beautifully I thought he'd better end on that.'

In a flash Mi felt again what she was made of. That she could take a decision for her horse's good and throw away her own honours.

'It was the right thing to do,' said Mi.

Edwina arrived. 'What made you miss the Stile?'

Velvet said nothing.

'People near me thought you'd funked it,' said Edwina half indignantly. 'You must have bin asleep to go and miss it.'

'She's no more asleep 'n my eye,' said Mi. And Mi's little eye, like an angry sapphire, raked Edwina till she shuffled her shoulder and itched.

'It's you, Edwina, now!' said Mally looking at the torn programme. 'On Mrs James. Bending.'

'A lot of chance I have!' said Edwina. 'Mrs James'll break every pole.'

'She gets rough and excited,' said Velvet.

'But it's Adults!' said Merry. 'They won't have nippy ponies. It'll be easier.'

But the Adults were seated on the smallest ponies they could ride. They looked like giants on dogs. Every grown-up was riding his sister's pony, and Mrs James, galloping like a wild animal, nostrils blowing and eye rolling, broke all the poles she could break. Edwina led her back without a word, disgusted and shamefaced.

It began to rain. Merry put a sack round her shoulders and pulled out the *Canary Breeder's Annual*. Edwina left them and went towards the tent.

'She got any money?' said Mally, looking after her keenly.

'Can't have,' said Velvet. 'She was broke yesterday.'

'P'raps she's got twopence for an Idris. Wish to God I had a Crunchie,' muttered Mally.

'Kandy Korner's got a stall here,' said Merry, reading. 'What's happening now?'

'It's the tea interval,' said Velvet gloomily. They had won nothing. They had made not a penny. They owed Mi thirty bob.

The rain slid, tapping, through the branches, and swept in windy puffs across the field.

It made a prison for them, it pressed them into a corner of life, a corner of the heart. They were hung up. Velvet was hung up in life. Where was she? A butcher's daughter, without money, in debt, under suzerainty, an amateur at her first trial of skill, destined that night to a bed of disappointment among the sleeping canaries. She did not think like that. But cared only that the piebald had jumped one jump as she had dreamt he might jump, with power, with crashing confidence. He was ignorant but he had no stage nerves. Of her own powers she had no thought.

Staring out into the lines of rain lightly she lifted her hands and placed them together in front of her, as though she held the leathers. So acute was the sensation of the piebald beneath her that she turned with surprise to see him standing under the dripping branches. A look of simplicity and adoration passed into her face, like the look of the mother of a child who has won honours. She had for him a future.

The rain came down in long knitting needles. Backwards and forwards blew the needles, as the wind puffed. Wet horses, wet mackintoshes, wet dogs, wet flapping of tents, and then as the storm was rent a lovely flushing of light in the raindrops. Wind blew the sky into hollows and rents.

'That Violet that Mi met, she's at Kandy Korner,' said Merry. 'Serving with them for a week on appro.'

'We can't borrow from her if she's only on appro. She'll get into trouble.'

'Mi,' said Velvet, looking round the tree, 'you round there? Is it dryer there?'

'No.'

'Your Violet's with Kandy Korner. Got a stall down here.'

Silence. Displeasure.

'You couldn't touch her for another twopence?'

'Not till I see daylight with that thirty bob.'

Edwina had gone off with one of the mackintoshes. The saddles were heaped under the other. Merry, Mally, and Velvet flattened themselves, shivering, against the treetrunk.

'There's mother!' said Velvet suddenly.

Across the field, swaying like a ship at sea, came the red and yellow meat van.

'She's brought tea!' said Merry.

'She'll thread my needle!' said Velvet.

Mally ran out into the open and waved. The van nosed and swayed towards them.

'Father's driving! If he stops . . . He'll never let you race, Velvet!'

'Stop him buying the programme if you can! Here, tear ours . . . give him the wrong half! Then he won't buy another.'

Velvet snatched up the programme and tore a little piece out with her thumb-nail. The van drew up under the tree. Mi opened the door and the giant bulk of Mrs Brown descended backwards.

'We've done nothing, mother! Nothing at all!' said Mally.

'That's bad,' said Mrs Brown. 'Here's your tea.'

'I'm not stopping,' said Mr Brown, from the wheel. 'There's a sugar box in the back. Pull it out for your mother to sit on. You're wet through, the lot of you. You ought to come home.'

'Coats is soppy,' said Mrs Brown. 'How's your vests?'

'Dry,' said Velvet, edging away. 'Dry's a bone.'

'You stay for one more race or whatever you call it,' said Mr Brown, 'an' then you'll take them horses home. I'll be back to fetch Mother.'

'But we've PAID . . .' began Velvet in horror. The self-starter whirred and he was gone.

'Does he mean it, mother?'

'You're dripping,' said Mrs Brown, cutting up a Madeira cake. 'Mi, come round here an' get some food.'

The cake grew wet even as they ate it.

'What's the next?' said mother. 'Gimme the list.' She studied it for a moment.

'That's next, mother,' said Velvet, pointing.

'Was your name in it?' asked Mrs Brown looking at the hole.

'Yes . . . it was. 'Tis.'

There was a long pause and Mrs Brown slowly stroked her chin. Mi looked down on her old felt hat in which a pool of rain was settling. Velvet ran one nail under the other and shot out a piece of earth.

'I'll thread your needle,' said Mrs Brown at last.

Velvet looked into the heavy eyes and smiled. The eyes blinked with the violence and worship of the glance.

The voice of the Broadcaster came roughly through the wind and rain.

'Event Number Five,' said the Voice . . . 'Competitors for Event Number Five . . . go to the Collecting Ring.'

Sir Pericles was saddled and Mrs Brown rose to her feet.

'Where'd I stand?' she asked.

'Mi'll take you. Mi! It's right far up there.'

Mrs Brown walked like a great soldier up the field.

In Velvet's heat she was the only child. She rode out of the gate of the Collecting Ring with four others—two livery-stable-men from Worthing, a grizzled woman with short hair and a hanging underlip, and a young man in checks on a hired horse with poverty streaks.

'I've plenty of chance,' she thought, 'I'm lighter than any of them.' All the horses were dripping and began to steam with excitement.

'Be slippery at the corner there,' said one of the livery-stable-men.

They reached the starting post, and the sodden Starter came down towards them.

The faces, shining in the rain, looked back at him. The young man in the check suit lay up on the inside against the rail. The woman with the hanging lip scowled at him and edged her horse nearer. Velvet came next, and on the outside the two stable-men. The flag was raised. Before it could fall the young man made a false start. While he was getting back into position the grizzled woman took his place.

'Don't shove!' said the young man, but the woman made no reply. Up went the flag again and the bounding of Velvet's heart swept Sir Pericles forward.

'Get back . . . that child!' shouted the Starter.

Velvet swung Sir Pericles back behind the line and brought him up. The flag fell again neatly as she got him square. She drove for the centre of the first hurdle. Out of the corner of her eye she saw the grizzled woman's horse run out. The young man in the checks she never saw again. Perhaps he never started. As she landed she saw a horse and man on the ground beside her. The heat was between Velvet and one livery-stable-man.

Sir Pericles, the little creature, brilliant and honest, never looked to right or left but stayed where Velvet drove him, straight at the middle of each hurdle. He fled along the grass, jumping as neatly as a cat, swung round the sharp, uphill corner towards the table where the sewers stood, Velvet kicking the stirrups free, neck and neck with the livery-man on a blue roan. The roan drew ahead. The sewers' table neared. Velvet flung herself off as they drew up; her feet ran in the air, then met the ground and ran beside the horse.

'What have you got off for? said Mrs Brown calmly, as she began to sew.

Velvet glanced with horror at her rival, leaning from his saddle while a tall girl sewed at his sleeve. 'Oh . . .' she breathed. She had forgotten the instructions. She had no need to dismount.

But Mrs Brown's needle flashed in and out, while the blue roan fidgeted and danced, and the tall girl pivoted on her feet.

It was an easy win for Velvet. She was in the saddle, off, and had time to glance behind, before the roan had started. She heard his galloping feet behind her but he never caught her up and Sir Pericles went steadily down the grassy slope, jumping his hurdles with willing care.

A burst of clapping and cheers went up.

'Stay in the field!' said a Steward. 'Wait for the other heats to be run.' Velvet sat alone in the rain, in a cloud of steam from the excited horse. One by one the winners of the three heats joined her.

The first was a boy of about nineteen, with a crooked jaw. Steaming and shining and smiling he rode up to her on a brown horse with a hunter-build, long tail and mane.

'You did a good one!' he said to her.

'I'd only one to beat,' she said, 'and even then it was the button that did it.'

'That's a beautiful little horse,' said the boy. 'He's *neat*.'

They turned to watch the finish of the next heat.

They were joined by a fat little man in a bowler hat, a dark grey riding coat, and soaking white breeches. He took off his bowler as he rode towards them and mopped his shining bald head. His horse was a grey.

'What a horse . . .' he said as he rode up. 'I hired him. Couldn't hold him fer a minute. Just went slap round as though he'd got a feed at the winning post. I'll never pull it off a second time, not unless he chooses to! Lands on his head, too, every time. Not a bit of shoulder.'

'The saddle looks too big for him,' said the boy. 'It's right up his neck. But he's a grand goer.'

'It's right up his neck, an' so'm I,' said the little man, dismounting. 'It's the way he jumps. Next round I'll be down and off and rolling out of your light! Here's the last! It's Flora Banks!'

'Who's she?' said the boy.

'Tough nut from Bognor,' said the little man under his breath.

Flora Banks wore a yellow waistcoat, had a face like a wet apple and dripping grey hair. She rode astride on a bay horse that looked like a racer, lean and powerful and fully sixteen hands. Velvet's heart sank.

'My poor Flora,' said the little man calmly, bringing out a match, 'you've got an overreach. You're out of it!'

The Tough Nut was off her bay in a second, flung her cigarette into the grass, and knelt and took the bleeding forefoot tenderly in her hands. The big bay hung his head like a disappointed child. He was out of it. She led him, limping, away.

'Makes us three,' said the little man, mopping his head. 'Two really. I can't last another round. You go it, little girl, an' get the fiver. Hi, they're calling us.'

Down went the three horses to the starting post, reins slipping in cold fingers, rain whirling in puffs. Velvet's breath would not sink evenly on the downward stroke. She shuddered as she breathed.

'Lay up against the rails, little girl,' said the bowler hat. 'I'm so fast you can't beat me whatever you do, but I'm coming off. Where's that Starter? Goin' to keep our hearts beating while he drinks his coffee? Hi, where's that Starter? The blighter's drinkin' coffee!'

The Starter burst out of a little tent wiping his mouth and ran through the raindrops, that suddenly grew less. The miraculous sun broke all over the soaking field. The freshness was like a shout. Velvet shaded her eyes, for the start was into the west. Water, filled with light, shone down the grass. The flag was raised and fell.

The boy on the brown horse got a bad start. Velvet and the little man rose together at the first hurdle. Velvet had the inside and the grey lay behind her. At the second hurdle she heard him breathe, then lost him. At the slight curve before the third hurdle he had drawn up on her inside, between her and the rail. She had lost her advantage.

Suddenly the boy on the brown appeared on her left. Both the grey and the brown drew ahead and Velvet strung out a near third. Like hounds over a wall they rose, one, two, three over the fourth hurdle and went sweeping round the uphill curve to the table.

Mrs Brown stood like an oak tree. Velvet galloped and drew up in a stagger beside her, throwing the single rein loose on Sir Pericles' neck. She stooped and hung over him, kicking both feet free from the stirrups to steady him. Trembling, panting, his sides heaving in and out he stood, his four feet still upon the ground, like a bush blown by a gale but rooted. Mrs Brown's needle flashed.

Velvet was off, stirrups flying, down the grass hill, the blazing light no longer in her eyes, going east. First the grey, then the brown, were after her. At the fifth hurdle the grey passed her, but the brown never drew near. The grey was wound up to go. Its hind quarters opened and shut like springs in front of her. She saw it rise at the sixth hurdle just ahead of her, and come down almost upon its head. It slowed. As she drew up she saw the little man was done, stretched up unnaturally on its neck. He took a year falling. She passed him while he was still at it—jumped the seventh and eighth hurdles and whispered to herself as the noise went up behind the ropes, 'A fiver . . .' And the piebald's glistening future spread like a river before her, the gates of the world all open. She pulled up, flung herself off Sir Pericles and glanced down at his feet.

He was all right. And the Steward was examining her button . . . That was all right too! Here came the sisters . . . The little man in the bowler, unhurt, was leading his horse down the track. Mrs Brown . . . Where was mother? Mi was by her side.

'Lead him off! Don't stand there! You look daft,' said Mi lovingly, and his little blue eyes winked and shone. 'Good girl, Velvet!' said Mr Croom as she neared the exit. And hands patted her and voices called.

The ruthless voice of the Broadcaster was gathering competitors for the next event.

'Thirty shilling is yours, Mi.'

'You'll have to give me forty. I want ten to get me teeth out of pawn.'

'You put them in again?'

'I had to. Hadn't nothing.'

'How is it they're so valuable, Mi?'

'Mass o' gold. My old Dad got 'em done. He said, "You always got money on you if you got gold in your mouth." I can raise ten shillings on them most towns.'

'You whistle better without them.'

'Yes, I do,' said Mi. 'Where's that Jacob?'

It was the evening, before supper. They had turned the horses into the field after a good meal, and the piebald in with them. He had shown no sign of kicking. He trotted happily about among the new companions, his tail raised in an arch and his nostrils blown out with excitement. Velvet leant on the gate and Mi stood beside her. The others had gone home before them down the road, clinking the buckets.

'Sir Pericles was lovely,' said Velvet for the twentieth time. Mi was tired of grunting assent. The reddest sun that ever sank after a wet day went down behind them and sent streams of light through rushes and branches. Mi shaded his eyes to look for Jacob, that thorn in his side.

'Was The Lamb really only fourteen-two?' asked Velvet casually.

'Some say fourteen-two. Some say fifteen.'

'Smallest horse ever won the National, wasn't he?'

'Won it twice.'

'You ever bin round there?'

'The course? Know every stick. Been on it hundreds a times.'

'What's the highest jump?'

Mi gazed into the field. He stuck his chin towards the piebald. 'He jumped as high as any today.'

'I thought he did,' said Velvet, low and happy.

There was a long silence. The fields rolled uphill. The hedge at the top of the field was indigo. Sir Pericles was cropping, like a tawny shadow against it. The piebald, disturbed and excited, cantered the length of the hedge, neighing. Sir Pericles looked up, kicked gaily at the empty air, and cantered too. Mrs James rolled an eye and laid her ears back.

Evenings after triumphs are full of slack and fluid ecstasy. The air swims with motes, visions dip into reach like mild birds willing to be caught. Things are heavenly difficult, but nothing is impossible. Here stood gazing into the field in the sunset the Inspirer, the Inspired, and, within the field, the Medium.

Under his boil of red hair Mi's thoughts were chattering 'Why not?'

And beside him Velvet looked, throbbing with belief, at her horse.

'Pity *you* don't ride,' said Velvet at last.

'The rider's all right,' said Mi mystically.

'What rider?'

'You.'

A pause.

The heat was between Velvet and one livery-stable man.

'There's jockeys from Belgium,' said Mi following the insane thread of thought, 'no one's ever seen before. Who's to know?'

'You think he could do it?'

'The two of you could do it.'

'Mi . . . oh, Mi . . .'

Pause.

'Who'd you write to? For entries.'

'Weatherby's.'

'Where are they?'

'Telephone book. London somewhere.'

'Weatherby's.'

There are evenings, full of oxygen and soft air, evenings after rain (and triumph) when mist curls out of the mind, when reason is asleep, stretched out on a low beach at the bottom of the heart, when something sings like a cock at dawn, a longdrawn wild note.

Velvet and Mi dreamed a boldness bordering on madness.

The race was being run in stage light, under the lamps of the mind. The incandescent grass streamed before Velvet's eyes. There was an unearthly light around the horses, their rumps shone. The white of the painted rails was blue-white like ice. The grass snaked in green water under the horses' feet. There was a thunder rolling in the piebald like a drum. His heart, beating for the great day of his life.

'Weatherby's,' said Velvet again. The word was a gateway to a great park. You could touch it, crisp, crested, full of carving . . . *Weatherby's*. Green grass, white rails, silk jackets. Through the arch of Weatherby's.

'Who's to know I'm a girl?' said Velvet, very very far along the road.

Mi was not far behind her.

'Just wants thinking out,' he said. His belly felt hollow with the night air. 'Supper, Velvet.' Slowly they left the gate and walked towards the village.

A EUROPEAN TITLE

Genevieve Murphy

'Then I went to Canada in May, and in the middle of July, I was in hospital.' This was the start of Princess Anne's account of the events between Badminton at the end of April and the European Championships at Burghley in early September—and it sounded as deceptively simple as the beginning of a Hemingway novel.

The Canadian tour had been pre-planned and pre-announced, it was all part of the accepted pattern; but the Princess's admission to hospital for an operation was outside the bounds of normality and it was therefore the event which made banner headlines. But, among the followers of three-day eventing, it was not so much a sensational fact as a cause for speculation: would she be out and ready and fit in time for the final trial at Eridge, six weeks later?

Most people thought not. Alison Oliver didn't believe there was any possibility that her Royal pupil could be fit in time. 'Until, that is, I went to see her in hospital and realized that she was utterly determined to go ahead. I think it was then that I really appreciated the extent of her dedication and knew that she was made of the right stuff.'

'I had a little trouble in hospital,' said Princess Anne, 'because I couldn't persuade any of the doctors to believe that I really did intend to try for Eridge and Burghley. I'd say: "Aren't there such people as physiotherapists?" And they'd say: "Yes, of course, but let's worry about that a little later."

'When I came out, I went to see two people who had put my family together after various illnesses. One of them was a physiotherapist and when she heard that I'd been given no "physio" treatment at all in hospital, she said: "*What?* They do it for everyone else!" She then gave me a book of exercises and, for the only time in my life, I actually did them.

'Later I went to Balmoral for about a week and did as much walking as I could up and down hills. Then I had a week on the yacht, during which I tried to take as much reasonable exercise as possible. When I got back, about four days before the final trial at Eridge, I was saying to myself: "Well, it feels all right at the moment but, if I do get a twinge, I won't bother to go on." Doublet led after the dressage at Eridge, but he was a bit bold going through that funny water jump and he couldn't get out over the rail. And then I fell off.'

'You would have won otherwise,' said Mark.

'Of course,' said Princess Anne. '*The old story*. I would have won if the horse hadn't stopped and I hadn't fallen off. Actually, in spite of that and for the first time in history, I had the equal fastest time of the day—and nobody was more surprised than I was. I know I made a bit of a mess of the cross-country but I was still thrilled, because the horse had gone very well and I wasn't feeling any the worse for wear. So then I thought it would probably be all right for Burghley.'

Mark Phillips had meanwhile won the advanced class of the Eridge Horse Trials on Great Ovation, thereby adding what little confirmation was needed to the inevitability of his selection for the British team. His own moment of near-disaster was, however, still to come for on the journey from Eridge to the training venue at Ascot, Great Ovation, somehow lost his feet in the trailer. He was travelling with Rock On, who was just back in harness and had finished seventh at Eridge, and between them the two horses made a formidable commotion. Mark, alone at the steering wheel, listened to it in horror.

'I had to pull up in the middle of East Grinstead,' he said. 'When I let the ramp down, Rock On came charging out and he disappeared down East Grinstead High Street, followed by a policeman. The partition had been kicked into matchwood by the stage and Great Ovation was still on the floor. When I eventually managed to get him back on his feet, I discovered that he had taken all the skin off one hip. But fortunately he was otherwise unharmed—and Rock On, who was finally caught in a pub car park, was all right as well.'

The period of collective training was supposed to be exclusively for the four riders who had been chosen for the team, and the two reserves. But Princess Anne, although she didn't come into this category, did most of her training with them, 'because I was living next-door, so to speak'. Windsor Castle is not 'next door' to Ribblesdale Park in the suburban sense of the term but, since the team were using Windsor Great Park for their training, they were (so to speak) sharing the same back garden.

When Bill Thompson's European Championship course was finally unveiled, it looked eminently fair, beautifully constructed and more than a little testing. 'I can remember thinking that I'd never in my life seen anything as big,' said Princess Anne, with feeling.

'It wasn't as big as Badminton,' Mark told her, matter-of-factly.

'Well *you* may not have thought so. But there were those three spread fences after the coffin and they were certainly wider than anything I'd seen before. They worried me because I'd never thought that Doublet was particularly good at spreads, and I didn't think he'd enjoy the hard going very much either.'

Alison Oliver, who had put in much dedicated background work in order to have the horse fit to run for his life on cross-country day, mentioned the problem imposed by the spread fences more specifically. 'Doublet was marvellous in many ways; he was very agile and clever; he was honest and bold. But he hadn't the limitless scope of Goodwill or Columbus who, if they meet a spread from a long way off, can throw an enormous leap. Therefore it demanded more accurate riding and Princess Anne was aware that she couldn't afford to meet the spreads too far out.' Alison was, however, conscious of a 'certain excitement' as she walked the course with her pupil: 'Here was the challenge and one thought that it might just work out right.'

The preceding dressage was expected to give the Princess a good start, for Doublet had already shown that he had an outstanding aptitude for this particular phase. 'In the end, you could more or less have shoved him in a big arena,' said Princess Anne, 'and he would have done a good test almost on his own.' This was obviously an over-simplification, since the Princess was rather more than a passenger, but she probably was flattered by the horse in that she didn't have to work as hard before and during the dressage as most other riders.

As Mark pointed out: 'There aren't that many Doublets around and most good tests don't just happen. To do a really good test, I think you have to start with a horse that has a natural cadence and a natural presence; then it's just a matter of temperament. But it can be very hard work. Great Ovation was leading in the dressage at Badminton that year, but I'd gone in with my shirt literally sticking to me from all the exertion beforehand. It was a good deal wetter when I came out!'

Doublet possessed the cadence and the presence and the

temperament. He also had that element of showmanship that belongs to all the truly great horses: he loved an audience. Princess Anne recalled one occasion at Badminton, when they were waiting in the cold and the drizzle, and Doublet seemed thoroughly disenchanted with the whole event. But, as soon as he walked into the arena and surveyed the crowds and the television cameras, he was in his element.

He was in his element, too, at Burghley, where enormous crowds had gathered to watch the European Championships in general and the Princess in particular. Unlike most horses who tend to be distracted or (worse still) intoxicated by large crowds, Doublet had a remarkable ability to concentrate on the job in hand. He produced a lovely rhythmic and accurate test and finished the first phase in the lead. This was something of a revelation to the overseas competitors who had arrived from Italy, France, Russia, Switzerland, Ireland and Holland (as full teams) and from West Germany and Sweden (as individuals). They had been intrigued by the Princess's Royal title but they hadn't even thought of rating her as a serious competitor.

Most people probably weren't convinced even then for, while dressage could be considered a suitable sport for princesses, the speed, endurance and cross-country test certainly could not. It covered more than seventeen miles and culminated in a four-and-three-quarter-mile cross-country section over thirty-three big solid fences. Everybody still expected that gruelling cross-country day would change the top placings, including Princess Anne herself.

'I set off thinking I might just about get round,' she said. 'Then, after all the worries about Doublet not liking the hard ground, I realized that he was thoroughly enjoying himself; he thought it was lovely from the word go. I actually began rather to enjoy it myself, once I'd jumped those three big fences and survived the Trout Hatchery. I tried—how I tried!—to trot into the Trout Hatchery, but Doublet wouldn't have it. He then created so much spray cantering through the water that he got one leg completely left behind and had nothing to push off with when he reached the bank on the other side.'

That one near-squeak was to be much analysed in Press reports and in television action replays. Some of them, perhaps, were a bit too lyrical, for the Princess simply did what any good rider would do; she gave her horse every assistance to get himself out of trouble by taking her weight off the saddle and giving him plenty of rein. I have seen Princess Anne make one or two genu-inely spectacular recoveries from heart-in-the-mouth situations, but that wasn't one of them.

Once he had heaved himself out of the water, Doublet recap-tured his rhythmic, ground-eating stride. Most riders exuded an air of grim purpose; Princess Anne made it look like a carefree holiday spin. Her round on Doublet was to leave a lasting impres-sion of lightness and speed and agility. It was also to leave the Russian assistant-director of sports medicine, who had travelled with the Soviet team, in a state of worried perplexity. Those members of his all-male team who had succeeded in completing the course looked thoroughly exhausted, whereas Princess Anne, and most of the other British girls, appeared to take it all in their stride. Like Victorian ladies, they were not sweating or perspiring, but merely glowing.

As she finished the Princess hoped, rather than knew, that her time would prove a fast one. 'I was dead ignorant about that sort of thing. I just knew that the horse had gone very well and that we'd been a bit faster than we were at Badminton. But I certainly didn't expect to be the second fastest.' The only rider to achieve a better time was Stewart Stevens, another British individual, but he had incurred a hefty deficit in the dressage arena with Classic Chips and was still more than forty points behind, in fourth place.

News of Doublet's score percolated rapidly. 'It was very boring for the rest of us,' Mark told his wife, 'because, no matter how well any of us had gone, we couldn't have beaten you.' In fact, Mark was to make a decision for which he has probably been kicking himself ever since. At the penultimate fence, he aimed Great

Princess Anne at the European Championships at Burghley.

Ovation at a V-shaped corner, which could be taken as one jump, rather than settle for the slower but safer route' over the two separate arms of the obstacle. Great Ovation thus marred an otherwise clear round with a run-out that cost him twenty penalties and second place.

At the end of cross-country day, Princess Anne held a lead of 27·8 points. It seemed substantial enough to the rest of us, but the Princess with the prize so nearly in her grasp and with all the attendant pressures that that implies, simply felt 'worried sick' about the show jumping. She was, she readily admits, far more nervous before the final phase than at any other stage of the competition. Even though a single mistake by Debbie West on Baccarat had increased her lead by another ten points, she was taking nothing for granted.

'Doublet was never particularly good at show jumping,' she said, 'and I was determined not to take chances with the first few fences, as I had done in other events. People said he jumped pawkily, which indeed he did, but that was because I'd decided that he took time to warm up and that there was no point in asking him to crack on until he was ready. When he cleared the third last, which a good many horses had down, I remember thinking that if we splashed into the water and crashed through the last (as long as we didn't fall) we would still win the Championship.' As it transpired she won with a clear round and later received the Raleigh Trophy from her delighted mother.

The Princess's victory naturally overshadowed the success of the British team, who beat Russia by a thumping great margin of 422·2 points. The four team members finished in close proximity in the individual placings: Debbie West was second on Baccarat, Mary Gordon-Watson fourth on Cornishman V, Richard Meade fifth on The Poacher and Mark Phillips sixth on Great Ovation, despite his débâcle at the penultimate cross-country fence.

'Afterwards,' said Princess Anne, 'everybody kept telling me that it was, of course, the team success that really mattered!'

Be that as it may, it was the Princess's victory that gave three-day eventing a far more prominent place on the sporting map of Britain. Those of us who write for newspapers had a special cause for gratification; the difference between the various equestrian disciplines was now clearly established and sub-editors no longer wrote 'show jumping' at the top of our three-day event reports.

That year, the Princess scooped all the 'personality' prizes. She won the Sportswriters' Award, was named the *Daily Express* Sportswoman of the Year and the BBC Television Sports Personality of the Year. Then there was an entertaining, totally irrelevant shindy—for which Harvey Smith, with his special flair for attracting maximum publicity from minor statements, was once again responsible.

'In her own class she is the best there is,' he said, 'but that is nowhere near Olympic standards. I certainly wouldn't like to see them pick her for the Olympics, despite the way the Press is clamouring for it.' It could have been argued that to be 'the best there is' in a sport which happens to be included in the Olympic Games might actually justify selection, but to produce logical argument would have been to miss all the fun. Instead there were urgent phone calls to the gentlemen of three-day eventing, who made gallant statements on Princess Anne's behalf.

More serious, in some eyes, was the fact that Harvey (not content with knocking the Princess) had the unforgivable effrontery to knock the sport as well. He claimed, in a quite remarkable display of *lèse-majesté*, that a fourth-rate professional show jumper entering Princess Anne's sport 'would clear the deck of every prize, in every event, every time'. Richard Meade challenged him to put his money where his mouth was, so to speak, by riding for a wager at Badminton. The challenge wasn't publicly declined but, since all good things must come to an end, the whole thing had died a natural death by the time the 1972 Badminton came around.

By then we were all involved in the feverish business of predicting who might be chosen for the Olympics. The Princess obviously came into the reckoning, but, though some writers awarded her a place on the team without further ado, most of us maintained that she would have to back up her European title with a good performance at Badminton.

It was not then generally known that Doublet had developed leg trouble at Burghley, which wasn't considered serious at the time. Princess Anne believes that the problem stemmed from the efforts to extricate himself from the Trout Hatchery ('I think he must have trodden on himself getting out') but there was still every reason to hope that he would be fit in time for Badminton. His preparations were almost complete when Alison decided to give him a thorough work-out, after which it was decided that the sprained tendon wouldn't stand Badminton or the Olympics. So the horse was withdrawn from Badminton less than a week before the competition was due to start and he was turned away for the year.

'Almost my most vivid impression of that time,' said Princess Anne, 'was Doublet's reaction to being roughed off. He seemed thoroughly depressed and looked at one with eyes that said: "What have I done wrong?"'

THE CONNEMARA DONKEY

Eleanor Farjeon

One morning just as usual, Danny O'Toole's mother buttoned on his coat, pulled his green beret over his ears, and saw him as far as the door. The rest of the way to school Danny went by himself. He was seven years old, and there was only one crossing.

'Be careful over the road,' said Mrs O'Toole. 'Look both ways, mind.'

'I will so,' promised Danny.

'Isn't that the best advice in the breadth of the world,' called Mr O'Toole from the kitchen, where they all had breakfast. 'If you look both ways, you'll be missing nothing so, from a stray cat to a king.'

'Never mind cats and kings,' said Mrs O'Toole. 'You look out for motor-cars and bicycles.'

'I will so,' promised Danny, and set out for Larchgrove Road Junior and Infants' Mixed.

Mrs O'Toole went back to the kitchen, where Mr O'Toole was packing his first pipe of the morning. 'What a lot of nonsense you tell the child,' she smiled. 'You stuff him as full of tales as you stuff your pipe with baccy.'

'What else would ye stuff a pipe with, or a child?' asked Mr O'Toole. He was Irish and she was English, and that was the difference. But the English either smile or scold at what they don't exactly understand, and Mr O'Toole, when he came to live in England, had been careful to pick a smiling one. She was smiling now as she piled up the breakfast-cups. Mr O'Toole got ready to go to work. He worked at the Coronation Theatre round the corner. At home he wore his shirt-sleeves like other men, but at work he wore a touch of splendour on his uniform that set him apart. Last Christmas Danny had been to see his first pantomime at the Coronation Theatre, and he had lost his heart to the beautiful Dick Whittington, and to his wonderful Cat, the Seven Fairy Belles, and the Programme Girl who brought him a vanilla ice after Part One. But when he lay awake at night thinking about it, till he fell asleep and dreamed about it, what he remembered as much as anything was the look of his own little father, opening the doors of motor-cars and whistling to taxis, dressed in something he never wore at home.

'My father has gold on his coat,' he told the children in school.

'Ho, very likely!' scoffed Albert Briggs, who was not Danny's favourite person at all. 'Tell that to the Marines.' Albert had heard his uncle say this lately, and he had faith in everything his uncle said, just as Danny had faith in everything his father told him. 'Gold on his coat, hoo!' scoffed Albert. 'You tell that to the Marines.'

'I will so,' said Danny stoutly. 'My father *does* have gold on his shoulders and all down his fronts.'

'Tell us where your father was born, Danny,' giggled Maisie Bonnington.

'My father was born in Connemara!' shouted Danny fiercely. This was the question which always ended the talk about Danny's father. The children screamed with laughter at the funny word, ever since Danny first said it. The school poet had made up a little chant about it:

'Danny's father! Danny's father!
Doesn't live in Connemara!'

'No he does not then,' shouted Danny, 'but he did before that.'

'Before what?' teased Maisie. 'There isn't such a place as Connemara.'

'There is then!'

'You made it up.'

'I did not then! and my father does have gold on his coat.'

'Tell that to the Marines,' repeated Albert Briggs rudely.

'The Marines *knows*,' said Danny, inspired. For all Albert Briggs knew about the Marines was that they were told things, and now Danny had collared them as if they were old friends. The school bell put an end to the talk, which happened after the Christmas holidays, when the pantomime was in full swing. But the day when Mr O'Toole said that about the cats and kings was in the summer, as far away as it could be from Christmas and pantomimes. It was summer holidays coming, and everybody was telling where they were going, or would like to go, or where they went last year.

At the crossing Danny looked both ways very carefully, and when the road was quite clear he scuttled across and in another minute was in the playground of Larchgrove Road Infant and Junior Mixed. And how funny that his father should have picked that very day to talk of cats, for there was Maisie Bonnington with a kitten in her arms. The other children were crowding round her, all trying to touch the kitten, who had a purple bow tied round its pale grey neck. It was mostly very soft whitey-grey, with dark markings and scared blue eyes, and when the children fondled it it pushed its nose under Maisie's armpit and tried to hide itself.

'It's a chinchilla kitten,' said Maisie proudly.

'Let me see!' said Danny O'Toole.

'Let Danny see!' mimicked Albert Briggs. 'He ain't never seed a chilla kitten before; they don't have chilla kittens in Connemara.'

'They has other things,' said Danny stoutly.

'What has they then?'

'I shan't tell you.'

'You don't know,' scoffed Albert Briggs.

This was only too true. Danny hedged till he could get information at the source. 'I'll tell you tomorrow.'

'No you won't.'

'I will so.'

'You won't, because,' crowed Albert triumphantly, 'there ain't no such a place as Conny-onny-mara!'

The children shrieked with delight, bringing Miss Daly to the door to see what it was all about. She was the new junior mistress, nice to look at, and very popular. She clapped her hands at them.

'Come along, come along, what's the joke? What have you got there, Maisie?'

'It's my chinchilla kitten, Miss. It was give me last night.'

'Given me, Maisie. How sweet. But I don't think you can bring it to school, you know.'

'Oh, Miss!'

Miss Daly shook her head. 'It's not school-age yet.'

The children giggled. 'We'll make it cosy and find it some milk. Aren't you the little sweet.' Miss Daly snuggled the soft grey ball under her chin. 'Gracious look at the time! Get a move on, children, quick!'

'S'pose it gets out and is lost, Miss,' quavered Maisie.

'I promise it won't. You can take it home at dinner-time.'

The thought of the chinchilla kitten permeated the lessons that morning. Maisie Bonnington basked in the glory of ownership, fawned on and envied by her school-fellows.

At tea-time Danny asked his father, 'What does they have in Connemara, Dad?'

'In Connemara is the greenest hills in Ireland, and the blackest bogs, and lakes like looking-glass you can see the clouds go by in.'

'Is there kittens I mean?'

'Just wait till you get there!'

'When?'

'Some day or other.' Mr O'Toole sugared his tea. 'Some day you an' me'll go to your grandfather's farm where I was born.'

This was a standard promise, often repeated. Suddenly Danny was curious about the farm he had never seen. 'Is there cats and kittens?'

'Cats and kittens is it? You couldn't step for kittens.'

'Of your very own was they?'

'If I'd wanted. But why me, with a donkey of my very own?'

'A donkey!'

'As white as pear-blossom.'

'A *donkey*.'

'And two eyes like red rubies.' (*Terence!* from Mrs O'Toole.)

Danny said, 'Maisie's chilla kitten's got blue eyes. She bringed her kitten to school today.'

'Did she so?' Mr O'Toole sugared his tea again, absent-mindedly. Out of the corner of his eye he was watching Danny's quivering lower lip.

'Albert says there's no chilla kittens in Connemara.'

Mr O'Toole stirred his cup of tea. 'You tell Albert Briggs, with me very best Sunday compliments, you've got a donkey of your own in Connemara.'

'*Me?*'

'Who else? Amn't I giving you him this very minute?'

'*I've*,' breathed Danny, 'got a donkey!'

'You have so.' Mr O'Toole stood up. It was time to get back to the Coronation, two turnings away, very convenient for slipping home to tea. Danny followed him down the street.

'How big is he, Dad?'

'About so big,' Mr O'Toole's hand sketched the air. 'Just the size for a boy the like of you.'

'Will I see him?'

'Some day or other.'

'Will I ride on his back?'

'Will you not!'

'Does he go quick?'

'As the four winds in one.'

'Does there be a saddle?'

'Sky-blue plush with silver knobs like stars. You turn back now. Herself won't wish you to be crossing twice.'

'Does there be reins?'

'Scarlet leather,' called Mr O'Toole from the middle of the road.

'Dad, dad!' Mr O'Toole paused on the far pavement. 'What's his name, Dad?'

'His name,' shouted Mr O'Toole, 'is Finnigan O'Flanagan. Go home now I'm saying.'

'Let's have a look at you,' said Mrs O'Toole, when Danny came dancing in, cheeks flushed, eyes shining. 'You haven't got a sore throat, have you?' She searched him anxiously for signs of fever.

'Finnigan O'Flanagan!' cried Danny.

Mrs O'Toole suspected delirium at once.

'My donkey's name is Finnigan O'Flanagan, Ma!'

'Get along!' she laughed. *It's his father's delirium he's got a touch of.* 'Up to bed with you, and don't forget to say your prayers.'

Danny went to bed, and took his donkey with him. His prayers first and last were for Finnigan O'Flanagan.

He ran breathless to school next morning, but only managed to clutch Albert Briggs in the passage leading to their different classrooms.

'In Connemara is donkeys.'

'Wossat?'

'One's mine.'

'Wossat?'

'A donkey. I've got one of my own. It's Finnigan—'

Education parted them, but somehow before the morning break a dozen children knew that Danny O'Toole was the owner of a donkey in Connemara. At least, he said so. But if there was no such place as Connemara, how could there be a donkey in it? This was put forcibly to Danny in the playground. Danny piled on the circumstantial evidence.

'He's got a blue saddle.'

'Coo!' from the Believers.

'And red reins and silver knobs.'

'Hoo!' from the Unbelievers.

'He's a white donkey.'

'There's no white donkey,' asserted Albert Briggs.

'There is so. He's got rubies for eyes. His name is Finnigan O'Flanagan.'

'Finnigan O'Flanagan!' Derision reached its peak in Albert's voice. 'Tell that to the Marines.'

The Disbelievers had it by an overwhelming majority. The children scampered about the playground shouting the ridiculous syllables. Finnigan O'Flanagan! A white donkey with ruby eyes. The Marines would never swallow it. His Muse took the school poet by the throat. 'Danny's wonky! So's his donkey!' chanted the poet.

'Danny's wonky, so's his donkey!' yelled the school as one child. They plugged this theme song till lessons were resumed.

In class Miss Daly said smiling, 'Handkerchief, Danny!' Sitting right under her nose on the front bench, he was trying to wipe his own without being noticed. He used the back of his hand. It isn't easy to suffer a broken heart in full view of teacher's bright blue eyes. Danny pulled out his handkerchief, and contrived to smear his own eyes with it while blowing his nose. There is nothing shameful about a good hard nose-blow, but eyes are a different matter. Miss Daly smiled again encouragingly, and went on with the lesson, wondering what was upsetting Danny O'Toole. For a reason of her own he was one of her pets, but if you have favourites it doesn't do to show it; and when children are numbered by the score, one must expect tears now and then. At dinner-time she beckoned Danny to her, and tucked a scrap of green in his button-hole.

'Shamrock for luck, Danny.' It had come to her by post only that morning.

'Thank you, Miss. Miss.'

'Yes, Danny?'

'Did you see a white donkey?'

'A white donkey! Where?'

'Isn't there white donkeys, Miss?'

'Indeed and there is then. I don't think I ever actually *saw* one, Danny. They're a rare kind of donkey, you know.'

'What's rare?' asked Danny.

'Special,' said Miss Daly.

Danny strutted out into the playground, fortified with lucky green shamrock. Passing Albert Briggs he shouted, 'White donkeys is special, Miss Daly says. Finnigan O'Flanagan's *special*.'

Next day he had specialities to impart. 'His four hoofs shine like gold. He swings a rose on his tail.'

'Coo!'

'Hoo!'

From then on there were tidings every day, gleaned from Danny's father every night. Believers and Unbelievers crowded to hear that Finnigan O'Flanagan had run in the races and beaten all the colts by seven necks. Finnigan O'Flanagan had met a mad bull in the lane and hee-hawed at him till he turned tail, thus saving the life of the Princess of Galway, for which he got a medal from the Mayor. Finnigan O'Flanagan could bray so loud it frighted all the Banshees out of Connemara. Brave as a lion was Finnigan O'Flanagan, gentle as a dove, and wise as an ould barn owl. He would carry a sleeping baby ten miles and never wake it, but he could smell out a villain among twenty honest men, and if that one mounted Finnigan he'd find himself on his back in a bog before you could say 'Whisht!'

'Coo!' breathed the Believers, while the Unbelievers hooted 'Hoo!'

But they were all greedy for more, for a good tale is a good tale, whether it's true or not. If Finnigan O'Flanagan wasn't an accepted fact in Larchgrove Road School, he was at least an accepted legend.

Then end of term approached. Interest in the Connemara donkey became somewhat submerged in the excitement of the holidays. 'Where you going?' 'Where *you* going, Maisie?' 'You goin' anywhere, Bert?'

'Southend. Two weeks.'

'Lucky boy!' called Miss Daly, scurrying by with her arms full of copybooks.

'Where *you* going, Miss?'

'Ballynahinch!' Miss Daly scurried on, followed by the children's gleeful laughter.

Pressed to say where *he* was going, on the day before school broke up, Danny said he wasn't going anywhere.

'Then you're going to Connemara,' sneered Albert Briggs, ''cos shall I tell you why, 'cos Connemara ain't nowhere.'

'I'll fight you!' Danny doubled his small fists.

'You shut up,' said Maisie surprisingly to Albert. Wasn't she spending the holidays with her auntie at Shoreham, and wasn't Bert going to Southend for two whole weeks? Well then! She chose Danny to go with as the children clattered through the gates, and asked him consolingly, 'What's Finnigan been up to?' Danny took the bait.

'One time Dad was lost and it was as black as pitch and so his lantern blowed out and there was bogs and so Finnigan's eyes shined red like traffic lights all the way a hundred miles. Dad was ever so hungry and he would of starved to death if Finnigan—'

'He could have shot some rabbits,' shouted Albert in the rear.

'He could not then, he didn't have a gun.'

'Why didn't he?'

'He was only as little as me.'

'When your dad was lost?'

'Yes, and Finnigan—'

'How old's your dad?' demanded Albert Briggs.

Danny dashed at it. 'Fifty-two.'

'Hoo! Finnigan's dead then.'

Danny turned and stared at him. Albert grinned round the group of home-going children. 'Donkeys don't live *twenty* years. Finnigan's a deader. Danny ain't never had no donkey. He's wonky.'

'So's his donkey!' chanted the poet.

'Danny's wonky, so's his donkey!' yelled the children.

It wasn't true, it wasn't true, it *couldn't* be true. His father would know. Danny doubled his fists again, wavered, then rushed out of earshot, rushed home with streaming eyes. At the crossing he forgot to look both ways.

It was Maisie who brought word to school next morning why Danny was absent on the last day of the term.

That evening Miss Daly appeared on Mrs O'Toole's doorstep. 'I've come to ask after Danny, Mrs O'Toole. We're all so dreadfully sorry. Is he—?'

'Oh, Miss, he's very poorly. Would you like to see him?'

But Danny didn't know who Miss Daly was. He seemed to be speaking to somebody who wasn't there, somebody he called Finnigan. Suddenly he stared at Miss Daly and doubled his fists. 'Finnigan's *not* a deader. I'll fight you!' he cried.

'I'd better go,' whispered Miss Daly. 'Don't come down. I'll find my way out.'

She went downstairs feeling very much upset. Mr O'Toole was hanging about the passage. He looked at her vaguely. 'Is it the nurse ye are?' Miss Daly recognized her native accent, and her heart went out instantly to Danny's father, as it had gone out instantly to his son.

'I'm Danny's schoolmistress, Kitty Daly,' she said. 'Mr O'Toole, who's Finnigan?'

Mr O'Toole told her. He told her everything, from the rose on Finnigan's tail to his non-existence. 'It's an ould fool I am to be

stuffin' the child's brain with legends,' he mourned, 'but such
store he set by that lily-white ass I went on and on with it, like a
man follows a wandering light in the dark.' Then Mr O'Toole
cried, and Miss Daly cried too.

'I'll write,' she said. 'I'll be going home tomorrow, but I'll write.
I'll want to know.'

Miss Daly did write, but not as soon as she meant to. When you
return home after quite a long time there's so much to catch you
from moment to moment, and then that business of crossing the
Irish Channel is more than just putting a space between you and
England, it's putting one life in place of another. To make things
worse, it happened that a young naval officer, called Frank,
arrived in her village the day after she did. He had been on the
same ship as her brother, so once she had met him, and now, by a
funny chance, he had turned up to spend a holiday where she was
spending hers. They spent the first week saying how curious it
was. Frank's hobby was taking snapshots, and he took them by the
reel of everything she showed him about her home. The only thing
he didn't take was Miss Daly. He wanted to, but something got
into her, and the more he urged the more she wouldn't let him. It
wasn't till the seventh day, when they were leaning over a gate,
feeding thistles to Paddy, the peat-cutter's old grey donkey, that
Miss Daly exclaimed, 'Oh dear!'

'What's the matter?' asked Frank, rather anxiously.

'I never wrote!'

'To whom?'

'To Danny, the darlint.'

'Who's Danny?' asked Frank, rather fiercely.

'He's my pet pupil, and he had an accident. I'll write this very
day.'

Three days later, Frank found Miss Daly crying her eyes out
over a letter from England.

'Kitty! Kitty dear—what is it?'

'Danny—' she choked.

'He isn't—?'

'No, but he's very bad indeed, he's in hospital, and he keeps crying and crying for Finnigan.'

'Finnigan?'

Miss Daly told Frank everything about Finnigan, everything that Mr O'Toole had told her; and how Danny's whole heart was set upon his Connemara donkey, white as snow, with ruby eyes and gold hoofs and a rose on his tail, his very own donkey whom he had never seen. 'And of course,' sobbed Miss Daly, 'there's no such donkey at all, and never was, and there's Danny crying out that Finnigan's died, and nothing his father tells him makes any difference. Wouldn't I be giving him a white donkey the like of Finnigan if I had one?'

Miss Daly felt her hand pressed gently. 'Indeed it's good of you to feel so for poor Danny,' she sighed, 'but it's only the sight of his donkey will do him any good.'

'Why not?' said Frank, whose only thought was to stop the tears flowing from Miss Daly's beautiful blue eyes.

The tears did stop flowing, and the blue eyes looked with great surprise into his brown ones. 'What do you mean by that?'

'You'll see what I mean,' said Frank, 'if you'll be in Mike's paddock at twelve o'clock tomorrow—and Kitty—'

'Well then?'

'Pray for a sunny day with all your might.'

Miss Daly must have spent the whole night praying, for the day was one of the sunniest ever seen. She couldn't wait till noon to get to the peat-cutter's paddock, but Frank was ready for her. And so was Paddy—but no! this was never Paddy? Mike had surely got himself a brand-new donkey, gleaming like snow on the top of a sunshiny mountain. As she came near, Frank was just finishing tying a big pink cabbage rose to the tail of this white wonder with a ribbon the colour of Kitty Daly's eyes.

'Allow me to introduce you,' said Frank gravely, 'to Finnigan O'Flanagan. Don't come too near, I'm not sure if he's quite dry yet. What do you think of him?'

'Oh, he's beautiful!' whispered Miss Daly. 'Where's your camera now?' She had jumped to it without being told. 'You must photograph him against Mike's old black shed, he'll show up like an angel so.'

'I hope he'll stand still,' said Frank. 'He's tried to kick me twice, and he's kicked over the whitewash can already.'

'He'll not kick me,' said Miss Daly. 'We're old friends, aren't we, Paddy boy?'

'Splendid!' said Frank. 'Then if you'll just stand by him and keep him still—'

'Ah, get away with you! I'll not be photographed.'

'Not even to please poor little Danny?'

'It's not me he's crying after.'

'No,' said Frank, 'but if you're in the picture he'll know that Finnigan is as alive as you are.' Miss Daly wavered. Frank had an inspiration. 'I tell you what! Lift up the donkey's tail, and be smelling the rose.'

Miss Daly gave in. With a face full of laughter she lifted Finnigan's tail daintily and sniffed the cabbage rose. The camera clicked. 'Right!' cried Frank. 'Just one more to make sure.' The camera clicked again. 'We'll have an enlargement made of the best of them, and send it by air.'

'Oh,' cried Kitty Daly, 'I could hug you!'

'Why not?' said Frank.

But it was two enlargements he ordered of the Connemara donkey with a rose on its tail.

When the autumn term started at Larchgrove Road Junior and Infants' Mixed, Danny O'Toole was not there. But half-way through the term he was well enough to come. Everybody knew he was coming, and Miss Daly who had visited him already at home, knew what he was bringing to school with him. She hovered in the background while he displayed the flat brown-paper parcel he carried so carefully under his small armpit.

'Wossat?' demanded Albert Briggs at sight.

'It's my donkey,' said Danny, 'it's Finnigan O'Flanagan.'

The children crowded round to see as he took off the outer wrapping, and opened the large stiff envelope which contained the photograph of a donkey as white as pear-blossom, as snow on the mountain-tops, or as whitewash. The children gasped with wonder; the black shed threw up the angelic donkey into dazzling relief, but as well as that his eyes glowed as red and his hoofs as gold as luminous paint could make them. And if anyone had still been inclined to doubt, there at Finnigan's rump stood their own Junior Mistress, smelling the rose on Finnigan's tail.

'Coo!' gasped Believers and Unbelievers in one breath.

'It's Miss Daly!' said Maisie Bonnington. She called eagerly to the Junior Mistress, 'Miss, Miss! That's you in the picture.'

'To be sure it's me.'

'And that's—is that akshually Finnigan?'

'Who else would it be? There was never a donkey the like of Finnigan O'Flanagan.'

And she started to tell them wonders that outstripped the stories of Mr O'Toole, yet they carried a conviction his had not. For his were tales of fifty years ago, but here was Miss Daly telling of a donkey she had seen with her own eyes only last month. Among the group of excited listeners, Albert Briggs chewed the bitter cud of thought. When Miss Daly paused for breath, he broke in.

'Miss.'

'What is it, Bert?'

'Danny said his donkey was in Connemara.'

'It is so!' declared Danny.

'But, Miss—you said you was going to Ballyninch.'

'Well then, goofy! Ballynahinch is just another name for Connemara,' laughed Miss Daly.

'Is there really such a place as Connemara, Miss?' asked Maisie.

'Well I should think there is! Wasn't I born there?'

Then Albert knew he had staked all and lost; and so did the rest of the Infants and Juniors of Larchgrove Road School. The fickle poet, seeing how the land lay, began to chant:

With a face full of laughter she lifted Finnigan's tail daintily and sniffed the cabbage rose.

'Bert's wonky!
Bert's a donkey!'

And the school took up the chant.

Danny's triumph did not end even there. It had been noticed that Miss Daly came back from Ireland with a ring on her left hand that hadn't been there during the summer term; and one day the exciting news ran round that Miss Daly had been called for by a naval officer, a Lieutenant in the *Marines*! He came down presently from the staff room, where he had been talking to the mistresses; and now he wanted to talk to the children—as many of them as could get near him, and weren't too shy to touch him. And the *things* he told them about Finnigan O'Flanagan! Things which outstripped all Mr O'Toole's and Miss Daly's tales put together. The Marines, it appeared, could tell even more things than they were told. But one thing he told made them all rather sad; it seemed that their Junior Mistress wouldn't be coming back to teach them next term. 'She's going to teach me instead,' groaned the Marine. 'Won't it be awful to be a class of one? I shan't ever be able to escape her eye.'

That made the children laugh. Maisie Bonnington reassured him. 'She's ever so nice, sir, she's scarcely never cross.'

'I'm relieved to hear it,' said the Marine Lieutenant. Then he told them something that brightened them up again. As a Christmas Treat he was going to take them to the Pantomime at the Coronation Theatre one Saturday in January, when he and Miss Daly would collect them all in a bunch.

The Marine was as good as his word, and *Aladdin* at the Coronation was past all expectation. But among the golden wonders of Aladdin's cave, none stuck more vividly in Albert Briggs's mind than the glitter on the coat of an important little man who helped to usher the party of children to their seats; a little man who, catching sight of Danny, winked solemnly, while Danny whispered in passing, 'Hullo Dad!'—a little man who was Danny O'Toole's father, and who wore gold on his fronts.

THE COOP

Edgar Wallace

Sometimes they referred to Mr Yardley in the newspapers as 'the Wizard of Stotford', sometimes his credit was diffused as the 'Yardley Confederation'; occasionally he was spoken of as plain 'Bert Yardley' but invariably his entries for any important handicaps were described as 'The Stotford Mystery'. For nobody quite knew what Mr Yardley's intentions were until the day of the race. Usually after the race, for it is a distressing fact that the favourite from his stable was usually unplaced, and the winner—also from his stable—started amongst the '100 to 7 others'.

After the event was all over and the 'weighed in' had been called, people used to gather in the paddock in little groups and ask one another what this horse was doing at Nottingham, and where were the stewards, and why Mr Yardley was not jolly well warned off. And they didn't say 'jolly' either.

For it is an understood thing in racing that, if an outsider wins, its trainer ought to be warned off. Yet neither Bert Yardley, nor Colonel Rogersman, nor Mr Lewis Feltham—the two principal owners for whom he trained—were so much as asked by the stewards to explain the running of their horses. Thus proving that the Turf needed reform, and that the stipendiary steward was an absolute necessity.

Mr Bert Yardley was a youngish man of thirty-five, who spoke very little and did his betting by telegram. He had a suite at the Midland Hotel, and was a member of a sedate and respectable club in Pall Mall. He read extensively, mostly such classics as *Races to Come*, and the umpteenth volume of the Stud Book, and he leavened his studies with such lighter reading as the training reports from the daily sporting newspapers—he liked a good laugh.

His worst enemy could not complain of him that he refused information to anybody.

'I think mine have some sort of chance, and I'm backing them both. Tinpot? Well, of course, he may win; miracles happen, and I shouldn't be surprised if he made a good show. But I've had to ease him in his work and when I galloped him on Monday he simply wouldn't have it—couldn't get him to take hold of his bit. Possibly he runs better when he's a little above himself, but he's a horse of moods. If he'd only give his running, he'd trot in! Lampholder, on the other hand, is as game a horse as ever looked through a bridle. A battler! He'll be there or thereabouts.'

What would you back on that perfectly candid, perfectly honest information straight, as it were, from the horse's mouth?

Lampholder, of course; and Tinpot would win. Even stipendiary stewards couldn't make Lampholder win, not if they got behind and shoved him. And that, of course, is no part of a stipendiary steward's duties.

That night he pulled in Nosey Boldin.

Mr Bert Yardley was dressing for dinner one March evening when he discovered that a gold watch had disappeared. He called his valet, who could offer no other information than that it had been there when they left Stotford for Sandown Park.

'Send for the police,' said Mr Yardley, and there came to him Detective-Sergeant Challoner.

Mr Challoner listened, made a few notes, asked a few, a very few, questions of the valet and closed his book.

'I think I know the person,' he said, and to the valet: 'A big nose—you're sure of the big nose?'

The valet was emphatic.

'Very good,' said The Miller. 'I'll do my best, Mr Yardley. I hope I shall be as successful as Amboy will be in the Lincoln Handicap.'

Mr Yardley smiled faintly.

'We'll talk about that later,' he said.

The Miller made one or two inquiries and that night pulled in Nosey Boldin, whose hobby it was to pose as an inspector of telephones and who, in this capacity, had made many successful experiments. On the way to the station, Nosey, so-called because of a certain abnormality in that organ, delivered himself with great force and venom.

'This comes of betting on horse races and follering Educated Evans's perishin' five-pound specials! Let this be a warning to you, Miller!'

'Not so much lip,' said The Miller.

'He gave me one winner in ten shots, and *that* started at 11 to 10 on,' ruminated Nosey. 'Men like that drive men to crime. There ought to be a law so's to make the fifth loser a *felony*! And after the eighth loser he ought to 'ang! That'd stop 'em.'

The Miller saw his friend charged and lodged for the night and went home to bed. And in the morning, when he left his rooms to go to breakfast, the first person he saw was Educated Evans, and there was on that learned man's unhappy face a look of pain and anxiety.

'Good morning, Mr Challoner. Excuse me if I'm taking a liberty, but I understand that a client of mine is in trouble?'

'If you mean Nosey, he is,' agreed The Miller. 'And what's more, he attributes his shame and downfall to following your tips. I sympathize with him.'

Educated Evans made an impatient clicking sound, raised his eyebrows and spread out his hand.

'Bolsho,' he said simply.

'Eh?' The Miller frowned suspiciously. 'You didn't give Bolsho?'

'Every guaranteed client received "Bolsho: fear nothing," ' said Evans even more simply; 'following Mothegg (ten to one, beaten a neck, hard lines), Toffeetown (third, hundred to eight, very unlucky), Onesided (won, seven to two, what a beauty!), followin' Curds and Whey (won, eleven to ten—can't help the price). Is that fair?'

'The question is,' said The Miller deliberately, 'Did Nosey subscribe to your guarantee wire, your five pound special, or your Overnight nap?'

'That,' said Educated Evans diplomatically, 'I can't tell till I've seen me books. The point is this: if Nosey wants bail, am I all right? I don't want any scandal, and you know Nosey. He ought to have been in advertisin''.'

The advertising propensities of Nosey were, indeed, well known to The Miller. He had the knack of introducing some startling feature into the very simplest case, and attracting to himself the amount of newspaper space usually given to scenes in the House and important murders.

It was Nosey who, by his startling statement that pickles were a greater incentive to crime than beer, initiated a press correspondence which lasted for months. It was Nosey who, when charged with hotel larceny—his favourite aberration—made the pronouncement that buses were a cause of insanity. Upon the peg of his frequent misfortunes it was his practice to hang a showing up for somebody.

The case of Nosey was dealt with summarily. Long before the prosecutor had completed his evidence he realized that his doom was sealed.

'Anything known about this man?' asked the magistrate.

A jailer stepped briskly into the box and gave a brief sketch of Nosey's life, and Nosey, who knew it all before, looked bored.

'Anything to say?' asked the magistrate.

Nosey cleared his throat.

'I can only say, your worship, that I've fell into thieving ways owing to falling in the hands of unscrupulous racing tipsters. I'm ruined by tips, and if the law was just, there's a certain party who ought to be standing here by my side.'

Educated Evans, standing at the back of the court, squirmed.

'I've got a wife, as true a woman as ever drew the breath of life,' Nosey went on. 'I've got two dear little children, and I ask your worship to consider me temptation owing to horse-racing, and betting and this here tipster.'

'Six months,' said the magistrate, without looking up.

Outside the court Mr Evans waited patiently for the appearance of The Miller.

'Nosey never had more than a shilling on a horse in his life,' he said bitterly, 'and he *owes*! Here's the bread being took out of my mouth by slander and misrepresentation; do you think they'll put it in the papers, Mr Challoner?'

'Certain,' said The Miller cheerfully, and Educated Evans groaned.

'That man's worse than Lucreature Burgia, the celebrated poisoner,' he said, 'that Shakespeare wrote a play about. He's a snake in the grass and viper in the bosom. And to think I gave him Penwiper for the Manchester November, and he never so much as asked me if I was thirsty! Mr Challoner.'

Challoner, turning away, stopped.

'Was that Yardley? I mean the trainer?'

The Miller looked at him reproachfully.

'Maybe I'm getting old and my memory is becoming defective,' he said, 'but I seem to remember that when you gave me Tellmark the other day, you said that you were a personal friend of Mr Yardley's, and that the way he insisted on your coming down to spend the week-ends was getting a public nuisance.'

Educated Evans did not bat a lid.

'That was his brother,' he said.

'He must have lied when he told me he had no brothers,' said The Miller.

'They've quarrelled,' replied Educated Evans frankly. 'In fact, they never mention one another's names. It's tragic when brothers quarrel, Mr Challoner. I've done my best to reconcile 'em—but what's the use? He didn't say anything about Amboy, did he?'

'He said nothing that I can tell you,' was his unsatisfactory reply, and he left Mr Evans to consider means and methods by which he might bring himself into closer contact with the Wizard of Stotford.

All that he feared in the matter of publicity was realized to the full. One evening paper said:

RUINED BY TIPSTERS
Once prosperous merchant goes to prison for theft.

And in the morning press one newspaper may be quoted as typical of the rest:

TIPSTER TO BLAME
Pest of the Turf wrecks a home.

Detective-Sergeant Challoner called by appointment at the Midland Hotel, and Mr Yardley saw him.

'No, thank you, sir,' The Miller was firm.

Mr Yardley put back the fiver he had taken from his pocket.

'I'll put you a tenner on anything I fancy,' he said. 'Who's this tipster, by the way?—the man who was referred to by the prisoner?'

The Miller smiled.

'Educated Evans,' he said, and when he had finished describing him Mr Yardley nodded.

He was staying overnight in London en route for Lincoln and he was inclined to be bored. He had read the *Racing Calendar* from the list of the year's races to the last description of the last selling hurdle race on the back page. He had digested the surprising qualities of stallions and he could have almost recited the forfeit list from Aaron to Znosberg. And he was aching for diversion when the bell boy brought a card.

It was a large card, tastefully bordered with pink and green roses: its edge was golden and in the centre were the words:

J. T. EVANS
(better known as 'Educated Evans'!!)
The World's Foremost and Leading Turf
Adviser and Racing Cricit
c/o Jockey Club, Newmarket or direct:
92 Bayham Mews, N.W.1
'The Man Who Gave Braxted!!
What a beauty!'—*vide* Press.

Mr Yardley read, lingering over the printer's errors.

'Show this gentleman up, page,' he said.

Into his presence came Educated Evans, a solemn purposeful man.

'I hope the intrusion will be amply excused by the important nature or character of my business,' he said. This was the opening he had planned.

'Sit down, Mr Evans,' said Yardley, and Educated Evans put his hat under the chair and sat.

'I've been thinking matters over in the privacy of my den—' began Evans, after a preliminary cough.

'You're a lion tamer as well?' asked the Wizard of Stotford, interested.

'By "den" I mean "study,"' said Evans, gravely. 'To come to the point without beating about the bush—to use a well-known expression—I've heard of a coop.'

'A what?'

'A coop,' said Evans.

'A chicken coop?' asked the puzzled Wizard.

'It's a French word, meaning "ramp",' said Evans.

'Oh yes, I see. "Coup"—it's pronounced "coo", Mr Evans.'
Educated Evans frowned.

'It's years since I was in Paris,' he said; 'and I suppose they've
altered it. It used to be "coop" but these French people are always
messing and mucking about with words.'

'And who is working this coop?' asked the trainer.

'Higgson.'

Educated Evans pronounced the word with great emphasis.
Higgson was another mystery trainer. His horses also won when
least expected. And after they won, little knots of men gathered in
the paddock and asked one another if the Stewards had eyes, and
why wasn't Higgson warned off?

'You interest me,' said the trainer of Amboy. 'Do you mean that
he's winning with St Kats?'

Evans nodded more gravely still.

'I think it's me duty to tell you,' he said. 'My information'—
he lowered his voice and glanced round to the door to be sure that
it was shut—'comes from the boy who does this horse!'

'Dear me!' said Mr Yardley.

'I've got correspondents everywhere,' said Educated Evans
mysteriously. 'My man at Stockbridge sent me a letter this morning—I daren't show it to you—about a horse in that two-year-old
race that will win with his ears pricked.'

Mr Yardley was looking at him through half-closed eyes.

'With his ears pricked?' he repeated, impressed. 'Have they
trained his ears too? Extraordinary! But why have you come to tell
me about Mr Higgson's horse?'

Educated Evans bent forward confidentially.

'Because you've done me many a turn, sir,' he said; 'and I'd like
to do you one. I've got the information. I could shut my mouth
an' make millions. I've got nine thousand clients who'd pay me the
odds to a pound—but what's money?'

'True,' murmured Mr Yardley, nodding. 'Thank you, Mr Evans. St Kats, I think you said? Now, in return for your kindness, I'll give you a tip.'

Educated Evans held his breath. His amazingly bold plan had succeeded.

'Change your printer,' said Mr Yardley, rising. 'He can't spell. Good night.'

Evans went forth with his heart turned to stone and his soul seared with bitter animosity.

Mr Yardley came down after him and watched the shabby figure as it turned the corner, and his heart was touched. In two minutes he had overtaken the educated man.

'You're a bluff and a fake,' he said, good humouredly, 'but you can have a little, a very little, on Amboy.'

Before Educated Evans could prostrate himself at the benefactor's feet Mr Yardley was gone.

The next day was a busy one for Educated Evans. All day Miss Higgs, the famous typist of Great College Street, turned her duplicator, and every revolution of the cylinder threw forth, with a rustle and a click, the passionate appeal which Educated Evans addressed to all clients, old and new. He was not above borrowing the terminology of other advertisement writers.

> You want the best winners—I've got them.
> Bet in Evans' way! Eventually, why not now?
> I've got the winner of the Lincoln!
> > What a beauty!
> > What a beauty!
> > What a beauty!
> Confidentially! From the trainer! This is the coop
> of the season! Help yourself! Defeat ignored!

To eight hundred and forty clients this moving appeal went forth.

On the afternoon of the race Educated Evans strolled with confidence to the end of the Tottenham Court Road to wait for the

Star. And when it came he opened the paper with a quiet smile. He was still smiling, when he read:

Tenpenny, 1
St Kats, 2
Ella Glass, 3
All probables ran.

'Tenpenny?—never heard of it,' he repeated, dazed, and produced his noon edition. Tenpenny was starred as a doubtful runner.

It was trained by—Yardley.

For a moment his emotions almost mastered him.

'That man ought to be warned off,' he said hollowly, and dragged his weary feet back to the stable yard.

In the morning came a letter dated from Lincoln.

Dear Mr Evans,—What do you think of my coop?—
Yours, H. YARDLEY.

There was a P.S. which ran:

I put a fiver on for you. Your enterprise deserved it.

Evans opened the cheque tenderly and shook his head.

'After all,' he said subsequently to the quietly jubilant Miller, 'clients can't expect to win *every* time—a Turf Adviser is entitled to his own coops.'

Tenpenny started at 25 to 1.

MY EARLY HOME

Anna Sewell

The first place that I can well remember was a large pleasant meadow with a pond of clear water in it. Some shady trees leaned over it, and rushes and water-lilies grew at the deep end. Over the hedge on one side we looked into a ploughed field, and on the other we looked over a gate at our master's house, which stood by the roadside; at the top of the meadow was a plantation of fir trees, and at the bottom a running brook overhung by a steep bank.

While I was young I lived upon my mother's milk, as I could not eat grass. In the day time I ran by her side, and at night I lay down close by her. When it was hot, we stood by the pond in the shade of the trees, and when it was cold, we had a nice warm shed.

As soon as I was old enough to eat grass, my mother used to go out to work in the day time, and came back in the evening.

There were six young colts in the meadow besides me; they were older than I was; some were nearly as large as grown-up horses. I used to run with them, and had great fun; we used to gallop all together round and round the field, as hard as we could go. Sometimes we had rather rough play, for they would frequently bite and kick as well as gallop.

One day, when there was a good deal of kicking, my mother whinnied to me to come to her, and then she said:

'I wish you to pay attention to what I am going to say to you. The colts who live here are very good colts, but they are cart-horse colts, and, of course, they have not learned manners. You have been well bred and well born; your father has a great name in these parts, and your grandfather won the cup two years at the New-market races; your grandmother had the sweetest temper of any horse I ever knew, and I think you have never seen me kick or bite. I hope you will grow up gentle and good, and never learn bad ways; do your work with a good will, lift your feet up well when you trot, and never bite or kick even in play.'

I have never forgotten my mother's advice; I knew she was a wise old horse, and our master thought a great deal of her. Her name was Duchess, but he often called her Pet.

Our master was a good, kind man. He gave us good food, good lodging, and kind words; he spoke as kindly to us as he did to his little children. We were all fond of him, and my mother loved him very much. When she saw him at the gate, she would neigh with joy, and trot up to him. He would pat and stroke her and say, 'Well, old Pet, and how is your little Darkie?' I was a dull black, so he called me Darkie; then he would give me a piece of bread, which was very good, and sometimes he brought a carrot for my mother. All the horses would come to him, but I think we were his favourites. My mother always took him to the town on a market day in a light gig.

There was a ploughboy, Dick, who sometimes came into our

field to pluck blackberries from the hedge. When he had eaten all he wanted, he would have, what he called, fun with the colts, throwing stones and sticks at them to make them gallop. We did not much mind him, for we could gallop off; but sometimes a stone would hit and hurt us.

One day he was at this game, and did not know that the master was in the next field; but he was there, watching what was going on: over the hedge he jumped in a snap, and catching Dick by the arm, he gave him such a box on the ear as made him roar with the pain and surprise. As soon as we saw the master, we trotted up nearer to see what went on.

'Bad boy!' he said, 'bad boy! to chase the colts. This is not the first time, nor the second, but it shall be the last—there—take your money and go home, I shall not want you on my farm again.' So we never saw Dick any more. Old Daniel, the man who looked after the horses, was just as gentle as our master, so we were well off.

The hunt

Before I was two years old, a circumstance happened which I have never forgotten. It was early in the spring; there had been a little frost in the night, and a light mist still hung over the plantations and meadows. I and the other colts were feeding at the lower part of the field when we heard, quite in the distance, what sounded like the cry of dogs. The oldest of the colts raised his head, pricked his ears, and said, 'There are the hounds!' and immediately cantered off, followed by the rest of us to the upper part of the field, where we could look over the hedge and see several fields beyond. My mother, and an old riding horse of our master's, were also standing near, and seemed to know all about it.

'They have found a hare,' said my mother, 'and if they come this way, we shall see the hunt.'

And soon the dogs were all tearing down the field of young wheat next to ours. I never heard such a noise as they made. They did not bark, nor howl, nor whine, but kept on a 'yo! yo, o, o! yo!

yo, o, o!' at the top of their voices. After them came a number of men on horseback, some of them in green coats, all galloping as fast as they could. The old horse snorted and looked eagerly after them, and we young colts wanted to be galloping with them, but they were soon away into the fields lower down; here it seemed as if they had come to a stand; the dogs left off barking, and ran about every way with their noses to the ground.

'They have lost the scent,' said the old horse; 'perhaps the hare will get off.'

'What hare?' I said.

'Oh! I don't know *what* hare; likely enough it may be one of our own hares out of the plantation; any hare they can find will do for the dogs and men to run after,' and before long the dogs began their 'yo! yo, o, o!' again, and back they came altogether at full speed, making straight for our meadow at the part where the high bank and hedge overhang the brook.

'Now we shall see the hare,' said my mother; and just then a hare wild with fright rushed by, and made for the plantation. On came the dogs, they burst over the bank, leapt the stream, and came dashing across the field, followed by the huntsmen. Six or eight men leaped their horses clean over, close upon the dogs. The hare tried to get through the fence; it was too thick, and she turned sharp round to make for the road, but it was too late; the dogs were upon her with their wild cries: we heard one shriek, and that was the end of her. One of the hunstmen rode up and whipped off the dogs, who would soon have torn her to pieces. He held her up by the leg torn and bleeding, and all the gentlemen seemed well pleased.

As for me, I was so astonished that I did not at first see what was going on by the brook; but when I did look, there was a sad sight; two fine horses were down, one was struggling in the stream, and the other was groaning on the grass. One of the riders was getting out of the water covered with mud, the other lay quite still.

'His neck is broke,' said my mother.

'And serve him right too,' said one of the colts.

I thought the same and said so, but my mother did not join with us.

'Well! no,' she said, 'you must not say that; but though I am an old horse, and have seen and heard a great deal, I never yet could make out why men are so fond of this sport; they often hurt themselves, often spoil good horses, and tear up the fields, and all for a hare or a fox, or a stag, that they could get more easily some other way; but we are only horses, and don't know.'

While my mother was saying this, we stood and looked on. Many of the riders had gone to the young man; but my master, who had been watching what was going on, was the first to raise him. His head fell back and his arms hung down, and every one looked very serious. There was no noise now; even the dogs were quiet, and seemed to know that something was wrong. They carried him to our master's house. I heard afterwards that it was young George Gordon, the Squire's only son, a fine, tall young man, and the pride of his family.

There was now riding off in all directions to the doctor's, to the farrier's, and no doubt to Squire Gordon's, to let him know about his son. When Mr Bond, the farrier, came to look at the black horse that lay groaning on the grass, he felt him all over, and shook his head; one of his legs was broken. Then some one ran to our master's house and came back with a gun; presently there was a loud bang and a dreadful shriek, and then all was still; the black horse moved no more.

My mother seemed much troubled; she said she had known that horse for years, and that his name was 'Rob Roy'; he was a good bold horse, and there was no vice in him. She never would go to that part of the field afterwards.

Not many days after, we heard the church bell tolling for a long time; and looking over the gate we saw a long strange black coach that was covered with black cloth and was drawn by black horses; after that came another and another and another, and all were black, while the bell kept tolling, tolling. They were carrying young Gordon to the churchyard to bury him. He would never ride again.

We saw a long strange black coach drawn by black horses.

What they did with Rob Roy I never knew; but 'twas all for one little hare.

My breaking in

I was now beginning to grow handsome; my coat had grown fine and soft, and was bright black. I had one white foot, and a pretty white star on my forehead. I was thought very handsome; my master would not sell me till I was four years old; he said lads ought not to work like men, and colts ought not to work like horses till they were quite grown up.

When I was four years old, Squire Gordon came to look at me. He examined my eyes, my mouth, and my legs; he felt them all down; and then I had to walk and trot and gallop before him; he seemed to like me, and said, 'When he has been well broken in, he will do very well.' My master said he would break me in himself, as he should not like me to be frightened or hurt, and he lost no time about it, for the next day he began.

Every one may not know what breaking in is, therefore I will describe it. It means to teach a horse to wear a saddle and bridle and to carry on his back a man, woman, or child; to go just the way they wish, and to go quietly. Besides this, he has to learn to wear a collar, a crupper, and a breeching, and to stand still while they are put on; then to have a cart or a chaise fixed behind him, so that he cannot walk or trot without dragging it after him: and he must go fast or slow, just as his driver wishes. He must never start at what he sees, nor speak to other horses, nor bite, nor kick, nor have any will of his own; but always do his master's will, even though he may be very tired or hungry; but the worst of all is, when his harness is once on, he may neither jump for joy nor lie down for weariness. So you see this breaking in is a great thing.

I had of course long been used to a halter and a headstall, and to be led about in the field and lanes quietly, but now I was to have a bit and a bridle; my master gave me some oats as usual, and after a good deal of coaxing, he got the bit into my mouth, and the bridle fixed, but it was a nasty thing! Those who have never had a bit in their mouths cannot think how bad it feels; a great piece of cold hard steel as thick as a man's finger to be pushed into one's mouth, between one's teeth and over one's tongue, with the ends coming out at the corner of your mouth, and held fast there by straps over your head, under your throat, round your nose, and under your chin; so that no way in the world can you get rid of the nasty hard thing; it is very bad! yes, very bad! at least I thought so; but I knew my mother always wore one when she went out, and all horses did when they were grown up; and so, what with the nice oats, and what with my master's pats, kind words, and gentle ways, I got to wear my bit and bridle.

Next came the saddle, but that was not half so bad; my master put it on my back very gently, whilst old Daniel held my head; he then made the girths fast under my body, patting and talking to me all the time; then I had a few oats, then a little leading about, and this he did every day till I began to look for the oats and the saddle. At length, one morning my master got on my back and rode me round the meadow on the soft grass. It certainly did feel queer; but I must say I felt rather proud to carry my master, and as he continued to ride me a little every day, I soon became accustomed to it.

The next unpleasant business was putting on the iron shoes; that too was very hard at first. My master went with me to the smith's forge, to see that I was not hurt or got any fright. The blacksmith took my feet in his hand one after the other, and cut away some of the hoof. It did not pain me, so I stood still on three legs till he had done them all. Then he took a piece of iron the shape of my foot, and clapped it on, and drove some nails through the shoe quite into my hoof, so that the shoe was firmly on. My feet felt very stiff and heavy, but in time I got used to it.

And now having got so far, my master went on to break me to harness; there were more new things to wear. First, a stiff heavy collar just on my neck, and a bridle with great side-pieces against my eyes called blinkers, and blinkers indeed they were, for I could not see on either side, but only straight in front of me; next there was a small saddle with a nasty stiff strap that went right under my tail; that was the crupper. I hated the crupper—to have my long tail doubled up and poked through that strap was almost as bad as the bit. I never felt more like kicking, but of course I could not kick such a good master, and so in time I got used to everything, and could do my work as well as my mother.

I must not forget to mention one part of my training, which I have always considered a very great advantage. My master sent me for a fortnight to a neighbouring farmer's, who had a meadow which was skirted on one side by the railway. Here were some sheep and cows, and I was turned in amongst them.

I shall never forget the first train that ran by. I was feeding quietly near the pales which separated the meadow from the railway, when I heard a strange sound at a distance, and before I knew whence it came—with a rush and a clatter, and a puffing out of smoke—a long black train of something flew by, and was gone almost before I could draw my breath. I turned, and galloped to the further side of the meadow as fast as I could go, and there I stood snorting with astonishment and fear. In the course of the day many other trains went by, some more slowly; these drew up at the station close by, and sometimes made an awful shriek and groan before they stopped. I thought it very dreadful, but the cows went on eating very quietly, and hardly raised their heads as the black frightful thing came puffing and grinding past.

For the first few days I could not feed in peace; but as I found that this terrible creature never came into the field, or did me any harm, I began to disregard it, and very soon I cared as little about the passing of a train as the cows and sheep did.

Since then I have seen many horses much alarmed and restive at the sight or sound of a steam engine; but thanks to my good master's care, I am as fearless at railway stations as in my own stable.

Now if any one wants to break in a young horse well, that is the way.

My master often drove me in double harness with my mother

because she was steady, and could teach me how to go better than a strange horse. She told me the better I behaved, the better I should be treated, and that it was wisest always to do my best to please my master; 'but,' said she, 'there are a great many kinds of men; there are good, thoughtful men like our master, that any horse may be proud to serve; but there are bad, cruel men, who never ought to have a horse or dog to call their own. Beside, there are a great many foolish men, vain, ignorant, and careless, who never trouble themselves to think; these spoil more horses than all, just for want of sense; they don't mean it, but they do it for all that. I hope you will fall into good hands; but a horse never knows who may buy him, or who may drive him; it is all a chance for us, but still I say, do your best wherever it is, and keep up your good name.'

LEARNING TO RIDE

Frances Hodgson Burnett

Cedric Errol and his widowed mother leave New York and come to live in England when it is discovered that seven year old Cedric is an heir. As Little Lord Fauntleroy he lives with his grandfather, the Earl of Dorincourt, at Dorincourt castle.

Lord Dorincourt had occasion to wear his grim smile many a time as the days passed by. Indeed as his acquaintance with his grandson progressed, he wore the smile so often that there were moments when it almost lost its grimness. There is no denying that before Lord Fauntleroy had appeared on the scene, the old man had been growing very tired of his loneliness and his gout and his seventy years. After so long a life of excitement and amusement, it was not agreeable to sit alone even in the most splendid room, with one foot on a gout-stool, and with no other diversion than flying into a rage, and shouting at a frightened footman who hated the sight of him. The old Earl was too clever a man not to know

perfectly well that his servants detested him, and that even if he
had visitors, they did not come for love of him—though some
found a sort of amusement in his sharp, sarcastic talk, which
spared no one. So long as he had been strong and well, he had
gone from one place to another, pretending to amuse himself,
though he had not really enjoyed it; and when his health began to
fail, he felt tired of everything and shut himself up at Dorincourt
with his gout and his newspapers and his books. But he could not
read all the time, and he became more and more 'bored', as he
called it. He hated the long nights and days, and he grew more and
more savage and irritable. And then Fauntleroy came; and when
the Earl saw the lad, fortunately for the little fellow, the secret
pride of the grandfather was gratified at the outset. If Cedric had
been a less handsome little fellow the old man might have taken so
strong a dislike to the boy that he would not have given himself
the chance to see his grandson's finer qualities. But he chose to
think that Cedric's beauty and fearless spirit were the results of
Dorincourt blood and a credit to the Dorincourt rank. And then
when he heard the lad talk, and saw what a well-bred little fellow
he was, notwithstanding his boyish ignorance of all that his new
position meant, the old Earl liked his grandson more, and actually
began to find himself rather entertained. It had amused him to
give into those childish hands the power to bestow a benefit on
poor Higgins. My lord cared nothing for poor Higgins, but it
pleased him a little to think that his grandson would be talked about
by the country people and would begin to be popular with the
tenantry, even in his childhood. Then it had gratified him to drive
to church with Cedric and to see the excitement and interest
caused by the arrival. He knew how the people would speak of the
beauty of the little lad; of his fine, strong, straight little body; of
his erect bearing, his handsome face, and his bright hair, and how
they would say (as the Earl had heard one woman exclaim to
another) that the boy was 'every inch a lord'. My lord of Dorincourt
was an arrogant old man, proud of his name, proud of his rank,
and therefore proud to show the world that at last the House of

Dorincourt had a worthy heir.

The morning the new pony had been tried the Earl had been so pleased that he had almost forgotten his gout. When the groom had brought out the pretty creature, which arched its brown glossy neck and tossed its fine head in the sun, the Earl had sat at the open window of the library and had looked on while Fauntleroy took his first riding lesson. He wondered if the boy would show signs of timidity. It was not a very small pony, and he had often seen children lose courage in making their first essay at riding.

Fauntleroy mounted in great delight. He had never been on a pony before, and he was in the highest spirits. Wilkins, the groom, led the animal by the bridle up and down before the library window.

'He's a well plucked un, he is,' Wilkins remarked in the stable afterwards with many grins. 'It weren't no trouble to put *him* up. An' a old un wouldn't ha' sat any straighter when he *were* up. He ses—ses he to me, "Wilkins," he ses, "am I sitting up straight? They sit up straight at the circus," ses he. And I ses, "As straight as a arrer, your lordship!"—an' he laughs, as pleased as could be, an' he ses "That's right," he ses, "you tell me if I don't sit up straight, Wilkins." '

But sitting up straight and being led at a walk were not altogether and completely satisfactory. After a few minutes Fauntleroy spoke to his grandfather—watching him from the window.

'Can't I go by myself?' he asked: 'and can't I go faster? The boy on Fifth Avenue used to trot and canter!'

'Do you think you could trot and canter?' said the Earl.

'I should like to try,' answered Fauntleroy.

His lordship made a sign to Wilkins, who at the signal brought up his own horse and mounted it and took Fauntleroy's pony by the leading-rein.

'Now,' said the Earl, 'let him trot.'

The next few minutes were rather exciting to the small equestrian. He found that trotting was not so easy as walking, and the faster the pony trotted, the less easy it was.

'It j-jolts a g-goo-good deal—do-doesn't it?' he said to Wilkins.

'D-does it j-jolt y-you?'

'No, my lord,' answered Wilkins. 'You'll get used to it in time. Rise in your stirrups.'

'I'm ri-rising all the t-time,' said Fauntleroy.

He was both rising and falling rather uncomfortably and with many shakes and bounces. He was out of breath and his face grew red, but he held on with all his might, and sat as straight as he could. The Earl could see that from his window. When the riders came back within speaking distance, after they had been hidden by the trees a few minutes, Fauntleroy's hat was off, his cheeks were like poppies, and his lips were set, but he was still trotting.

'Stop a minute!' said his grandfather. 'Where's your hat?'

Wilkins touched his. 'It fell off, your lordship,' he said, with evident enjoyment. 'Wouldn't let me stop to pick it up, my lord.'

'Not much afraid, is he?' asked the Earl, dryly.

'Him, your lordship!' exclaimed Wilkins. 'I shouldn't say as he knowed what it meant. I've taught young gen'lemen to ride afore, an' I never see one stick on more determiner.'

'Tired?' said the Earl to Fauntleroy. 'Want to get off?'

'It jolts you more than you think it will,' admitted his young lordship frankly. 'And it tires you a little too; but I don't want to get off. I want to learn how. As soon as I've got my breath I want to go back for the hat.'

The cleverest person in the world, if he had undertaken to teach Fauntleroy how to please the old man who watched him, could not have taught him anything which would have succeeded better. As the pony trotted off again towards the avenue, a faint colour crept up in the fierce old face, and the eyes, under the shaggy brows, gleamed with a pleasure such as his lordship had scarcely expected to know again. And he sat and watched quite eagerly until the sound of the horses' hoofs returned. When they did come, which was after some time, they came at a faster pace. Fauntleroy's hat was still off, Wilkins was carrying it for him; his cheeks were redder than before, and his hair was flying about his ears, but he came at quite a brisk canter.

'There,' he panted, as they drew up, 'I c-cantered. I didn't do it as well as the boy on the Fifth Avenue, but I did it, and I stayed on!'

He and Wilkins and the pony were close friends after that. Scarcely a day passed on which the country people did not see them out together, cantering gaily on the highroad or through the green lanes. The children in the cottages would run to the door to look at the proud little brown pony with the gallant little figure sitting so straight in the saddle, and the young lord would snatch off his cap and swing it at them, and shout, 'Hullo! Good morning!' in a very unlordly manner, though with great heartiness. Sometimes he would stop and talk with the children, and once Wilkins came back to the Castle with a story of how Fauntleroy had insisted on dismounting near the village school, so that a boy who was lame and tired might ride home on his pony.

'An' I'm blessed,' said Wilkins, in telling the story at the stables, —I'm blessed if he'd hear of anything else! He wouldn't let me get down, because he said the boy mightn't feel comfortable on a big horse. An' ses he, "Wilkins," ses he, "that boy's lame and I'm not, and I want to talk to him too." And up the lad has to get, and my lord trudges alongside of him with his hands in his pockets, and his cap on the back of his head, a-whistling and talking as easy as you please! And when we come to the cottage, an' the boy's mother come out all in a taking to see what's up, he whips off his cap an' ses he, "I've brought your son home, ma'am," ses he, "because his leg hurt him, and I don't think that stick is enough for him to lean on; and I'm going to ask my grandfather to have a pair of crutches made for him." An' I'm blest if the woman wasn't struck all of a heap, as well she might be! I thought I should 'a' hex-plodid, myself!'

When the Earl heard the story, he was not angry, as Wilkins had been half afraid that he would be; on the contrary, he laughed outright, and called Fauntleroy up to him, and made him tell all about the matter from beginning to end, and then he laughed again. And actually, a few days later, the Dorincourt carriage

'It j-jolts a g-goo-good deal—do-doesn't it?' said Fauntleroy.

stopped in the green lane before the cottage where the lame boy
lived, and Fauntleroy jumped out and walked up to the door,
carrying a pair of strong, light, new crutches, shouldered like a
gun, and presented them to Mrs Hartle (the lame boy's name was
Hartle) with these words: 'My grandfather's compliments, and if
you please, these are for your boy, and we hope he will get better.'

'I said your compliments,' he explained to the Earl when he
returned to the carriage. 'You didn't tell me to, but I thought
perhaps you forgot. That was right, wasn't it?'

And the Earl laughed again, and did not say it was not. In fact,
the two were becoming more intimate every day, and every day
Fauntleroy's faith in his lordship's benevolence and virtue
increased. He had no doubt whatever that his grandfather was the
most amiable and generous of elderly gentlemen. Certainly, he
himself found his wishes gratified almost before they were uttered;
and such gifts and pleasures were lavished upon him, that he was
sometimes almost bewildered by his own possessions. Apparently,
he was to have everything he wanted, and to do everything he
wished to do. And though this would certainly not have been a
very wise plan to pursue with all small boys, his young lordship
bore it amazingly well. Perhaps, notwithstanding his sweet nature,
he might have been somewhat spoiled by it, if it had not been for
the hours he spent with his mother at Court Lodge. That 'best
friend' of his watched over him very closely and tenderly. The two
had many long talks together, and he never went back to the Castle
with her kisses on his cheeks without carrying in his heart some
simple, pure words worth remembering.

There was one thing, it is true, which puzzled the little fellow
very much. He thought over the mystery of it much oftener than
anyone supposed; even his mother did not know how often he
pondered on it; the Earl for a long time never suspected that he did
so at all. But being quick to observe, the little boy could not help
wondering why it was that his mother and grandfather never
seemed to meet. He had noticed that they never did meet. When
the Dorincourt carriage stopped at Court Lodge, the Earl never

alighted, and on the rare occasions of his lordship's going to church, Fauntleroy was always left to speak to his mother in the porch alone, or perhaps to go home with her. And yet, every day, fruit and flowers were sent to Court Lodge from the hot-houses at the Castle. But the one virtuous action of the Earl's which had set him upon the pinnacle of perfection in Cedric's eyes, was what he had done soon after that first Sunday when Mrs Errol had walked home from church unattended. About a week later, when Cedric was going one day to visit his mother, he found at the door, instead of the large carriage and prancing pair, a pretty little brougham and a handsome bay horse.

'That is a present from you to your mother,' the Earl said abruptly. 'She cannot go walking about the country. She needs a carriage. The man who drives will take charge of it. It is a present from *you*.'

Fauntleroy's delight could but feebly express itself. He could scarcely contain himself until he reached the lodge. His mother was gathering roses in the garden. He flung himself out of the little brougham and flew to her.

'Dearest!' he cried, 'could you believe it? This is yours! He says it is a present from me. It is your own carriage to drive everywhere in!'

He was so happy that she did not know what to say. She could not have borne to spoil his pleasure by refusing to accept the gift, even though it came from the man who chose to consider himself her enemy. She was obliged to step into the carriage, roses and all, and let herself be taken for a drive, while Fauntleroy told her stories of his grandfather's goodness and amiability. They were such innocent stories that sometimes she could not help laughing a little, and then she would draw her little boy closer to her side and kiss him, feeling glad that he could see only good in the old man who had so few friends.

The very next day after that, Fauntleroy wrote to Mr Hobbs. He wrote quite a long letter, and after the first copy was written, he brought it to his grandfather to be inspected.

'Because,' he said, 'it's so uncertain about the spelling. And if you'll tell me the mistakes, I'll write it out again.'

This was what he had written:

'My dear mr hobbs i want to tell you about my granfarther he is the best earl you ever new it is a mistake about earls being tirents he is not a tirent at all i wish you new him you would be good friends i am sure you would he has the gout in his foot and is a grate sufrer but he is so pashent i love him more every day becaus no one could help loving an earl like that who is kind to every one in this world i wish you could talk to him he knows everything in the world you can ask him any question but he has never plaid base ball he has given me a pony and a cart and my mamma a bewtifle carige and i have three rooms and toys of all kinds it would serprise you you would like the castle and the park it is such a large castle you could lose yourself wilkins tells me wilkins is my groom he says there is a dungon under the castle it is so pretty every thing in the park would serprise you there are such big trees and there are deers and rabbits and games flying about in the cover my granfarther is very rich but he is not proud and orty as you thought earls always were i like to be with him the people are so polite and kind they take of their hats to you and the women make curtsies and sometimes say god bless you i can ride now but at first it shook me when i troted my granfarther let a poor man stay on his farm when he could not pay his rent and mrs mellon went to take wine and things to his sick children i should like to see you and i wish dearest could live at the castle but I am very happy when i dont miss her too much and i love my granfarther every one does plees write soon

'your afechshnet olf friend
'CEDRIC ERROL

'p s no one is in the dungon my granfarther never had any one langwishin in there

'p s he is such a good earl he reminds me of you he is a unerversle favrit'

'Do you miss your mother very much?' asked the Earl when he had finished reading this.

'Yes,' said Fauntleroy, 'I miss her all the time.'

He went and stood before the Earl and put his hand on his knee looking up at him.

'*You* don't miss her, do you?' he said.

'I don't know her,' answered his lordship rather crustily.

'I know that,' said Fauntleroy, 'and that's what makes me wonder. She told me not to ask you any questions, and—and I won't, but sometimes I can't help thinking, you know, and it makes me all puzzled. But I'm not going to ask any questions. And when I miss her very much, I go and look out of my window to where I see her light shine for me every night through an open place in the trees. It is a long way off, but she puts it in her window as soon as it is dark and I can see it twinkle far away, and I know what it says.'

'What does it say?' asked my lord.

'It says, "Good-night, God keep you all the night!"—just what she used to say when we were together. Every night she used to say that to me, and every morning she said, "God bless you all the day!" So you see I am quite safe all the time——"

'Quite, I have no doubt,' said his lordship dryly. And he drew down his beetling eyebrows and looked at the little boy so fixedly and so long that Fauntleroy wondered what he could be thinking of.

BAREBACK

Meindert Dejong

A tornado hits the district, causing devastation everywhere. Mark is left alone in charge of the farm, and goes
to the rescue of his neighbour Mr Sayers when looters
raid his house. Mrs Sayers, known as Mama, is hurt and
Mark decides to take her to the hospital.

They were hardly started when the wagon hit a rain-bared root,
the front wheels stuttered over it, but the whole body of the
wagon screaked and groaned. Mr Sayers stopped Creek before
the hind wheels could bounce over the same root. He looked back,
shook his head. 'It isn't hurting Mama now, but a few more jolts
like that and this whole thing could fall apart, and then where
would we be? My old eyes aren't any good for this, and this silly
little flashlight is no good at all.'

Mark clambered up to sit beside the old man, but Mr Sayers in
the meanwhile must have had another thought. He turned the
wagon around and they went back the way they'd come. 'I've got

to find the sergeant,' the old man was muttering, 'see if I can beg that big flashlight away from him.'

The man wasn't hard to find. He stood alone in the field beyond the woodlot, talking orders and directions into his walkie-talkie. The four soldiers had scattered far afield.

At the sound of the wagon the man shone his flash.

'Sergeant,' Mr Sayers called out, 'I bounced this wagon over a tree root, and it all but came apart. Could we have your flashlight? The little ones we've got don't pick out the holes and bumps for me. And I got to thinking . . . Wouldn't it be something if we made it to Mason Road and they wouldn't see our little toy flashlights, and we'd get run down by an ambulance?'

The sergeant laughed. 'Shrewd thinking to get my flashlight away from me.' He came over to the wagon.

'It's really Mark I'm thinking of. He's got to come back alone to an empty house.'

'I'm not scared,' Mark protested. 'Not with Creek—and not when we're going back to Colonel. If I'm scared in the house, I'll stay in the barn with them.'

'Good boy!' the sergeant said. 'Just don't take them into the *living* room with you.' Laughing, he handed up his flashlight and took Mr Sayers' tiny one. 'No good to me either but I'll take it until I find another one. You can find about anything on a night like this, even a pailful of dimes.'

'Don't go making fun of Mama's dimes. They're going to put the roof back on our house, maybe buy us a bed—if they don't, we'll sleep in the oats in the grain bin.'

'Don't worry, you'll get help,' the sergeant assured him. 'The Red Cross is already in Stanton. Things will soon straighten out. Now on your way lest Mama comes to before you get to the Mason Road. She's quite a girl, that wife of yours. She didn't whimper but she must have gone through holy hell until I gave her that shot. Almost tempted to give her a booster but I'd better not, I don't know enough about that kind of stuff, so make it fast to an ambulance.'

'Sergeant,' Mark spoke up, 'could you give Creek a hypo in her leg? She's limping bad.'

The big man shook his head. 'All I could do would be to put her to sleep so she'd lie down. You ask the men on the ambulance, they're doctors. They may have something to ease the pain. They'll do it for you if they can. I'll give out the word on my walkie-talkie to my first contact.'

'But suppose Creek gets crippled forever?'

The big man smiled at him. 'And suppose Mama doesn't get to the hospital, suppose Mr Sayers doesn't find out about your dad, suppose he doesn't get to see your mother, "suppose" . . .'

Mark grinned sheepishly. 'All right, I get it. Giddap, Creek.'

The old man handed him the flashlight. 'You shine the way and pick out the best way across the field. When I get back we'll spend the rest of the night doctoring Creek. I'm an old horseman, raised horses all my life, doctored 'em too—that's what the oats in the grain bin were from.'

Oats! Mother had been going to bring some for Colonel, but instead the tornado had come. Now there were oats in the bin. They'd make Colonel strong and maybe help heal Creek's cut.

They zigzagged through the fields, now they'd soon come to the Mason Road. Mama was still sleeping and the milk wagon moved smoothly through the grass. The tornado hadn't touched down here at all. Then the flash beam picked a grey line far out ahead. 'The Mason Road,' Mark yelled.

'About time,' the old man said.

And then they were in the gravel road. Creek rested and Mark jumped down to look at her bandaged leg. Mr Sayers came down stiffly from the wagon and studied it, too. The bandage was still in place but above it the flesh was puffed out and swollen. 'That's from the tight bandage—but it's got to be. The moment I get to your house we'll loosen the bandage, but while you're there alone don't you touch it no matter how badly it swells. If she's hurting, she'd kick like a mule. Understand?'

Mark nodded. He hated Creek to be hurting.

He walked her on the grassy edge of the road.

They stood and stood and nothing moved along the road. Nothing came. 'The sergeant said it might be a long wait—we're not the only ones,' Mr Sayers cautioned Mark. But finally he became impatient himself. Suddenly he could stand no more. 'What if no ambulance comes for hours, and Mama comes to, and then still we have to go all the miles into the hospital? You get in the back with the light. Keep shining it from wheel to wheel and watch the wires. We'll stop before the last one wears through, but we'll at least be doing something instead of standing here. The sergeant said this road was clear so I won't need any light ahead. You keep it on the wheels and watch like a hawk.'

'But what'll I do going back without any wires on the wheels?'

'Have you ever ridden a real riding horse bareback?'

Mark gave him a startled look. 'Yes, yes I have. I never told anyone, but on the way to school there's a house with a field for their riding horse. I used to feed him sugar. Once I climbed the fence and got on his back. He threw me. I fell under him and he stepped right over me and he came back and nuzzled me until I remembered and reached a cube of sugar up to him. Then he let me get on again and we rode and rode. I was late to school but it was worth it.'

'Threw you and you got on again! You'll be all right with horses! Look, if you ride Creek back, it'll be a lot easier on her than dragging the wagon. This wagon isn't important, we'll leave it at the side of the road when the ambulance comes.'

'What'll we do with Dad's tool box?'

'We'll hide it back of bushes in a ditch. Now hop in and watch the rims.'

As Mr Sayers said the words there was a roar and an ambulance came hurtling out of the night and they hadn't put the wagon across the road to block it. Mark waved the flashlight but the ambulance shot by. Mr Sayers groaned and said, 'Kick me for being such a wise guy and knowing better than the sergeant.'

They went on down the road at a slow careful pace because of Creek's bad limp. Mark stood in the box of the wagon shining the flash from wheel to wheel and then on Creek's awful limp. It scared him but it scared him to look at Mama lying there so dead-looking. He knew they had to get to the hospital.

The steel-rimmed wheels dug into the gravel. Then came the first sharp ping as the tightly wound wire snapped and sprang away. After the first one they all seemed to go. At last Mark said, 'We'll have to stop.'

The old man looked around. One of the rims was riding off the wheel. He stopped Creek. There was no sound anywhere, nothing moved. The few stars of the evening had gone away. The old man clucked to Creek and turned the wagon crosswise in the road. They waited.

It seemed hours before there was a roaring far down the road. 'Now wave the flashlight in circles and up and down. It's got to see us long before it gets here if it's going to stop in time. Be ready to jump if I have to drive down in the ditch.'

Then there was time for nothing. The ambulance roared down on them, squealed to a stop and slewed in the gravel. It was scary for a moment, then two men jumped down.

They had the tailgate down by the time Mr Sayers struggled down from the seat.

'Good,' one of the men said, 'she's on a mattress. We'll take mattress and all, because all the room left is on the floor.'

'Your wife?' the other man asked. 'Then you sit on the floor with her and hold her steady. Do the best you can. We've got a man in there badly hurt—whole church caved in on him. What about this kid?'

'He's going back. Mark, once you get to a level spot unhitch the wagon and let it stand. Keep Creek's harness on—if her leg gives out and she goes down, you'll have something to hang on to. . . . My wife's had a hypo a while back, the sergeant thought maybe she'd need a booster.'

The man shook his head. 'No, better wait. Don't want to interfere with what the docs might give her. We'll be in the hospital in a few minutes.'

'Please, mister,' Mark said. 'Couldn't you give Creek the hypo you're not going to give Mama? It's a long way back home and she's limping bad.'

'Creek? Oh, the horse.'

'Could you?' Mr Sayers said urgently.. 'Mark's never ridden her and if she went wild with pain . . . wouldn't it slow her down?'

The man shrugged. 'I'm no horse doctor, still it probably would make her more manageable.'

Mark held Creek's head while the man jabbed the needle into her leg. He jabbed it in a circle around the puffing. 'Ought to make her more comfortable. Lots of luck, son. This is the kind of crazy thing you do on a night like this—horse doctor!'

He jumped back in the ambulance. Mr Sayers was already inside by Mama. The ambulance roared away. It was gone and Mark was alone with Creek.

He walked her on the grassy edge of the road. When they came to a brush pile he stopped, pulled the tool box out and hid it back of the bushes. Then he led Creek away from the brush pile so the abandoned wagon wouldn't give the tool box away. But he didn't go far. Creek's slow weary limp worried him. He unhitched her and put the flashlight on the wagon seat so he could reach out for it after he had mounted.

They went along the grassy side of the road until at last there were the wagon tracks leading out of the field. Now he wouldn't get lost. He could find his way back by the crushed tracks the wagon wheels had made in the grass.

It was so still, so alone. But he had a flashlight and there would be Colonel when they got home and all three of them would stay together in the barn until Mr Sayers came. It was better to think about that than to think about who might be in the silent fields. Now only one more road to cross, then through the Sayers' farm and across the single field and then Colonel would neigh a welcome from the barn because he would hear Creek.

It seemed that this whole night—everything they'd gone through together—had made Creek his. Why, he'd told the sergeant that his dad had given her to him for his birthday and the big man hadn't questioned it. It had to be so.

Oh, what if in the hospital the first thing Dad said to Mother was: 'Did you find that horse I got for Mark? I left her in the woodlot.'

And then faintly across the dark fields there was the walkie-talkie voice. He listened closely but he must have imagined it. There was nothing but silence.

Suddenly Mark was uneasy. Suppose the big sergeant was at some farm down the road and a man there was saying, 'I lost my horse. She ran away in the tornado. She's a brown riding horse, have you seen her?'

And the sergeant would say, 'A brown horse, with a star on her forehead?'

'That's her,' the man would say.

'Funny, we saw a horse like that pulling a crazy little wagon. Didn't seem to go together—horse was too fine. But the boy said he'd just got her for his birthday. Well, if she's your horse, she won't be hard to find. It's a farm on the Stanton road. The man said it hadn't been touched by the tornado—it'll be one of the few that wasn't. Give it a try. It might be your horse.'

Mark shuddered and was glad he'd left the wagon on the road. He stared ahead. Maybe the man was out looking for Creek right now.

He'd made it all up from imagining the walkie-talkie, but now it was as real as the night. He wouldn't take Creek home to the barn. He'd go to the woodlot—that's what he'd do. He'd lead Creek down the gully to the same crook that had held Colonel. Nobody'd see her down there in the dark—she was dark, too. But he'd stay with her. He'd stay until Mr Sayers came. Mr Sayers wouldn't let anybody take Creek away from him. Maybe by that time he'd find out from Dad that Dad had bought her.

Mark lay over Creek and whispered in her ear. Together they went quietly through the deep dark to their own woodlot trees on their own farm.

EBONY JOINS THE CIRCUS

Josephine Pullein-Thompson

I wasn't the clean and elegant horse when I left Clarendon Mews that I had been on arrival. In fact I was dirty and unfit, with a staring coat and a mane and tail that needed pulling, when Percy put an old rope halter on me and led me to the horse sale. Worst of all for an old horse I had no reputation left and not even a respectable stud groom to vouch for my character.

I was tied to a ring in the wall between a shivering and half-starved pony and a stout carthorse and a round paper with a number on it was stuck to my quarters. I turned as far as my rope would allow me and watched the scene. There was a great many people, mostly farmers and tradesmen, but also some very rough-looking men and boys who swore and spat a good deal.

The noise was very great. The sellers were telling everyone what good animals they were offering. The frightened horses were all whinneying and there was an endless clattering of hoofs and cracking of whips as they were run up to show their paces to likely buyers. There were a few men already drunk, though it was not yet twelve, and they were shouting and singing.

It was very unpleasant having my mouth forced open by complete strangers who wanted to see my teeth. Some of them felt my legs, slapped my flank and pulled out my tail as well, before making a disparaging remark about my age and walking on.

The farmers all thought me too well-bred. 'You got to cosset that sort,' they said, or, 'I 'aven't the time to look after a blood 'orse.' The tradesmen all asked if I was broken to harness and Percy, who didn't know any better, said no, I was a hunter. The occasional person looking for a cheap hunter was always horrified by my age. The cart horse next to me was having a better time. The farmers all said that 'he was a likely sort'. He told me that he'd been working on the canals, towing barges, he enjoyed the life but more and more goods were going by rail instead of by water so he and many more like him, were out of a job. But, he added placidly, that he would be quite happy to work on a farm.

At last two men came who didn't dismiss me as useless. The younger was tall and thin with an eager, handsome face, the other short and fat, wearing rather old fashioned clothes and smoking a cigar. The young one, Felix, stood back studying me carefully and then said, 'I think we've found him, Alf. He's got presence, look at him, and breeding. Trimmed up a bit, well-groomed, he'd be exactly right; stupendous!'

'Except that he's not a mare,' said Alf. He looked at my teeth, 'Past his second youth. Is he sound? That's the question. And can he jump?'

'Oh yes, he can jump all right,' said Percy coming forward and he told them about my riderless hunt.

Felix laughed a lot. 'There, that clinches it,' he said. 'I knew at once he was the horse for us. Personality, looks quiet, friendly; a great jumper and any amount of character.'

Alf seemed less certain. 'We'll see what he fetches; I'm not paying much for a horse of his age. Here, boy, trot him out and let's see how he moves.'

I liked the look of Felix, I felt that he would be a considerate master and all that talk of jumping was music to my ears, but I hoped that he didn't want to hunt me in a fast country for I knew that I wasn't up to that sort of work any more.

Presently my turn to be sold came. I was walked and then trotted up and down amid a sea of white faces and brandishing whips, while the auctioneer called for bids. There was no great eagerness to buy me. A few of the people who'd looked at me bidded; one sounded like the undertaker, another voice could have belonged to the cats' meat man, the third was obviously a farmer. Then I saw Alf waving his catalogue in a lordly manner. At last the auctioneer's hammer fell and I was led away and tied up. The half starved pony was being sold; I hoped he would go to someone who would give him a square meal, and not for cat's meat. Then Felix came up carrying a saddle and bridle. 'We got you for a song, old horse,' he told me. 'Now, where's that boy? I want to know your name.' Percy seemed pleased that Felix was to have me. He put on the saddle, while Felix adjusted the bridle to fit my head, then he sobbed a tear or two as he stroked my neck, but Felix gave him sixpence and told him I should have a good home.

As Felix mounted and rode out of the sale yard I knew that he was a good rider. He felt confident and easy, he didn't attempt to impose his will on me, but just rode me quietly forward while he learned what I was like. In no time we were partners, it was as though I had Fanny or Ned back again and my heart rose as we left the town.

It was a frosty day but the sun was high and warm and had already thawed most of the bone from the ground. Felix sang as we walked and trotted along and altogether he seemed very pleased and cheerful.

We passed through several villages and then we cantered over a short stretch of moor and came to a long lane, between stone walls, that brought us down to a grey stone farm in the valley.

It was rather a tumble down place and the yard instead of being full of pigs or cattle, had a whole collection of living vans within its walls; like gipsy vans they had little chimneys, two windows and shafts for the horse, but the people who came to greet us weren't gipsies, though there may have been one or two among them. There were a great many children playing everywhere and a smell of paint and cooking filled the air.

Felix led me into a stable. I saw with pleasure that it was quite a large loosebox and when I looked over the low partition into the next box I found the smallest pony I had ever seen. He was skew-bald and much smaller than The Giant. He could not have been more than eight hands. He said at once that his name was Tom Thumb, that he was the smallest pony in the world and came from the Shetland Isles. Felix was rubbing me down, someone was spreading straw, someone else brought a bucket of water and yet another came running with a rug so I was soon very comfortably settled. When the humans had gone away and I had eaten my feed, Tom Thumb asked me what I did. I answered that I was a hunter and he didn't seem to find that at all satisfactory.

'I wonder what you'll do here, then,' he said. 'Oh well I suppose they'll teach you something. I jump through hoops, lie down, take handkerchiefs from my master's pocket, chase a boy round the ring and do numerous other tricks. I'm billed as The Clever Pony as well as The Smallest Horse in the World; people pay good money to watch me.'

I felt rather alarmed at this, but Tom Thumb, who seemed very pleased to have a companion, talked on and on. It seemed that he and his master Andrew had belonged to a circus, but there had been a fire and the equipment had all been lost so now they had joined this fair and soon we would all be travelling round the countryside performing.

I asked if he knew what Felix did and he answered that he was an actor and that sometimes a whole company of them went round with a fair, but he thought that Felix was the only one and he had been talking about an equestrian act. Then I asked about Alf and Tom Thumb said he was the Guv'ner and usually called 'His Nibs'. He settled the quarrels and arranged the fairgrounds and lent everyone money.

Felix seemed a very thoughtful master. The very next morning he spent a long time sawing and hammering at my door and when he had finished it was in two halves and the top one fastened back and enabled me to look out and see all the activities in the farmyard. I can't describe the pleasure that gave me. Being tied up in a stall is all very well for a short time and it's not so bad for a horse that is out all day doing slow work and only in his stall at night. But when a hunter or hack is condemned to spend twenty-two out of twenty-four hours, six or seven days a week, facing the same black wall, well, it's no wonder that horses are driven to crib biting, wind-sucking and other nervous disorders.

After the boredom of the mews I was delighted with my view and made Tom Thumb so jealous with my accounts of all I could see that he began to work on the bolt of the door between our boxes. He got the head up and then slid it back with his teeth and pushed the door open and came in with me. Of course he wasn't tall enough to see over the door and he had to balance with one toe on the cross bar. When Felix found our two heads looking out he laughed and fetched a stout box for Tom Thumb's forefeet.

For a few days Felix just took me for rides in the countryside We jumped some walls and hurdles and a gate and he seemed very pleased with me and always told everyone that I was 'just the thing'.

Then one day he took me into the barn. The floor was scattered with peat and a ring was marked out in the middle; it was rather a small space, but I was well enough balanced to canter round it quite fast, which pleased Felix. We practised entering at a wild gallop and stopping dead in the centre. He was very careful of my mouth and threw his weight back as a signal instead of pulling on the reins and, as soon as I understood what he wanted, I did it all on my own. Then we started work on the whole act. After the gallop in Felix would make a speech all about his wonderful mare Black Bess and then another man called King would come in on one of the caravan horses and he and Felix, who was Dick Turpin, plotted together.

Then a very old coach came in, drawn by four very hairy horses and it was robbed by Turpin and King, several people fell dead and everyone fired pistols which made us horses jump at first though we soon became used to it. After that the police came and they captured King, and he called to Turpin to shoot the men who held him, but Turpin missed and killed King by mistake.

Then a great chase began. I would go round and round the ring at a gallop, rush out and come in again from the other side and the pursuers were doing the same though they never caught up with us. We robbed another coach; it was the same one really, but they put a different name on the doors and dressed the people differently, and there was some more firing of pistols.

The next exciting part was when a toll gate was put up in the ring. As Turpin and I came galloping in the keeper shut it to stop us, but Felix would give a shout and I would soar over. After that I had to show signs of tiring and when I could only proceed at a weary trot with my head low we stopped at an Inn and I was given a drench of brandy or ale or something from a bottle, only the bottle was always empty.

Then we came to the city of York and a large cardboard spire was put up and bells began to ring. I was reduced to a walk and Felix dismounted and led me and then it seemed I was supposed to fall down dead. This wasn't easy to learn. Tom Thumb could do it and I was made to watch him, but I found all his advice very irritating and really got on better when Felix taught me alone.

He would take me to a nice soft spot and strap up one of my forelegs, then he would tap my other knee with a whip until I bent it and kneeled down. The moment I did it I was praised and given oats or carrots. Gradually I learned to kneel without the strap and whenever he pointed at my knees. All he had to do then was to turn my head towards him and gently push my shoulder until I gave way and lay down on my side. I wouldn't have done it for Hopkins, but Felix was kind to me and made all my lessons enjoyable, so I decided to oblige.

I soon knew the routine and when we reached York and the bells began to ring, I would watch for the signal. When I had died Felix would make a long speech over my dead body and then the pursuers would come up and there was another fight. The first time this happened I raised my head to see what was going on, but this caused a great outcry from the watching children and Felix came and told me I had to stay dead.

The next problem was carrying me out. A great yard door was brought in and slid under as six strong men lifted me, then about twelve of them carried me out. I always hated this part but Felix would walk by my head and stroke my neck to keep me calm, so I put up with it.

Though there were stablehands among the fair people, Felix looked after me himself and by the start of the season I was a picture. Too round and well-covered to be hunting fit I was just right for a public performance, my coat shone, my mane and tail, neatly trimmed, were beautifully brushed out and this was just as well, for there were some very extravagent tributes to Black Bess's beauty in the verses Felix had to say.

On the day we moved out of our winter quarters all the carts and wagons and vans left very early in the morning. Felix and I started much later for we could take a short cut across country instead of going by the roads.

When we reached the fairground which was just outside a large town, Felix rode me to a tent with a large notice about Tom Thumb the Clever Pony and another saying that Captain Felix Fanshawe, late Royal Hussars, would present the stupendous equestrian drama *Dick Turpin's ride to York* with many spectacular fights and a thrilling performance by his famous horse Black Bess.

Inside was our usual ring and the cardboard Inn and spire and the toll gate and a couple more jumps were all ready at the side. I began to feel nervous but Felix rode me round until I was used to the tent and the lights and then he took me out to see the fairground. There were stalls for Hoop-la and ranges for shooting and coconut shies. There was a huge roundabout with brightly coloured and richly gilded horses and a steam engine to work it. There were many little booths with fortune tellers and fireproof ladies and fat ladies inside. There was Professor Lopescu's Flea Circus from Rumania and a Punch and Judy Show and many slides and swings and entertainments of all sort.

As it grew darker more and more lights came on and the steam engines sent sparks and smoke up into the dark sky. There was a smell of burning coal and hot engines. Then a great steam organ started up. It was painted in bright colours and gilded like the horses and the noise from it was tremendous, as though a whole brass band was playing close at hand. I stood looking at the scene, turning this way and that to take it all in and Felix sat on my back laughing at my amazement.

When we went to the stable tent that I was to share with Tom he was being got ready for his act. He wore a silver and orange bridle, roller and crupper and from his forelock rose a very handsome orange plume. I wondered if I had to dress up, but no, it was Felix who came disguised. He had a curly moustache, a green coat and cocked hat, a belt full of pistols. Andrew was impossible to recognize with his face covered in white, a huge mouth and a false nose; he was dressed as a clown, and the small fat boy Tom had to chase had been made to look fatter than ever by very tight clothes.

When Tom left for the ring one of the stable hands put the finishing touches to my appearance, then Felix stopped brushing his coat and mounted and we walked over to the ring tent and waited in a dark corner.

Tom was pretending to become angrier and angrier with the fat boy and finally he chased him round the ring and out in a ferocious manner. His Nibs, wearing black trousers, a scarlet coat and a top hat announced Dick Turpin, and Felix took me well back so that we could get up speed for our entrance.

We whirled in and round and came to a very dashing halt in the centre. Felix took off his hat and bowed low, I stared at the lights and the white faces all round me. Then Felix began the verses on how much he loved his bonny Black Bess. As he came to the last verse:

> *'Mark that skin, sleek as velvet and dusky at night,*
> *With its jet undisfigured by one spot of white;*
> *That throat branched with veins, prompt to charge or caress.*
> *Now, is she not beautiful? Bonny Black Bess!'*

King came riding in and they began to plan robberies.

We held up the coach, the horses were all looking a good deal smarter than they had at rehearsal and the guard had a horn to blow. There were the usual shootings and several deaths and then we made off with some bags labelled MONEY. King had taken too many and could not control his horse, which was why the police got him.

When Felix's shot killed him all the audience groaned in horror but cheered up when we took one of the extra jumps and galloped away. These brush fences were not very big but though I was supposed to leap over perfectly the pursuers, especially the police were meant to run into each other, fall off and generally make a hash of things and this pleased the audience very much.

Then we robbed the second coach and came to the toll gate. It had grown larger at every practice and was now a big jump, about five feet. I took it carefully for the lights were casting strange shadows and made finding the right take-off difficult. The people cheered and clapped as I soared over. We stopped at the Inn and Felix had another long verse to say which ended:

> *'By moonlight, in darkness, by night or by day,*
> *Her headlong career there is nothing can stay.*
> *She cares not for distance, she knows not distress,*
> *Can you show me the courser to match with Black Bess?'*

The people cheered and clapped as I soared over the toll gate.

Then I began to slow down and hang my head; soon I was only walking and then as the spire was put up and the bells began to ring, Felix led me. Right in the middle of the ring he pointed at my knees and I fell dead. The audience were very upset; I think some of them thought I really had died. Turpin was very upset too:

'Art thou gone, Bess? Gone—gone!' he cried out very dramatically. 'And I have killed the best steed that was ever crossed.

'O'er highway and byeway, in rough or smooth weather,
Some thousands of miles have we journeyed together;
Our couch the same straw, our meals the same mess;
No couple more constant than I and Black Bess.'

They fought the last fight and I managed to lie still and not look though it was very hard. Then the door came and they called for volunteers from the audience to help carry out poor dead Bess and I'm certain a great many people went home wondering whether I was really dead or not.

All the fair people thought the performance a great success and Felix kept patting me and saying 'Old horse, you're a natural, a born actor; stupendous!'

After that he became even more ambitious and besides adding new touches to our present act he was always thinking of other acts we could perform in the future and talking about *The Taylor of Brentford* and *The High-Mettled Racer* or, *The Fat Farmer*, who wore layers and layers of clothes and undressed as he galloped round the ring.

We seemed to be doing well. We moved from place to place, sometimes only staying for one day and night, sometimes for five. By the summer we had reached the west country and I was jumping the toll keeper as he ran to bar the way, as well as the gate; we were practising for *The Taylor of Brentford* which called for a lot of acting on my part as I had to push Felix around and make disagreeable faces and pretend to bite him.

In some places our audiences were so large that we had to do

Dick Turpin three times over every evening. I did get very bored at having to go through it so often and we had to think of new things to do to keep up our interest. Felix invented that I should raise my head and give my thoughtless master a kiss with my lips before I died; this upset the audiences very much.

In the autumn we came near to London and the idea was that we would work our way north and back to winter quarters, except for those who had special Christmas engagements.

Then one night some men came round to the stable when the performance was over. The stablehand was rubbing me down and Felix was unsticking his moustache. They introduced themselves and asked him out to supper. He seemed very excited and changing quickly he went off with them leaving me to the stablehand.

Next day Felix seemed very thoughtful and he had a long talk with His Nibs. Our show went on as usual but we gave up rehearsing *The Taylor's Ride*. I sensed that something was wrong and I lost some of my enthusiasm. But he didn't say anything until one morning when we had just come to a new town. Then he came rushing into my tent; he was dressed very smartly in his best suit. He put his arms round my neck and said, 'I'm sorry, Ebony, I feel a brute, a complete cad doing this to you. You've been magnificent, you did everything you could to make the show a success, you never let me down once and now I'm walking out on you. But you see, old horse, it's the chance of a lifetime, you *can't* refuse a part like this. You just can't!

'If I had the ready cash I'd buy you from His Nibs and take you with me, but I haven't and no stable to put you in either. I'm truly sorry old horse.' He gave me a carrot and ran out of my stable. I couldn't believe that our happy times together had ended as suddenly and finally as this. For a day or two I thought he might come back. I would look for him in the mornings and when the time for our performance came, I felt sure that he would come bursting in, sticking on his moustache and telling me some new plan. Sometimes I thought I heard his voice and would whinny excitedly, but he never came.

Then I learned, from the talk of the stablehands, that he had been offered a good part at a big London theatre and might well become rich and famous. For a time I clung to the idea that His Nibs was finding another Dick Turpin to ride me and things would go on much as before, but men appeared who looked at my teeth and felt my legs and had me trotted up so I knew I was to be sold.

'Too old for a hunter,' they all said, and 'who wants a circus horse, he'll be doing tricks in the road.' And they haggled with His Nibs over the price.

At last a man with very fair hair came; he said that he owned a large riding school and livery stable in London and needed a reliable, well-mannered horse for his lady clients and was willing to pay a good price for the right animal. So I changed hands again and now belonged to Mr Chandler.

THE QUEEN MEETS THE LIPIZZANERS

Alois Podhajsky

The Lipizzaner stallions of the Spanish Riding School in Vienna are a cross of Andalusian, Arab and Barbary horses, first bred at the Royal Stud founded in 1580 by Archduke Charles of Austria. The purity of the strain has been carefully nurtured ever since.

While the riders and horses were approaching the Channel coast to cross via the Hook of Holland and Harwich on their way to London I flew in with my wife from Düsseldorf. As the plane flew across the Channel on this fine summer's day I could not help remembering my flight in similar circumstances four years earlier. Then too the International Horse Show was the object of my journey, but this time success depended not on me alone, but on the efforts of my companions. Above all, the meeting of the past with the present awaited me. It was with such thoughts that we landed at London Airport, were met and given a warm welcome by the President of the British Horse Society, Colonel

Williams, and his wife. What a wonderful feeling of true friendship! We had not seen each other for a long time, but they both greeted us as kindly and affectionately as if we had been away only a few days. Of course we must go with them to their glorious place, East Burnham Park, and we found everything just the same as four years earlier, including Simon, who leapt joyfully up at us, and the exotic giant ducks waddling over the English grass.

The next day with Colonel Williams I inspected the White City stadium and the arrangements made for the Lipizzaner. Roomy boxes for the sixteen stallions had been prepared in tented stabling right next to the ring, covered with peat-litter, as the use of straw was prohibited by the fire-prevention authorities. When I said I was afraid that my white horses might turn canary colour after a night on this 'bed', sawdust was immediately substituted for the peat, and I was told with a smile that hay was allowed for fodder. My Lipizzaner would be so plentifully supplied with roughage that this too might be useful for bedding, so the noble stallions were virtually bedded down in hay.

In the White City I found a clean turf square prepared for our performances just opposite the Royal Box and surrounded with flowering shrubs. Colonel Williams informed me that this space would be kept permanently free of obstacles, so that the grass would not be too badly worn by the jumping. Above all care would be taken that the effect of our performances should not be marred by obstacles being too close, and the Lipizzaner would be clearly visible from all sides. This thoughtfulness after our recent experiences did me as much good as the reception of the horses on their arrival on 15 July by members of the British Horse Society, who had appeared with the journalists and supervised the immediate transfer of the Lipizzaner by horse-box to their stabling. This was typical of the Spanish Riding School's welcome in England. The picture on the cover of the programme was a full-page coloured photograph of me on Neopolitano Africa in the *passage*. In other ways, too, I was constantly made aware that this horse and his earlier efforts here in London had not been forgotten.

Unfortunately, Neopolitano Africa could not come this time, and his substitute, Maestoso Alea, was still far from following in the footsteps of his gallant predecessor. He was a handsome and unusually nimble Lipizzaner, but very difficult. An important factor in giving him such a complex nature was his use when young for stud. He could make a convincing picture of a riding horse— when he wanted to—and he could, if something did not please him, be so uncooperative as to be barely recognizable. In London the ponies affected him particularly and drove him mad. I usually had to warm him up for a long time and give him a great deal of exercise, and often thought with longing of my faithful Neopolitano Africa as I carried out this exhausting work.

On the second day we met the Press photographers in the stadium. The excellent shots taken on this occasion, including some perfect *caprioles*, were then published as half- or full pages in the English papers and magazines, but they went abroad too, and the same pictures appeared in German, American, French, Dutch, Spanish, and even Moroccan publications.

On 19 July we showed excerpts from our programme in a live television broadcast that was to last ten minutes. I compiled a programme ending with the quadrille, and, as this was the easiest to adapt to the time limit, we arranged for a signal when time was nearly up, as I wanted to line up and finish the broadcast with a salute. As arranged, I began the shortened programme, knowing that it was too late to make alterations now, for we were already appearing on many hundreds of thousands of screens. Everything went without a hitch, we were approaching the quadrille, and I was just waiting for the prearranged warning signal. It seemed a great deal longer than ten minutes, but when no sign came and the variations of the quadrille were finished I decided on the spot to line up, salute, and thus wind up the broadcast. Then the television staff rushed towards me, overwhelmed me with praise and congratulations, and explained that the programme had been so marvellous that they had not had the heart to give the signal after nine minutes. The broadcast had lasted seventeen.

The next day saw the opening of the thirty-fourth International Horse Show. There were afternoon and evening performances on all six days; at each one we showed different parts of our programme for half an hour. The musical accompaniment was once more provided—as for my exhibition rides in 1949—by a Royal Marine band under the direction of the head of the Royal Marine Music School, Major V. Dunn, but this time the bandsmen had to play concert pieces unfamiliar to them, the Austrian compositions that always accompanied the Lipizzaner. The music of Mozart's Symphony in G minor, the accompaniment for the *Pas de Trois*, was missing, and the substitute of Haydn chosen by Major Dunn did not quite fit in with the horses' movements. Afterwards he listened to the symphony we wanted on our tape-recorder, and left the arena deep in thought.

I could scarcely believe my ears when on the opening day the strains of Mozart instead of Haydn greeted our entry for the *Pas de Trois*—so perfectly played that at first I thought it was the tape-recorder, until I traced it to Major Dunn's full band; an achievement showing not only goodwill but also great musical ability.

Signs of the Spanish Riding School's success began to be evident after its very first appearance. The Lipizzaner appealed to the crowds—the papers said later that the Horse Show had had the largest attendance ever, more than a hundred thousand spectators —and soon became the accepted idols of the English.

On the evening of 22 July the young Queen Elizabeth II came to the White City, and at the express wish of the organizers was shown two items from our programme: all the gaits and turns of the *haute école* demonstrated by Pluto Theodorosta, and the school quadrille. There was a heavy shower just before the evening performance, and it almost seemed as if we should have to perform for the Queen in the rain, but it cleared up just as we rode in, and there was a happy feeling of excitement and expectancy in the packed stadium.

I rode Pluto Theodorosta on a curb in a difficult programme of *pirouettes*, changes of leg, *piaffes*, the *passage*, and other movements, holding the reins in my left hand only, which was sometimes difficult as the surface was rough and covered with large puddles. However, Pluto Theodorosta went magnificently, although I had not been able to ride him much since Aachen because of an injury, and was enthusiastically applauded. The quadrille was very well received too. When we finally reached the saddling enclosure the horses and their riders were spattered with mud from head to foot as if they had just come in from hunting over heavy ground.

After the performance I was summoned to the Royal Box and presented to the Queen, and was very struck by her appearance. In all her disciplined movements and speech she revealed her queenliness in spite of her youth. Holding out her hand she said, 'I have not seen anything for a long time that has impressed me as much as this performance by the Spanish Riding School.'

After the presentation Colonel Williams asked me to go on to a reception at Kensington Palace arranged by the Duke of Beaufort. When we got there he told me that the Queen must have arrived already as her car was also waiting outside, and in fact she and her Consort, Prince Philip, were there with members of the aristocracy. She shook hands and remarked that she had already spoken to me at the White City. While my wife was being presented the Duke of Edinburgh, standing beside the Queen, congratulated me on the performance. Then the Duke of Beaufort took me by the arm, led me into the next room, and gave me a glass of champagne.

'You have worked hard to-day; you must be very thirsty.'

The Duchess of Beaufort came up to me with a plate full of cakes, saying, 'You have given me such pleasure with your horses, and I hear that you like sweet things.'

As I stood holding the plate and my glass a man spoke to me, and, looking up, I recognized the Duke of Edinburgh, who had followed me. I had barely answered his first question when I heard a woman's voice on the other side of me, and, turning round, saw the Queen, and the three of us had a long conversation. The Queen, still lovelier than all her pictures with her wonderful English colouring, looked straight at me with her large shining eyes as she spoke. It seemed as if she combined in a rare harmony the naturalness of a charming woman with the dignity of a monarch. The Duke of Edinburgh too, tall and good-looking, looked intently at me as we talked, so that I was often in some doubt in answering the many questions which of the pairs of eyes I should meet.

The comparatively long talk with Queen Elizabeth II was for me a special experience. Although she was very fully occupied during the Coronation festivities with the countless banquets, parades, receptions, and presentations, she showed an incredible interest even in unimportant matters in those days, and in everything to do with horses. She inquired where the Lipizzaner had been during the War, what had happened to them afterwards, and how it had been possible for this once imperial riding-school to survive at all to the present day in spite of the collapse of the Austro-Hungarian Empire and all that had followed afterwards. I replied, 'Because the Spanish Riding School is a cultural institution which even after 1918 carried on an old and venerable tradition. But a tradition can survive only if it remains in its entirety and is saved from gradual decay. Even leaving off a glove is a sign of decay.'

At this the Queen turned to her husband and said emphatically, 'He's right, isn't he?'

I was more than a little astonished when she mentioned the behaviour of Maestoso Borina, who carried his rider magnificently in the *passage*, but only gave a sketch of this step with pupils. I had written about it in my book *The Vienna Spanish Riding School*, which the Queen had borrowed from the Duke of Beaufort because at that time it was out of print. And I was specially struck by her keen observation when she said of Pluto Theodorosta, who particularly attracted her, 'I was amazed that your horse, although he was only ridden with one hand on a curb, performed all those difficult exercises absolutely smoothly. What impressed me most, though, was that in the *passage*, although he trod in a puddle and splashed himself, he did not break his rhythm at all. Most horses would have tried to avoid the puddles.'

She asked me whether I always rode Pluto Theodorosta in this way or whether he could be ridden on a snaffle, and asked for information on many other points of schooling. In this connexion she inquired whether she too would be able to ride him, or whether the direction he was accustomed to was any different from that of riding in general. So I answered, 'Your Majesty, I should be greatly honoured if you would ride Pluto Theodorosta.'

The Queen hesitated a moment and did not give a definite answer, although the Duke of Edinburgh said, 'Go on, ride him, now that you have the chance.'

In the meantime the rest of the company had formed a semicircle round us and were listening in silence to the conversation. The Queen thanked me for my explanation and left the party. The Duke of Beaufort, who had escorted her to the door, came up to me at once and said, 'Her Majesty has asked me to find out whether the invitation to ride your horse was given merely out of politeness, or whether you really meant it. We are good friends you and I, so please tell me the truth.' When I replied that I had offered my horse in all seriousness, the Duke said he would inform the Queen.

Pluto Theodorosta's solo had impressed one man particularly: the landowner who had described me as far back as 1949 as the 'dressage rider with a soul'. He came next day to the saddling enclosure and was most insistent that I should ride Pluto Theodorosta once more in the show. This was not included in the programme, so I said that the prearranged order of events ought not to be changed, for in no circumstances did I want to create the impression that I was anxious to push myself forward with my solos. He begged my permission to put his request to the organizers, and the next day Colonel Ansell asked me to ride Pluto Theodorosta once more in place of the *Pas de Trois*. When I rode back to the saddling enclosure, cheered by the audience, the landowner came to me, shook my hand vigorously, and, looking at me with shining eyes, said simply, 'Thank you.'

After our penultimate performance I was bidden with the riders to the Royal Box. There the Duchess of Beaufort presented each

Bereiter with a souvenir medal of the Horse Show, and me with the Medal of Honour. This medal, awarded by the British Horse Society for outstanding services to riding in England, had only been given five times before; I was the first foreigner to receive it.

At the close of this little ceremony the Duchess invited me into the Royal Box, where I had a very pleasant surprise. As I stepped in I at once noticed the former Governor-General of Canada, Lord Alexander, who stood up, held out his hand, and said, 'You probably will not remember me, but I am Lord Alexander, and met you in Toronto and had a talk with you.' What greatness and modesty for a man in his high position! How often I had met smaller people who made no secret of their resentment that I had not at once recognized them.

The intention of Queen Elizabeth to ride a Lipizzaner stallion had caught the imagination of the ordinary citizens of London more than I could have believed possible. The pros and cons were argued right up to the time when the horses were actually on their way to Buckingham Palace. The opponents of this 'riding experiment' argued that it was irresponsible for the Queen in the middle of the Coronation festivities and just before her world tour to be exposed to the possible danger of injury from a foreign horse from a foreign country.

Pluto Theodorosta and four other Lipizzaner were taken with their riders by horse-box to the Palace, but the Duke of Beaufort warned me not to be disappointed if the Queen did not in the end actually ride as the objections had not completely died down. However, she would certainly come at 10.30 a.m. into the covered school to watch the handling and the 'Airs Above the Ground', as she had not yet seen these items. Just the same I made complete preparations for the Queen's ride. Luckily, among the many details, I thought that my stirrup leathers might not have enough reserve holes to shorten them sufficiently, which would naturally have been rather an unfortunate discovery to make in the Queen's presence. The Duke of Beaufort, to whom I confessed my anxiety, sent for the stirrups from one of the Queen's own saddles.

The covered school at Buckingham Palace is unusually long and quite simply equipped. The iron girders across the roof were decorated with the various flags of the Commonwealth.

Punctually at 10.30 Queen Elizabeth, followed by the Duke of Edinburgh, their two children, and Princess Margaret, entered the room outside the school where the Duke and Duchess of Beaufort, the Crown Equerry, Sir Dermot McMorrough Kavanagh, and Colonel Williams with their wives and my wife had assembled. I noticed at once that the Queen was in riding clothes and therefore intended to ride Pluto Theodorosta. She greeted us individually, beginning with the Duchess of Beaufort. I shall never forget how the two women met. First they embraced and kissed each other on the cheek, then the white-haired Duchess, an aunt of the Queen, took one step backward, made a deep curtsy and kissed the young Queen's hand—the first greeting was for near relatives, the curtsy or bow and kissing of Her Majesty's hand for every one regardless of age or relationship.

I now asked the Queen whether I might show her the stallions trained for 'Airs Above the Ground', and explained that the horses learnt these exercises first on the rein without their riders, and then with them. I showed *levades*, *caprioles*, and *courbettes* with three unmounted Lipizzaner, and then had the same movements repeated with their riders. Everybody followed this demonstration with obvious interest, and all were amazed at the exceptional willingness of the horses. After this short introduction I asked the Queen, remembering what I had said at Kensington Palace, whether she wanted to ride Pluto Theodorosta on a curb or a snaffle. She replied, 'I prefer the snaffle,' so I decided to ride him first on a snaffle, as he had become accustomed during our tours to being ridden only on a curb, so that I could make certain how this rather temperamental horse would behave under these conditions. When I had taken him through every step and the hardest movements I galloped up to the Queen and begged her to take my place. My groom quickly changed the stirrups, the Queen stepped forward and mounted.

When she was in the saddle and had taken the reins she asked me who besides myself rode Pluto Theodorosta, and when I replied that he was only led when I was away said, 'Shall I really be the first strange rider he has carried?'

When the Queen began her ride I went into the middle of the school, keeping level with her, ready to jump forward if necessary, for I was very conscious of my heavy responsibility, but walking and trotting went fine, the Queen followed my suggestions promptly and finally broke into a gallop. During a breather she said, 'How supple this horse is and how willing he is to gallop in either direction. My horse is not so easy in the gallop; he always wants to go to the right.'

When the Queen had tried out some more basic steps, delighted with her success so far, I asked her if she would like to try the *piaffe* and *passage*. She said, 'Oh, yes, I should love to, but I don't know what I have to do.'

I gave her a few instructions and helped a little with my switch, and Pluto Theodorosta changed into the two steps of the *haute école*. Her Majesty's cheeks grew rosy, and when she finally stopped she called out excitedly, 'I am thrilled!' And I, too, was pleasantly stimulated and happy. She dismounted and asked, 'Might my husband also ride him? Then he can see how lovely it is to sit on a well-trained horse!' So the Duke of Edinburgh mounted Pluto Theodorosta, and rode him for a long time, but not so sensitively and quietly as the Queen, rather more in polo style. After the first quick parade I was horrified to see the increasing resistance of Pluto Theodorosta, and was glad when the Duke dismounted before there was any serious difference between horse and rider.

Then at the Duke's request I put Prince Charles on Pluto Theodorosta and led him round walking and trotting. Then seeing how longingly she watched her elder brother, I finally lifted Princess Anne on to the Lipizzaner's back.

When I had set her down the Royal Family crowded admiringly round Pluto Theodorosta, inspecting him closely, while the

The Lipizzaner appealed to the crowds—and soon became the idol of the English.

children, quite unafraid, offered him carrots and sugar.

Then something delightful happened. When I had heard that the Queen had had to borrow my book from the Duke of Beaufort I asked if I might present her with a copy. He said that she did not generally accept gifts, but if I did not mind I could give him a signed copy and he would try to find out whether I should be permitted to present it to the Queen. While we were exchanging a few words after the ride he suddenly pushed the book under my arm from behind, so I knew that I might offer it to the Queen and did so. The effect was magical. She took the book in both hands, looked at the title, and clasped it to her, saying, 'I am absolutely delighted to have a copy of my own of your book about the beautiful horses. I was sorry to have to give back the one I borrowed.'

She turned to Princess Margaret and said, 'Look, now I have one of my own!' And, bending her knees to make herself smaller, she showed the open book to her children.

'See! This lovely book belongs to Mummy.'

This little episode will always remain with me: the fêted Queen of England, cheered by millions of people during the Coronation festivities, had lost none of her warm, feminine charm!

When I came later to the White City and was asked for my impressions by Colonel Llewellyn I described the incident with enthusiasm. He smiled and said, 'One more conquest! This Coronation is really nothing more than the adoration of millions of people for a Queen!'

The same afternoon some journalists asked for a few of my impressions of England, and especially for my experiences in London. I naturally omitted completely the morning at Buckingham Palace, and talked of many other things, but not a word about the Queen's ride, so I was very astonished to read next day an account of the visit of the Lipizzaner to the Palace, ending with my expressed comment that 'The Queen impressed me by her remarkably light hands and her sensitive and intelligent riding. The Duke of Edinburgh, on the other hand, rode like a polo player.'

Later it was discovered that these remarks had been made by someone present, and had been picked up by a reporter and attributed to me to make the story better. Somehow it must have got out that the Queen had ridden a Lipizzaner, for that same afternoon a sizeable crowd came to the stables, and everybody wanted to see Pluto Theodorosta, whose name became so well known that some months later I received a letter intended for me addressed to 'Mr Pluto Theodorosta, Wels.' The writer explained that he had not remembered my name, so he had used that of my horse, and the postal officials in Wels knew—full marks to them!— that it could only be intended for a member of the school. When we returned to Vienna one of the many reporters and photographers from all over the world was Mr Armstrong Jones, later to marry Princess Margaret. He said he did not want to take the usual pictures of the performance, but the portraits of Pluto Theodorosta and me.

Queen Elizabeth II's ride seemed to me to set the crown on my work as a rider. The purpose of any dressage work must be so to train a horse that it is agreeable to ride at any time for any rider, without his having to discover any special secrets about it.

The Horse Show closed its doors on 25 July after our quadrille. Once again I watched with emotion the closing ceremony displaying all the pomp of a world power, with the fascinating musical exercises of the Royal Marine Band, the extinguishing of the lights, the slow lowering of the flag, and the sound of 'God Save the Queen', which everybody heard with moist eyes and bared heads. As I stood there feeling a little sad I thought gratefully of the series of wonderful successes there had been for the Spanish Riding School and myself. I thanked God that I had been permitted to ride once again for Austria here in London, and I was happy that this time I could return from my triumphs in good health.

The success of the Spanish Riding School was more enduring than ever before. *The Times* said that 'the last quadrille by the Spanish Riding School only made everyone still greedier for more', and when in 1958 we were invited to another festival the official letter said that our performances had been so impressive that the British Horse Society had abandoned all other exhibition items, as they had only proved disappointing. Without a doubt, therefore, 1953 brought our greatest success, and the subsequent visits to Salzburg and Passau were quite overshadowed by our English appearances, in spite of the presence of illustrious visitors from all over the world.

As the year drew to its close I looked back with satisfaction that the white horses of Austria had maintained their high standards and added many new friends to the crowds of old ones. Alongside the actual events and experiences certain disadvantages of these long tours were becoming increasingly obvious. I grew still more reluctant to accept the many invitations from abroad, and managed to get the Ministry to refuse a tremendous number of official ones: a visit to Belgrade and Athens; a tour of the four Scandinavian countries; a repeat of the performances in Hamburg and Rotterdam, and a tour planned several years before to San Francisco and Los Angeles. These measures were unavoidable because the Spaniards, after agitating for years, had at last obtained permission for a festival tour of the Vienna Riding School in 1954.

On the same grounds I at first stood firm in my refusal of an invitation to a second Horse Show in the new Westphalia Hall in Dortmund, although this was proof of the great success of the white horses' previous appearance, but when the President of the Dortmunder Reitverein protested that any other exhibition number at the resuscitated Westphalian Horse Show would be an anticlimax I relented. I realized that a repetition of our previous programmes might easily prove disappointing, so I suggested modifying and shortening them, and this worked out very well.

Seven nations took part in the International Horse Show in March, and the rebuilding had progressed enormously. This time the Lipizzaner were able to go direct to the stables erected close to the hall, which was completely sold out for the last three days. The papers spoke of a total of 64,000, and the Lipizzaner did not prove in any way disappointing, delighting thousands of spectators and inspiring the Press to give extensive coverage, and using such phrases as 'aesthetic calming of the nerves'—as a matter of interest, the same remark that the London papers had used—and 'creatures like statues that awoke at the sound of Mozart's music and became ballet-dancers on four legs'.

My wife and I were invited to an intimate lunch at the house of the President of the Deutscher Sportbund, Herr Daume, at which the President of the Republic, Dr Theodor Heuss, also appeared. I found the German Head of State a jovial scholar with a pronounced sense of humour, a clever man with a penetrating eye for the tasks of the present day. I was struck by his directness and simplicity in all that he did and said. When my wife looked round for her place card the President said with a smile, 'It's all right, Frau Podhajsky, just come up to me. To-day your place is here on my right.' With these few words and a simple gesture he announced what was in fact a great honour.

When the Spanish Riding School ended the programme that day, performing before 14,000 people, the riders lined up after the big school quadrille in front of the German President's box for a small ceremony. Herr Wörneke, who was responsible for providing the musical accompaniment for us, recorded this event on tape and gave it to me as a present. Through his quick thinking, an example of German efficiency and a warm heart, I have preserved for me in sound one of the memorable moments of my life.

I saluted, and then the President made a speech outlining my career and bestowed on me, amid thunderous applause, the Grand Service Cross of the Service Order of the German Republic. Then he shook my hand warmly and congratulated me, while Herr Daume put the ribbon of the order round my neck.

After a few choked words of thanks I climbed back into the saddle and left the arena at the head of my riders in the *passage*, cheered by the audience, which clapped in time to the horses' steps. Our visit to Dortmund, where we had once again been received with great kindness, thus ended in honourable and triumphant splendour.

SILVER BLAZE

Sir Arthur Conan Doyle

'**I** am afraid, Watson, that I shall have to go,' said Holmes, as we sat down together to our breakfast one morning.

'Go! Where to?'

'To Dartmoor—to King's Pyland.'

I was not surprised. Indeed, my only wonder was that he had not already been mixed up in this extraordinary case, which was the one topic of conversation through the length and breadth of England. For a whole day my companion had rambled about the room with his chin upon his chest and his brows knitted, charging and re-charging his pipe with the strongest black tobacco, and absolutely deaf to any of my questions or remarks. Fresh editions of every paper had been sent up by our newsagent only to be glanced over and tossed down into a corner. Yet, silent as he was, I knew perfectly well what it was over which he was brooding. There was but one problem before the public which could challenge his powers of analysis, and that was the singular disappearance of the favourite for the Wessex Cup, and the tragic murder of its trainer. When, therefore, he suddenly announced his intention of setting out for the scene of the drama, it was only what I had both expected and hoped for.

'I should be most happy to go down with you if I should not be in the way,' said I.

'My dear Watson, you would confer a great favour upon me by coming. And I think that your time will not be mis-spent, for there are points about this case which promise to make it an absolutely unique one. We have, I think, just time to catch our train at Paddington, and I will go further into the matter upon our journey. You would oblige me by bringing your very excellent field-glass.'

And so it happened that an hour or so later I found myself in the corner of a first-class carriage, flying along, en route for Exeter, while Sherlock Holmes, with his sharp, eager face framed in his earflapped travelling cap, dipped rapidly into the bundle of fresh papers which he had procured at Paddington. We had left Reading far behind us before he thrust the last of them under the seat, and offered me his cigar case.

'We are going well,' said he, looking out of the window, and glancing at his watch. 'Our rate at present is fifty-three and a half miles an hour.'

'I have not observed the quarter-mile posts,' said I.

'Nor have I. But the telegraph posts upon this line are sixty yards apart, and the calculation is a simple one. I presume that you have already looked into this matter of the murder of John Straker and the disappearance of Silver Blaze?'

'I have seen what the *Telegraph* and the *Chronicle* have to say.'

'It is one of those cases where the art of the reasoner should be used rather for the sifting of details than for the acquiring of fresh evidence. The tragedy has been so uncommon, so complete, and of such personal importance to so many people that we are suffering from a plethora of surmise, conjecture, and hypothesis. The difficulty is to detach the framework of fact—of absolute, undeniable fact—from the embellishments of theorists and reporters. Then, having established ourselves upon this sound basis, it is our duty to see what inferences may be drawn, and which are the special points upon which the whole mystery turns. On Tuesday evening I received telegrams, both from Colonel Ross, the owner of the horse, and from Inspector Gregory, who is looking after the case, inviting my cooperation.'

'Tuesday evening!' I exclaimed. 'And this is Thursday morning. Why did you not go down yesterday?'

'Because I made a blunder, my dear Watson—which is, I am afraid, a more common occurrence than anyone would think who only knew me through your memoirs. The fact is that I could not believe it possible that the most remarkable horse in England could long remain concealed, especially in so sparsely inhabited a place as the north of Dartmoor. From hour to hour yesterday I expected to hear that he had been found, and that his abductor was the murderer of John Straker. When, however, another morning had come and I found that, beyond the arrest of young Fitzroy Simpson, nothing had been done, I felt that it was time for me to take action. Yet in some ways I feel that yesterday has not been wasted.'

'At least I have a grip of the essential facts of the case. I shall enumerate them to you, for nothing clears up a case so much as stating it to another person, and I can hardly expect your cooperation if I do not show you the position from which we start.'

I lay back against the cushions, puffing at my cigar, while Holmes, leaning forward, with his long thin forefinger checking off the points upon the palm of his left hand, gave me a sketch of the events which had led to our journey.

'Silver Blaze,' said he, 'is from the Isonomy stock, and holds as brilliant a record as his famous ancestor. He is now in his fifth year, and has brought in turn each of the prizes of the turf to Colonel Ross, his fortunate owner. Up to the time of the catastrophe he was first favourite for the Wessex Cup, the betting being three to one on. He has always, however, been a prime favourite with the racing public, and has never yet disappointed them, so that even at short odds enormous sums of money have been laid upon him. It is obvious, therefore, that there were many people who had the strongest interest in preventing Silver Blaze from being there at the fall of the flag next Tuesday.

'This fact was, of course, appreciated at King's Pyland, where the Colonel's training stable is situated. Every precaution was taken to guard the favourite. The trainer, John Straker, is a retired jockey, who rode in Colonel Ross's colours before he became too heavy for the weighing chair. He has served the Colonel for five years as jockey, and for seven as trainer, and has always shown himself to be a zealous and honest servant. Under him were three lads, for the establishment was a small one, containing only four horses in all. One of these lads sat up each night in the stable, while the others slept in the loft. All three bore excellent characters. John Straker, who is a married man, lived in a small villa about two hundred yards from the stables. He has no children, keeps one maid-servant, and is comfortably off. The country round is very lonely, but about half a mile to the north there is a small cluster of villas which have been built by a Tavistock contractor for the use of invalids and others who may wish to enjoy the pure Dartmoor air. Tavistock itself lies two miles to the west, while across the moor, also about two miles distant, is the larger training establishment of Capleton, which belongs to Lord Backwater, and is managed by Silas Brown. In every other direction the moor is a complete wilderness, inhabited only by a few roaming gipsies. Such was the general situation last Monday night, when the catastrophe occurred.

'On that evening the horses had been exercised and watered as usual, and the stables were locked up at nine o'clock. Two of the lads walked up to the trainer's house, where they had supper in the kitchen, while the third, Ned Hunter, remained on guard. At a few minutes after nine the maid, Edith Baxter, carried down to the stables his supper, which consisted of a dish of curried mutton. She took no liquid, as there was a water-tap in the stables, and it was the rule that the lad on duty should drink nothing else. The maid carried a lantern with her, as it was very dark, and the path ran across the open moor.

'Edith Baxter was within thirty yards of the stables when a man appeared out of the darkness and called to her to stop. As he stepped into the circle of yellow light thrown by the lantern she saw that he was a person of gentlemanly bearing, dressed in a grey suit of tweed with a cloth cap. He wore gaiters, and carried a heavy stick with a knob to it. She was most impressed, however, by the extreme pallor of his face and by the nervousness of his manner. His age, she thought, would be rather over thirty than under it.

'"Can you tell me where I am?" he asked. "I had almost made up my mind to sleep on the moor when I saw the light of your lantern."

'"You are close to the King's Pyland training stables," she said.

'"Oh, indeed! What a stroke of luck!" he cried. "I understand that a stable boy sleeps there alone every night. Perhaps that is his supper which you are carrying to him. Now I am sure that you would not be too proud to earn the price of a new dress, would you?" He took a piece of white paper folded up out of his waistcoat pocket. "See that the boy has this to-night, and you shall have the prettiest frock that money can buy."

'She was frightened by the earnestness of his manner, and ran past him to the window through which she was accustomed to hand the meals. It was already open, and Hunter was seated at the small table inside. She had begun to tell him of what had happened, when the stranger came up again.

'"Good evening," said he, looking through the window, "I wanted to have a word with you." The girl has sworn that as he spoke she noticed the corner of the little paper packet protruding from his closed hand.

'"What business have you here?" asked the lad.

'"It's business that may put something into your pocket," said the other. "You've two horses in for the Wessex Cup—Silver Blaze and Bayard. Let me have the straight tip, and you won't be a loser. Is it a fact that at the weights Bayard could give the other a hundred yards in five furlongs, and that the stable have put their money on him?"

'"So you're one of those damned touts," cried the lad. "I'll show you how we serve them in King's Pyland." He sprang up and rushed across the stable to unloose the dog. The girl fled away to the house, but as she ran she looked back, and saw that the stranger was leaning through the window. A minute later, however, when Hunter rushed out with the hound he was gone, and though the lad ran all round the buildings he failed to find any trace of him.'

'One moment!' I asked. 'Did the stable boy, when he ran out with the dog, leave the door unlocked behind him?'

'Excellent, Watson; Excellent!' murmured my companion. 'The importance of the point struck me so forcibly, that I sent a special wire to Dartmoor yesterday to clear the matter up. The boy locked the door before he left it. The window, I may add, was not large enough for a man to get through.

'Hunter waited until his fellow grooms had returned, when he sent a message up to the trainer and told him what had occurred. Straker was excited at hearing the account, although he does not seem to have quite realized its true significance. It left him, however, vaguely uneasy, and Mrs Straker, waking at one in the morning, found that he was dressing. In reply to her inquiries, he said that he could not sleep on account of his anxiety about the horses, and that he intended to walk down to the stables to see that all was well. She begged him to remain at home, as she could hear the rain pattering against the windows, but in spite of her entreaties he pulled on his large mackintosh and left the house.

'Mrs Straker awoke at seven in the morning, to find that her husband had not yet returned. She dressed herself hastily, called the maid, and set off for the stables. The door was open; inside, huddled together upon a chair, Hunter was sunk in a state of absolute stupor, the favourite's stall was empty, and there were no signs of his trainer.

'The two lads who slept in the chaff-cutting loft above the harness-room were quickly roused. They had heard nothing during the night, for they are both sound sleepers. Hunter was obviously under the influence of some powerful drug; and, as no sense could be got out of him, he was left to sleep it off while the two lads and the two women ran out in search of the absentees. They still had hopes that the trainer had for some reason taken out the horse for early exercise, but on ascending the knoll near the house, from which all the neighbouring moors were visible, they not only could see no signs of the favourite, but they perceived something which warned them that they were in the presence of a tragedy.

'About a quarter of a mile from the stables, John Straker's overcoat was flapping from a furze bush. Immediately beyond there was a bowl-shaped depression in the moor, and at the bottom of this was found the dead body of the unfortunate trainer. His head had been shattered by a savage blow from some heavy weapon, and he was wounded in the thigh, where there was a long, clean cut, inflicted evidently by some very sharp instrument. It was clear, however, that Straker had defended himself vigorously against his assailants, for in his right hand he held a small knife, which was clotted with blood up to the handle, while in his left he grasped a red and black silk cravat, which was recognized by the maid as having been worn on the preceding evening by the stranger who had visited the stables.

'Hunter, on recovering from his stupor, was also quite positive as to the ownership of the cravat. He was equally certain that the same stranger had, while standing at the window, drugged his curried mutton, with the intention of depriving the stables of their watchman.

'As to the missing horse, there were abundant proofs in the mud which lay at the bottom of the fatal hollow, that he had been there at the time of the struggle. But from that morning he has disappeared; and although a large reward has been offered, and all the gipsies of Dartmoor are on the alert, no news has come of him. Finally an analysis has shown that the remains of his supper, left by the stable lad, contain an appreciable quantity of powdered opium, while the people of the house partook of the same dish on the same night without any ill effect.

'Those are the main facts of the case stripped of all surmise and stated as baldly as possible. I shall now recapitulate what the police have done in the matter.

'Inspector Gregory, to whom the case has been committed, is an extremely competent officer. Were he but gifted with imagination he might rise to great heights in his profession. On his arrival he promptly found and arrested the man upon whom suspicion naturally rested. There was little difficulty in finding him, for he was thoroughly well known in the neighbourhood. His name, it appears, was Fitzroy Simpson. He was a man of excellent birth and education, who had squandered a fortune upon the turf, and who lived now by doing a little quiet and genteel bookmaking in the sporting clubs of London. An examination of his betting-book shows that bets to the amount of five thousand pounds had been registered by him against the favourite.

'On being arrested he volunteered the statement that he had come down to Dartmoor in the hope of getting some information about the King's Pyland horses, and also about Desborough, the second favourite, which was in charge of Silas Brown, at the Capleton stables. He did not attempt to deny that he had acted as described upon the evening before, but declared that he had no sinister designs, and had simply wished to obtain first-hand information. When confronted with the cravat he turned very pale, and was utterly unable to account for its presence in the hand of the murdered man. His wet clothing showed that he had been out in the storm of the night before, and his stick, which was a Penang lawyer, weighted with lead, was just such a weapon as might, by repeated blows, have inflicted the terrible injuries to which the trainer had succumbed.

'On the other hand, there was no wound upon his person, while the state of Straker's knife would show that one, at least, of his assailants must bear his mark upon him. There you have it all in a nutshell, Watson, and if you can give me any light I shall be infinitely obliged to you.'

I had listened with the greatest interest to the statement which Holmes, with characteristic clearness, had laid before me. Though most of the facts were familiar to me, I had not sufficiently appreciated their relative importance, nor their connection with each other.

'Is it not possible,' I suggested, 'that the incised wound upon Straker may have been caused by his own knife in the convulsive struggles which follow any brain injury?'

'It is more than possible; it is probable,' said Holmes. 'In that case, one of the main points in favour of the accused disappears.'

'And yet,' said I, 'even now I fail to understand what the theory of the police can be.'

'I am afraid that whatever theory we state has very grave objections to it,' returned my companion. 'The police imagine, I take it, that this Fitzroy Simpson, having drugged the lad, and having in some way obtained a duplicate key, opened the stable door, and took out the horse, with the intention, apparently, of kidnapping him altogether. His bridle is missing, so that Simpson must have put it on. Then, having left the door open behind him, he was leading the horse away over the moor, when he was either met or overtaken by the trainer. A row naturally ensued, Simpson beat out the trainer's brains with his heavy stick without receiving any injury from the small knife which Straker used in self-defence, and then the thief either led the horse on to some secret hiding-place, or else it may have bolted during the struggle, and be now wandering out on the moors. That is the case as it appears to the police, and improbable as it is, all other explanations are more improbable still. However, I shall very quickly test the matter when I am once upon the spot, and until then I really cannot see how we can get much further than our present position.'

It was evening before we reached the little town of Tavistock, which lies, like the boss of a shield, in the middle of the huge circle of Dartmoor. Two gentlemen were awaiting us at the station; the one a tall fair man with lion-like hair and beard, and curiously penetrating light blue eyes, the other a small alert person, very neat and dapper, in a frock-coat and gaiters, with trim little side-whiskers and an eye-glass. The latter was Colonel Ross, the well-known sportsman, the other Inspector Gregory, a man who was rapidly making his name in the English detective service.

'I am delighted that you have come down, Mr Holmes,' said the Colonel. 'The Inspector here has done all that could possibly be suggested; but I wish to leave no stone unturned in trying to avenge poor Straker, and in recovering my horse.'

'Have there been any fresh developments?' asked Holmes.

'I am sorry to say that we have made very little progress,' said the Inspector. 'We have an open carriage outside, and as you would no doubt like to see the place before the light fails, we might talk it over as we drive.'

A minute later we were all seated in a comfortable landau and were rattling through the quaint old Devonshire town. Inspector Gregory was full of his case, and poured out a stream of remarks, while Holmes threw in an occasional question or interjection. Colonel Ross leaned back with his arms folded and his hat tilted over his eyes, while I listened with interest to the dialogue of the two detectives. Gregory was formulating his theory, which was almost exactly what Holmes had foretold in the train.

'The net is drawn pretty close round Fitzroy Simpson,' he remarked, 'and I believe myself that he is our man. At the same time, I recognize that the evidence is purely circumstantial, and that some new development may upset it.'

'How about Straker's knife?'

'We have quite come to the conclusion that he wounded himself in his fall.'

'My friend Dr Watson made that suggestion to me as we came down. If so, it would tell against this man Simpson.'

'Undoubtedly. He has neither a knife nor any sign of a wound. The evidence against him is certainly very strong. He had a great interest in the disappearance of the favourite, he lies under the suspicion of having poisoned the stable boy, he was undoubtedly out in the storm, he was armed with a heavy stick, and his cravat was found in the dead man's hand. I really think we have enough to go before a jury.'

Holmes shook his head. 'A clever counsel would tear it all to rags,' said he. 'Why should he take the horse out of the stable? If he wished to injure it, why could he not do it there? Has a duplicate key been found in his possession? What chemist sold him the powdered opium? Above all, where could he, a stranger to the district, hide a horse, and such a horse as this? What is his own explanation as to the paper which he wished the maid to give to the stable boy?'

'He says that it was a ten-pound note. One was found in his purse. But your other difficulties are not so formidable as they seem. He is not a stranger to the district. He has twice lodged at Tavistock in the summer. The opium was probably brought from London. The key, having served its purpose, would be hurled away. The horse may lie at the bottom of one of the pits or old mines upon the moor.'

'What does he say about the cravat?'

'He acknowledges that it is his, and declares that he had lost it. But a new element has been introduced into the case which may account for his leading the horse from the stable.'

Holmes pricked up his ears.

'We have found traces which show that a party of gipsies encamped on Monday night within a mile of the spot where the murder took place. On Tuesday they were gone. Now, presuming that there was some understanding between Simpson and these gipsies, might he not have been leading the horse to them when he was overtaken, and may they not have him now?'

'It is certainly possible.'

'The moor is being scoured for these gipsies. I have also examined every stable and outhouse in Tavistock, and for a radius of ten miles.'

'There is another training stable quite close, I understand?'

'Yes, and that is a factor which we must certainly not neglect. As Desborough, their horse, was second in the betting, they had an interest in the disappearance of the favourite. Silas Brown, the trainer, is known to have had large bets upon the event, and he was no friend to poor Straker. We have, however, examined the stables, and there is nothing to connect him with the affair.'

'And nothing to connect this man Simpson with the interests of the Capleton stable?'

'Nothing at all.'

Holmes leaned back in the carriage and the conversation ceased. A few minutes later our driver pulled up at a neat little red-brick villa with overhanging eaves, which stood by the road. Some distance off, across a paddock, lay a long grey-tiled out-building. In every other direction the low curves of the moor, bronze-coloured from the fading ferns, stretched away to the sky-line, broken only by the steeples of Tavistick, and by a cluster of houses away to the westward, which marked the Capleton stables. We all sprang out with the exception of Holmes, who continued to lean back with his eyes fixed upon the sky in front of him, entirely absorbed in his own thoughts. It was only when I touched his arm that he roused himself with a violent start and stepped out of the carriage.

'Excuse me,' said he, turning to Colonel Ross, who had looked at him in some surprise. 'I was day-dreaming.' There was a gleam in his eyes and a suppressed excitement in his manner which convinced me, used as I was to his ways, that his hand was upon a clue, though I could not imagine where he had found it.

'Perhaps you would prefer at once to go on to the scene of the crime, Mr Holmes?' said Gregory.

'I think that I should prefer to stay here a little and go into one or two questions of detail. Straker was brought back here, I presume?'

'Yes, he lies upstairs. The inquest is to-morrow.'

'He has been in your service some years, Colonel Ross?'

'I have always found him an excellent servant.'

'I presume that you made an inventory of what he had in his pockets at the time of his death, Inspector?'

'I have the things themselves in the sitting-room if you would care to see them.'

'I should be very glad.'

We all filed into the front room and sat round the central table, while the Inspector unlocked a square tin box and laid a small heap of things before us. There was a box of vestas, two inches of tallow candle, an ADP briar-root pipe, a pouch of sealskin with half an ounce of long-cut Cavendish, a silver watch with a gold chain, five sovereigns in gold, an aluminium pencil-case, a few papers, and an ivory-handled knife with a very delicate inflexible blade marked Weiss and Co., London.

'This is a very singular knife,' said Holmes, lifting it up and examining it minutely. 'I presume, as I see bloodstains upon it, that it is the one which was found in the dead man's grasp. Watson, this knife is surely in your line.'

'It is what we call a cataract knife,' said I.

'I thought so. A very delicate blade devised for very delicate work. A strange thing for a man to carry with him upon a rough expedition, especially as it would not shut in his pocket.'

'The tip was guarded by a disc of cork which we found beside his body,' said the Inspector. 'His wife tells us that the knife had lain for some days upon the dressing-table, and that he had picked it up as he left the room. It was a poor weapon, but perhaps the best that he could lay his hand on at the moment.'

'Very possibly. How about these papers?'

'Three of them are receipted hay-dealers' accounts. One of them is a letter of instructions from Colonel Ross. This other is a milliner's account for thirty-seven pounds fifteen, made out by

Madame Lesurier, of Bond Street, to William Darbyshire. Mrs Straker tells us that Darbyshire was a friend of her husband's, and that occasionally his letters were addressed here.'

'Madame Darbyshire had somewhat expensive tastes,' remarked Holmes, glancing down the account. 'Twenty-two guineas is rather heavy for a single costume. However, there appears to be nothing more for us to learn here, and we may now go down to the scene of the crime.'

As we emerged from the sitting-room a woman who had been waiting in the passage took a step forward and laid her hand upon the Inspector's sleeve. Her face was haggard, and thin, and eager; stamped with the print of a recent horror.

'Have you got them? Have you found them?' she panted.

'No, Mrs Straker; but Mr Holmes, here, has come from London to help us, and we shall do all that is possible.'

'Surely I met you in Plymouth, at a garden party, some little time ago, Mrs Straker,' said Holmes.

'No, sir; you are mistaken.'

'Dear me; why, I could have sworn to it. You wore a costume of dove-coloured silk with ostrich feather trimming.'

'I never had such a dress, sir,' answered the lady.

'Ah; that quite settles it,' said Holmes; and, with an apology, he followed the Inspector outside. A short walk across the moor took us to the hollow in which the body had been found. At the brink of it was the furze bush upon which the coat had been hung.

'There was no wind that night, I understand,' said Holmes.

'None; but very heavy rain.'

'In that case the overcoat was not blown against the furze bushes, but placed there.'

'Yes, it was laid across the bush.'

'You fill me with interest. I perceive that the ground has been trampled up a good deal. No doubt many feet have been there since Monday night.'

'A piece of matting has been laid here at the side, and we have all stood upon that.'

'Excellent.'

'In this bag I have one of the boots which Straker wore, one of Fitzroy Simpson's shoes, and a cast horseshoe of Silver Blaze.'

'My dear Inspector, you surpass yourself!'

Holmes took the bag, and descending into the hollow he pushed the matting into a more central position. Then stretching himself upon his face and leaning his chin upon his hands he made a careful study of the trampled mud in front of him.

'Halloa!' said he, suddenly, 'what's this?'

It was a wax vesta, half burned, which was so coated with mud that it looked at first like a little chip of wood.

'I cannot think how I came to overlook it,' said the Inspector, with an expression of annoyance.

'It was invisible, buried in the mud. I only saw it because I was looking for it.'

'What! You expected to find it?'

'I thought it not unlikely.' He took the boots from the bag and compared the impressions of each of them with marks upon the ground. Then he clambered up to the rim of the hollow and crawled about among the ferns and bushes.

'I am afraid that there are no more tracks,' said the Inspector. 'I have examined the ground very carefully for a hundred yards in each direction.'

'Indeed!' said Holmes, rising, 'I should not have the impertinence to do it again after what you say. But I should like to take a little walk over the moors before it grows dark, that I may know my ground to-morrow, and I think that I should put this horseshoe into my pocket for luck.'

Colonel Ross, who had shown some signs of impatience at my companion's quiet and systematic method of work, glanced at his watch.

'I wish you would come back with me, Inspector,' said he. 'There are several points on which I should like your advice, and especially as to whether we do not owe it to the public to remove our horse's name from the entries for the Cup.'

'Certainly not,' cried Holmes, with decision; 'I should let the name stand.'

The Colonel bowed. 'I am very glad to have had your opinion, sir,' said he. 'You will find us at poor Straker's house when you have finished your walk, and we can drive together into Tavistock.'

He turned back with the Inspector, while Holmes and I walked slowly across the moor. The sun was beginning to sink behind the stables of Capleton, and the long sloping plain in front of us was tinged with gold, deepening into rich, ruddy brown where the faded ferns and brambles caught the evening light. But the glories of the landscape were all wasted upon my companion, who was sunk in the deepest thought.

'It's this way, Watson,' he said, at last. 'We may leave the question of who killed John Straker for the instant, and confine ourselves to finding out what has become of the horse. Now, supposing that he broke away during or after the tragedy, where could he have gone to? The horse is a very gregarious creature. If left to himself his instincts would have been either to return to King's Pyland or go over to Capleton. Why should he run wild upon the moor? He would surely have been seen by now. And why should gipsies kidnap him? These people always clear out when they hear of trouble, for they do not wish to be pestered by the police. They could not hope to sell such a horse. They would run a great risk and gain nothing by taking him. Surely that is clear.'

'Where is he, then?'

'I have already said that he must have gone to King's Pyland or to Capleton. He is not at King's Pyland, therefore he is at Capleton. Let us take that as a working hypothesis, and see what it leads us to. This part of the moor, as the Inspector remarked, is very hard and dry. But it falls away towards Capleton, and you can see from here that there is a long hollow over yonder, which must have been very wet on Monday night. If our supposition is correct, then the horse must have crossed that, and there is the point where we should look for his tracks.'

We had been walking briskly during this conversation, and a

few more minutes brought us to the hollow in question. At Holmes' request I walked down the bank to the right, and he to the left, but I had not taken fifty paces before I heard him give a shout, and saw him waving his hand to me. The track of a horse was plainly outlined in the soft earth in front of him, and the shoe which he took from his pocket exactly fitted the impression.

'See the value of imagination,' said Holmes. 'It is the one quality which Gregory lacks. We imagined what might have happened, acted upon the supposition, and find ourselves justified. Let us proceed.'

We crossed the marshy bottom and passed over a quarter of a mile of dry, hard turf. Again the ground sloped and again we came on the tracks. Then we lost them for half a mile, but only to pick them up once more quite close to Capleton. It was Holmes who saw them first, and he stood pointing with a look of triumph upon his face. A man's track was visible beside the horse's.

'The horse was alone before,' I cried.

'Quite so. It was alone before. Halloa! what is this?'

The double track turned sharp off and took the direction of King's Pyland. Holmes whistled, and we both followed along after it. His eyes were on the trail, but I happened to look a little to one side, and saw to my surprise the same tracks coming back again in the opposite direction.

'One for you, Watson,' said Holmes, when I pointed it out; 'you have saved us a long walk which would have brought us back on our own traces. Let us follow the return track.'

We had not to go far. It ended at the paving of asphalt which led up to the gates of the Capleton stables. As we approached a groom ran out from them.

'We don't want any loiterers about here,' said he.

'I only wished to ask a question,' said Holmes, with his finger and thumb in his waistcoat pocket. 'Should I be too early to see your master, Mr Silas Brown, if I were to call at five o'clock to-morrow morning?'

'Bless you, sir, if any one is about he will be, for he is always the first stirring. But here he is, sir, to answer your questions for himself. No, sir, no; it's as much as my place is worth to let him see me touch your money. Afterwards, if you like.'

As Sherlock Holmes replaced the half-crown which he had drawn from his pocket, a fierce-looking elderly man strode out from the gate with a hunting-crop swinging in his hand.

'What's this, Dawson?' he cried. 'No gossiping! Go about your business! And you—what the devil do you want here?'

'Ten minutes' talk with you, my good sir,' said Holmes, in the sweetest of voices.

'I've no time to talk to every gadabout. We want no strangers here. Be off, or you may find a dog at your heels.'

Holmes leaned forward and whispered something in the trainer's ear. He started violently and flushed to the temples.

'It's a lie!' he shouted. 'An infernal lie!'

'Very good! Shall we argue about it here in public, or talk it over in your parlour?'

'Oh, come in if you wish to.'

Holmes smiled. 'I shall not keep you more than a few minutes, Watson,' he said. 'Now, Mr Brown, I am quite at your disposal.'

It was quite twenty minutes, and the reds had all faded into greys before Holmes and the trainer reappeared. Never have I seen such a change as had been brought about in Silas Brown in that short time. His face was ashy pale, beads of perspiration shone upon his brow, and his hands shook until the hunting-crop wagged like a branch in the wind. His bullying, overbearing manner was all gone too, and he cringed along at my companion's side like a dog with its master.

'Your instructions will be done. It shall be done,' said he.

'There must be no mistake,' said Holmes, looking round at him. The other winced as he read the menace in his eyes.

'Oh, no, there shall be no mistake. It shall be there. Should I change it first or not?'

Holmes thought a little and then burst out laughing. 'No, don't,' said he. 'I shall write to you about it. No tricks now or . . .'

'Oh, you can trust me, you can trust me!'

'You must see to it on the day as if it were your own.'

'You can rely upon me.'

'Yes, I think I can. Well, you shall hear from me tomorrow.' He turned upon his heel, disregarding the trembling hand which the other held out to him, and we set off in the direction of King's Pyland.

'A more perfect compound of the bully, coward and sneak than Master Silas Brown I have seldom met with,' remarked Holmes, as we trudged along together.

'He has the horse, then?'

'He tried to bluster out of it, but I described to him so exactly what his actions had been upon that morning, that he is convinced that I was watching him. Of course, you observed the peculiarly square toes in the impressions, and that his own boots exactly corresponded to them. Again, of course, no subordinate would have dared to have done such a thing. I described to him how when, according to his custom, he was the first down, he perceived a strange horse wandering over the moor; how he went out to it, and his astonishment at recognizing from the white forehead which has given the favourite its name that chance had put in his power the only horse which could beat the one upon which he had put his money. Then I described how his first impulse had been to lead him back to King's Pyland, and how the devil had shown him how he could hide the horse until the race was over, and how he had led it back and concealed it at Capleton. When I told him every detail he gave it up, and thought only of saving his own skin.'

'But his stables had been searched.'

'Oh, an old horse-faker like him has many a dodge.'

'But are you not afraid to leave the horse in his power now, since he has every interest in injuring it?'

'My dear fellow, he will guard it as the apple of his eye. He knows that his only hope of mercy is to produce it safe.'

'Colonel Ross did not impress me as a man who would be likely to show much mercy in any case.'

'The matter does not rest with Colonel Ross. I follow my own methods, and tell as much or as little as I choose. That is the advantage of being unofficial. I don't know whether you observed it, Watson, but the Colonel's manner has been just a trifle cavalier to me. I am inclined now to have a little amusement at his expense. Say nothing to him about the horse.'

'Certainly not, without your permission.'

'And, of course, this is all quite a minor case compared with the question of who killed John Straker.'

'And you will devote yourself to that?'

'On the contrary, we will both go back to London by the night train.'

I was thunderstruck by my friend's words. We had only been a few hours in Devonshire, and that he should give up an investigation which he had begun so brilliantly was quite incomprehensible to me. Not a word more could I draw from him until we were back at the trainer's house. The Colonel and the Inspector were awaiting us in the parlour.

'My friend and I return to town by the midnight express,' said Holmes. 'We have had a charming little breath of your beautiful Dartmoor air.'

The Inspector opened his eyes, and the Colonel's lips curled in a sneer.

'So you despair of arresting the murderer of poor Straker,' said he.

Holmes shrugged his shoulders. 'There are certainly grave difficulties in the way,' said he. 'I have every hope, however, that your horse will start upon Tuesday, and I beg that you will have your jockey in readiness. Might I ask for a photograph of Mr John Straker?'

The Inspector took one from an envelope in his pocket and handed it to him.

'My dear Gregory, you anticipate all my wants. If I might ask you to wait here for an instant, I have a question which I should like to put to the maid.'

'I must say that I am rather disappointed in our London consultant,' said Colonel Ross, bluntly, as my friend left the room. 'I do not see that we are any further than when he came.'

'At least, you have his assurance that your horse will run,' said I.

'Yes, I have his assurance,' said the Colonel, with a shrug of his shoulders. 'I should prefer to have the horse.'

I was about to make some reply in defence of my friend, when he entered the room again.

'Now, gentlemen,' said Holmes, 'I am now quite ready for Tavistock.'

As we stepped into the carriage one of the stable lads held the door open for us. A sudden idea seemed to occur to Holmes, for he leaned forward and touched the lad upon the sleeve.

'You have a few sheep in the paddock,' he said. 'Who attends to them?'

'I do, sir.'

'Have you noticed anything amiss with them of late?'

'Well, sir, not of much account; but three of them have gone lame, sir.'

I could see that Holmes was extremely pleased, for he chuckled and rubbed his hands together.

'A long shot, Watson; a very long shot!' said he, pinching my arm. 'Gregory, let me recommend to your attention this singular epidemic among the sheep. Drive on, coachman!'

Colonel Ross still wore an expression which showed the poor opinion which he had formed of my companion's ability, but I saw by the Inspector's face that his attention had been keenly aroused.

'You consider that to be important?' he asked.

'Exceedingly so.'

'Is there any other point to which you would wish to draw my attention?'

'To the curious incident of the dog in the night-time.'

'The dog did nothing in the night-time.'

'That was the curious incident,' remarked Sherlock Holmes.

Four days later Holmes and I were again in the train bound for Winchester, to see the race for the Wessex Cup. Colonel Ross met us, by appointment, outside the station, and we drove in his drag to the course beyond the town. His face was grave and his manner was cold in the extreme.

'I have seen nothing of my horse,' said he.

'I suppose that you would know him when you saw him?' asked Holmes.

The Colonel was very angry. 'I have been on the turf for twenty years, and never was asked such a question as that before,' said he. 'A child would know Silver Blaze with his white forehead and his mottled off fore leg.'

'How is the betting?'

'Well, that is the curious part of it. You could have got fifteen to one yesterday, but the price has become shorter and shorter, until you can hardly get three to one now.'

'Hum!' said Holmes. 'Somebody knows something, that is clear!'

As the drag drew up in the enclosure near the grandstand, I glanced at the card to see the entries. It ran:—

Wessex Plate. 50 sovs. each, h ft, with 1,000 sovs. added, for four and five-year olds. Second £300. Third £200. New course (one mile and five furlongs).

1. Mr Heath Newton's The Negro (red cap, cinnamon jacket).
2. Colonel Wardlaw's Pugilist (pink cap, blue and black jacket).
3. Lord Backwater's Desborough (yellow cap and sleeves).
4. Colonel Ross's Silver Blaze (black cap, red jacket).
5. Duke of Balmoral's Iris (yellow and black stripes).
6. Lord Singleford's Rasper (purple cap, black sleeves).

'We scratched our other one and put all hopes on your word,' said the Colonel. 'Why, what is that? Silver Blaze favourite?'

'Five to four against Silver Blaze!' roared the ring. 'Five to four against Silver Blaze! Fifteen to five against Desborough! Five to four on the field!'

'There are the numbers up,' I cried. 'They are all six there.'

'All six there! Then my horse is running,' cried the Colonel, in great agitation. 'But I don't see him. My colours have not passed.'

'Only five have passed. This must be he.'

As I spoke a powerful bay horse swept out from the weighing enclosure and cantered past us, bearing on its back the well-known black and red of the Colonel.

'That's not my horse,' cried the owner. 'That beast has not a white hair upon its body. What is this that you have done, Mr Holmes?'

'Well, well, let us see how he gets on,' said my friend, imperturbably. For a few minutes he gazed through my field-glass. 'Capital! An excellent start!' he cried suddenly. 'There they are, coming round the curve!'

From our drag we had a superb view as they came up the straight. The six horses were so close together that a carpet could have covered them, but half way up the yellow of the Capleton stable showed to the front. Before they reached us, however, Desborough's bolt was shot, and the Colonel's horse, coming away with a rush, passed the post a good six lengths before its rival, the Duke of Balmoral's Iris making a bad third.

'It's my race anyhow,' gasped the Colonel, passing his hand over his eyes. 'I confess that I can make neither head nor tail of it. Don't you think that you have kept up your mystery long enough Mr Holmes?'

'Certainly, Colonel. You shall know everything. Let us all go round and have a look at the horse together. Here he is,' he continued, as we made our way into the weighing enclosure where only owners and their friends find admittance. 'You have only to wash his face and his leg in spirits of wine and you will find that he is the same old Silver Blaze as ever.'

'You take my breath away!'

'I found him in the hands of a faker, and took the liberty of running him just as he was sent over.'

'My dear sir, you have done wonders. The horse looks very fit and well. It never went better in its life. I owe you a thousand apologies for having doubted your ability. You have done me a great service by recovering my horse. You would do me a greater still if you could lay your hands on the murderer of John Straker.'

'I have done so,' said Holmes, quietly.

The Colonel and I stared at him in amazement. 'You have got him! Where is he, then?'

'He is here.'

'Here! Where?'

'In my company at the present moment.'

The Colonel flushed angrily. 'I quite recognize that I am under obligations to you, Mr Holmes,' said he, 'but I must regard what you have just said as either a very bad joke or an insult.'

Sherlock Holmes laughed. 'I assure you that I have not associated you with the crime, Colonel,' said he; 'the real murderer is standing immediately behind you!'

He stepped past and laid his hand upon the glossy neck of the thoroughbred.

'The horse!' cried both the Colonel and myself.

'Yes, the horse. And it may lessen his guilt if I say that it was done in self-defence, and that John Straker was a man who was entirely unworthy of your confidence. But there goes the bell; and as I stand to win a little on this next race, I shall defer a more lengthy explanation until a more fitting time.'

We had the corner of a Pullman car to ourselves that evening as we whirled back to London, and I fancy that the journey was a short one to Colonel Ross as well as to myself, as we listened to our companion's narrative of the events which had occurred at the Dartmoor training stables upon that Monday night, and the means by which he had unravelled them.

'I confess,' said he, 'that any theories which I had formed from the newspaper reports were entirely erroneous. And yet there were indications there, had they not been overlaid by other details which concealed their true import. I went to Devonshire with the conviction that Fitzroy Simpson was the true culprit, although, of course, I saw that the evidence against him was by no means complete.

'It was while I was in the carriage, just as we reached the trainer's house, that the immense significance of the curried mutton occurred to me. You may remember that I was distrait, and remained sitting after you had all alighted. I was marvelling in my own mind how I could possibly have overlooked so obvious a clue.'

'I confess,' said the Colonel, 'that even now I cannot see how it helps us.'

'It was the first link in my chain of reasoning. Powdered opium is by no means tasteless. The flavour is not disagreeable, but it is perceptible. Were it mixed with any ordinary dish, the eater would undoubtedly detect it, and would probably eat no more. A curry was exactly the medium which would disguise this taste. By no possible supposition could this stranger, Fitzroy Simpson, have caused curry to be served in the trainer's family that night, and it is surely too monstrous a coincidence to suppose that he happened to come along with powdered opium upon the very night when a dish happened to be served which would disguise the flavour. That is unthinkable. Therefore Simpson becomes eliminated from the case, and our attention centres upon Straker and his wife, the only two people who could have chosen curried mutton for supper that night. The opium was added after the dish was set aside for the stable boy, for the others had the same for supper with no ill effects. Which of them, then, had access to that dish without the maid seeing them?

'Before deciding that question I had grasped the significance of the silence of the dog, for one true inference invariably suggests others. The Simpson incident had shown me that a dog was kept in the stables, and yet, though someone had been in and had fetched out a horse, he had not barked enough to arouse the two lads in the loft. Obviously the midnight visitor was someone whom the dog knew well.

'I was already convinced, or almost convinced, that John Straker went down to the stables in the dead of the night and took

'I only wished to ask a question,' said Holmes.

out Silver Blaze. For what purpose? For a dishonest one, obviously, or why should he drug his own stable boy? And yet I was at a loss to know why. There have been cases before now where trainers have made sure of great sums of money by laying against their own horses, through agents, and then prevented them from winning by fraud. Sometimes it is a pulling jockey. Sometimes it is some surer and subtler means. What was it here? I hoped that the contents of his pockets might help me to form a conclusion.

'And they did so. You cannot have forgotten the singular knife which was found in the dead man's hand, a knife which certainly no sane man would choose for a weapon. It was, as Dr Watson told us, a form of knife which is used for the most delicate operations known in surgery. And it was to be used for a delicate operation that night. You must know, with your wide experience of turf matters, Colonel Ross, that it is possible to make a slight nick upon the tendons of a horse's ham, and to do it subcutaneously so as to leave absolutely no trace. A horse so treated would develop a slight lameness which would be put down to a strain in exercise or a touch of rheumatism, but never to foul play.'

'Villain! Scoundrel!' cried the Colonel.

'We have here the explanation of why John Straker wished to take the horse out on to the moor. So spirited a creature would have certainly roused the soundest of sleepers when it felt the prick of the knife. It was absolutely necessary to do it in the open air.'

'I have been blind!' cried the Colonel. 'Of course, that was why he needed the candle, and struck the match.'

'Undoubtedly. But in examining his belongings, I was fortunate enough to discover, not only the method of the crime, but even its motives. As a man of the world, Colonel, you know that men do not carry other people's bills about in their pockets. We have most of us quite enough to do to settle our own. I at once concluded that Straker was leading a double life, and keeping a second establishment. The nature of the bill showed that there was a lady in the case, and one who had expensive tastes. Liberal as you are with your servants, one hardly expects that they can buy twenty-guinea walking dresses for their women. I questioned Mrs Straker as to the dress without her knowing it, and having satisfied myself that it had never reached her, I made a note of the milliner's address, and felt that by calling there with Straker's photograph, I could easily dispose of the mythical Darbyshire.

'From that time on all was plain. Straker had led out the horse to a hollow where his light would be invisible. Simpson, in his flight, had dropped his cravat, and Straker had picked it up with some idea, perhaps, that he might use it in securing the horse's leg. Once in the hollow he had got behind the horse, and had struck a light, but the creature, frightened at the sudden glare, and with the strange instinct of animals feeling that some mischief was intended, had lashed out, and the steel shoe had struck Straker full on the forehead. He had already, in spite of the rain, taken off his overcoat in order to do his delicate task, and so, as he fell, his knife gashed his thigh. Do I make it clear?'

'Wonderful!' cried the Colonel. 'Wonderful! You might have been there.'

'My final shot was, I confess, a very long one. It struck me that so astute a man as Straker would not undertake this delicate tendon-nicking without a little practice. What could he practice on? My eyes fell upon the sheep, and I asked a question which, rather to my surprise, showed that my surmise was correct.'

'You have made it perfectly clear, Mr Holmes.'

'When I returned to London I called upon the milliner, who at once recognized Straker as an excellent customer, of the name of Darbyshire, who had a very dashing wife with a strong partiality for expensive dresses. I have no doubt that this woman had plunged him over head and ears in debt, and so led him into this miserable plot.'

'You have explained all but one thing,' cried the Colonel. 'Where was the horse?'

'Ah, it bolted and was cared for by one of your neighbours. We must have an amnesty in that direction, I think. This is Clapham

279

Junction, if I am not mistaken, and we shall be in Victoria in less than ten minutes. If you care to smoke a cigar in our rooms, Colonel, I shall be happy to give you any other details which might interest you.'

A HORRIBLY HORSEY DAUGHTER

Josephine Pullein-Thompson

It was going to be a dull weekend, thought Miranda Cummings.
Prep, television, books from the library, but nothing really to
do, except for her ride, one hour on Saturday morning. *Now*, if
she had a pony of her own . . . But it was no use wasting time
on that old fantasy; for years she'd been looking up places to ride
to on the map, for years she'd imagined herself schooling, riding
perfect half passes, seen herself in the show ring, jumping clear
rounds. And there wasn't a chance of any of it coming true; it
was just a stupid dream.

It wasn't as though they were poor, it wasn't as though they
lived in the centre of a huge city. Their house stood in the same

road as a riding school and there was plenty of room beside the garage for a loose-box, Miranda had often paced it out. No, it was simply that her father had convinced himself that horsey girls were dull, stupid and generally horrible. He could never see beautiful girls riding gracefully on Anglo-Arabs. It was always large, fat, ugly girls slumped on ponies too small for them to which he pointed triumphantly saying: 'There, that's what you'd look like if I let you do all this riding.' And when Miranda's mother, who was on Miranda's side, pointed out that she was really quite pretty, with long dark hair and brown eyes, and that she must be intelligent to have won the scholarship to St Catherine's, her father would answer, 'Oh I'm quite contented with her as she *is*. It's just that I won't take the risk of her changing. I don't want a horsey daughter who talks about ponies at every meal. And anyway she's no good at it,' he would add to Miranda's annoyance, for how could she improve when she only rode for one hour a week?

All the time she'd been working for the scholarship, Miranda had encouraged herself with the idea that her father might reward her with a pony, but when, delighted with the result, he'd merely taken her out to lunch at the most expensive restaurant in Cranbourne, she had given up hope. Since then she had tried not to dream of becoming a superb rider, because dreams which couldn't be realized were a waste of time, but just occasionally when there was only a dreary weekend ahead, all the old longings came back in full force. And that was how it was when Liz Holder telephoned and asked for her help.

Mr Cummings was away on business so Miranda went in search of her mother. She was arranging the dining room for her Oxfam Bring and Buy sale next day.

'Mummy, Miss Barnes has gone to Yorkshire for her niece's wedding and Anne Ashmore who was supposed to help Liz run the stables this weekend has let her down. Liz wants me to help instead; she says she's desperate, can I?'

Mrs Cummings looked undecided. 'But would you be any use?' she asked. 'I mean you're not very experienced yourself.'

'She's asked me,' answered Miranda, feeling slightly offended that her parents always thought her so useless.

'Yes, well, Daddy doesn't like you hanging round the stables but this is an emergency; one must help people in trouble. Anyway, he doesn't come back from Germany until Sunday evening. Yes, that's all right, darling . . .'

'Oh, *thank you*,' called Miranda as she rushed back to the telephone.

Liz had said that she could manage the stable work so there was no need for Miranda to be early, but Miranda wasn't going to miss a minute of her horsey weekend and she was hurrying along the road just after eight on Saturday morning. It was a dismal-looking day. Yellow leaves drifted through the grey light and landed on the road and pavement with tiny exhausted sighs, but it wasn't raining or freezing, thought Miranda with relief. . .

Liz was mucking out the three stabled horses: Stardust, Jasper and Coot. 'Hullo, you're early,' she said. 'Well, you can fetch up the ponies as soon as Andrew and Chris come and meanwhile if you'd like to give Stardust some clean straw. . .'

Miranda spread straw until Chris, who was eleven with red hair, arrived on her bicycle. Then they collected head collars and pony nuts while they waited for Andrew. He was only nine, with blue eyes and a large face that always wore a deadpan expression; he lived opposite the stable gates.

'Miranda, if you ride one and lead one you'll be able to bring them all up in two goes,' called Liz.

Most of the ponies were waiting at the field gate and they had quite a job to get the first four through without letting the whole lot out. Chris and Andrew had chosen their favourites, piebald Domino and little brown Filbert. Miranda rode Max, a stately grey of 14.2, and led Blackberry who was thickset and obstinate and no one's favourite. On the second trip Andrew chose the other little pony, Fudge, while Chris had roan Punch, and Miranda rode Rugus and led Pepsi who was Punch's twin in appearance, but not so sweet-tempered.

Liz fed the larger ponies and they groomed the smaller ones, who only had haynets, until the feeds were eaten. Then the large ones were groomed too, great clouds of dust rising from their mud-caked coats.

Miranda rode Rufus for her official ride. Liz took them in the school and gave them quite an exciting time with more jumping than Miss Barnes usually allowed. They were the best ride of the day and afterwards the standard fell steeply. When Miranda saw the eleven o'clock ride trying to put themselves up she understood why Liz had asked for her help. She was to take Clare, who was seven and had only ridden five times, on the leading rein. And besides Clare there were two other beginners, large girls of about sixteen, who were to ride Coot and Jasper. Then there was Andrew on Filbert, a very nervous boy on Rufus, a bossy girl with huge teeth and straight hair on Blackberry and three fairly efficient-looking girls on Pepsi, Punch and Domino. Chris helped with the stirrups and held Fudge and Clare while Miranda led out Max and mounted. When Liz had checked all the girths and stirrups she mounted Stardust and led the cavalcade down the road and then along the lane towards the common. Clare was quite chatty; she said that she liked Filbert better than Fudge and that she could rise to the trot. Miranda taught her some easy points of the horse, crest and withers and knee, and told her about keeping her legs back and riding with a perpendicular stirrup leather.

Liz didn't take them over the high, open part of the common, but along the sandy tracks through the woods and presently she halted at the start of a long, grassy track and said, 'If you and Clare will trot up there and wait at the top, Miranda, I'll send the people who want to canter up in ones and twos so that the ponies don't get excited.'

Jean and Hazel, the large beginners, didn't want to canter, nor did the nervous boy. The bossy girl on Blackberry began to laugh at them but Liz told her to shut up and sent them all on with Miranda.

No one fell off and Andrew, who had insisted on going last, was quite sure he had galloped, though no one else thought so. Liz took the lead again and they rode along narrow, winding paths between bracken and heather and birch trees.

Clare chattered about school and Miranda taught her how to halt and to trot with folded arms. They had almost completed their circle and were waiting to cross the one busy road between them and the stables, when the bossy girl, whose name was Carol, barged past Liz and announced that there was tons of time to cross.

'Come back,' shouted Liz. But Blackberry decided to carry on and as Carol tugged on the reins in the middle of the road, Liz called, 'Keep them together, Miranda,' and rode after Carol.

Miranda said, 'Wait everyone. Standstill.' And then there was a horrible crack as Blackberry lashed out. The other riders couldn't see whether it was Liz or Stardust who caught the full impact of the kick, but then Liz leaned forward, obviously in pain, and put one hand across her face. A man in a car driving past slowly shouted that she wasn't fit to be in charge of children. Miranda took over. She shepherded everyone across the road and then took Stardust's rein, for Liz seem dazed and not in control.

'I'll be all right in a minute,' she murmured. 'It's just my ankle.'

Away from the road, Miranda dismounted and looked for the damage, but jodpurs and boot concealed whatever had happened.

'It wasn't a hard kick,' said Carol. '*She'll* be all right.'

Jean and Hazel were suggesting doctors who lived near, Andrew offered to gallop to a telephone and dial 999. Miranda came to a decision. 'You go to the back,' she told Carol severely, 'and don't kick anyone else. Pat,' she asked, 'could you lead Max? He's friends with Domino. Then I'll walk with Clare and Liz.'

They walked slowly and sadly across the last stretch of the common and along the road to the stables, for they could all see that Liz was still in pain. Clare looked as though she was going to cry so Miranda had to assume a cheerful manner and explain that even if Liz's ankle was broken it would soon mend.

Chris met then at the yard gate.

'You take Clare,' said Miranda. There were several mothers waiting to collect their children; the riders explained about the kick, all talking at once.

'Will you put your ponies away, please,' called Miranda as the mothers crowded round her and Liz. 'I think if you undo the girth you can slide the rider off with the saddle, I read about it in a book,' Miranda told them.

'A splint first,' said a first-aiding mother and they made one with the crook of a hunting crop under the foot and fixed it with tail bandages. Then they slid Liz off and sat her in the nervous boy's mother's car. 'I'll drive her straight to the hospital,' said Mrs Giles. 'Come on, Nick.'

Miranda wrote down Liz's telephone number and promised to break the news to *her* mother gently and then, as the car drove away, she suddenly realized that she was in charge and alone. Well, not quite alone, Chris and Andrew would help her, but supposing anything else went wrong? She hadn't even Miss Barnes's telephone number.

'Aren't you going to book us up for next week?' asked Carol's bossy voice. 'You're not very efficient, are you? I think I'd better stay and help, especially as everyone says it was my fault.'

'There's no need,' Miranda told her hastily. 'Chris and Andrew are the regular helpers.' And grabbing the diary she wrote down the names of those who were coming next week.

'I hope *you'll* take me again,' said Clare.

The pupils gone, the ponies watered, Chris and Andrew came to her to ask about feeds; Miss Barnes always mixed them, they just took them round.

'I'll have to guess,' decided Miranda. 'We won't give them too many oats. They won't starve so long as they have plenty of hay and I don't want to give them colic or laminitis or get the pupils bucked off.'

As soon as all the horses were munching, Miranda telephoned Liz's mother.

'An accident?' she gasped.

'Just a small one,' Miranda repeated, 'just her ankle and Mrs Giles has taken her to the hospital for an X-ray.'

'To the hospital? Thank you, dear. I'll go down right away.'

Andrew went home to lunch so it was only Miranda and Chris who ate their sandwiches in the saddle room. As she ate Miranda inspected the diary. 'I'm sure Liz won't be back for days,' she told Chris. 'I'd better put everyone off. They won't like it if they've come miles and find no riding.' But it wasn't so easy to put them off. Miss Barnes didn't bother with surnames and how could you telephone 'Jenny T' or 'David' and the one name she had written down was 'Berry'. It would waste hours, Miranda thought, ringing every Berry in the phone book.

'I should just take them,' said Chris. 'After all, Liz let you teach Clare. This lot aren't much good, but they're not actual beginners.'

'I suppose I could take them for a hack,' said Miranda. That was what she did and, though it was dull for the ponies, she took them the same ride that they had gone with Liz that morning, for it was a good safe ride with no wild gallops.

Hearing of Liz's accident, all the pupils were extra nice and helpful and when Jenny T had asked her age Miranda had hastily instructed one of the younger riders to avoid answering for she felt certain that Jenny was at least as old as she was.

Afterwards the riders of the field ponies turned them out and some offered to carry down hay and help generally so the ponies were soon fed, but everyone spilled a good deal and the yard began to look a bit of a mess.

Chris and Andrew had worked hard while the ride was out; the boxes were bedded down and the stabled horses; water and haynets ready so, when Miranda had mixed another set of feeds, they fed the horses and gathered in the saddle room looking gloomily at the eleven dirty sets of tack.

'I have to go home at half past five,' said Andrew.

'We could just wash the bits,' suggested Chris. 'I know Miss Barnes does sometimes when there's an emergency and this *must* be one.'

'Yes, we'll do that,' agreed Miranda and then the telephone rang and it was Liz's mother.

'We're just back from the hospital,' she said. 'What a palaver! They had to put her in plaster but it's only a walking one. She's broken the smaller of the two bones in the leg—her fibula. It'll be six weeks, they say, but she'll be able to get about. How are things with you? Liz's worried to death over the horses. She wants me to drive her up now, but she's not allowed to walk for twelve hours, not till the plaster dries out.'

'Tell her everything is all right,' answered Miranda. 'Chris and Andrew have helped all day and the horses and ponies are fed etcetera. She needn't worry. I think we had better get in touch with Miss Barnes. It seems a pity to upset her trip and I'm sure she'll want to come home when she knows how things stand, but of course trains are few and far between on a Sunday, so if you could manage the feeding in the morning? Liz says not to worry about mess and muddle; it's just the well-being of the animals that matters.'

Miranda told Chris and Andrew about the broken fibula as they washed the bits and then when they'd gone home she topped up the horses' water buckets, checked their haynets and rugs and locked the saddle room before starting on her own rather weary walk through the dusk. She felt as though years and years had passed since that morning.

'Thirty-eight pounds, fifty-five pence for Oxfam,' announced Mrs Cummings proudly. 'Not bad, was it? And how did your day go, were you able to give a helping hand?'

Miranda explained about Liz's ankle. 'I'm in charge now.'

'Oh poor Liz. But you can't really be in charge, darling. Not of all those horses. I mean you don't know enough and some of them are enormous. I could ring the RSPCA and ask them to send a man round. Or that Mrs What's it who's secretary of the pony club, she'd know what to do.'

'I know what to do,' said Miranda, 'and it's all done. Anyway, it's only until tomorrow and then Miss Barnes will be back. Have you had tea? I'm terribly hungry.'

The eleven o'clock ride were in need of help.

Much as she hated early rising Miranda was at the stables at seven-fifteen on Sunday morning. She inspected her charges; Coot, the ugly black gelding, had no water, Stardust's rug had slipped, Jasper, who'd eaten every morsel of his hay neighed indignantly for breakfast, but otherwise they seemed all right. She watered and fed them.

By the time Chris and Andrew appeared it was raining. They ran to fetch in the ponies before their coats were wet. As they mucked out and groomed, it settled down to being a wet day.

'You'll have to take the ten o'clock ride in the school,' Chris told Miranda, 'no one will want to go for a hack in this.' They inspected the diary. Nine pupils at ten, nine at eleven.

'Some of the ten o'clock are good,' said Chris.

'And some of the elevens are terrible,' added Andrew. 'That girl Sandra screams.'

Miranda's heart was sinking. It wasn't the screaming Sandra who frightened her, but the accomplished ten o'clocks; they probably rode far better than she did. 'I don't think I *can* take them, I'm not experienced enough,' she was telling Chris when Carol's head came round the saddle room door.

'Hullo, how are you getting on? I hear Liz's leg is broken so I've come to help. I'll take a ride out.'

'No you won't,' answered Chris. 'Miranda was put in charge and she's taking them in the school.'

'Yes, that's right,' Miranda was forced to agree. 'And Miss Barnes has written down which ponies they are all to ride, so we only have to tack up.'

'I'll saddle Stardust,' said Carol, grabbing tack.

'That's Coot's bridle,' Andrew told her coldly.

Miranda's feelings of inadequacy increased as the ten o'clock pupils, all looking tall and competent and quite as old as her, arrived. Chris told them of Liz's accident and how Miranda had been put in charge and Miranda unwillingly dragged her leaden legs and hollow-feeling stomach into the centre of the school, which had suddenly assumed cathedral-like proportions. She spurred herself on with the knowledge that Carol would rush forward and take over if she faltered.

The ride walked round quarrelling mildly. Peter wanted to lead and so did Fiona. Miranda said firmly that the horses were to go first and Blackberry last. With a cross sigh Peter found himself a place in the middle.

Knowing the terrible boredom of just going round and round, Miranda had thought up a full lesson. She whirled her pupils into circles and serpentines, took them from turns on the forehand and reining back into riding without stirrups. They all seemed to know the aids for everything, but Marilyn had her legs too far forward and Fiona would look down. All went well until Patsy failed to get Blackberry on the right leg and then quite suddenly everyone began to give advice, including Carol from the gallery. Above the babble Jill's voice wailed that 'Surely it was time to jump?' The other riders immediately took up the cry. Peter dismounted and prepared to carry in the jumps.

'Wait a minute,' shouted Miranda above the uproar. 'Blackberry is very stiff and shoulder-in would improve her so we're going to practise it before we jump. Who knows the aids?' To her delight no one did, so she had the ride under control and listening again. When everyone, even Blackberry, had managed to do a few steps the riders sat patting their ponies and feeling quite pleased with themselves while Andrew, Chris and Carol helped to arrange cavalletti for trotting. After that they did grid-jumping and then a twisty little course. Miranda was just presenting imaginary rosettes to the winners when a flood of eleven o'clock pupils into the gallery told her that it was time to stop.

Outside it was still raining. The second ride took over the ponies but some of the horses weren't needed. The first ride wanted to book up and the second ride needed help with its stirrups and the Alsop girls said they couldn't put their horses away because their father was waiting. Miranda was struggling with the bookings with Stardust and Jasper's rains draped round her, when down the gallery steps, helped by her mother, came Liz.

'Well *done*, Miranda!' she called. 'That was fabulous, I couldn't have done it better myself.'

'Thank you,' said Miranda, still puzzling over the diary. 'Is it OK if I book a friend of Patsy's for next Sunday? It'll make ten but she's small and could ride Fudge.'

At that moment Sandra began to let out the most piercing screams. Her pony was stationary, but she had dropped her reins and was clinging to the pommel with both hands. Her face wore a look of terror. Miranda flung the diary at Liz and the reins of the horses to the nearest uninjured person, who, she saw with some surprise, was her own father, and rushed to Sandra's aid. 'What happened? What's the matter?'

'Punch made a horrid face at Filbert,' Sandra wailed tearfully, 'I thought he was going to eat us.'

Explaining that horses were not carnivorous and that if you hung on to your reins you could prevent their petty quarrels, Miranda led her across the yard. Order was beginning to prevail, the pupils were riding into the school, Liz had coped with the diary and Chris and Andrew were putting away the spare horses.

'I thought you weren't coming back until tonight, Daddy?' said Miranda accusingly. 'And I hope you don't want me because I'm terribly busy.'

'So I see,' said Mr Cummings. 'It's all right. You carry on, my business can wait.'

This was a very different ride to instruct. Some of them seemed so unsafe that Miranda didn't dare let them canter much or jump, but she organized races at the trot which were very popular. Sandra won the garden path competition, mostly because Filbert had the smallest and neatest hoofs, and announced that it was the loveliest ride she had ever had, which made up for a complaining girl who said she only liked hacking.

As they came out of the school, there was Miss Barnes looking unfamiliar in ordinary clothes.

'Oh, you're back,' said Miranda, feeling suddenly deflated.

'I flew,' explained Miss Barnes. 'It took no time at all. Oh

Miranda, you have been marvellous. I can't thank you enough. You've coped brilliantly.'

Miranda stood, uncertain what to say. 'Chris and Andrew did most of the work,' she answered. 'Now what about the ponies you don't need this afternoon, shall we turn them out?'

'No, you've done your bit and I promised your father I'd pack you off home as soon as you'd finished the lesson. I had a talk with him, but he'll tell you about that.'

Miranda walked home slowly; everything seemed so flat. Prep, television, she thought. Perhaps a hasty change into a dress, a smart lunch out. I like *doing* things, she thought. Her parents seemed pleased to see her.

'You really were in charge then, darling,' said her mother. 'Daddy was *most* impressed. I wish I'd come along to see you in all your glory, but I was in a panic over lunch with him turning up so unexpectedly.'

'I had a talk with Miss Barnes,' said Miranda's father. 'She was telling me that riding offers scope at various levels: stupid people just muddle through on instinct but to the intelligent it's an art with a history and a future like any other art; quite interesting. Anyway she wants to borrow you for the next few weekends while Liz is laid up. I said you'd be delighted to help out, and after that we might think about a horse.'

'A horse? Do you mean a horse for me?' asked Miranda in amazement.

'We'll think about it,' said Mr Cummings, 'but you'll have to promise not to become . . .

'Once I have one I'll never mention it,' promised Miranda throwing her arms round him and silencing him with a smacking kiss.

Jumper

Nicholas Kalashnikoff

No one doubted, least of all Jumper, that he was his master's darling and the favourite of the whole yard. Every motion he made had in it a proud consciousness of his superiority. Whether in rare repose or in action he always succeeded in drawing attention to himself. With the instinct of a showman he could display his grotesquely lean body, his heavy mane, and his showy trumpet of a tail so that they appeared inordinately graceful.

'You see how handsome I am,' his flashing eyes said.

But if Jumper was a favourite through a conscious exercise of his charms, he became a hero quite by accident when on a bitter night in January his fleet legs saved the master and the boy from certain death.

That day the master came to the stable early, and hitched Jumper to a light sleigh. Something special was afoot: his Sunday clothes, freshly scrubbed face, and neatly combed beard indicated a holiday outing of some sort.

The master was in gay spirits and sang as he worked on the leather fastenings. When the last buckle was in place the old man called to the boy, who also was dressed in his best, and in high good humour they climbed into the sleigh. Instinctively Jumper responded to the festive mood of his friends, as he carried them swiftly along the hard-packed road to a nearby village which he remembered visiting before. The contented voices and occasional laughter behind him, and the bright, clear sky above, lent strength to his legs. He was completely happy.

But when they arrived in the village Jumper, still hitched to the sleigh, was left standing under a rude shelter. No one came near to speak to him or to bring him food. Every now and then he neighed, demanding attention, but only some neighbouring horses responded half-heartedly. Despite the blanket with which he was covered he was chilled to the bone, and the hunger made him irritable. The aroma of fresh hay and the sound of a horse munching it reached him through a window of a nearby stable. From the street came the sounds of hilarious singing voices, the jangling of tambourines, the trampling of feet, and the screech of sleigh runners on snow.

Jumper had learned that holidays were easily distinguishable from work-days. There was always more noise of a different and happier kind, and very often the master's behaviour underwent a subtle change. He started the day joyously, and the joy apparently spread from his head to his feet, until they began to perform odd and unpredictable antics. On such occasions he was very affectionate and embarrassingly playful. 'You are my true friend, Jumper—my only friend,' he would insist loudly, flinging his arms around the colt's neck. Sometimes he wept, while at other times he amused himself by crawling under the colt's belly and tickling him.

Jumper's mind associated holidays with a foreign odour that mingled with the familiar scent of strong tobacco. He didn't like or understand it, but he had learned to regard it as a warning, and a signal for caution. When the master smelled and acted in this unaccountable manner Jumper knew he had to be patient and cautious.

On this occasion it was quite dark when he at last heard the familiar voices. They were some distance away, but they were coming nearer, accompanied by a large group of strangers.

'Hee-ee-ee-aa-a!' Jumper welcomed them, and pawed the snow to make them hurry.

There was no response except the humming of voices, as a dozen men assisted the master into the sleigh. He sprawled where they had flung him, and shouted unintelligible words. Then Jumper felt the reins grow taut.

'Giddap.'

Obedient as always, in spite of being hungry and neglected, Jumper swung carefully into the road. He knew it was the boy and not the master who held the reins. The hands were not as firm and experienced, and the young voice that reached him above the screech of the runners was affectionate and a little anxious. As Jumper gathered speed a warmth spread through his body, and the pleasant sensation made him forget his hunger.

The night was eerie. Except for an occasional grove of black trees the gently rolling earth was concealed under a covering of snow. A bright moon lighted the scene and cast weird and moving shadows.

Behind Jumper the master's hoarse voice rose in a song. Then the singing stopped, and was followed by snores.

'Faster, Jumper. Hurry home . . . home . . . home,' the boy was saying.

Jumper pricked up his ears. 'Home' was a word he knew well, and, besides, there was an urgent note in the thin voice that conveyed fear. He increased his pace. The road was familiar. Beyond the small woods, now visible in the distance, was a turn

'On, Jumper—on!'

and a slight incline. Then nothing but a straight, clear stretch to the village.

They reached the woods, passed through them, and were approaching the turn at the foot of the hill when an ear-splitting howl broke the quiet, and shadowy forms spread fan-wise behind the sleigh. Jumper did not need the boy's terrified cry nor the slap of the reins to start him sprinting at top speed. The hill up which he had to go was neither long nor steep, but it slowed him down, and gave the pursuing pack an advantage. At the crest he was sure that the wolves would close in on him in another second. Their triumphant howls sounded frighteningly near. The shadows took on a definite form, and acquired cruel, fiery pinpoints for eyes, and gaping jaws with lolling tongues.

Straining every muscle, now that the climb was over, Jumper raced down hill along the final stretch of road. The weeping boy frantically told him that the danger was great, and that only he— could save them. But this was not what he needed to give him confidence. He needed the master's calm voice and firm grip on the reins.

Try as he would, he could not gain on his pursuers. Several wolves were racing alongside the sleigh, waiting for an opportune moment to attack. Their pungent odour maddened him.

Then, when all hope seemed gone, the howling of the wolves, the anguished cries of the boy, and the swaying of the sleigh finally roused the master. Instantly he grasped the situation and took charge.

'On, Jumper—on, dear fellow. You can do it.'

His voice pleaded, but it was neither excited nor frightened. Jumper, taking new courage, found strength to redouble his efforts.

In the ensuing race everything was a wild confusion. To shake the pursuit the master tossed a blanket out of the sleigh. Several of the wolves attacked it hungrily, and in doing so fell behind. But one, an enormous beast, refused to be fooled. With great leaps he kept gaining on the sleigh in an effort to reach Jumper's head.

He seemed to know that his only hope of stopping them was in getting at the horse.

Closer he came, pounding the firm snow at Jumper's side. A little more, and he would make a lunge. Instinctively Jumper sensed the new danger and pressed forward, his long neck extended, his ears flattened, and every nerve poised for the attack.

'On, Jumper—on!'

The wolf now was aware of Jumper's determination, and with the village only a short distance away he had to take a desperate chance. He lunged, missed, crashed against the shaft, and fell under Jumper's speeding hoofs.

It all happened in a single terrifying moment. Jumper felt the bump and something crunching underfoot, heard the blood-chilling cry of pain, and then the gleeful howl of the pack as they fell on their crushed leader.

They were out of danger, but Jumper did not relax until he was well within the limits of the village. He pulled up at the gate of his own yard. The dog met and greeted him boisterously, and the horses in the stable neighed, welcoming him home.

Only now he realized how deathly tired he was. But before he could enjoy the snug comfort of the stable he had to submit to a thorough rub down. Then the master walked him up and down the yard until his overheated body had cooled down.

In the meantime the household came to life, and people gathered around to hear about the adventure, and to pay their respects to the hero.

'Jumper, you are a wonder! . . .'

'Jumper, you are the finest horse in all the world! . . .'

Delighted to be the centre of such admiring attention, he longed to prance and to show off, but he was too exhausted. Meekly he accepted the congratulations and affectionate pats, and settled under a warm blanket for the night.

He was content, not because he was a hero but because these people to whom he belonged loved him and in some unaccountable way were pleased.

JANE EYRE MEETS Mr ROCHESTER

Charlotte Brontë

Jane Eyre, a humble and plain orphan, has had a hard, though genteel, life in a charitable boarding school. She has found a new post as governess to a little girl, Adèle, and has gone to live at Thornfield Hall. Jane has not yet met the master, Mr Rochester.

The promise of a smooth career, which my first calm introduction to Thornfield Hall seemed to pledge, was not belied on a longer acquaintance with the place and its inmates. Mrs Fairfax turned out to be what she appeared, a placid-tempered, kind-natured woman, of competent education and average intelligence. My pupil was a lively child, who had been spoilt and indulged, and therefore was sometimes wayward; but as she was committed entirely to my care, and no injudicious interference from any quarter ever thwarted my plans for her improvement, she soon forgot her little freaks, and became obedient and teachable. She had no great talents, no marked traits of character, no peculiar development of feeling or taste which raised her one inch above the ordinary level of childhood; but neither had she any deficiency or vice which sunk her below it. She made reasonable progress, entertained for me a vivacious, though perhaps not very profound, affection; and by her simplicity, gay prattle, and efforts to please, inspired me, in return, with a degree of attachment sufficient to make us both content in each other's society.

This, *par parenthèse*, will be thought cool language by persons who entertain solemn doctrines about the angelic nature of children, and the duty of those charged with their education to conceive for them an idolatrous devotion: but I am not writing to flatter paternal egotism, to echo cant, or prop up humbug; I am merely telling the truth. I felt a conscientious solicitude for Adèle's welfare and progress, and a quiet liking to her little self; just as I cherished towards Mrs Fairfax a thankfulness for her kindness, and a pleasure in her society proportionate to the tranquil regard she had for me, and the moderation of her mind and character.

Anybody may blame me who likes, when I add further, that, now and then, when I took a walk by myself in the grounds; when I went down to the gates and looked through them along the road; or when, while Adèle played with her nurse, and Mrs Fairfax made jellies in the store-room, I climbed the three staircases, raised the trap-door of the attic, and having reached the leads, looked out afar over sequestered field and hill, and along dim sky-line—that then I longed for a power of vision which might overpass that limit; which might reach the busy world, towns, regions full of life I had heard of but never seen, that then I desired more of practical experience than I possessed; more of intercourse with my kind, of acquaintance with variety of character, than was here within my reach. I valued what was good in Mrs Fairfax and Adèle; but I believed in the existence of other and more vivid kinds of goodness, and what I believed in I wished to behold.

Who blames me? Many, no doubt; and I shall be called discontented. I could not help it: the restlessness was in my nature; it agitated me to pain sometimes. Then my sole relief was to walk along the corridor of the third story, backwards and forwards, safe in the silence and solitude of the spot, and allow my mind's eye to dwell on whatever bright visions rose before it—and, certainly, they were many and glowing; to let my heart be heaved by the exultant movement, which, while it swelled it in trouble, expanded it with life; and, best of all, to open my inward ear to a tale that was never ended—a tale my imagination created, and narrated continuously; quickened with all of incident, life, fire, feeling, that I desired and had not in my actual existence.

It is in vain to say human beings ought to be satisfied with tranquillity: they must have action; and they will make it if they cannot find it. Millions are condemned to a stiller doom than mine, and millions are in silent revolt against their lot. Nobody knows how many rebellions besides political rebellions ferment in the masses of life which people earth. Women are supposed to be very calm generally: but women feel just as men feel; they need exercise for their faculties, and a field for their efforts as much as their brothers do; they suffer from too rigid a constraint, too absolute a stagnation, precisely as men would suffer; and it is narrowed-minded in their more privileged fellow-creatures to say that they ought to confine themselves to making puddings and knitting stockings, to playing on the piano and embroidering bags. It is thoughtless to condemn them, or laugh at them, if they seek to do more or learn more than custom has pronounced necessary for their sex.

When thus alone, I not unfrequently heard Grace Poole's laugh: the same peal, the same low, slow ha! ha! which, when first heard, had thrilled me: I heard, too, her eccentric murmurs; stranger than her laugh. There were days when she was quite silent; but there were others when I could not account for the sounds she made. Sometimes I saw her: she would come out of her room with a basin, or a plate, or a tray in her hand, go down to the kitchen and shortly return, generally (oh, romantic reader, forgive me for telling the plain truth!) bearing a pot of porter. Her appearance always acted as a damper to the curiosity raised by her oral oddities:

hard-featured and staid, she had no point to which interest could attach. I made some attempts to draw her into conversation, but she seemed a person of few words: a monosyllabic reply usually cut short every effort of that sort.

The other members of the household, viz., John and his wife, Leah the housemaid, and Sophie the French nurse, were decent people; but in no respect remarkable: with Sophie I used to talk French, and sometimes I asked her questions about her native country; but she was not of a descriptive or narrative turn, and generally gave such vapid and confused answers as were calculated rather to check than encourage inquiry.

October, November, December passed away. One afternoon in January, Mrs Fairfax had begged a holiday for Adèle, because she had a cold; and, as Adèle seconded the request with an ardour that reminded me how precious occasional holidays had been to me in my own childhood, I accorded it, deeming that I did well in show-ing pliability on the point. It was a fine, calm day, though very cold; I was tired of sitting still in the library through a whole long morning: Mrs Fairfax had just written a letter which was waiting to be posted, so I put on my bonnet and cloak and volunteered to carry it to Hay; the distance, two miles, would be a pleasant winter afternoon walk. Having seen Adèle comfortably seated in her little chair by Mrs Fairfax's parlour fireside, and given her best wax doll (which I usually kept enveloped in silver paper in a drawer) to play with, and a story-book for change of amusement; and having replied to her 'Revenez bientôt, ma bonne amie, ma chère Mdlle Jeannette,' with a kiss, I set out.

The ground was hard, the air was still, my road was lonely; I walked fast till I got warm, and then I walked slowly to enjoy and analyse the species of pleasure brooding for me in the hour and situation. It was three o'clock; the church bell tolled as I passed under the belfry; the charm of the hour lay in its approaching dimness, in the low-gliding and pale-beaming sun. I was a mile from Thornfield, in a lane noted for wild roses in summer, for nuts and blackberries in autumn, and even now possessing a few coral treasures in hips and haws, but whose best winter delight lay in its utter solitude and leafless repose. If a breath of air stirred, it made no sound here; for there was not a holly, not an evergreen to rustle, and the stripped hawthorn and hazel bushes were as still as the white, worn stones which causewayed the middle of the path. Far and wide, on each side, there were only fields, where no cattle now browsed; and the little brown birds, which stirred occasionally in the hedge, looked like single russet leaves that had forgotten to drop.

This lane inclined up-hill all the way to Hay: having reached the middle, I sat down on a stile which led thence into a field. Gathering my mantle about me, and sheltering my hands in my muff, I did not feel the cold, though it froze keenly; as was attested by a sheet of ice covering the causeway, where a little brooklet, now congealed, had overflowed after a rapid thaw some days since. From my seat I could look down on Thornfield: the grey and battlemented hall was the principal object in the vale below me; its woods and dark rookery rose against the west. I lingered till the sun went down amongst the trees, and sank crimson and clear behind them. I then turned eastward.

On the hill-top above me sat the rising moon; pale yet as a cloud, but brightening momently: she looked over Hay, which, half lost in trees, sent up a blue smoke from its few chimneys; it was yet a mile distant, but in the absolute hush I could hear plainly its thin murmurs of life. My ear too felt the flow of currents; in what dales and depths I could not tell: but there were many hills beyond Hay, and doubtless many becks threading their passes. That evening calm betrayed alike the tinkle of the nearest streams, the sough of the most remote.

A rude noise broke on these fine ripplings and whisperings, at once so far away and so clear: a positive tramp, tramp; a metallic clatter, which effaced the soft wave-wanderings; as, in a picture, the solid mass of a crag, or the rough boles of a great oak drawn in dark and strong on the foreground, efface the aërial distance of azure hill, sunny horizon, and blended clouds.

The din was on the causeway: a horse was coming; the windings of the lane yet hid it, but it approached. I was just leaving the stile; yet, as the path was narrow, I sat still to let it go by. In those days I was young, and all sorts of fancies bright and dark tenanted my mind: the memories of nursery stories were there amongst other rubbish; and when they recurred, maturing youth added to them a vigour and vividness beyond what childhood could give. As this horse approached, and as I watched for it to appear through the dusk, I remembered certain of Bessie's tales, wherein figured a North-of-England spirit, called a 'Gytrash'; which, in the form of horse, mule, or large dog, haunted solitary ways, and sometimes came upon belated travellers, as this horse was now coming upon me.

It was very near, but not yet in sight; when, in addition to the tramp, tramp, I heard a rush under the hedge, and close down by the hazel stems glided a great dog, whose black and white colour made him a distinct object against the trees. It was exactly one mask of Bessie's Gytrash—a lion-like creature with long hair and a huge head: it passed me, however, quietly enough; not staying to look up, with strange pretercanine eyes, in my face, as I half expected it would. The horse followed—a tall steed, and on its back a rider. The man, the human being, broke the spell at once. Nothing ever rode the Gytrash: it was always alone; and goblins, to my notions, though they might tenant the dumb carcasses of beasts, could scarce covet shelter in the common-place human form. No Gytrash was this—only a traveller taking the short cut to Millcote. He passed, and I went on; a few steps, and I turned: a sliding sound and an exclamation of 'What the deuce is to do now?' and a clattering tumble, arrested my attention. Man and horse were down; they had slipped on the sheet of ice which glazed the causeway. The dog came bounding back, and seeing his master in a predicament, and hearing the horse groan, barked till the evening hills echoed the sound, which was deep in proportion to his magnitude. He snuffed round the prostrate group, and then he ran up to me; it was all he could do—there was no other help at hand to summon. I obeyed him, and walked down to the traveller, by this time struggling himself free of his steed. His efforts were so vigorous, I thought he could not be much hurt; but I asked him the question:—

'Are you injured, sir?'

I think he was swearing, but am not certain; however, he was pronouncing some formula which prevented him from replying to me directly.

'Can I do anything?' I asked again.

'You must just stand on one side,' he answered as he rose, first to his knees, and then to his feet. I did; whereupon began a heaving, stamping, clattering process, accompanied by a barking and baying which removed me effectually some yards distance; but I would not be driven quite away till I saw the event. This was finally fortunate; the horse was re-established, and the dog was silenced with a 'Down, Pilot!' The traveller, now stooping, felt his foot and leg, as if trying whether they were sound; apparently something ailed them, for he halted to the stile whence I had just risen, and sat down.

I was in the mood for being useful, or at least officious, I think, for I now drew near him again.

'If you are hurt, and want help, sir, I can fetch someone either from Thornfield Hall or from Hay.'

'Thank you; I shall do: I have no broken bones—only a sprain;' and again he stood up and tried his foot, but the result extorted an involuntary 'Ugh!'

Something of daylight still lingered, and the moon was waxing bright: I could see him plainly. His figure was enveloped in a riding cloak, fur collared, and steel clasped; its details were not apparent, but I traced the general points of middle height, and considerable breadth of chest. He had a dark face, with stern features and a heavy brow; his eyes and gathered eyebrows looked ireful and thwarted just now; he was past youth, but had not reached middle age; perhaps he might be thirty-five. I felt no fear of him, and but little shyness. Had he been a handsome, heroic-looking young

The rider passed, and I went on.

gentleman, I should not have dared to stand thus questioning him against his will, and offering my services unasked. I had hardly ever seen a handsome youth; never in my life spoken to one. I had a theoretical reverence and homage for beauty, elegance, gallantry, fascination; but had I met those qualities incarnate in masculine shape, I should have known instinctively that they neither had nor could have sympathy with anything in me, and should have shunned them as one would fire, lightning, or anything else that is bright but antipathetic.

If even this stranger had smiled and been good-humoured to me when I addressed him; if he had put off my offer of assistance gaily and with thanks, I should have gone on my way and not felt any vocation to renew inquiries: but the frown, the roughness of the traveller set me at my ease: I retained my station when he waved to me to go, and announced:—

'I cannot think of leaving you, sir, at so late an hour, in this solitary lane, till I see you are fit to mount your horse.'

He looked at me when I said this: he had hardly turned his eyes in my direction before.

'I should think you ought to be at home yourself,' said he, 'if you have a home in this neighbourhood; where do you come from?'

'From just below; and I am not at all afraid of being out late when it is moonlight: I will run over to Hay for you with pleasure, if you wish it; indeed, I am going there to post a letter.'

'You live just below—do you mean at that house with the battlements?'—pointing to Thornfield Hall, on which the moon cast a hoary gleam, bringing it out distinct and pale from the woods, that, by contrast with the western sky, now seemed one mass of shadow.

'Yes, sir.'

'Whose house is it?'

'Mr Rochester's.'

'Do you know Mr Rochester?'

'No, I have never seen him.'

'He is not resident, then?'

'No.'

'Can you tell me where he is?'

'I cannot.'

'You are not a servant at the hall, of course. You are . . .' He stopped, ran his eye over my dress, which, as usual, was quite simple: a black merino cloak, a black beaver bonnet; neither of them half fine enough for a lady's maid. He seemed puzzled to decide what I was: I helped him.

'I am the governess.'

'Ah, the governess!' he repeated; 'deuce take me, if I had not forgotten! The governess!' and again my raiment underwent scrutiny. In two minutes he rose from the stile: his face expressed pain when he tried to move.

'I cannot commission you to fetch help,' he said; 'but you may help me a little yourself, if you will be so kind.'

'Yes, sir.'

'You have not an umbrella that I can use as a stick?'

'No.'

'Try to get hold of my horse's bridle and lead him to me: you are not afraid?'

I should have been afraid to touch a horse when alone, but when told to do it, I was disposed to obey. I put down my muff on the stile, and went up to the tall steed; I endeavoured to catch the bridle, but it was a spirited thing, and would not let me come near its head; I made effort on effort, though in vain: meantime, I was mortally afraid of its trampling forefeet. The traveller waited and watched for some time, and at last he laughed.

'I see,' he said, 'the mountain will never be brought to Mahomet, so all you can do is to aid Mahomet to go to the mountain; I must beg of you to come here.'

I came. 'Excuse me,' he continued, 'necessity compels me to make you useful.' He laid a heavy hand on my shoulder, and leaning on me with some stress, limped to his horse. Having once caught the bridle, he mastered it directly, and sprang to his saddle; grimacing grimly as he made the effort, for it wrenched his sprain.

'Now,' said he, releasing his under lip from a hard bite, 'just hand me my whip; it lies there under the hedge.'

I sought it and found it.

'Thank you; now make haste with the letter to Hay, and return as fast as you can.'

A touch of a spurred heel made his horse first start and rear, and then bound away; the dog rushed in his traces: all three vanished,

> 'Like heath that, in the wilderness,
> The wild wind whirls away.'

I took up my muff and walked on. The incident had occurred and was gone for me: it *was* an incident of no moment, no romance, no interest, in a sense; yet it marked with change one single hour of a monotonous life. My help had been needed and claimed; I had given it: I was pleased to have done something; trivial, transitory though the deed was, it was yet an active thing, and I was weary of an existence all passive. The new face, too, was like a new picture introduced to the gallery of memory; and it was dissimilar to all the others hanging there: firstly, because it was masculine; and, secondly, because it was dark, strong, and stern. I had it still before me when I entered Hay, and slipped the letter into the post-office; I saw it as I walked fast down hill all the way home. When I came to the stile, I stopped a minute, looked round and listened, with an idea that a horse's hoofs might ring on the causeway again, and that a rider in a cloak, and a Gytrash-like Newfoundland dog, might be again apparent: I saw only the hedge and a pollard willow before me, rising up still and straight to meet the moonbeams; I heard only the faintest waft of wind roaming fitful among the trees round Thornfield, a mile distant; and when I glanced down in the direction of the murmur, my eye, traversing the hallfront, caught a light kindling in a window: it reminded me that I was late, and I hurried on.

I did not like re-entering Thornfield. To pass its threshold was to return to stagnation; to cross the silent hall, to ascend the darksome staircase, to seek my own lonely little room, and then to meet tranquil Mrs Fairfax, and spend the long winter evening with her, and her only, was to quell wholly the faint excitement wakened by my walk—to slip again over my faculties the viewless fetters of an uniform and too still existence; of an existence whose very privileges of security and ease I was becoming incapable of appreciating. What good it would have done me at that time to have been tossed in the storms of an uncertain struggling life, and to have been taught by rough and bitter experience to long for the calm amidst which I now repined! Yes, just as much good as it would do a man tired of sitting still in a 'too easy chair' to take a long walk: and just as natural was the wish to stir, under my circumstances, as it would be under his.

I lingered at the gates; I lingered on the lawn; I paced backwards and forwards on the pavement: the shutters of the glass door were closed; I could not see into the interior; and both my eyes and spirit seemed drawn from the gloomy house—from the grey hollow filled with rayless cells, as it appeared to me—to that sky expanded before me—a blue sea absolved from taint of cloud; the moon ascending it in solemn march; her orb seeming to look up as she left the hill tops, from behind which she had come, far and farther below her, and aspired to the zenith, midnight-dark, in its fathomless depth and measureless distance: and for those trembling stars that followed her course; they made my heart tremble, my veins glow when I viewed them. Little things recall us to earth: the clock struck in the hall; that sufficed; I turned from moon and stars, opened a side-door, and went in.

The hall was not dark, nor yet was it lit, only by the high-hung bronze lamp: a warm glow suffused both it and the lower steps of the oak staircase. This ruddy shine issued from the great dining-room, whose two-leaved door stood open, and showed a genial fire in the grate, glancing on marble hearth and brass fire-irons, and revealing purple draperies and polished furniture, in the most pleasant radiance. It revealed, too, a group near the mantelpiece: I had scarcely caught it, and scarcely become aware of a cheerful mingling of voices, when the door closed.

I hastened to Mrs Fairfax's room: there was a fire there too, but no candle, and no Mrs Fairfax. Instead, all alone, sitting upright on the rug, and gazing with gravity at the blaze, I beheld a great black and white long-haired dog, just like the Gytrash of the lane. It was so like it that I went forward and said,—

'Pilot,' and the thing got up and came to me and snuffed me. I caressed him, and he wagged his great tail: but he looked an eerie creature to be alone with, and I could not tell whence he had come. I rang the bell, for I wanted a candle; and I wanted, too, to get an account of this visitant. Leah entered.

'What dog is this?'

'He came with master.'

'With whom?'

'With master—Mr Rochester—he is just arrived.'

'Indeed! and is Mrs Fairfax with him?'

'Yes, and Miss Adela; they are in the dining-room, and John is gone for a surgeon: for master has had an accident; his horse fell and his ankle is sprained.'

'Did the horse fall in Hay Lane?'

'Yes, coming down the hill; it slipped on some ice.'

'Ah! Bring me a candle, will you, Leah?'

Leah brought it; she entered, followed by Mrs Fairfax, who repeated the news; adding that Mr Carter the surgeon was come, and was now with Mr Rochester: then she hurried out to give orders about tea, and I went upstairs to take off my things.

THE
PONY EXPRESS

Mark Twain

The American Express Postal Service was started in 1860. In spite of the five-dollars-an-ounce charge, the scheme was a financial failure and lasted only eighteen months.

In a little while all interest was taken up in stretching our necks and watching for the 'pony-rider'—the fleet messenger who sped across the Continent from St Joe to Sacramento, carrying letters nineteen hundred miles in eight days!

The pony-rider was usually a little bit of a man, brimful of spirit and endurance. No matter what time of the day or night his watch came on, and no matter whether it was winter or summer, raining, snowing, hailing or sleeting, or whether his 'beat' was a level straight road or a crazy trail over mountain crags and precipices, or whether it led through peaceful regions or regions that swarmed with hostile Indians, he must always be ready to leap into the saddle and be off like the wind!

There was no idling-time for a pony-rider on duty. He rode fifty miles without stopping, by daylight, moonlight, starlight, or through the blackness of darkness—just as it happened. He rode a splendid horse that was born for a racer and fed and lodged like a gentleman; kept him at his utmost speed for ten miles, and then, as he came crashing up to the station where stood two men holding fast a fresh, impatient steed, the transfer of rider and mail bag was made in the twinkling of an eye, and away flew the eager pair and were out of sight before the spectator could get hardly the ghost of a look. Both rider and horse went 'flying light', the rider's dress was thin, and fitted close . . . he carried no arms—he carried nothing that was not absolutely necessary, for even the postage on his literary freight was worth *five dollars a letter*. He got but little frivolous correspondence to carry—his bag had letters in it, mostly. His horse was stripped of all unnecessary weight, too. He wore a little wafer of a racing saddle, and no visible blanket. He wore light shoes, or none at all. The little flat mail-pockets strapped under the rider's thighs would each hold about the bulk of a child's primer. They held many an important business chapter and news-paper letter, but these were written on paper as airy and thin as gold-leaf, nearly, and thus bulk and weight were economized.

The Stage Coach travelled about a hundred to a hundred and twenty-five miles a day (twenty-four hours), and the pony-rider about two hundred and fifty. There were about eighty pony-riders in the saddle all the time, night and day, stretching in a long, scattering procession from Missouri to California, forty flying eastwards, and forty towards the west, and among them making four hundred gallant horses earn a stirring livelihood and see a great deal of scenery every single day in the year.

We had had a consuming desire, from the beginning, to see a pony-rider, but somehow all that passed us and all that met us managed to streak by in the night, and so we heard only a whiz and a hail, and the swift phantom of the desert was gone before we could get our heads out of the windows. But now we were

The man and horse burst past us and winged away like a belated fragment of a storm.

expecting one along every moment, and would see him in broad daylight. Presently the driver exclaims: 'Here he comes!'

. . . Away across the endless dead level of the prairie a black speck appears against the sky, and it is plain that it moves. . . In a second or two it becomes a horse and rider, rising and falling, rising and falling—sweeping towards us nearer and nearer—growing more and more distinct, more and more sharply defined—nearer and still nearer, and the flutter of hoofs comes faintly to the ear—another instant a whoop and a hurrah, from our upper deck, a wave of the rider's hand, but no reply, and man and horse burst past our excited faces, and go winging away like a belated fragment of a storm!

FOLLYFOOT FARM

Monica Dickens

Follyfoot Farm is a home of rest for horses, which viewers of the television series based on the books may be familiar with.

Steve works and lives at Follyfoot; so does Dora, and Callie whose stepfather the Colonel runs the place.

Since last year, when Cobbler's Dream had captured a thief and saved his own life by clearing the impossible spiked park fence, Steve had begun to jump him again.

The Cobbler had once been a famous juvenile show jumper. When the girl who trained him grew too big, he was bought by a hard-handed child who wanted a vehicle for winning championships, rather than a pony to love. Steve worked for her father. He had to see the marvellous pony making mistakes because of the child. Finally he had to see him blinded in one eye by a blow from a whip. He had taken him away then, and brought him to the farm, and they had both stayed here.

The other eye became half blind, but Cobby had adapted so well that he was almost as surefooted as before, and his fantastic leap over the Manor park fence had proved that he had acquired some kind of sixth sense to judge a jump. He would jump almost anything if you took him slow and let him get the feel of it.

Steve put up some sheep hurdles in one of the fields, and he and Dora made a brush jump with gorse stuck through a ladder. Most of the other horses were too old and stiff to jump, so Dora was teaching the mule Willy, who had no mouth at all, and either rushed his jumps or stopped dead and let Dora jump without him.

Steve and Dora had the afternoon off, so they took the Cobbler and Willy through the woods on the other side of their hill, where there were fallen tree trunks across the rides. Cobby jumped them all without checking his canter, bunching his muscles, arching his back, smoothly away on his landing stride with his ears pricked for the next jump. Willy jumped the smaller trees. If they did not reach right across the path, he whipped round them with his mouth open, yawing at the bit. If they were too big, he dug in his toes, and Dora had to get off and lead him over. He would jump his front end, stand and stare with the tree trunk under his middle, and then heave his rear end over with a grunt like an old man getting out of the bath.

Near the far edge of the wood, Cobby shortened his stride, trotting with his head high, and turned to the side, listening.

'What does he hear?'

There were people who came to the woods with guns and shot at rabbits and foxes and anything that moved. Sometimes they shot each other.

Steve and Dora both stopped and listened. Only the continual sigh of the breeze moving through the tops of the tall trees.

'I don't hear anything.'

'Cobb does. His hearing is sharper now that he can't see much. So is his nose.'

The chestnut pony had his nostrils squared, as if he were getting a message.

Steve pushed him on, over two more jumps, but he slowed down again, listening.

'There is something. Let's go the way he wants to.'

They rode out of the wood and along the edge of a cornfield. In a grassy lane beyond the hedge, a grey horse was grazing in a patch of clover.

It was a calm horse. It stood still and exchanged blown breaths with Cobby, and then the ritual squeal and striking out. The mule laid back his long ears like a rabbit and said nothing. He distrusted strange horses. When he was turned out with a new one, he would communicate for the first two weeks only with his heels.

The grey horse wore a head collar. It let Steve slip his belt through the noseband, and trotted quietly beside Cobby back to the farm.

The Colonel did not recognize the horse. 'Someone will be worried though,' he said. 'It's a nice-looking horse and well kept.' The grey looked like a hunter, coat clean and silky, whiskers and heels neatly trimmed, tail and mane properly pulled. 'Better ring the police, Steve.'

Sergeant Oddie said at once, 'Oh no! Not that grey again. Look here, I've got the big wedding to worry about, two men off on a drug raid, a three-car crash on the Marston road and some nippers have set fire to the bus shelter. That horse is the last thing I need.'

'It's been out before?'

'Time and again. The neighbours are on my neck about it day and night. Regular wasps' nest, it's stirred up. Here, I'll give you Mrs Jordan's number, and I wish you'd tell her how to build a fence to keep a horse in.'

'But we have,' Mrs Jordan said. 'It's not our fault, or the horse's. Oh dear. I'll come and get him.'

'I'll ride him home, if you could bring me back,' Steve said.

The grey horse looked like a lovely ride, and he was, well schooled, a beautiful mover, quickly responsive, but you could stop him by flexing your wrist.

Steve was surprised when he saw where he came from. The Jordans's house on the edge of a small town had obviously once stood in fields, but new houses had been built close all round, and the fenced paddock was not much bigger than a tennis court. The fence was strong and high enough. The gate looked sound.

'It's they who are doing it,' Mrs Jordan told Steve. 'They used to do it at night, but they're getting bolder now, and they've begun to do it in the daytime if I go out.'

'Who do what?'

'The neighbours. The people in that pink house with gnomes in the garden and plastic flowers in the windowboxes. They open the gate and let David out, then they quickly ring the police and complain that the horse is loose and trampling on people's gardens.'

'How do you know?'

'Oh, I know all right.' Mrs Jordan was a faded, once beautiful woman, with lines of work and worry round her big sad eyes and her full, drooping mouth. 'When the police were here last time— they were nice enough at first, but now they're getting fed up—I saw that front curtain move, and another time, the woman was standing in the window, blatantly watching and laughing.'

'Why don't you padlock the gate?'

'We have. But she somehow prised the rails loose at night, and then got them back up after she'd chased David out. It's her, not her husband. He's not so bad, but she's a fanatic. She hates horses, because she thinks they're something that rich people have. Rich! She's much better off than us. Her husband is a plumber. But she's the kind of person who can't stand anybody having something she hasn't got, even if she doesn't want it. She wants to buy that piece of land where David's paddock is, and breed chinchillas.'

'Chinchillas!' She looked at Steve with her tragic eyes. 'On what was once our back lawn, where the girls used to have their summer house and swings.'

After they had put the grey horse away in the open shed in the corner of the paddock, Mrs Jordan made Steve go into the house for something to eat before she would drive him home. She seemed lonely, glad of someone to talk to. He sat in a comfortable shabby armchair and listened. He had learned from the Colonel that if you will only shut up and listen, people will tell you things they won't tell to someone who is trying to keep up their end of the conversation.

It was a tragic story. Her husband had been a trainer and show judge. A car crash had killed their younger daughter and left him unable to work for a long time. They had to borrow money on their house and land. Their other daughter Nancy left college and went to work, and Mrs Jordan got a job in an old people's nursing home, but they could not pay the interest on the mortgage. Four acres of their land had been seized, and sold to the builder who had put up all these ugly little houses where the pastures and stables had been.

All the horses had gone, of course, except David, who had belonged to the dead girl.

'How could we part with him? Nancy rides him occasionally, but she has so little time, and she's always so tired. We're all tired, Steve. My husband has a part-time job now, but it doesn't pay much, and he's not well enough even for that. I lie awake night after night wondering what will happen when they take our house in the end and that horrible woman gets David's paddock—our last bit of land—and keeps her wretched chinchillas in prison cages.'

'Death row.' Steve nodded. 'Only one way out.'

'I hate her.'

'So do I,' Steve said with feeling, although he had never seen the woman with the plaster gnomes in her garden.

'Sergeant Oddie rang me up after he talked to you, and said if the horse got out again, we'd have to get rid of him.'

'I thought the sergeant was so busy,' Steve said.

'Not too busy to tell me *that*. And that's what that woman wants.'

'Why don't you turn her in?'

'I can't prove it. She's cunning. I've never been able to catch her.'

'Mind if I try?'

'It's not much use.'

'You all go out some night. Make a big noise about driving off in the car, so she knows. But I'll be here. I'll be in the shed with David.'

No need to tell the Colonel. Not that he would mind, but . . . no need to worry him.

'I can't risk any trouble,' he had said. He had his own problems with neighbours. 'We've got to stay on the right side of the law.'

Well, this was the right side, but . . . no need to tell him, Steve thought.

Steve did not tell Dora either, or anyone at the farm.

The next evening, after the horses had been bedded down and fed and watered, Steve asked if he could use the truck.

'All right,' the Colonel said. 'What for?'

'I'm going out.'

'Who with?' Dora's rumpled head came over the top of a stable door, where she was rubbing liniment on Dolly's chronic foreleg.

'A girl I know.'

'You don't know any girls.'

'How do you know?'

'You'd tell me.'

Dora rested her chin on the door. Old Doll put her head out beside her and laid back her ears at Steve. She had once been so badly abused by a man that she still only liked women. It was Dolly who had kicked the Colonel in the head.

'You'd be the last person I'd tell.' Steve laughed. 'You'd want to come too, and sit between us and talk all through the film.'

'Are you going to a film?'

'Yes.'

'I want to come too.'

'No.'

'What's her name?'

'Nancy.'

'I don't believe you're going out with a girl,' Dora said, but more doubtfully.

When he drove off, Dora was sitting on the wall by the gate, polishing a snaffle bit and kicking her heels against the bricks. Her face looked closed and sulky, her lower lip stuck out. Steve waved. She did not wave back or look up.

Mr Jordan was a grey, stooped man, with a mouth stiffened by pain of body and heart. Nancy was a bright-cheeked girl with thick bouncing hair and good legs, the kind of girl Steve would have gone to the cinema with if he had been going to the cinema with a girl.

They made the necessary noise about leaving. Racing the engine, slamming the doors, going back for a coat, calling out that they would be late.

'The film starts at eight!' Mrs Jordan called from behind the wheel, to let her neighbours know that they would be away at least two hours.

In the pink house with the window-boxes full of impossible flowers that never bloomed in the spring, nor even in England at all, a shadow moved behind the curtain.

Steve sat in the straw of the open shed and talked to the grey horse and thought about things long gone. Other nights of adventure when you waited, with your nerves on edge and your hair pricking on your scalp. The night when he had stolen Cobby away to safety with sacking wrapped round his hooves.

About nine-thirty, with the family still in the cinema, David raised his head from his hay and swung his small ears forward. Steve listened, holding his breath.

Were there footsteps on the soft ground? Did the night breeze shiver that bush, or was someone behind it? Steve watched, motionless in the dark corner.

David, who liked people, walked out of the shed in a rustle of straw and into the paddock. A thick woman in tight pants was climbing through the fence. She held out her hand as the horse went up to her and gave him something. In the still night, Steve heard his teeth on the sugar. He followed the woman as she moved quickly across the small paddock to the gate.

Steve waited. It was too dark to see much. She had her back to him, but he heard the clink of the chain on the gate. He got up quickly, went silently up behind her and said in her ear, 'Can I help you?'

'Oh my God!' The woman jumped round with a hand on the ample shelf over her heart. As she moved, Steve was almost sure that he saw her fist clench over a piece of metal that could be a key.

'What do you want?' She was breathing fast, and he could see behind her dark fringe tomorrow's imagined headlines chasing each other through her head.

WOMAN FOUND STRANGLED. HOUSEWIFE KILLED IN NEIGHBOUR'S GARDEN. SUBURBAN SLAYING, MYSTERY GROWS.

'What you—what are you doing here?' The woman must be bold to have done as much as she had, but her mouth was twitching now with nerves, because Steve was looming over her threateningly.

'I'm a friend of the family,' he said. 'The horse looked as if he might be headed for colic, so I was watching he didn't lie down. Someone might have slipped him something. People round here have been making trouble, you wouldn't believe it.'

'Oh, I know.' The woman relaxed. 'The poor Jordans, it's dreadful for them, on top of all their bad luck. I try to keep an eye on things for them, when they're not here. That's why I came out, to check on the gate fastening.'

'Oh, I see,' said Steve. 'To check the gate.'

'That's right.' The woman started to move towards her house. 'To check the gate.'

'You keep an eye on things. That's nice.'

'Well,' she said, 'one does what one can. We were all put in this world to help each other, that's what I say.'

'Oh so do I.' With a hand on the neck of the grey horse, Steve

A grey horse was grazing in a patch of clover.

watched the woman climb through the paddock fence and go back into her own house, waggling her bottom righteously, like a good neighbour who has done her duty.

'So that's what you ought to do,' Steve told the Jordans.

They looked at each other. 'I'm no hand with electricity.' The father looked baffled.

'I'll do it.'

'She'll see you.' Mrs Jordan glanced towards the pink house. 'She sees everything.'

'I'll do it after dark. There's no moon. She won't try anything on tomorrow after the scare she got tonight. If I use a rubber hammer, I can get the insulators on without making any noise, and I'll put the battery behind the shed so she won't hear it ticking.'

Next day, Steve offered to do Anna's shopping, and bought the battery and thin wire and the insulators while he was in town.

In the evening, when he asked casually for the truck, Dora did not ask him where he was going. She had not allowed herself to ask him about the film last night, which was a good thing because he had forgotten to find out what was on.

At the Jordans he rigged up two strands of electric wire close to the paddock rails where it could not be seen. Then he turned on the battery and waited at the side of the shed.

He chirruped softly. The horse came up to the rail, put out his nose, then jumped back and snorted.

'Sorry, David.' The grey horse stood in the middle of the paddock, looking very offended. 'I had to test it.'

Two nights Steve waited in the straw, with the battery ticking softly on the other side of the shed. He dozed and woke and dozed, but he was sleepy in the daytime, and Dora made embittered remarks about people who stayed out too late with girls.

Why not tell her and let her watch with him in the shed and share the adventure? Because she kept saying things like, 'When are we going to see this famous Nancy? Not that I care. Or is she too hideous to bring here?' Talking herself out of the adventure.

'She's gorgeous, as a matter of fact,' Steve said, irritated. 'Marvellous legs.' He winked at Slugger.

'Can't go far wrong with that.' Slugger winked at the horse he was grooming. ' "When judgin' a woman *or* a horse, you gotta look at the legs, of course." That's what me grandad used to say.'

'Anyone can have good legs.' Dora's, which were rather muscular and boyish, were covered in torn faded blue jeans, which she refused to let Anna patch, or hem at the bottom.

On the third night, Steve went to bed early—'What's the matter? She sick of you already?'—and got up again at midnight after everyone was asleep. He stopped the truck before he got to the Jordans', and walked quietly through what was left of their garden and round the side of the house to the shed.

When he whispered, to show the horse he was there, a voice answered him.

'Nancy?'

'I couldn't sleep.' She was lying covered with straw, only her face and hair showing.

'I wanted to do this alone.' Steve came in and sat beside her.

'Why?'

'It was my idea.'

'It's my horse.'

They lay side by side in the straw and talked softly. Nancy told him about the man at work she thought she was in love with. Girls always started to tell you about other men just when you were getting interested.

Steve wriggled his fingers through the straw, trying to find her hand.

'But he's almost old enough to be my father,' Nancy said.

Steve took her hand, and at that moment there was a blood-curdling scream from the other side of the paddock.

David jumped. Steve and Nancy scrambled up. The plump woman in the tight pants was sitting on the ground with her arms wrapped round herself like a straitjacket, rocking backwards and forwards and moaning.

'It can't have been that bad.' Steve and Nancy slid carefully under the fence and went across to her.

'Oh, I'm killed,' the woman moaned. 'Oh, my heart—'

'Just going to check up on the gate, eh?'

She looked up at Steve, her hair, disordered from bed, standing wildly up as if the electricity had gone right through it.

'Yes,' she croaked. 'One does what one can. But there are some people—' she glowered up at Nancy, still rocking and holding herself as if she might fall apart—'some people who don't know the meaning of the word gratitude.'

After this, Steve did take Nancy to the farm at the weekend, to show her the horses.

The Colonel was delighted with her. He conducted her round himself, hands behind his back, cap over his eyes, very military. Callie was pleased with her because she asked the right questions and said, 'How lucky for Miss to have Callie to look after her,' when they visited Miss America, queening it in the orchard so that the other horses would not disturb the healing wound.

Dora was rather gruff. She took a long look at Nancy's legs, then went off to greet a family of visitors and became very busy giving them a conducted tour of all the horses.

The family, who had only come to see the donkey which had once belonged to their Uncle Fred, kept saying, 'Well, better be getting along,' but Dora dragged them on from horse to horse, so as not to have to talk to Nancy.

Soon after this, Steve got a letter from Mrs Jordan. Their telephone had been cut off because they couldn't pay the bill.

The plump woman and the plumber had put the pink house up for sale and gone away. Two days later—'*If she'd only waited two days, she could have had her revenge in chinchillas*'—Mr Jordan was asked by a friend in Australia to go out and join him on the ranch where he was breeding horses.

'*So we're all going, Steve. A new life. Free passage out if we stay two years, and they can have this poor house and make it into a pub or a Bingo hall or whatever they want. No regrets. Except about David. We sail next week. Please find him a good home and use the sale money for the farm. The best home only. I trust you.'*

David could stay out at night, so the Colonel let Steve bring him to the farm.

'What's *that*?' Dora made a face at the grey as he backed neatly out of the horse box and stood with his fine head up and his mane and tail blowing like an Arab, staring at some of the old horses, who were drawn up in the field, all pointing the same way like sheep, observing him.

'It's the horse we found on the other side of the wood. You know.'

'Nancy's horse.'

'Yes,' Steve said. 'They're—'

'It's too long in the back,' Dora said, 'and I don't like the look of that near hock.'

'They're going to Australia. With Nancy.'

'But other than that, it's the best-looking horse we've ever had here.' Dora grinned. 'Can we ride him?'

'Till we can find the right home.'

'Let's not start looking yet.'

'We've got to work with him a bit,' they told the Colonel. 'He hasn't worked for so long, we'll have to school him before we can show him to anyone.'

And every day when the Colonel, during his morning rounds, asked, 'You got a prospect for that grey?', they said, 'He's still a bit tricky. We want him perfect.'

David already was perfect. They had never had such a marvellous horse to ride. They were not going to let him go in a hurry.

'Got to work with him a bit longer.'

Mr Sponge's
Sporting Tour

R. Surtees

Early to bed and early to rise being among Mr Sponge's maxims, he was enjoying the view of the pantiles at the back of his hotel shortly after daylight the next morning, a time about as difficult to fix in a November day as the age of a lady of a 'certain age'. It takes even an expeditious dresser ten minutes or a quarter of an hour extra the first time he has to deal with boots and breeches; and Mr Sponge, being quite a pattern card in his peculiar line, of course took a good deal more to get himself 'up'.

An accustomed eye could see a more than ordinary stir in the streets that morning. Riding-masters and their assistants might be seen going along with strings of saddled and side-saddled screws; flies began to roll at an earlier hour, and natty tigers to kick about in buckskins prior to departing with hunters.

Each man had told his partner at Miss Jumpheavy's ball of the capital trick they were going to play the stranger; and a desire to see the stranger, far more than a desire to see the trick, caused many fair ones to forsake their downy couches who had much better have kept them.

The world is generally very complaisant with regard to strangers, so long as they *are* strangers, generally making them out to be a good deal better than they really are, and Mr Sponge came in for his full share of stranger credit. They not only brought all the twenty horses Leather said he had scattered about to Laverick Wells, but made him out to have a house in Eaton Square, a yacht at Cowes, and a first-rate moor in Scotland, and some said a peerage in expectancy. No wonder that he 'drew', as theatrical people say.

Let us now suppose him breakfasted, and ready for a start.

He was 'got up' with uncommon care in the most complete style of the severe order of sporting costume. It being now the commencement of the legitimate hunting season—the first week in November—he availed himself of the privileged period for turning out in everything new. Rejecting the now generally worn cap, he adhered to the heavy, close-napped hat, described in our opening chapter, whose connection with his head, or back, if it came off, was secured by a small black silk cord, hooked through the band by a fox's tooth, and anchored to a button inside the haven of his low coat-collar. His neck was enveloped in the ample folds of a large white silk cravat, tied in a pointing diamond tie, and secured with a large silver horse-shoe pin, the shoe being almost large enough for the foot of a young donkey.

His low, narrow-collared coat was of the infinitesimal order; that is to say, a coat, and yet as little of a coat as possible—very near a jacket, in fact. The seams, of course, were outside, and were it not for the extreme strength and evenness of the sewing and the evident intention of the thing, an ignorant person might have supposed that he had had his coat turned. A double layer of cloth

extended the full length of the outside of the sleeves, much in the
fashion of the stage-coachmen's greatcoats in former times; and
instead of cuffs, the sleeves were carried out to the ends of the
fingers, leaving it to the fancy of the wearer to sport a long cuff or
a short cuff, or no cuff at all—just as the weather dictated. Though
the coat was single-breasted, he had a hole made on the button
side, to enable him to keep it together by means of a miniature
snaffle, instead of a button. The snaffle passed across his chest,
from whence the coatee, flowing easily back, displayed the broad
ridge and furrow of a white cord waistcoat, with a low step collar,
the vest reaching low down his figure, with large flap pockets and
a nick out in front, like a coachman's. Instead of buttons, the waistcoat was secured with foxes' tusks and catgut loops, while a heavy
curb chain, passing from one pocket to the other, raised the
impression that there was a watch in one and a bunch of seals in
the other. The waistcoat was broadly bound with white binding,
and, like the coat, evinced great strength and powers of resistance.
His breeches were of a still broader furrow than the waistcoat,
looking as if the ploughman had laid two ridges into one. They
came low down the leg, and were met by a pair of well-made, well
put on, very brown topped boots, a colour then unknown at
Laverick Wells. His spurs were bright and heavy, with formidable
necks and rowels, whose slightest touch would make a horse wince,
and put him on his good behaviour.

Nor did the great slapping brown horse, Hercules, turn out less
imposingly than his master. Leather, though not the man to work
himself, had a very good idea of work, and right manfully he made
the helpers at the Eclipse livery and bait stables strap and groom his
horses. Hercules was a fine animal. It did not require a man to be
a great judge of a horse to see that. Even the ladies, though perhaps
they would rather have had him a white or a cream colour, could
not but admire his nut-brown muzzle, his glossy coat, his silky
mane, and the elegant way in which he carried his flowing tail. His
step was delightful to look at—so free, so accurate, and so easy.
And that reminds us that we may as well be getting Mr Sponge

up—a feat of no easy accomplishment. Few hack hunters are without their little peculiarities. Some are runaways—some kick—some bite—some go tail first on the road—some go tail first at their fences—some rush as if they were going to eat them, others baulk them altogether—and few, very few, give satisfaction. Those that do, generally retire from the public stud to the private one. But to our particular quadruped, 'Hercules'.

Mr Sponge was not without his misgivings that, regardless of being on his preferment, the horse might exhibit more of his peculiarity than would forward his master's interests, and, independently of the disagreeableness of being kicked off at the cover side, not being always compensated for by falling soft, Mr Sponge thought, as the meet was not far off, and he did not sport a cover hack, it would look quite as well to ride his horse quietly on as go in a fly, provided always he could accomplish the mount—the mount—like the man walking with his head under his arm—being the first step to everything.

Accordingly, Mr Leather had the horse saddled and accoutred as quietly as possible—his warm clothing put over the saddle immediately, and everything kept as much in the usual course as possible, so that the noble animal's temper might not be ruffled by unaccustomed trouble or unusual objects. Leather having seen that the horse could not eject Mr Sponge even in trousers, had little fear of his dislodging him in boots and breeches; still it was desirable to avoid all unseemly contention, and maintain the high character of the stud, by which means Leather felt that his own character and consequence would best be maintained. Accordingly, he refrained from calling in the aid of any of the stable assistants, preferring for once to do a little work himself, especially when the rider was up to the trick, and not 'a gent' to be cajoled into 'trying a horse'. Mr Sponge, punctual to his time, appeared at the stable, and after much patting, whistling, so—so—ing, my man, and general ingratiation, the redoubtable nag was led out of the stable into a well-littered straw-yard, where, though he might be gored by a bull if he fell, the 'eyes of England' at all events would not

333

witness the floorer. Horses, however, have wonderful memories and discrimination. Though so differently attired to what he was on the occasion of his trial, the horse seemed to recognize Mr Sponge, and independently of a few snorts as he was led out, and an indignant stamp or two of his foot as it was let down, after Mr Sponge was mounted he took things very quietly.

'Now,' said Leather, in an undertone, patting the horse's arched neck, 'I'll give you a hint; they're a goin' to run a drag to try what he's made on, so be on the look-out.'

'How do you know?' asked Mr Sponge, in surprise, drawing his reins as he spoke.

'*I know,*' replied Mr Leather with a wink.

Just then the horse began to plunge, and paw, and give symptoms of uneasiness, and not wishing to fret or exhibit his weak points, Mr Sponge gave him his head, and passing through the side-gate was presently in the street. He didn't exactly understand it, but having full confidence in his horsemanship, and believing the one he was on required nothing but riding, he was not afraid to take his chance.

Not being the man to put his candle under a bushel, Mr Sponge took the principal streets on his way out of town. We are not sure that he did not go rather out of his way to get them in, but that is neither here nor there, seeing he was a stranger who didn't know the way. What a sensation his appearance created as the gallant brown stepped proudly and freely up Coronation Street, showing his smart, clean, well-put-on head up and down on the unrestrained freedom of the snaffle.

'Oh, d—n it, there he is!' exclaimed Mr Spareneck, jumping up from the breakfast-table, and nearly sweeping the contents off by catching the cloth with his spur.

'Where?' exclaimed half-a-dozen voices, amid a general rush to the windows.

'What a fright!' exclaimed little Miss Martindale, whispering into Miss Beauchamp's ear: 'I'm sure anybody may have him for me,' though she felt in her heart that he was far from bad looking.

'I wonder how long he's taken to put on that choker,' observed Mr Spareneck, eyeing him intently, not without an inward qualm that he had set himself a more difficult task than he imagined, to 'cut him down', especially when he looked at the noble animal he bestrode, and the masterly way he sat him.

'What a pair of profligate boots,' observed Captain Whitfield, as our friend now passed his lodgings.

'It would be the duty of a right-thinking man to ride over a fellow in such a pair,' observed his friend, Mr Cox, who was breakfasting with him.

'Ride over a fellow in such a pair!' exclaimed Whitfield. 'No well-bred horse would face such things, I should think.'

'He seems to think a good deal of himself!' observed Mr Cox, as Sponge cast an admiring eye down his shining boot.

'Shouldn't wonder,' replied Whitfield; 'perhaps he'll have the conceit taken out of him before night.'

'Well, I hope you'll be in time, old boy!' exclaimed Mr Waffles to himself, as looking down from his bedroom window, he espied Mr Sponge passing up the street on his way to cover. Mr Waffles was just out of bed, and had yet to dress and breakfast.

One man in scarlet sets all the rest on the fidget, and without troubling to lay 'that or that' together, they desert their breakfasts, hurry to the stables, get out their horses, and rattle away, lest their watches should be wrong, or some arrangement made that they are ignorant of. The hounds, too, were on, as was seen, as well by their footmarks, as by the bob, bob, bobbing of sundry black caps above the hedges, on the Borrowdon road, as the huntsman and whips proceeded at that pleasant post-boy trot, that has roused the wrath of so many riders against horses that they could not get to keep in time.

Now look at old Tom, cocked jauntily on the spicey bay, and see what a different Tom he is to what he was last night. Instead of a battered, limping, shabby-looking, little old man, he is all alive, and rises to the action of his horse, as though they were all one. A fringe of grey hair protrudes beneath his smart velvet cap, which sets off a weather-beaten, but keen and expressive face, lit up with little piercing black eyes. See how chirpy and cheery he is; how his right arm keeps rising and falling with his whip, beating responsive to the horse's action with the butt-end against his thigh. His new scarlet coat imparts a healthy hue to his face, and good boots and breeches hide the imperfections of his bad legs. His hounds seem to partake of the old man's gaiety, and gather round his horse, or frolic forward on the grassy sidings of the road, till, getting almost out of earshot, a single 'yooi doit!—Arrogant!'—or 'here again, Brusher!' brings them cheerfully back to whine and look in the old man's face for applause. Nor is he chary of his praise. 'G—oood betch!—Arrogant!—g—oood betch!' says he, leaning over his horse's shoulder towards her, and jerking his hand to induce her to proceed forward again. So the old man trots gaily on, now making of his horse, now coaxing a hound, now talking to a 'whip', now touching or taking off his cap as he passes a sportsman, according to the estimation in which he holds him.

As the hounds reach Whirleypool Windmill, there is a grand rush of pedestrians to meet them. First comes a velveteen-jacketed, leather-legginged keeper, with whom Tom (albeit suspicious of his honesty) thinks it prudent to shake hands; the miller and he, too, greet; and forthwith a black bottle with a single glass make their appearance, and pass current with the company. Then the earth-stopper draws nigh, and, resting a hand on Tom's horse's shoulder, whispers confidentially in his ear. The pedestrian sportsman of the country, too, has something to say; also a horse-breaker; while groups of awe-stricken children stand staring at the mighty Tom, thinking him the greatest man in the world.

Railways and fox-hunting make most people punctual, and in less than five minutes from the halting of the hounds by the Windmill, the various roads leading up to it emit dark-coated grooms, who, dismounting, proceed to brush off the mud sparks, and rectify any little derangement the horses or their accoutrements may have contracted on the journey. Presently Mr Sponge, and such other gentlemen as have ridden their own horses on, cast up, while

Though so differently attired, the horse seemed to recognize Mr Sponge.

from the eminence the road to Laverick Wells is distinctly traceable with scarlet coats and flys, with furs and flaunting feathers. Presently the foremost riders begin to canter up the hill, when

> *All around is gay, men, horses, dogs,*
> *And in each smiling countenance appears*
> *Fresh blooming health and universal joy.*

Then the ladies mingle with the scene, some on horseback, some in flies, all chatter and prattle as usual, some saying smart things, some trying, all making themselves as agreeable as possible, and of course as captivating. Some were in ecstasies at dear Miss Jumpheavy's ball—she was such a *nice* creature—such a charming ball, and so well managed, while others were anticipating the delights of Mrs Tom Hoppey's, and some again were asking which was Mr Sponge. Then up went the eyeglasses, while Mr Sponge sat looking as innocent and as killing as he could. 'Dear me!' exclaimed one, 'he's younger than I thought.' 'That's him, is it?' observed another; 'I saw him ride up the street'; while the propriety-playing ones praised his horse, and said it was a beauty.

The hounds, which they all had come to see, were never looked at.

Mr Waffles, like many men with nothing to do, was most unpunctual. He never seemed to know what o'clock it was, and yet he had a watch, hung in chains, and gewgaws, like a lady's chatelaine. Hunting partook of the general confusion. He did not profess to throw off till eleven, but it was often nearly twelve before he cast up. Then he would come up full tilt, surrounded by 'scarlets', like a general with his staff; and once at the meet, there was a prodigious hurry to begin, equalled only by the eagerness to leave off. On this auspicious day he hove in sight, coming best along the road, about twenty minutes before twelve, with a more numerous retinue than usual. In dress, Mr Waffles was the light, butterfly order of sportsman—once-round tie, French polish, paper boots, and so on. On this occasion he sported a shirt-collar with three or four blue lines, and then a white space followed by three or more blue lines, the whole terminating in blue spots about the size of fourpenny pieces at the points; a once-round blue silk tie, with white spots and flying ends. His coat was a light, jackety sort of thing, with little pockets behind, something in the style of Mr Sponge's (a docked dressing-gown), but wanting the outside seaming, back strapping, and general strength that characterized Mr Sponge's. His waistcoat, of course, was a worked one—heart's-ease mingled with foxes' heads, on a true blue ground, the gift of—we'll not say who—his leathers were of the finest doe-skin, and his long-topped, pointed-toed boots so thin as to put all idea of wet or mud out of the question.

Such was the youth who now cantered up and took off his cap to the rank, beauty, and fashion, assembled at Whirleypool Windmill. He then proceeded to pay his respects in detail. At length, having exhausted his 'nothings', and said the same thing over again in a dozen different ways to a dozen different ladies, he gave a slight jerk of the head to Tom Towler, who forthwith whistled his hounds together, and attended by the whips, bustled from the scene.

Epping Hunt, in its most palmy days could not equal the exhibition that now took place. Some of the more lively of the horses, tired of waiting, perhaps pinched by the cold, for most of them were newly clipped, evinced their approbation of the move, by sundry squeals and capers, which being caught by others in the neighbourhood, the infection quickly spread, and in less than a minute there was such a scene of rocking, and rearing, and kicking, and prancing, and neighing and shooting over heads, and rolling over tails, and hanging on by manes, mingled with such screamings from the ladies in the flies, and such hearty-sounding kicks against splash boards and fly bottoms, from sundry of the vicious ones in harness, as never was witnessed. One gentleman, in a bran-new scarlet, mounted on a flourishing piebald, late the property of Mr Batty, stood pawing and fighting the air, as if in the saw-dust circle, his unfortunate rider clinging round his neck, expecting to have the beast back over upon him. Another little wiry chestnut, with abundance of rings, racing martingale, and tackle generally, just turned tail on the crowd and ran off home as hard as ever he could lay legs to the ground; while a good steady bay cob, with a barrel like a butt, and a tail like a hearth-brush, having selected the muddiest, dirtiest place he could find, deliberately proceeded to lie down, to the horror of his rider, Captain Greatgun, of the royal navy, who, feeling himself suddenly touch mother earth, thought he was going to be swallowed up alive, and was only awoke from the delusion by the shouts of the foot people, telling him to get clear of his horse before he began to roll.

Hercules would fain have joined the truant set, and, at the first commotion, up went his great back, and down went his ears, with a single lash out behind that meant mischief, but Mr Sponge was on the alert, and just gave him such a dig with his spurs as restored order, without exposing anything that anybody could take notice of.

The sudden storm was quickly lulled. The spilt ones scrambled up; the loose riders got tighter hold of their horses; the screaming fair ones sank languidly in their carriages; and the late troubled ocean of equestrians fell into irregular line *en route* for the cover.

Bump, bump, bump; trot, trot, trot; jolt, jolt, jolt; shake, shake, shake; and carriages and cavalry got to Ribston Wood somehow or other. It is a long cover on a hill-side, from which parties, placing themselves in the green valley below, can see hounds 'draw', that is to say, run through with their noses to the ground, if there are any men foolish enough to believe that ladies care for seeing such things. However, there they were.

'Eu leu, in!' cries old Tom, with a wave of his arm, finding he can no longer restrain the ardour of the pack as they approach, and thinking to save his credit, by appearing to direct. 'Eu leu, in!' repeats he, with a heartier cheer, as the pack charge the rotten fence with a crash that echoes through the wood. The whips scuttle off to their respective points, gentlemen feel their horses' girths, hats are thrust firmly on the head, and the sherry and brandy flasks begin to be drained.

'Tally ho!' cries a countryman at the top of the wood, hoisting his hat on a stick. At the magic sound, fear comes over some, joy over others, intense anxiety over all. What commotion! What indecision! What confusion! 'Which way?—Which way?'

'Twang, twang, twang,' goes old Tom's horn at the top of the wood, whither he seems to have flown, so quick has he got there.

A dark-coated gentleman on a good family horse solves the important question—'Which way?'—by diving at once into the wood, crashing along till he comes to a cross-road that leads to the top, when the scene opening to 'open fresh fields and pastures new', discloses divers other sections struggling up in long drawn files, following other leaders, all puffing, and wheezing and holding on by the manes, many feeling as if they had had enough already— 'Quick!' is the word, for the tail-hounds are flying the fence out of the first field over the body of the pack, which are running almost mute at best pace beyond, looking a good deal smaller than is agreeable to the eyes of a sportsman.

'F—o—o—r—rard!' screams old Tom, flying the fence after them, followed by jealous jostling riders in scarlet and colours, some anxious, some easy, some wanting to be at it, some wanting to look as if they did, some wishing to know if there was anything on the far side.

Now Tom tops another fence, rising like a rocket and dropping like a bird; still 'F—o—o—r—rard!' is the cry—away they go at racing pace.

The field draws out like a telescope, leaving the largest portion at the end, and many—the fair and fat ones in particular—seeing the hopelessness of the case, pull up their horses, while yet on an eminence that commands a view. Fifteen or twenty horsemen enter for the race, and dash forward, though the hounds rather gain on old Tom, and the further they go the smaller the point of the telescope becomes. The pace is awful; many would give in but for the ladies. At the end of a mile or so, the determined ones show to the front, and the spirters and 'make-believes' gladly avail themselves of their pioneering powers.

Mr Sponge, who got well through the wood, has been going at his ease, the great striding brown throwing the large fields behind him with ease, and taking his leaps safely and well. He now shows to the front, and old Tom, who is still 'F—o—o—r—rarding' to his hounds, either rather falls back to the field or the field draws upon him. At all events they get together somehow. A belt of Scotch fir plantation, with a stiffish fence on each side, tries their mettle and the stoutness of their hats: crash they get through it, the noise they make among the thorns and rotten branches resembling the outburst of a fire. Several gentlemen here decline under cover of the trees.

'F—o—o—r—rard!' screams old Tom, as he dives through the stiff fence and lands in the field outside the plantation. He might have saved his breath, for the hounds were beating him as it was. Mr Sponge bores through the same place, little aided, however, by anything old Tom has done to clear the way for him, and the rest follow in his wake.

The field is now reduced to six, and two of the number, Mr Spareneck and Caingey Thornton, become marked in their attention to our hero. Thornton is riding Mr Waffles's crack steeplechaser 'Dare-Devil', and Mr Spareneck is on a first-rate hunter belonging to the same gentleman, but they have not been able to get our friend Sponge into grief. On the contrary, his horse, though lathered goes as strong as ever, and Mr Sponge, seeing their design, is as careful of him as possible, so as not to lose ground. His fine, strong, steady seat, and quiet handling, contrasts well with Thornton's rolling bucketing style, who has already begun to ply a heavy cutting whip, in aid of his spurs at his fences, accompanied with a half frantic 'g—u—r—r—r along!' and inquires of the horse if he thinks he stole him?

The three soon get in front; fast as they go, the hounds go faster, and fence after fence is thrown behind them, just as a girl throws her skipping-rope.

Tom and the whips follow, grinning with their tongues in their cheeks, Tom still screeching 'F—o—o—o—rard!' at intervals.

A big stone wall, built with mortar, and coped with heavy blocks of stone, is taken by the three abreast, for which they are rewarded by a gallop up Stretchfurrow pasture, from the summit of which they see the hounds streaming away to a fine grass country below, with pollard willows dotted here and there in the bottom.

'Water!' says our friend Sponge to himself, wondering whether Hercules would face it. A desperate black bullfinch, so thick that they could hardly see through it, is shirked by consent, for a gate which a countryman opens, and another fence or two being passed, the splashing of some hounds in the water, and the shaking of others on the opposite bank, show that, as usual, the willows are pretty true prophets.

Caingey, grinning his coarse red face nearly double, and getting his horse well by the head, rams in the spurs, and flourishes his cutting whip high in air, with a 'g—u—u—ur along! do you think I'—the 'stole you' being lost under water just as Sponge clears the brook a little lower down. Spareneck then pulls up.

When Nimrod had Dick Christian under water in the Whissendine in his Leicestershire run, and someone more humane than the rest of the field observed, as they rode on,

'But he'll be drowned.'

'Shouldn't wonder,' exclaimed another.

'But the pace,' Nimrod added, 'was too good to inquire.'

Such, however, was not the case with our watering-place cock, Mr Sponge. Independently of the absurdity of a man risking his neck for the sake of picking up a bunch of red herrings, Mr Sponge, having beat everybody, could afford a little humanity, more especially as he rode his horse on sale, and there was now no one left to witness the further prowess of the steed. Accordingly, he availed himself of a heavy, newly-ploughed fallow, upon which he landed as he cleared the brook, for pulling up, and returned just as Mr Spareneck, assisted by one of the whips, succeeded in landing Caingey on the taking-off side. Caingey was not a pretty boy at the best of times—none but the most partial parents could think him one—and his clumsy-featured, short, compressed face, and thick, lumpy figure, were anything but improved by a sort of pea-green net-work of water-weeds with which he arose from his bath. He was uncommonly well soaked, and had to be held up by the heels to let the water run out of his boots, pockets, and clothes. In this undignified position he was found by Mr Waffles and such of the field as had ridden the line.

'Why, Caingey, old boy! you look like a boiled porpoise with parsley sauce!' exclaimed Mr Waffles, pulling up where the unfortunate youth was spluttering and getting emptied like a jug. 'Confound it!' added he, as the water came gurgling out of his mouth, 'but you must have drunk the brook dry,' and with this he laughed heartily.

Caingey would have censured his inhumanity, but knowing the imprudence of quarrelling with his bread and butter, and also aware of the laughable, drowned-rat figure he must then be cutting, he thought it best to laugh, and take his change out of Mr Waffles another time. Accordingly, he chuckled and laughed too, though his jaws nearly refused their office, and kindly transferred the blame of the accident from the horse to himself.

'He didn't put on steam enough,' he said.

Meanwhile, old Tom, who had gone on with the hounds, having availed himself of a well-known bridge, a little above where Thornton went in, for getting over the brook, and having allowed a sufficient time to elapse for the proper completion of the farce, was now seen rounding the opposite hill, with his hounds clustered about his horse, with his mind conning over one of those imaginary runs that experienced huntsmen know so well how to tell, when there is no one to contradict them.

Having quartered his ground to get at his old friend the bridge again, he just trotted up with well-assumed gaiety as Caingey Thornton spluttered the last piece of green weed out from between his great thick lips.

'Well, Tom!' exclaimed Mr Waffles, 'what have you done with him?'

'Killed him, sir,' replied Tom, with a slight touch of his cap, as though 'killing' was a matter of every-day occurrence with them.

'Have you, indeed!' exclaimed Mr Waffles, adopting the lie with avidity.

'Yes, sir,' said Tom gravely; 'he was nearly beat afore he got to the brook. Indeed, I thought Vanquisher would have had him in it; but, however, he got through, and the scent failed on the fallow, which gave him a chance; but I held them on to the hedgerow beyond, where they hit it off like wildfire, and they never stopped again till they tumbled him over at the back of Mr Plummey's farm-buildings, at Shapwick. I've got his brush,' added Tom, producing a much tattered one from his pocket, 'if you'd like to have it?'

'Thank you, no—yes—no,' replied Waffles, not wanting to be bothered with it; 'yet stay,' continued he, as his eye caught Mr Sponge, who was still on foot beside his vanquished friend; 'give it to Mr What-de-ye-call-'em,' added he, nodding towards our hero.

'Sponge,' observed Tom, in an undertone, giving the brush to his master.

'Mr Sponge, will you do me the favour to accept the brush?' asked Mr Waffles, advancing with it towards him; adding, 'I am sorry this unlucky bather should have prevented your seeing the end.'

Mr Sponge was a pretty good judge of brushes, and not a bad one of camphire; but if this one had smelt twice as strong as it did —indeed, if it had dropped to pieces in his hand, or the moths had flown up in his face, he would have pocketed it, seeing it paved the way to what he wanted—an introduction.

'I'm very much obliged, I'm sure,' observed he, advancing to take it—'very much obliged, indeed; been an extremely good run, and fast.'

'Very fair—very fair,' observed Mr Waffles, as thought it were nothing in their way; 'seven miles in twenty minutes, I suppose, or something of that sort.'

'*One*-and-twenty,' interposed Tom, with a laudable anxiety for accuracy.

'Ah! one-and-twenty,' rejoined Mr Waffles. 'I thought it would be somewhere thereabouts. Well, I suppose we've all had enough,' added he, 'may as well go home and have some luncheon, and then a game at billiards, or rackets, or something. How's the old water-rat?' added he, turning to Thornton, who was now busy emptying his cap and mopping the velvet.

The water-rat was as well as could be expected, but did not quite like the new aspect of affairs. He saw that Mr Sponge was a first-rate horseman, and also knew that nothing ingratiated one man with another so much as skill and boldness in the field. It was by that means, indeed, that he had established himself in Mr Waffles' good graces—an ingratiation that had been pretty serviceable to him, both in the way of meat, drink, mounting, and money. Had Mr Sponge been, like himself, a needy, penniless adventurer, Caingey would have tried to have kept him out by some of those plausible, admonitory hints, that poverty makes men so obnoxious to; but in the case of a rich, flourishing individual, with such an astonishing stud as Leather made him out to have, it was clearly Caingey's policy to knock under and be subservient to Mr Sponge also. Caingey, we should observe, was a bold, reckless rider, never seeming to care for his neck, but he was no match for Mr Sponge, who had both skill and courage.

Caingey being at length cleansed from his weeds, wiped from his mud, and made as comfortable as possible under the circum-stances, was now hoisted on to the renowned steeple-chase horse again, who had scrambled out of the brook on the taking-off side, and, after meandering the banks for a certain distance, had been caught by the bridle in the branch of a willow—Caingey, we say, being again mounted, Mr Sponge also, without hindrance from the resolute brown horse, the first whip put himself a little in advance, while old Tom followed with the hounds, and the second whip mingled with the now increasing field, it being generally understood (by the uninitiated, at least) that hounds have no business to go home so long as any gentleman is inclined for a scurrey, no matter whether he has joined early or late. Mr Waffles, on the contrary, was very easily satisfied, and never took the shine off a run with a kill by risking a subsequent defeat. Old Tom, though keen when others were keen, was not indifferent to his comforts, and soon came into the way of thinking that it was just as well to get home to his mutton-chops at two or three o'clock, as to be groping his way about bottomless bye-roads on dark winter nights.

As he retraced his steps homeward, and overtook the scattered field of the morning, his talent for invention, or rather stretching, was again called into requisition.

'What have you done with him, Tom?' asked Major Bouncer, eagerly bringing his sturdy collar-marked cob alongside of our huntsman.

'Killed him, sir,' replied Tom, with the slightest possible touch of the cap. (Bouncer was no tip.)

'Indeed!' exclaimed Bouncer, gaily, with that sort of sham satisfaction that most people express about things that can't concern them in the least. 'Indeed! I'm deuced glad of that! Where did you kill him?'

'At the back of Mr Plummey's farm-buildings, at Shapwick,' replied Tom; adding, 'but, my word, he led us a dance afore we got there—up to Ditchington, down to Somerby, round by Temple Bell Wood, cross Goosegreen Common, then away for Stubbington Brooms, skirtin' Sanderwick Plantations, but scarce goin' into 'em, then by the round hill at Camerton leavin' great Heatherton to the right, and so straight on to Shapwick, where we killed, with every hound up . . .'

'God bless me!' exclaimed Bouncer, apparently lost in admiration, though he scarcely knew the country; 'God bless me!' repeated he, 'what a run! The finest run that ever was seen.'

'Nine miles in twenty-five minutes,' replied Tom, tacking on a little both for time and distance.

'B-o-y JOVE!' exclaimed the major.

Having shaken hands with, and congratulated Mr Waffles most eagerly and earnestly, the major hurried off to tell as much as he could remember to the first person he met, just as the cheese-bearer at a christening looks out for someone to give the cheese to. The cheese-getter on this occasion was Doctor Lotion, who was going to visit old Jackey Thompson, of Woolleyburn. Jackey being then in a somewhat precarious state of health, and tolerably advanced in life, without any very self-evident heir, was obnoxious to the attentions of three distinct litters of cousins, someone or other of whom was constantly 'baying him'. Lotion, though a sapient man, and somewhat grinding in his practice, did not profess to grind old people young again, and feeling he could do very little for the body corporate, directed his attention to amusing Jackey's mind, and anything in the shape of gossip was extremely acceptable to the doctor to retail to his patient. Moreover, Jackey had been a bit of a sportsman, and was always extremely happy to see the hounds—*on anybody's land but his own.*

So Lotion got primed with the story, and having gone through the usual routine of asking his patient how he was, how he had slept, looking at his tongue, and reporting on the weather, when the old posing question, 'What's the news?' was put, Lotion replied, as he too often had to reply, for he was a very slow hand at picking up information.

'Nothin' particklar, I think, sir,' adding, in an off-hand sort of way, 'you've heard of the gr*eet* run, I s'pose, sir?'

'Great run!' exclaimed the octogenarian, as if it was a matter of the most vital importance to him; 'great run, sir; no, sir, not a word!'

The doctor then retailed it.

Old Jackey got possessed of this one idea—he thought of nothing else. Whoever came, he out with it, chapter and verse, with occasional variations. He told it to all the 'cousins in waiting'; Jackey Thompson, of Carrington Ford; Jackey Thompson, of Houndesley; Jackey Thompson, of the Mill; and all the Bobs, Bills, Sams, Harrys, and Peters, composing the respective litters;

MR SPONGE'S SPORTING TOUR

—forgetting where he got it from, he nearly told it back to Lotion himself. We sometimes see old people affected this way—far more enthusiastic on a subject than young ones. Few dread the aspect of affairs so much as those who have little chance of seeing how they go.

But to the run. The cousins reproduced the story according to their respective powers of exaggeration. One tacked on two miles, another ten; and so it went on and on, till it reached the ears of the great Mr Seedeyman, the mighty WE of the country, as he sat in his den penning his 'stunners' for his market-day *Mercury*. It had then distanced the great sea-serpent itself in length, having extended over thirty-three miles of country, which Mr Seedeyman reported to have been run in one hour and forty minutes.

Pretty good going, we should say.

RED RUM'S
FIRST NATIONAL

Ivor Herbert

Three times winner of the Grand National, Red Rum, a horse who is already a legend in his lifetime, and a great favourite with the public, will certainly be among the famous horses of history as time goes by.

Betting was particularly heavy, unusually accurate in its selection and, for once, quite beneficial to the punters. Those who prefer the bookie-free methods of racing finance practised in the world's other major racing countries noted that William Hill's boasted of £700,000 being staked with their organization on the race. Ladbroke's with their money-minting nationwide net of betting shops, claimed even more: 1½ million punters had wagered more than £1 million on the race. 'Undoubtedly a record,' murmured a Ladbroke's official comfortably.

Nearly £2 million bet on one race with must a couple of betting organizations seems a maniacal amount of money for a nation somnambulating towards bankruptcy. But the British as a whole would rather gamble than work. We are the world's biggest (and so poorest) punters, the Grand National is the lottery of the year, and nowhere on the globe have there ever existed bookmakers as rich as ours.

Beryl McCain, wife of Red Rum's trainer, had no bet. She hardly ever does. Nor does she often watch a race with 'Ginger', particularly with Red Rum. 'We stand apart.' She went up onto the roof on her own.

'Don McCain,' said Brian Fletcher, the jockey, 'did not give me any orders. I just said I was going to sit in the middle on the outside on the first circuit and hunt round. Then ride a race past the stands.'

'Brian's plan,' said McCain, 'was to stay out of trouble on the first circuit to get the horse settled and running nicely. Then, once you're over The Chair' (just coming up to the stands) 'to sit down and ride a jockey's race. This is pretty well what he did.'

Fletcher makes another point. 'I was trying to help Jongo, 'cos he was having his first ride round Aintree. He was on my "inner" till he fell. In all the 'Nationals I've ridden in, I always try to get a clear run on the first circuit, trying to dodge the fallers. Luck went with me.'

So did Red Rum's intelligence and his own instinct for keeping out of trouble and on his feet. He is simply that often-described but rare conveyance 'a safe jumper'. So was Arkle. So are nearly all steeplechasing stars. Without Red Rum's literally boundless stamina, even without his courage he would still be getting round and winning when the others fell. As it is, he gallops on and on, growing incredibly stronger while his ordinary rivals weaken.

'He is not in my opinion,' Brian Fletcher decides, 'a particularly brave *jumper*. He doesn't just take hold of his bit and go from A to B.' Jumping crackles with such terrifying tearaways. 'He watches what he's doing,' as Fletcher describes it. 'He sidesteps any bother, provided he has time to see it. If there's any trouble near him, he'll dodge out of it. He's a very *clever* horse. A horse with *brains*.'

Brains then, and a strong sense (often quite absent in moronic horses) of self-preservation. Quickness of reflex. Observance of trouble ahead. Balance—Bobby Renton's 'beautiful proportions'. These things combine to make what he is: a natural jumper. Yet there is no vestige of 'jumping blood' in his pedigree. Battered by man he certainly was in some ways, but the tough school taught him not delinquency but survival. And he was helped. Tim Molony's little circular loose school was his kindergarten. Sandra Kendall, as was, schooled him on. Dozens of different jockeys doing different things made him, as a young man learns to cope with different bosses, utterly self-reliant. And finally his foot stopped hurting and he loved his supremacy on the long wide sands, and he found in battle-scarred Brian Fletcher someone who wouldn't badger and bother him, but let him settle.

The ground on 31 March 1973 was exactly as Red Rum loves it: firm. Brian Fletcher had warmed up with a 4th in the first race, the BP Shield Handicap Hurdle. Don McCain was relieved to see him safe round and home.

Thirty-eight runners paraded for the Grand National. It was worth £25,486 and, three minutes late at 3.18 p.m., the field leapt forward on the start of a journey of four miles and 856 yards which only 17 would complete. The firmness of the ground strongly suggested a fast pace. The jockeys had received their customary half-heard cautionary warning against going a mad gallop early on. No one believed that records were about to be broken.

Nothing accelerated steeplechasing's soaring popularity more than its television coverage by the cool and competent BBC. Its leading racing commentator Peter O'Sullevan is a legend in his lifetime. A victorious owner himself on the highest level both on the flat and under NH Rules, he knows the game from the muck-yard up to its rich and noble patrons. His commentaries set a standard so far unequalled. And he begins:

'They're off. And Rouge Autumn starts fast on the inside, with Sunny Lad and Go-Pontinental moving up on the outside with Beggar's Way, then comes Black Secret with General Symons on his outside and Richeleau and Glenkiln. Crisp has gone right up there with Sunny Lad on the inside, then comes Hurricane Rock, then Mill Door over on the far side with Endless Folly, Beggar's Way and Black Secret, and with Rouge Autumn disputing it, they come to the first.'

John Hanmer takes up the commentary:

'Black Secret over in the lead. There's a faller—Richeleau has gone at the first—and as they go towards the second, Grey Sombrero on the outside along with Ashville, then Glenkiln, then comes Black Secret, General Symons, then Highland Seal. . . Over the ditch and Grey Sombrero over first. There's a faller at that one— Ashville fell.'

Then shrewd Julian Wilson, beady-eyed, the intense and furrowed-browed skilled television interviewer, takes up the racing tale:

'And spread right across the course with Grey Sombrero the leader over that one, from Endless Folly in the centre, Black Secret towards the outside, Highland Seal just scrambled over that one. Crisp is right up there on the inside, as they race down towards the fifth. As they race down towards Bechers, it's the grey, Grey Sombrero, racing wide of the field, the clear leader from Crisp in second, Black Secret third. At Bechers—Grey Sombrero over— and *just* clears it—from Crisp in second, Black Secret third, Endless Folly fourth, Sunny Lad five, Rouge Autumn is sixth and Beggar's Way is a faller at Bechers. Over the next, with Crisp *now* the leader from Grey Sombrero, then Black Secret and Endless Folly . . . they come towards the Canal Turn. Nereo has been pulled up and Crisp is the leader from Grey Sombrero, Black Secret, Endless Folly . . . then comes Spanish Steps. Highland Seal has been pulled up as they jump the next. Crisp over it from Grey Sombrero, Black Secret. . .

John Hanmer resumes from his vantage point:

'As they go towards the next fence it's Crisp the clear leader from Grey Sombrero, Endless Folly, Black Secret, then comes Great Noise, Sunny Lad, then Rouge Autumn, then comes Tarquin Bid, behind Tarquin Bid is Red Rum, then Spanish Steps, then Hurricane Rock and Glenkiln as they go across the Melling Road.'

We pick up Peter O'Sullevan again as they turn onto the race-course.

. . . 'Crisp, well clear, over from Grey Sombrero who jumps it second, Endless Folly jumps it third, then Great Noise fourth, five is Black Secret, six is Rouge Autumn, seven is Spanish Steps and eight Tarquin Bid and nine is Red Rum and ten, on the inside, is Sunny Lad as they come to the next. Crisp over in the lead and clear. . . . Red Rum well in there' (he was 12th) 'and then comes Glenkiln . . . Coming to the Chair now—this is one of the biggest. Crisp, his ears pricked, jumps it beautifully in the lead—he just pecked a little bit, but got away with it. Grey Sombrero's gone at that one. Grey Sombrero's a faller, Glenkiln's a faller—'

Beryl McCain was staring from the top of the stand. 'I saw Red Rum on the wide outside all the way round. I saw Crisp. Then I saw poor "Glen" fall. We'd all got soft spots for him, 'cos he's a super and very kind horse. He fell at the Chair and I saw him struggle. He couldn't get up. His leg was stuck in the bottom of the fence. Canharis jumped over after him and clouted him on the back of the head. He got up. He was dazed. He jumped the water and fell in and the whole of his back legs were covered with the water. And he pulled himself out and they caught him by the stables. I hadn't watched Red Rum. And by the time Glen was out of the water, they'd jumped the first fence second time round and Crisp was still in the lead, but Red Rum was *second*!'

'Ginger' McCain was delighted to see Brian Fletcher really riding Red Rum along over the Chair and then the water. They improved five or six places very rapidly.

Thus away over the Melling Road with the giant Crisp loping

along in front, turning the enormous fences into hurdles, seeming as if he was cantering ahead of a pack of galloping ponies.

Fletcher says: 'From the third fence on the second circuit, from the ditch, I was chasing this horse in front of me. I didn't know what it was. I couldn't tell it was Crisp.'

John Hanmer calls the remnants as they thunder past him:

'Crisp at the ditch, the nineteenth, he stood right back, he jumped it well, he's right out in front still of Red Rum, second, Rouge Autumn is third, Spanish Steps fourth, Tarquin Bid is fifth, Great Noise is sixth, then Endless Folly and Black Secret.'

Julian Wilson's admiration of great Crisp sends his voice sailing:

'And Richard Pitman over that one on Crisp and what a fantastic ride he's having! I can't remember a horse so far ahead in the Grand National at this stage! Jumping that second was Red Rum, then Spanish Steps on the outside of Rouge Autumn, Great Noise made a mistake there, but coming to the next . . . Crisp is over that one, safely over the one before Bechers from Red Rum . . . Crisp comes on his own to Bechers Brook for the second time, Crisp the top weight. Richard Pitman over it in tremendous style and he's about twenty lengths clear from Red Rum in second place, behind comes Spanish Steps, then Hurricane Rock. Crisp is over the twenty-third *already*, and racing down to the Canal Turn, as Red Rum jumps the twenty-third in second place . . . Crisp jumps the Canal Turn, clear. He's still twenty lengths clear from Red Rum in second.'

'I just thought at the Canal Turn,' says 'Ginger' McCain, 'that we'd be second and how unlucky we were to meet Crisp . . .'

'Seeing the race afterwards,' reflects little Brian Fletcher, 'I've often said to myself that if I'd *ever* said "I'm going to be second", if I'd ever dropped my hands or eased off Red Rum for one moment, then I *would have been second*.'

Fletcher did not ease. Red Rum did not falter. Fletcher drew his whip at Anchor Bridge. He hit Red Rum twice, thrice, four times. The bay horse quickened. 'Knowing the horse would stay and jump,' says Fletcher, 'and had only 10st 5lb on his back, I never accepted he'd be second.'

John Hanmer saw the move, but Crisp was still, as Julian Wilson had shouted, 'a long long way ahead of Red Rum.' Hanmer called quickly, 'Crisp has got three to jump, he's well clear of Red Rum, who's made a bit of ground. Spanish Steps is third, Hurricane Rock is fourth. Over the third from home, Crisp over safely. Red Rum in second place, then Spanish Steps, Hurricane Rock just passing Spanish Steps . . . As they go across the Melling Road, with two to jump, it's Crisp with Red Rum in second place *making* ground, but a very long gap after that to Hurricane Rock, Spanish Steps and Rouge Autumn . . .'

Peter O'Sullevan takes up the saga of the slowly shrinking lead, Crisp conceding one stone nine pounds to his pursuer. 'It's Crisp in the lead from Red Rum, but Red Rum *still* making ground on him! Brian Fletcher on Red Rum chasing Dick Pitman on Crisp. Crisp still *well* clear with two fences left to jump in the 1973 National and this great Australian 'chaser, Crisp, with twelve stone on his back and ten stone five on the back of Red Rum, who's chasing him and they look to have it *absolutely* to themselves. At the second last . . . Crisp is over. And clear of Red Rum who's jumping it a long way back. In third place is Spanish Steps then Hurricane Rock and Rouge Autumn and L'Escargot. But coming to the final fence in the 'National now . . . and it's Crisp *still* going in great style with twelve stone on his back. He jumps it well. Red Rum is about fifteen lengths behind him as he jumps it. Dick Pitman coming to the elbow now in the 'National. He's got two hundred and fifty yards to run. But *Crisp is just wandering off the true line now. He's beginning to lose concentration.* He's been out there on his own for so long. *And Red Rum is making ground on him.* Still as they come to the line, it's a furlong to run now, two hundred yards now for Crisp, and Red Rum *still* closing on him, and Crisp is getting *very* tired, and Red Rum is pounding after him and Red Rum is the one who finishes the strongest. *He's going to get up! Red Rum is going to win the 'National!* At the line Red Rum has just *snatched* it from Crisp! *And Red Rum is the winner!* And Crisp is second and L'Escargot is just coming up to be third . . .

Beryl McCain was alone and shaking on the top of the stands. 'When Red Rum came back onto the racecourse I was getting excited that he was going to be *second*. This was fantastic. I started not being able to hold my glasses still. Then it became worse. And he jumped the last and I was getting very weepy and I just broke down. There was a lady stood in front of me and she got hold of me. And she let me put my head on her shoulder and I was crying my heart out. She said, "Which is yours?" and I said "It's Red Rum." She said "He's won. Are you all right?" and I said "Yes."'

'She came to me afterwards,' said Beryl McCain, 'and asked "Do you remember me?" I said, "Thank you very much for looking after me." She said, "I completely understand. I was the same when my husband rode the winner of the 'National in '69. I'm Eddie Harty's wife."'

Old Mr Le Mare was white. 'When he was catching up on Crisp, they're all cheering and shouting and bawling, and I just sit there and look . . .' But another owner of McCain's had watched him with some anxiety. 'He was shouting and cheering. His hands were in the air. I thought he'd have a heart attack.' McCain said afterwards, bringing out all his loving admiration for Noel Le Mare, 'The Guv'nor tells me his face never moved!'

'Hope your Guv'nor's all right?' a friend of 'Ginger''s gasped, running to congratulate him as the horse was mobbed by deliriously excited Jackie Grainger and Billy Ellison.

They ran at and round him hugging and slapping him, as if they would wrestle him to the ground. Red Rum was escorted in by the two police horses. Noel Le Mare, who claims he is only excited by women, got down in the unsaddling enclosure. They brought him a chair. He sat on it dazed with glory, his head a little slanted, his mouth smiling with the delight of having won something even more than the world's greatest steeplechase.

'All these people in my box,' said Mr Le Mare, 'jumping up and down like mad people!' He gave a twinkle. 'I never batted an eyelid,' he said.

It was only 67 years since Le Mare the engineer's apprentice had read about Ascetic Silver's Grand National and seen that American millionaire spinning sovereigns outside the Fleetwood Hotel. It was a normal man's lifetime since he'd made his three resolves. It seemed to him, in that euphoria of dreams come true, only a day or so back across the troubled years to McCain's first winner, San Lorenzo, here at Liverpool. Mr Le Mare had watched that race from the rails. 'The horse looked to me like a donkey amongst a lot of good animals, but he came storming in, and I lost my breath and everything to get to "Ginger".' When the third of his dreams came true, he struggled back to get to 'Ginger'.

As the horse came in McCain's grin beamed over the hubbub suitably like the Cheshire cat's: he has always loved that next-door county. There he stood all in brown with a furry collar, face alight, looking the nicest fellow in the world, murmuring 'I'm only a glorified amateur . . . Knew my feller would tackle him all the way . . . You can't get on top of him . . .'

Beryl recovered, not quite tear-stained but eyes enormous and shining, was there in her blue coat under her white Russian hat. The One Good Horse that 'Ginger' had been on about all these years, driving through Cheshire, pointing out the big places and the grand horses, the One Good Horse had come.

And Brian Fletcher, scarlet-faced, sweating, gap-toothed, triumphantly grinning, was trying inarticulately to recount his victory with much chopping and punching of his left hand. His mother, a charming-looking lady, all aglow had (as Brian would say) materialized suddenly at his side and had come in proudly with her son, squeezed by the mounted policemen. Brian murmured some good and loving things about her, and moistness of the eyes was added to the heated damp of victory.

McCain had watched the race from the top of the County Stand. 'I thought, honestly, we were going to win it even 50 yards off going to the last.' He said immediately in praise of Crisp, 'He didn't waver till after he'd jumped the last. Red Rum went absolutely straight compared to Crisp who definitely wandered off to the left.' The huge Australian, punch-drunk with fatigue, had tottered left towards the dolls like an exhausted explorer, at the end of his tether, struggling into sight of home. 'Ginger' said, 'Crisp was magnificent. The weight bogged him down. But I couldn't see the same thing happening to Red Rum. I think he would have kept going come what may. Till he dropped. Because this is him.'

Red Rum had smashed the generally accepted Grand National record time set up by Golden Miller in 1934. (In some record books Reynoldstown carrying 11st 4 lb in 1935 (the first year of his double) is credited with 9 min 20·2 sec compared with 'The Miller's' 9 min 20·4 sec carrying 12st 2lb.) Red Rum's time, an incredible half-a-minute quicker than the *average* time, was 9 min 1·9 sec—a speed over the 30 biggest obstacles in Britain of nearly 29 m.p.h.

The corks came out of the champagne bottles in a fusillade on the racecourse. Fletcher and McCain agreed to pay for a case each to go into the weighing room for the jockeys and valets. McCain remarked afterwards, 'Somehow I seemed to pay for both . . .' Charitably he put it down to the riotous moment of victory.

At last the McCain's party set off back for Birkdale.

'We were only about five minutes in front of the box,' says 'Ginger', 'and when we turned up the road I saw the road blocked. I thought there had been an accident. I saw police-cars, and there must have been four or five hundred people and the streets were jammed. The police weren't even *trying* to get people through. Everyone was at a standstill. But everybody was being marvellous about it. Then the box comes round the corner with its headlights on and all its lights flashing and the horns going. Jackie's driving and the boys are all hanging out of the cab . . . It was *grand*.'

McCain's face suddenly switches into one of sympathy. In the elation of victory he was thinking of the faller. 'But it was rather sad as well, because Glenkiln had had a desperate fall and was very, very sore.' The ramp went down, Red Rum came out and received a blast of tremendous cheering. McCain said to Billy Ellison, 'Take him up the road fifty yards for the people to see.' McCain grinned again at the delight of the greeting, then added, 'But while that's going on poor old Glenkiln slips out of the box and slides into the stable, very stiff, very sore. And he's such a good-hearted horse, that I felt very sad.'

The celebrations exploded down the streets and into the little yard. A tide of people shouting and cheering swept over the cobbles round Red Rum's box, then jostled into the McCains's small house. Strangers from the streets, magnetized by their new local hero, converged upon him and upon the celebratory drinks.

'Then everybody seemed to come into the house! I don't know where they came from.' 'Ginger' added, abashed, 'I'd had a couple of crates of champagne brought in before the race—got a bit carried away, I suppose . . .' He would never have admitted such confidence before. He went on, 'They got stuck into those. Then the toast-machine got started and everybody was eating toast. Of all things, toast and champagne! The yard was crammed full. The police had a few jars too.' The rejoicing continued for an hour and a half and then McCain decided that the horses needed a rest. 'We filtered the people out quietly and some went off. The Guv'nor was having a do at the Prince of Wales so we went off there. But I didn't feel like getting too involved in a party, so about ten of us went and had a quiet meal in the dining room of the Prince of Wales. I think the Guv'nor had a bill for around £800 for champagne. I think all of Southport had free drinks on him.'

But the pendulum reaction to the greatest triumph of 'Ginger' McCain's life began to swing. He is a quiet man, gratified but reluctant to be suddenly a hero. 'The dinner was a little bit of an anti-climax after it all. I would have preferred it to be *very* quiet with just a few close friends.'

'He's going to get up! Red Rum is going to win the "National"!'

He had moreover a small anxiety about Red Rum. During the race the record-breaking winner had struck into his near-fore and given himself a small, but very deep cut. The scar clearly remained fifteen months later. 'It was a nasty deep little cut,' said 'Ginger' McCain, 'and he was rather sore. We bandaged it and he stayed in his box for three days, resting.'

There was no rest on the morrow for the McCains. Noel Le Mare looked understandably, and in 'Ginger''s words, 'very peaky and very tucked up afterwards'. But on the Sunday 'Ginger''s and Beryl's house filled up again with celebrants and they decided to go down the street to their nearest pub, always known to its habitués for visible reasons as 'The Upsteps'.

It was already crowded, with a thunder of voices and collection of splendid Lancashire urban faces making 'Coronation Street' seem plastic rubbish. A rousing cheer exploded as 'Ginger''s tall frame squeezed in through the door and his now famous face beamed down on the hot, laughing throng. After a very great victory in a very great race, after defeating ill-luck and hardship, something magic attaches to the connections of the triumphant horse. Ordinary people want to touch them for luck and to record, '"Ginger" had a word wi' me this morning''.

'Ginger' rashly shouted out: 'Drinks all round twice!' He said, 'Everybody had drinks twice and twice again and so on and we'd been at the champagne that morning, anyway. Oh, it was a *good day*!'

If it had not been for Red Rum's over-reach he would have gone for the Scottish National that first year in 1973. With the wound, there was no question of running him again. After three days he was ridden out again deep into the sea. It cured his over-reach. It took away the soreness. He was sound again. He accepted homage as he passed through the town. 'It's not really a horsey town,' said 'Ginger', 'but he's about the greatest celebrity Southport's ever had.'

The season ended. Noel Le Mare toweringly topped the owners' list with stakes of £34,196 won by three horses in eight races (Red

Rum had won six of them). 'Ginger' McCain proved conclusively that he was no one-horse trainer by producing eight different winners of eighteen races worth £37,404. He ranked 6th in the trainers' table, finishing between the two large stables of Bob Turnell (5th) and David Barons (7th). Of Red Rum's jockeys that year, Ron Barry sailed away with the championship with 125 winners, Tommy Stack was 3rd with 71 and Brian Fletcher, now established as our hero's partner, ended up 6th with 47 winners. Of the perils of the sport there was lower down the list a poignant reminder. The late Doug Barrott, killed in action, had finished his season, and his life, with 43 winners.

SWEETBRIAR TURNS A SOMERSAULT

K. M. Peyton

Christina had a new habit made for her fifteenth birthday, the indefatigable Mary having let out Aunt Isabel's habit to its ultimate frayed dart during the last two winters. With some new stays to improve her waist, Christina turned herself round in front of her bedroom mirror with considerable satisfaction. Even if her stock of day dresses, supplied by Aunt Grace every spring and autumn, was not in the first flight of fashion, at least in her new habit she looked splendid, like a hard-riding débutante from the cream of the grass country. She lifted her chin, and pulled out some curls from under the brim of the new bowler to lie on her forehead. She had wanted to put her hair up, bundled at the back of her head so that the bowler would have to sit well forward at an angle Christina thought terribly dashing, but Mary was shocked at the suggestion, and would not hear of it.

'At your age, miss! Whatever next!'

Mark raised his eyebrows and whistled when he saw her.

'Who d'you think you are, then? Did you get Father to pay it?'

'Yes. For my birthday.'

'I didn't get anything when I was seventeen. Only a lecture about not getting girls into tr— about behaviour, I mean.' He grinned. 'Perhaps I could get a new pair of boots out of him.'

'You had new breeches for the point-to-point.'

Mark scowled. 'I'd rather have won in my old ones than lost in the new ones.'

'Next year,' Christina said.

In the spring Mark had ridden Treasure in the hunt races, but because of their joint inexperience, they had only come in fourth. Mark had been furious. His own enthusiasm had inflamed the already excitable Treasure, so that he had made several bad mistakes, but the horse was considered to have a big future, and already Mark was counting the days to the next race. Christina thought, secretly, that if Dick could have ridden Treasure, the horse would have won, for Dick had had a remarkably calming effect on Treasure during the three years he had cared for him.

Dick noticed her new habit too; she could tell by the way his eyes carefully did not look, after the first flare of surprise.

She laughed and said, 'Don't you think I look smart, Dick? I'm as smart as Drummer now.'

'Why, yes, miss. You're a right pair.' He smiled, flushing slightly. He did not chat any more—as he once had when they had ridden through the fields together. Christina had noticed, gradually, that he no longer started conversations, nor passed remarks, but only replied to her own observations. He had withdrawn, and she knew it was because of the convention that she had discussed with William. He treated her with more respect. A small part of Christina was flattered by this, but a larger, more logical part was grieved. She had wanted Dick to go on being a friend, as he had been when he had taught her to ride, but now the barrier between them was preventing it. What William had said, although she had laughed at him, had stuck in her mind, but Christina saw no way of bridging this gulf. She also felt that Dick was more anxious to keep it than she was herself, and she had a feeling that he wanted it in some way as a protection for himself, but as a protection from what, she had no idea. When she was older she realized what it was, but when she was fifteen she had only vague feelings which she could never pin down, nor analyse. She always admired William for the way he was able to explain everything with his mathematician's logic, but she did not think that even William could explain what some of her feelings meant, nor even what they were. She thought that Aunt Grace would have been more helpful, with her brisk, 'It's your age.'

Out hunting, she had no worries. Her horses were superb, and she was afraid of nothing. When people told her she was 'fearless', she sometimes wondered if it was because she had no imagination, as William had told her. But on Sweetbriar and Drummer she never had cause to be afraid; she was never foolhardy, like Mark, and would turn away from a fence if she decided that it was too big for her. If Mark had to do this it sent him into a frenzy, but Christina kept her head, having learned patience the hard way. Although she took several falls, she was never hurt. In the evenings, at dinner, she would discuss the day's sport with her uncle and Mark—and now she knew whether it was Ploughman or Rockwood who first owned the line, and Partridge who got into trouble over a hare—and Russell's eyes would flash over his wine-glass. William would sit silently, in a world of his own. In spite of his father's scorn, he never touched any drink but water. Christina, accustomed now to the Russell ways, stopped worrying about William.

Christina, like Mark, regretted the all too hasty passing of the winter days. By February one could almost count off the remaining hunting days on one's fingers. After a period of hard frost which cancelled three days' hunting, she rode with Mark to a meet at the 'Ferrers Arms' with the feeling that these next few weeks must make up for the week they had just missed and all the weeks to come.

'Summer's awful,' Mark agreed. 'After the point-to-point—nothing. Father thinks I ought to go up to Oxford. Can you imagine it?'

'No,' Christina said. 'William ought to go,' she added.

'He never said anything about William going. He's welcome to it, I say.'

It was a good day, cold and clear. Christina was on Drummer, and Mark on Treasure, and Dick was bringing on Woodpigeon and Sweetbriar as second horses. Drummer was on his toes—'He's as bad as Treasure,' Christina said.

'Good as, you mean,' Mark said.

Mr Lucas's hounds (many of them veterans bred by Russell when he owned them) were lean and fast. 'They would never win prizes for looks,' Russell had said often enough, 'but they know their job.' They drew a covert called Four Ashes, and were away in minutes, and Christina knew, with one of her 'feelings', that it was going to be a good day. The ground was firm, not too sticky, and the turned plough gleamed where the big horses had patiently worked over it. The farmer had left a wide edge of grass and Drummer went down it like an arrow from a bow, clods flying from his hoofs. All the rest of the field had gone away on the other side, but Christina, rather than wait in the hustle for the gate out of the wood, had decided to go round. If the fox ran left-handed up to Stag's Bushes, as he usually did, she would be right up with hounds on the other side. She knew this wood well. She pulled at Drummer to steady him, and he went over the timber at the bottom of the field as neatly as a cat. Here they could cross the spur of woodland unimpeded. The peaty ride was their own. Bending down to miss the branches, Christina smelt the leather and the sweat and the flying peat; Drummer was all lathery with excitement, taut and sweet beneath her. She steadied him again, because of the branches, and she thought of the hounds running ahead and laughed out loud. Sometimes when she felt like this she laughed, but half of her wanted to cry. The excitement went through her like a current.

The jump out of the wood was narrow, three plain bars covered with lichen, and high. It needed careful judgement, and she shut her lips tight as she rode at it, concentrating hard. Drummer pulled and raked out, too keen, but she had time to steady him; he saw the bars in plenty of time, and Christina got him just right, so that even as he took off she knew it was all right. It was beautiful, and clever, and filled her with wonderful satisfaction. There was no one to see, but she thought, 'If nothing more happens today, it has been worth it.'

But the glory of the day had barely started. The fox had turned left-handed, as Christina had hoped, and out of the wood she found only Mr Lucas and his huntsman ahead of her, and the best stretch of grass in the country under her heels. Hounds were running in a bunch, fast, along the bottom of the big sloping valley. For a moment she held Drummer, looking down on the two red coats and the rippling hounds, then the little bay leapt forward and started to gallop down the hill in pursuit. She only had to sit, hands still, and feel the cold air splintering past her face.

At the end of the valley there was a brief check which enabled the strung-out field to catch up, then they were away again across a field of kale. Christina found Mark, and they had time to grin at each other as they jumped a low hedge side by side into a lane. Mark, in his usual fashion, took Treasure out over a blind bank which Christina would not consider; she did not see him again until the next check on the edge of a piece of woodland, by which time the horses were tiring, and a large part of the field had disappeared. Mark rode up in a flurry of mud and said, 'If only that damned Dick would arrive with Woodpigeon!'

'If anyone can get them here, Dick will,' said Christina.

Treasure was black with sweat. Drummer's sides heaved. Christina would have dismounted, but was afraid hounds might go away again at any minute and leave her stranded.

'Perhaps if he goes out on the Fallowfield side we'll meet Dick on the road.'

'Listen!'

Somewhere in the wood a hound was owning the line again. A cold breeze rattled the branches. Christina was anxious, wanting to go, but knowing Drummer was getting tired.

'They'll go out of the far corner,' Mark said. 'Come on.'

'Yes, listen! They're away—'

'And up towards the road too.'

Treasure and Drummer, hearing hounds, broke into a trot. Mark went ahead, but Christina nursed Drummer, holding him. They went round the bottom of the wood and saw Mr Lucas going up the hill the other side, over rough pasture, hounds strung out over fifty yards ahead of him. Mark put Treasure into a canter again, but the going was heavy, and Christina knew she ought to pull Drummer out. She looked across towards the road, and to her delight saw Dick coming through the gate at the top with Wood-pigeon and Sweetbriar. Mark saw him at the same time, and altered course.

Christina started to canter for the gate. Dick had dismounted and as Mark rode up, instead of changing horses immediately, Dick said something to him, and they seemed to be having an argument. Christina, still some way behind, had guessed that something was wrong, because Dick had been riding Sweetbriar, and the cross-saddle was still on her. Usually he rode Woodpigeon, and led Sweetbriar, because Sweetbriar had the side-saddle. Christina eased the labouring Drummer. She saw Mark slip down from Treasure, throw the reins to Dick and jump up on to Sweetbriar.

'Whatever—?' Christina was filled with indignation. 'That's my horse! Mark!' she shouted. 'Mark!'

But as she rode up to Dick, Mark was already away, turning in his saddle to shout something which Christina could not catch. Christina's eyes blazed.

'What's he doing? Dick, why did he take Sweetbriar?'

'I told him, miss, Woodpigeon's gone lame. So he took Sweet-briar. I couldn't stop him.'

Dick was as angry as Christina.

'Oh, the beast! The beast!' Christina could have wept with rage. 'And hark at them, Dick! Hark at them!'

Hounds had doubled back. They had crossed the lane and were running back on the other side, throwing their tongues with an abandon that set all the horses jigging, even the weary Drummer. Mr Lucas and his huntsman were lost somewhere between the banks of the lane, and the only horseman in sight was Mark, coming down on the far side at a flat gallop. He was standing in his stirrups and quite oblivious of anything but the flying pack in front of him. With his fresh horse Christina knew just how he was feeling; a great sob of rage burst out of her.

'The beast! Oh, Dick, how could he?'

But she knew only too well how he could. She wondered, if she had been Mark, if she could have resisted the temptation herself. She watched Sweetbriar's flying white tail, and the big hedge that stood in her way at the bottom of the hill. Mark was going at it as he did with Treasure, fast, his hands up on the mare's neck. Christina, knowing Sweetbriar, frowned and said to Dick, 'Oh, the idiot! She'll go right through it.'

But, watching him, Christina could feel Sweetbriar's long stride, see the hedge as Mark saw it: a trifling obstacle between him and that galloping pack whose wild music was filling the valley. Seeing the hedge in cold blood, from up the hill, Christina shivered, and said, 'Oh, Dick, the mare!'

Even as Sweetbriar rose at it, Christina knew that she was watching disaster. She saw the gallant attempt at a take-off from a ditch lip of brimming mud, heard the crack of the rails as the mare hit them with her forelegs, then the cartwheel arc of her iron shoes as she catapulted out of sight through the crackling brush-wood. Christina looked at Dick. Even then, it was the mare's plight she was thinking of, not Mark's. Her own excitement was quenched; hounds were already out of sight in the woodlands along the bottom of the valley, and she felt cold at the sight of the accident.

'I reckon the mare'll be no better for that,' Dick said shortly.

He mounted Treasure, and pulled the lame Woodpigeon up beside him. 'We'd best go and see.'

They went out of the gate and rode down the metalled lane at a trot. Below the hedge where Sweetbriar had foundered there was a gate into the field. Christina opened it from Drummer, held it for Dick, then wheeled round and cantered ahead. Sweetbriar was lying where she had fallen, propped up on her forelegs half in and half out of the ditch, her eyes very wild, her flanks heaving. Mark was staggering out of the ditch beside her, his hands up to his face, not looking as if he knew quite where he was going. The sight of him on his feet, conscious, switched Christina's whole attention to the mare; for Mark her fear dissolved into a furious contempt.

'What have you done to her?' she shouted at him angrily. 'You've half-killed her!'

She slid off Drummer and ran towards Sweetbriar. But Dick came alongside and shouted, 'Leave her to me! You hold the horses.' He jumped off Treasure, and threw Christina the reins, so that she was suddenly entangled with the reins of three wheeling horses. She tried to calm them and watch Dick at the same time, trembling with indignation. Dick was standing by Sweetbriar's head, talking to her, encouraging her to get out of the ditch. She quietened with Dick by her, but her eyes were black with pain. Christina watched in an agony of fear for the mare.

'What's wrong? What's the matter with her, Dick?'

'Come on, old lady . . . come up out of there, my old dear. You'll be better when you're four-square, my old horse . . .' With Dick coaxing her, Sweetbriar scrabbled again and clawed with her trembling legs at the sliding earth.

'Now—up, my old lady! There's a girl!'

With a rush the mare came up on to the grass, but her legs were shaking so that she almost keeled over. Dick put his shoulder to hers and held her, talking to her all the while. Mark came up to

Christina, and Christina took her eyes off Sweetbriar for a moment to look at him. His face was covered with mud and his nose was pouring blood, which was spattering his white stock and disappearing into the scarlet of his jacket.

'Look what you've done to the mare!' Christina raged at him. 'You were mad to put her at that!'

'Look whad she's dod to be!' Mark muttered. 'Fool horse . . . Have you god something to mob it with? I—ugh . . .'

'You ought to lie down,' Christina said coldly. She turned back to look at Sweetbriar, and saw that she was steady now, her head drooping, one foreleg pointed out. Dick was feeling her shoulders and ribs, taking off her saddle.

'What's wrong with her?'

'I'm not sure, miss. I think it's her shoulder—possibly a rib cracked. She took the fall on her near shoulder, I think. Her leg, you see . . .' He stood back, and looked at her thoughtfully.

'Will she be all right?'

'I can't tell, miss. She'll need a vet.'

'What can we do with her now, though?'

'We'll have to see if she can get as far as the farm.' He nodded down the hill. 'Then get the vet up. Let's see if you can walk, old lady. Come on, my old girl. Try your old bones out . . .'

He coaxed Sweetbriar forward and she took a few paces stumbling on her near fore, trembling.

'She'll get there, I think, miss. If I take my time.'

'If we take the other horses home I can send Fowler out to help you,' Christina said. 'And call the vet. Would that be best?'

'Yes, miss. You go on now. It's doing those horses no good standing about. I'll see to the mare all right.'

Christina looked coldly at Mark.

'Here, take Treasure. And you can jolly well lead Woodpigeon too. He's your horse.'

Mark took Treasure's reins, and Christina, taking another look at him, relented a little. 'Here, take my handkerchief. It's not very big though. You do look queer.'

Mark's dark eyes looked balefully out of the mud and gore. He gathered up Treasure's reins and pulled himself up into the saddle with a groan. Christina maliciously handed him Woodpigeon's reins and said, 'Take your horse. All this is your own fault entirely so you can't complain. It was a dirty trick to play on me. If I'd done the same to you, you wouldn't have been very pleased. Apart from what you've done to the mare . . .'

'Nag, nag, nag,' said Mark.

Christina waited for Dick to come and give her a leg-up on Drummer. When she was settled, she said, 'I'll be as quick as I can and send you some help.'

'Thank you, miss.' He hesitated, then said awkwardly, 'If I'm held up here with the mare, late tonight, I mean, could you tell Violet what's happened? So my mother knows?'

'Violet?'

'My sister.'

'Oh, yes. Of course.'

'Thank you, miss.'

Christina put Drummer into a trot to catch up with Mark. On top of everything that had just happened, she found herself astonished to know that Violet was Dick's sister.

She said to Mark, 'Did you know Violet was Dick's sister?'

Mark looked at her as if she were mad. 'I wouldn't care at the moment if she was his mother-in-law,' he said. 'What are you talking about?'

'Dick's just said would I tell his sister, if he's held up—meaning Violet. I never knew they were brother and sister.'

'I don't see that it matters at all,' Mark said. With two horses to cope with, and one hand still mopping at his nose, he looked furious. 'That blasted mare of yours never even took off. Straight through it she went. I reckon she's broken my nose. Put her great hoof right in my face. I've never known a horse so clumsy.'

'You're lucky she didn't break your skull!' Christina said furiously. 'Riding at a place like that! The take-off was a sea of mud—what did you expect her to do but go right through it?

Treasure would have done just the same. It's imbecile the way you ride. I wonder you weren't killed long ago. And now poor Sweetbriar—because of you . . .'

'Who are you telling how to ride?' Mark said, equally furiously. 'The mare's past it, that's her trouble. She's not worth keeping if that shoulder's going to be troublesome.'

'What do you mean, not worth keeping? She carries me like a bird. I wouldn't change her for all the Treasures in England. She's got manners, at least. Which is more than you can say of any horse you've ridden for a bit. Look at Treasure now, for instance!'

Treasure was jogging along crabwise, pushing his quarters into the subdued Woodpigeon. Mark gave him an angry chuck on the mouth.

'What was that fool Dick thinking of to bring me a lame horse anyway? He's to blame for all this. Woodpigeon wouldn't have blundered.'

'You don't suppose Woodpigeon was lame when he set out, do you?' Christina said scathingly. 'Dick's not a soothsayer, to guess the horse is going to go lame, is he? Probably something to do with the way you rode him last Saturday.'

As they bickered it started to rain. Mark huddled down in his saddle. They had about eight miles to go, and as the roads slowly slipped away beneath the ringing hoofs Christina mellowed towards Mark and felt almost sorry for him. She had never known him so subdued and dejected. Then she thought of Sweetbriar, and Dick benighted in some dirty farm stable trying to make her comfortable, and she hardened again and set her lips.

When they got home Mark went indoors and she took the three horses round to the stables. She had rarely led one horse, let alone two before, and felt very competent as she clattered into the stable-yard. 'Just like Dick,' she thought. Fowler came running out in alarm at the sight of her, and she explained to him what had happened, while he stood pursing his lips and shaking his head.

'I'll go myself, at once. Dick will have his hands full. I know the place you mean.'

She saw Dick coming with Woodpigeon and Sweetbriar.

'And perhaps someone had better go for Dr Porter. Mark thinks his nose is broken.'

'Dear me, dear me.' Fowler clicked his tongue, full of concern. 'Harry will go, this instant. Leave it to me, miss. I'll see to it. You go up to the house now, and get yourself dry. I'll go straight out to Dick, so don't you worry.'

The boys took the horses. Christina looked into the stables and saw the glow of the lamps, the golden beds of straw, the boys, one to a horse, rubbing them down, hissing through their lips. It was warm and sweet-smelling, shining, the horses mellowed by lamplight. Christina was struck by the picture; the kindliness of it warmed her, and she ran back up to the house to get some comfort herself. Her hair was heavy with rain.

Mark was washing in the kitchen, as he usually did, but this time with much moaning and groaning. With the mud removed, his face was badly cut and swollen. Mary said, 'You must bathe that nose with cold water to get it down to size. Fetch a cloth, Violet, and a bowl.' Violet did as she was told. Christina, drying herself by the fire, looked up through the tangled curtain of her hair and saw Violet take the things to Mark, and stand by him with a towel. Her face—and now Christina saw the family likeness to Dick in it—seemed to shine with sympathy; her big green eyes were filled with a tenderness that shocked Christina. 'Why, she—she—' Christina's mind struggled with a conception completely new to her. She remembered Violet saying that Mark was handsome, but it had never occurred to her that Violet could—could— Christina could not even acknowledge that there was a name for Violet's feelings, so transparently evident as she stood over Mark. She was suddenly quite furious, crouched there beside the fire. She threw her hair back and stood up quickly.

'Violet, take some hot water up to my room.' She spoke with a sharpness that made Violet jump.

'Yes, miss.'

Christina went upstairs feeling utterly confused. 'Why did I speak like that?' she wondered. 'I must be tired.' But she knew she was jealous, and she could not understand why. Jealous of whom, she wondered, for how could anyone be jealous of Violet? Christina did not know. She felt angry and upset, and all for no reason that she understood. She pulled off her jacket.

'It must be my stays,' she thought. It was certainly bliss to undo them. Christina knew how well a small waist looked with a good riding habit, and had gradually been making hers smaller and smaller. 'Perhaps it is not very wise,' she thought. When Violet came in she gave her Dick's message, and Violet said, 'Thank you, miss,' and withdrew very quickly. To get back to Mark, Christina thought.

'Oh!' Christina was exasperated. She changed into her prettiest dress and tied her hair back with a black ribbon. 'I shall put it up next season. I don't care what Mary says,' she thought.

When dinner was served, William came in rather late. Christina could tell by the colour on his cheeks and his damp hair that he had been out, but Russell made no inquiries. He scarcely glanced at him, as he was giving his full attention to Mark's description of Sweetbriar's 'idiocy'. William looked at Mark, and a glint of amusement came into his face.

'Had a good day?' he said pointedly.

Mark's half-closed eyes darted him a murderous glance. Mary brought in some more gravy and said, 'Dr Porter's called, sir. Shall I tell him to wait?'

'Send him in. He can have a drink with us,' Russell said.

Dr Porter joined them, and drank several glasses of wine while they finished their dinner. To Christina it seemed a very long time since her first night at Flambards, when Dr Porter had last joined them for dinner. She remembered William on the stretcher—the only time she had ever seen him in hunting clothes—and Mark helping get the supper—the only time he had ever done so. After three glasses of port she could hardly remember the time before Flambards: Aunt Grace and Battersea.

'Where have you been?' she asked William when they left the table.

He grinned at her. He was not little any more, but taller than Christina by a head.

'Nowhere.'

'You were all wet.'

'The roof must leak.'

'Oh, you tell such lies!' Christina said. She went slowly up to her room. The rain was pattering steadily against the window and sliding off the ivy in drips from leaf to leaf. Christina pressed her nose against the glass, looked into the darkness and thought of Dick still working. And Violet going home through the rain, warm with love for Mark.

SHASTA SETS OUT ON HIS TRAVELS

C. S. Lewis

Shasta, a fisherman's son, meets a war horse, Bree, who can talk, and who teaches him to ride, and they decide to run away together. In the end Shasta arrives in the country of his forefathers and discovers he is the King's son.

This is the story of an adventure that happened in Narnia and Calormen and the lands between, in the Golden Age when Peter was High King in Narnia and his brother and his two sisters were King and Queens under him.

In those days, far south in Calormen on a little creek of the sea, there lived a poor fisherman called Arsheesh, and with him there lived a boy who called him Father. The boy's name was Shasta. On most days Arsheesh went out in his boat to fish in the morning, and in the afternoon he harnessed his donkey to a cart and loaded the cart with fish and went a mile or so southward to the village to sell it. If it had sold well he would come home in a moderately good temper and say nothing to Shasta, but if it had sold badly he would find fault with him and perhaps beat him. There was always something to find fault with for Shasta had plenty of work to do, mending and washing the nets, cooking the supper, and cleaning the cottage in which they both lived.

Shasta was not at all interested in anything that lay south of his home because he had once or twice been to the village with Arsheesh and he knew that there was nothing very interesting there. In the village he only met other men who were just like his father—men with long, dirty robes, and wooden shoes turned up at the toe, and turbans on their heads, and beards, talking to one another very slowly about things that sounded dull. But he was very interested in everything that lay to the North because no one ever went that way and he was never allowed to go there himself. When he was sitting out of doors mending the nets, and all alone, he would often look eagerly to the North. One could see nothing but a grassy slope running up to a level ridge and beyond that the sky with perhaps a few birds in it.

Sometimes if Arsheesh was there Shasta would say, 'O my Father, what is there beyond that hill?' And then if the fisherman was in a bad temper he would box Shasta's ears and tell him to attend to his work. Or if he was in a peaceable mood he would say, 'O my son, do not allow your mind to be distracted by idle questions. For one of the poets has said, "Application to business is the root of prosperity, but those who ask questions that do not concern them are steering the ship of folly towards the rock of indigence."'

Shasta thought that beyond the hill there must be some delightful secret which his father wished to hide from him. In reality, however, the fisherman talked like this because he didn't know what lay to the North. Neither did he care. He had a practical mind.

One day there came from the South a stranger who was unlike any man that Shasta had seen before. He rode upon a strong dappled horse with flowing mane and tail and his stirrups and bridle were inlaid with silver. The spike of a helmet projected from the middle of his silken turban and he wore a shirt of chain mail. By his side hung a curving scimitar, a round shield studded with bosses of brass hung at his back, and his right hand grasped a lance. His face was dark, but this did not surprise Shasta because all the people of Calormen are like that; what did surprise him was the man's beard which was dyed crimson, and curled and gleaming with scented oil. But Arsheesh knew by the gold ring on the stranger's bare arm that he was a Tarkaan or great lord, and he bowed kneeling before him till his beard touched the earth and made signs to Shasta to kneel also.

The stranger demanded hospitality for the night which of course the fisherman dared not refuse. All the best they had was set before the Tarkaan for supper (and he didn't think much of it) and Shasta, as always happened when the fisherman had company, was given a hunk of bread and turned out of the cottage. On these occasions he usually slept with the donkey in its little thatched stable. But it was much too early to go to sleep yet, and Shasta, who had never learned that it is wrong to listen behind doors, sat down with his ear to a crack in the wooden wall of the cottage to hear what the grown-ups were talking about. And this is what he heard.

'And now, O my host,' said the Tarkaan, 'I have a mind to buy that boy of yours.'

'O my master,' replied the fisherman (and Shasta knew by the wheedling tone the greedy look that was probably coming into his face as he said it), 'what price could induce your servant, poor though he is, to sell into slavery his only child and his own flesh? Has not one of the poets said, "Natural affection is stronger than soup and offspring more precious than carbuncles?"'

'It is even so,' replied the guest dryly. 'But another poet has likewise said, "He who attempts to deceive the judicious is already baring his own back for the scourge." Do not load your aged mouth with falsehoods. This boy is manifestly no son of yours, for your cheek is as dark as mine but the boy is fair and white like the accursed but beautiful barbarians who inhabit the remote North.'

'How well it was said,' answered the fisherman, 'that swords

381

can be kept off with shields but the Eye of Wisdom pierces through every defence! Know then, O my formidable guest, that because of my extreme poverty I have never married and have no child. But in that same year in which the Tisroc (may he live for ever) began his august and beneficent reign, on a night when the moon was at her full, it pleased the gods to deprive me of my sleep. Therefore I arose from my bed in this hovel and went forth to the beach to refresh myself with looking upon the water and the moon and breathing the cool air. And presently I heard a noise as of oars coming to me across the water and then, as it were, a weak cry. And shortly after, the tide brought to the land a little boat in which there was nothing but a man lean with extreme hunger and thirst who seemed to have died but a few moments before (for he was still warm), and an empty water-skin, and a child, still living. "Doubtless," said I, "these unfortunates have escaped from the wreck of a great ship, but by the admirable designs of the gods, the elder has starved himself to keep the child alive and has perished in sight of land." Accordingly, remembering how the gods never fail to reward those who befriend the destitute, and being moved by compassion (for your servant is a man of tender heart)—'

'Leave out all these idle words in your own praise,' interrupted the Tarkaan. 'It is enough to know that you took the child—and have had ten times the worth of his daily bread out of him in labour, as anyone can see. And now tell me at once what price you put on him, for I am wearied with your loquacity.'

'You yourself have wisely said,' answered Arsheesh, 'that the boy's labour has been to me of inestimable value. This must be taken into account in fixing the price. For if I sell the boy I must undoubtedly either buy or hire another to do his work.'

'I'll give you fifteen crescents for him,' said the Tarkaan.

'Fifteen!' cried Arsheesh in a voice that was something between a whine and a scream. 'Fifteen! For the prop of my old age and the delight of my eyes! Do not mock my grey beard, Tarkaan though you be. My price is seventy.'

At this point Shasta got up and tiptoed away. He had heard all he wanted, for he had often listened when men were bargaining in the village and knew how it was done. He was quite certain that Arsheesh would sell him in the end for something much more than fifteen crescents and much less than seventy, but he was also sure that he and the Tarkaan would take hours in getting to an agreement.

You must not imagine that Shasta felt at all as you and I would feel if we had just overheard our parents talking about selling us for slaves. For one thing, his life was already little better than slavery; for all he knew, the lordly stranger on the great horse might be kinder to him than Arsheesh. For another, the story about his own discovery in the boat had filled him with excitement and with a sense of relief. He had often been uneasy because, try as he might, he had never been able to love the fisherman, and he knew that a boy ought to love his father. And now, apparently, he was no relation to Arsheesh at all. That took a great weight off his mind. 'Why, I might be anyone!' he thought. 'I might be the son of a Tarkaan myself—or the son of the Tisroc (may he live for ever)—or of a god!'

He was standing out in the grassy place before the cottage while he thought these things. Twilight was coming on apace and a star or two was already out, but the remains of the sunset could still be seen in the west. Not far away the stranger's horse, loosely tied to an iron ring in the wall of the donkey's stable, was grazing. Shasta strolled over to it and patted its neck. It went on tearing up the grass and took no notice of him.

Then another thought came into Shasta's mind. 'I wonder what sort of a man that Tarkaan is,' he said out loud. 'It would be splendid if he was kind. Some of the slaves in a great lord's house have next to nothing to do. They wear lovely clothes and eat meat every day. Perhaps he'd take me to the wars and I'd save his life in a battle and then he'd set me free and adopt me as his son and give me a palace and a chariot and a suit of armour. But then he might be a horrid, cruel man. He might send me to work on the fields in chains. I wish I knew. How can I know? I bet this horse knows, if only he could tell me.'

The Horse had lifted its head. Shasta stroked its smooth-as-satin nose and said, 'I wish *you* could talk, old fellow.'

And then for a second he thought he was dreaming, for quite distinctly, though in a low voice, the Horse said, 'But I can.'

Shasta stared into its great eyes and his own grew almost as big, with astonishment.

'How ever did *you* learn to talk?' he asked.

'Hush! Not so loud,' replied the Horse. 'Where I come from, nearly all the animals talk.'

'Wherever is that?' asked Shasta.

'Narnia,' answered the Horse. 'The happy land of Narnia— Narnia of the heathery mountains and the thymy downs, Narnia of the many rivers, the plashing glens, the mossy caverns and the deep forests ringing with the hammers of the Dwarfs. Oh the sweet air of Narnia! An hour's life there is better than a thousand years in Calormen.' It ended with a whinny that sounded very like a sigh.

'How did you get here?' said Shasta.

'Kidnapped,' said the Horse. 'Or stolen, or captured—whichever you like to call it. I was only a foal at the time. My mother warned me not to range the southern slopes, into Archenland and beyond, but I wouldn't heed her. And by the Lion's Mane I have paid for my folly. All these years I have been a slave to humans, hiding my true nature and pretending to be dumb and witless like *their* horses.'

'Why didn't you tell them who you were?'

'Not such a fool, that's why. If they'd once found out I could talk they would have made a show of me at fairs and guarded me more carefully than ever. My last chance of escape would have been gone.'

'And why—' began Shasta, but the Horse interrupted him.

'Now look,' it said, 'we mustn't waste time on idle questions. You want to know about my master the Tarkaan Anradin. Well,

One day there came from the south a stranger.

he's bad. Not too bad to me, for a war horse costs too much to be
treated very badly. But you'd better be lying dead tonight than
go to be a human slave in his house tomorrow.'

'Then I'd better run away,' said Shasta, turning very pale.

'Yes, you had,' said the Horse. 'But why not run away with me?'

'Are you going to run away too?' said Shasta.

'Yes, if you'll come with me,' answered the Horse. 'This is the
chance for both of us. You see if I run away without a rider,
everyone who sees me will say "Stray horse" and be after me as
quick as he can. With a rider I've a chance to get through. That's
where you can help me. On the other hand, you can't get very far
on those two silly legs of yours (what absurd legs humans have!)
without being overtaken. But on me you can outdistance any other
horse in this country. That's where I can help you. By the way,
I suppose you know how to ride?'

'Oh yes, of course,' said Shasta. 'At least, I've ridden the donkey.'

'Ridden the *what*?' retorted the Horse with extreme contempt.
(At least, that is what he meant. Actually it came out in a sort of
neigh—'Ridden the wha-ha-ha-ha-ha.' Talking horses always
become more horsy in accent when they are angry.)

'In other words,' it continued, 'you *can't* ride. That's a draw-
back. I'll have to teach you as we go along. If you can't ride, can
you fall?'

'I suppose anyone can fall,' said Shasta.

'I mean can you fall and get up again without crying and mount
again and fall again and yet not be afraid of falling?'

'I—I'll try,' said Shasta.

'Poor little beast,' said the Horse in a gentler tone. 'I forget you're
only a foal. We'll make a fine rider of you in time. And now—we
mustn't start until those two in the hut are asleep. Meantime we
can make our plans. My Tarkaan is on his way North to the great
city, to Tashbaan itself and the court of the Tisroc—'

'I say,' put in Shasta in rather a shocked voice, 'oughtn't you
to say "May he live for ever?"'

'Why?' asked the Horse. 'I'm a free Narnian. And why should

I talk slaves' and fools' talk? I don't want him to live for ever, and I know that he's not going to live for ever whether I want him to or not. And I can see you're from the free North too. No more of this Southern jargon between you and me! And now, back to our plans. As I said, my human was on his way North to Tashbaan.'

'Does that mean we'd better go to the South?'

'I think not,' said the Horse. 'You see, he thinks I'm dumb and witless like his other horses. Now if I really were, the moment I got loose I'd go back home to my stable and paddock; back to his palace which is two days' journey South. That's where he'll look for me. He'd never dream of my going on North on my own. And anyway he will probably think that someone in the last village who saw him ride through has followed us to here and stolen me.'

'Oh hurrah!' said Shasta. 'Then we'll go North. I've been longing to go to the North all my life.'

'Of course you have,' said the Horse. 'That's because of the blood that's in you. I'm sure you're true Northern stock. But not too loud. I should think they'd be asleep soon now.'

'I'd better creep back and see,' suggested Shasta.

'That's a good idea, but take care you're not caught.'

It was a good deal darker now and very silent except for the sound of the waves on the beach, which Shasta hardly noticed because he had been hearing it day and night as long as he could remember. The cottage, as he approached it, showed no light. When he listened at the front there was no noise. When he went round to the only window, he could hear, after a second or two, the familiar noise of the old fisherman's squeaky snore. It was funny to think that if all went well he would never hear it again. Holding his breath and feeling a little bit sorry, but much less sorry than he was glad, Shasta glided away over the grass and went to the donkey's stable, groped along to a place he knew where the key was hidden, opened the door and found the Horse's saddle and bridle which had been locked up there for the night. He bent forward and kissed the donkey's nose. 'I'm sorry we can't take *you*,' he said.

'There you are at last,' said the Horse when he got back to it.
'I was beginning to wonder what had become of you.'

'I was getting your things out of the stable,' replied Shasta.
'And now, can you tell me how to put them on?'

For the next few minutes Shasta was at work, very cautiously
to avoid jingling, while the Horse said things like, 'Get that girth
a bit tighter,' or 'You'll find a buckle lower down,' or 'You'll need
to shorten those stirrups a good bit.' When all was finished it said:

'Now; we've got to have reins for the look of the thing, but you
won't be using them. Tie them to the saddle-bow: very slack so
that I can do what I like with my head. And, remember—you are
not to touch them.'

'What are they for, then?' asked Shasta.

'Ordinarily they are for directing me,' replied the Horse. 'But
as I intend to do all the directing on this journey, you'll please
keep your hands to yourself. And there's another thing. I'm not
going to have you grabbing my mane.'

'But I say,' pleaded Shasta. 'If I'm not to hold on by the reins
or by your mane, what *am* I to hold on by?'

'You hold on with your knees,' said the Horse. 'That's the
secret of good riding. Grip my body between your knees as hard
as you like; sit straight up, straight as a poker; and remember
to keep your elbows in. And by the way, what did you do with
the spurs?'

'Put them on my heels, of course,' said Shasta. 'I do know that
much.'

'Then you can take them off and put them in the saddlebag.
We may be able to sell them when we get to Tashbaan. Ready?
And now I think you can get up.'

'Ooh! You're a dreadful height,' gasped Shasta after his first,
and unsuccessful, attempt.

'I'm a horse, that's all,' was the reply. 'Anyone would think I
was a haystack from the way you're trying to climb up me! There,
that's better. Now sit *up* and remember what I told you about
your knees. Funny to think of me who has led cavalry charges and

won races having a potato-sack like you in the saddle! However, off we go.' It chuckled, not unkindly.

And it certainly began their night journey with great caution. First of all it went just south of the fisherman's cottage to the little river which there ran into the sea, and took care to leave in the mud some very plain hoof-marks pointing South. But as soon as they were in the middle of the ford it turned upstream and waded till they were about a hundred yards farther inland than the cottage. Then it selected a nice gravelly bit of bank which would take no footprints and came out on the Northern side. Then, still at a walking pace, it went Northward till the cottage, the one tree, the donkey's stable, and the creek—everything, in fact, that Shasta had ever known—had sunk out of sight in the grey summer-night darkness. They had been going uphill and now were at the top of the ridge—that ridge which had always been the boundary of Shasta's known world. He could not see what was ahead except that it was all open and grassy. It looked endless: wild and lonely and free.

'I say!' observed the Horse. 'What a place for a gallop, eh?'

'Oh don't let's,' said Shasta. 'Not yet. I don't know how to— please, Horse. I don't know your name.'

'Breehy-hinny-brinny-hoohy-hah,' said the Horse.

'I'll never be able to say that,' said Shasta. 'Can I call you Bree?'

'Well, if it's the best you can do, I suppose you must,' said the Horse. 'And what shall I call you?'

'I'm called Shasta.'

'H'm,' said Bree. 'Well, now, there's a name that's *really* hard to pronounce. But now about this gallop. It's a good deal easier than trotting if you only knew, because you don't have to rise and fall. Grip with your knees and keep your eyes straight ahead between my ears. Don't look at the ground. If you think you're going to fall just grip harder and sit up straighter. Ready? Now: for Narnia and the North.'

INTERNATIONAL SHOW JUMPING

Pat Smythe

Pat Smythe, the world famous show jumper, has travelled the world representing Britain at international show jumping events. She was a member of the British team in 1947 at the age of nineteen. This story is about one of her great victories in 1955.

I was thrilled to get home, but Tosca was fat and unfit from her holiday. Prince Hal arrived back at Stroud Station, and I went to meet him. I was certain that he would be better, but my heart sank as we led him out of the train box. He would hardly put his bad foot to the ground, and the usual stiffness from a long journey could not account for this. The White City, our most important international show, loomed ahead. I feared that Tosca would not be fit in time, and now Prince Hal looked a doubtful starter. The X-rays of Prince Hal's foot did not show much, but after a most serious consultation with Mr J. R. Brain, our friend and vet for the horses during the past two years, we came to a drastic conclusion. Prince Hal had to have complete rest for at least three months. I had had great hopes of competing in Paris and Brussels during the autumn. Prince Hal was at the height of his career and in his element jumping indoors, but it was doubtful if he would be right in time to get fit for these exacting competitions.

Tosca came to the White City with me, although she had not had much work to prepare her. The first competition was the Selby Cup, which she had won twice before. Luckily she really enjoys the White City, and in spite of not being fit she tried her best, and secured the lovely cup for the third time.

The honour of winning the Queen Elizabeth Cup has evaded me so far, and the next day we had this exciting contest. Tosca jumped faultlessly, and so did France's José Bonnaud on Charleston. In the jump-off on time Tosca nipped round the corners, and finished with a fast clear round. However, Charleston, last to go, galloped faster, and beat Tosca's time by a second. It was an exhilarating competition and exciting to watch.

Our National Championships were held at Blackpool, and again Tosca seemed to be in terrific form. But again we went from success to despair, as she developed some gland trouble on the last day and nearly died of internal poisoning. She took a long time to recuperate, and was still uncertain of herself by the time Harringay came round.

Before Tosca completely recovered, I went to Jersey for a day, and watched a horse show there. I was thrilled to find an enthusiastic and flourishing pony club on the island, in spite of the children having far less opportunity with the limited amount of land, and the difficulty of finding new ponies.

A week before Harringay, Prince Hal was allowed to start work. I did not think that he would be able to jump so soon. Tosca, too, was a doubtful starter. She had not really recovered her confidence after her illness, and I was afraid she would remember her fall at her last indoor show in America.

Horses have long memories, but luckily Tosca has happy ones of Harringay. It was a risk to take the two horses to Harringay, but this time it came off. Tosca won the BSJA Spurs again, and Hal, after winning the Diana Stakes, finished the show by winning the *Sunday Graphic* Cup, the Victor Ludorum Championship that Tosca had won the year before.

The rules for this championship ensure an exciting finish to the competition. The first round is jumped over a fairly big and long course. Then the jumps are altered to a test course with fewer and bigger fences. After the horses have jumped the second course, their faults for the two rounds are added together. This time there were five horses with no faults for jumping or time, so the fences were raised, and we jumped a third round. Our time counted on this final round if we were clear again. Miss Dawn Palethorpe jumped a fast clear round on Earlsrath Rambler, who had been going consistently well throughout the show. Then came Mr Wilf White on Nizefella, and in this round he wasted no time. He made the last turn as he landed over the triple bar, galloped to the last fence, taking off at an almost impossible distance from the wall. He was clear, and the crowd waited tensely for his time to be announced. It was half a second slower than Earlsrath Rambler.

The crowd were still clapping the last horse as the bell rang for Prince Hal to start his round. I was over two fences, before I heard people quieten and settle to watch the horse now in the ring. Although one notices the crowd's noises and reactions, I was concentrating on cutting every possible second off the time of our round. Hal was in great form, but he was nearly too excited to turn quickly after the triple bar. I thought that we had a second or two in hand from a quicker turn after the third fence—we galloped through the finish, I glanced up at the clock and saw that Prince Hal had won. What a compensation after the months of doubt, and the fears that he would not be able to jump again.

Tosca and Prince Hal left for Paris with Pauline two days before I joined them there. During the time after Harringay, they had had an easier time than I, but they were both fit, and in good form for the trip. Prince Hal especially had put on a lot of muscle with the three weeks of steady work. We were greeted in Paris with lovely weather. A further joy was to find the horses stabled in big comfortable boxes near to the Bois de Boulogne. Every other autumn we had competed at the indoor Paris show, the horses had not been stabled in luxury. Formerly, a storehouse had been converted into horse lines and the horses had to be tied up all the time. The horses usually developed coughs from the stuffy atmosphere, and they would not eat well. They could never rest peacefully with the noise of all the other horses, or lie down in comfort in their narrow stalls.

This had been the only place near the Vel d'Hiv, where the show was held, that could accommodate horses. With only a short time allotted in the morning for exercise in the small ring, it was difficult to give the horses enough work to prepare them for the evening performance. However, with the new arrangement and the comfortable boxes the horses were fit and happy. We could work them out of doors in the morning sun, and at night they were taken to the show. The articulated vans took six horses quite comfortably, although Tosca, being small, found the mangers a little high for her chin. The vans were built for racehorses like Prince Hal, so poor Tosca had to keep her head up while she was travelling.

On the first day of the show, I worked hard with both the horses in the morning. I have always found that they need to be extra obedient for the first competition, because they are more easily distracted by the strangeness of the surroundings. As they settle into the routine of jumping every evening, often with tiring jump-offs, so they need less work the following morning. Prince Hal is an exception to this, as he gets more and more energy the more work he has. So a great deal of surplus spirits have to be worked off every morning.

The first evening's jumping gave a good preview of the general standard for the show. The courses were big and yet all the horses jumped them well. There was plenty of excitement for the 15,000 spectators packed into the Vel d'Hiv. The crowd is always sympathetic and alive, most of them going there regularly to see any sport that is on, whether it be bicycle races, wrestling, boxing or the horse show.

Tosca was over-anxious and too careful in her competition, and lacked the necessary zip for the speed that counted on the first round. Prince Hal's class was for the horses that would be competing for the Grand Prix later in the week. The course was made up of combinations of fences with one or two strides between each.

There were four horses with clear rounds, and for the jump-off the fences were raised. The time counted on this round, and Prince Hal was first to go. He was clear again, but the other riders had seen the pace that he had set. They were also without a fault and only four-fifths of a second divided all our times. Prince Hal was fourth. It is only a win that counts for international prestige, although there was so little between these four horses. During the round the rider cannot afford to relax from complete concentration for a fraction of a second. One hesitation or slight mistake puts one out of the running, and even a perfect round cannot win a timed competition unless it is carried out with speed and accuracy. The rider has to be prepared to take risks. It is an advantage to see the other horses jumping first, then one knows how many risks are necessary in order to beat their time.

The following evening, I nearly took one risk too many. It was at a time that mattered desperately as it was the first part of the Grand Prix. The twelve best horses qualified for the final of the Grand Prix, according to their results in three other competitions. This first part was a speed competition over quite big fences. I knew that the standard would be high, so if Prince Hal wanted a ribbon, we would have to do a fast clear round. Already some very good rounds had been jumped before my turn came. After jumping the first fence quite fast, I turned Hal quickly to save the distance before the next fence. It was not a difficult fence, but I had decided to jump it at an angle. Hal had sensed that this was a speed competition and was excited and unsettled. As we turned, he was fighting the bit, and did not see the fence until the last moment. His surprise made him stop—and so a small risk that should have come off resulted in a refusal which lost the competition. We finished the round without touching a fence, but three faults for the refusal put us sixteenth in the final placing.

I was most depressed about this, as we would have to do extremely well in the other two competitions in order to get into the finals of the Grand Prix. In Paris, the only thing to do was to make the best of our unfortunate start. The next evening was free, so for the first time in my life I managed to get a seat for the Paris grand opera. The company were doing Weber's *Oberon*, with the ballet as well. The Opera House is an impressive sight, and every place was crammed before the curtain went up. With the opening scene, I found myself at the gates of fairyland. Two trees, standing like guardian dragons, showed the way to the gleaming white pinnacles of the fairy city. The ballet was like a dream and combined perfectly with the immense and beautifully dressed chorus. The splendours of the superb production reminded one of the extravagant days of Louis XV. After seeing the artistry of this performance and thinking of the work involved to produce such a fabulous combination of words, music and dancing, I went back to my job with renewed determination.

The next day Tosca was feeling herself on more familiar ground again. She was last to go in her speed class. The other competitors already knew their positions in the prize list, and Tosca had not shown enough form to worry them. However she did worry them when she scuttled round the fences, clear, and with the fastest time. The second part of the Grand Prix followed this and was again on time over a bigger course. This time I took no risks and Prince Hal was clear and placed fourth on time. I had one nasty moment when Hal thought he had to jump the left-hand of two fences placed side by side. We had taken off before I had persuaded him that our fence was on the right. He made an immense jump and cleared the right one. My heart was in my mouth, but we finished with a clear round.

This pulled us up a bit in the general placing, but our final position depended on the Puissance competition. On that evening the show was being televised for the English transmission. The BBC, used to our big international shows of Harringay and the White City with the split-second timing of the schedule and efficient military organization, had not realized that time is immaterial at foreign shows. Instead of giving the English public the thrilling finish to this Puissance competition, the people at home saw fences being moved, raised, lowered and moved again. Eventually before our television closed down, a few clear rounds had been jumped and so qualified for the jump-off but the most exciting part was yet to come.

The competition ended with a final jump-off over three huge fences. The first was a high wall with a bar beyond it. Voulette, a charming grey mare, the French hope, ridden by M Jonquères d'Oriola, who had won the gold medal at Helsinki, just hit the bar by not spreading enough for this high and wide fence. Then the large parallel bars needed accurate jumping without losing the necessary impetus for such a spread. The last fence was the test, a dead straight wall standing well over 6 ft with no marked ground line to make the horse jump it well. There had been no clear rounds over this final course when Prince Hal's turn came. He jumped the first two fences easily, but he was fighting with excitement when we turned for the wall. I thought that we were a little close on the take-off, but Prince Hal soared up and over to finish clear. Apart from the lovely deep blue Sèvres vase for this victory, he had ensured our place in the final twelve to jump for the Grand Prix.

By this time I knew that Prince Hal was in such fantastic form, that it would only be through a fault of mine if he did not fulfil my ambition for the year by winning the Paris Grand Prix. I felt my responsibility most terribly, and although one probably rides better when feeling calm and confident, I was tense and anxious. It is only too easy to get worked up about these jumping competitions. One is in the ring for about two minutes, and yet I frequently think over that round for the rest of the night. It is not only the winning round that is so exciting. Sometimes a horse

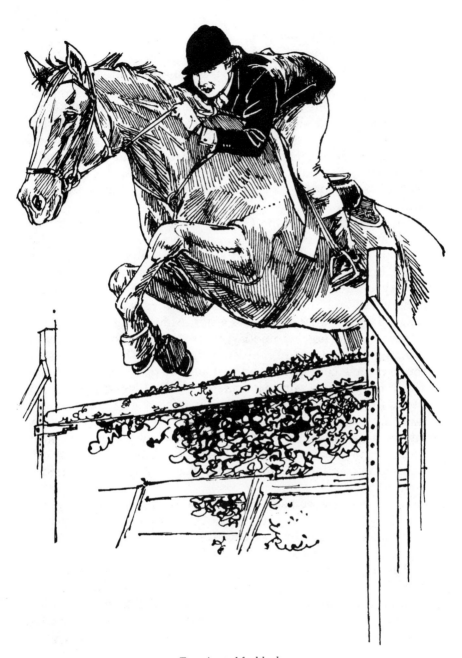

Tosca jumped faultlessly.

produces a complete feeling of happy co-operation, and a joy of jumping. Although through some small fault he may not have won, the rider gets the utmost stimulation and excitement from the round. At one show, I was thrilled with a round that Tosca had jumped over a course that did not suit her. We had not won, but she had done everything I could wish for, and we had really enjoyed it. Somebody came up to me and said, 'What is the matter with Tosca today?—not winning.' Luckily horses are not machines.

On the night before the Grand Prix, the show did not finish until the early hours. We had had no supper, but I was ready for bed, in order to have as much sleep as possible before the big event. En route for the hotel, the others decided that they were too hungry so we called in at a bar in St Germain des Prés. After having a sandwich, and joining in the dancing, there was little time left before I had to work the horses again. After riding in the Bois, I returned to the hotel at midday, where the draw for the order of jumping for the Grand Prix was to take place. The two prizes for the evening's competitions were being displayed at this official reception. I was certain that something would go wrong with my round for the Grand Prix, so I barely glanced at the superb cigar box that would be given to the winner. The prize that really attracted my attention was a lovely clock, with figures of little jumping horses round the dial. This could be won in Tosca's competition, and our dining-room at home so desperately needed a clock!

In the evening we had two reception parties before arriving at the show. I think that I was concentrating more on the evening performance ahead, than on social conversation around me. When we arrived at the Palais des Sports I went to see the horses. Paul was getting Tosca out of the van, ready for me to ride her into the ring. I was the first to go in the second section, so there was no hurry. After walking round the course, I was able to watch a few of the horses jumping in the first section. When I went to fetch Tosca we kept her as unexcited as possible. To warm her up, I trotted her down a side street, over the cobbles, away from the other horses. Then we were called into the ring. It was a touch and out competition with the horses jumping round the course until they made a fault. The winner had to jump the greatest number of fences in the time limit. Tosca was feeling in great form, and needed no winding up as she jumped fence after fence. Her time was nearly up, and she was very tired when I made a mistake and asked her to make too big an effort which finished our round. So far we were winning the competition, only there were still many more good horses to go. I could not wait to see the result of the other horses, as the Grand Prix followed immediately. Tosca was left in the collecting ring, and Paul took her saddle out for Prince Hal. I had to work him up and down a passage behind the Vel d'Hiv. He had been well drawn as eleventh to go out of the twelve horses. The only disadvantage being that he would be standing in the inside collecting ring, with no chance of moving until the other ten horses had jumped their rounds. Moreover the last of the twelve to go was the best of the French horses.

When Prince Hal had settled down outside, I rushed back to the arena, to see how Tosca's competition was faring. As I came through the door I heard a storm of clapping. This surely must be for a competitor that had beaten Tosca's time, or I thought that by then maybe she was out of the running. I tried not to appear too anxious as I asked people who was winning the competition. Nobody seemed to know. The competition was over, and I still did not know the results. The soldiers were already changing the course for the Grand Prix, when over the microphone the prize-winners were told to come into the ring immediately. Tosca had won by jumping two fences more than the others. I rushed excitedly to get her, only to find that she had no saddle. She was too hot from exertion and the stuffy atomosphere for me to ride her bareback, so we managed to borrow a military saddle for her just in time to collect our prize. The dining-room at Miserden was going to get its clock.

Prince Hal was waiting at the arena entrance as I rode Tosca out. I leapt straight on to him, and into the ring for a quick canter before standing him in the inner collecting ring. Then only a moment was left for me to walk round the course, and size up the many problems for this all-important competition. Time was endless while the ten horses before me jumped their rounds. After seeing two or three times at least that Prince Hal's tack was correctly fitted, it was time to get on him. Once in the ring he settled down quickly, and he was jumping out of his skin over the fences. There was never a doubt about his clear round. Several of the other horses were also clear, and we all had to jump a second round. Again, the wait, the agony of watching before going into the ring again. I had been misinformed that the result of the Grand Prix was to be decided on the accumulation of faults and time on the two rounds. Prince Hal flashed round with another clear. His time was the fastest—but no, he had not won, the microphone informed us that two other horses that had also jumped two clear rounds would again jump off with Prince Hal, with the time counting only in this third round. All the strain again—the fences were raised, the air got hotter and dustier, the horses were sweating, and I felt worn out. It was getting on for midnight.

The first horse in was the Swedish Lurifax. Again he went clear, and up went the Swedish flag, but I knew that I could beat his time. I took no risks, and Prince Hal was clear again, almost wasting time in the air as he was clearing his fences by so much. His time was faster than the Swede's, so down came the Swedish flag, and up went the Union Jack. The last horse to go was Vezelise. He had jumped brilliantly for Captain Guy Lefrant throughout the show, and was the favourite for this prize. Vezelise jumped a fast round, but he was tired, and did not jump quite high enough. He finished with eight faults, and the Union Jack stayed in its place. Prince Hal came into the ring followed by Lurifax and Vezelise. The anthem was played and I felt like following it up with 'Why, oh, why do I love Paris!'

I very nearly missed the train to Brussels. The horses were safely en route, but I tried to fit in more than was possible before leaving Paris. The traffic did all it could to hold us up on the way to the station, but by the time the train puffed out, I was on it.

The Palais des Sports in Brussels has a larger ring than Paris, although in both places there is a cycling track around the outside. The conditions were the same for the horses, and we worked them each morning in the woods outside Brussels, where they were stabled. In the evening they were transported to the show by huge vans, and before they came into the inner collecting ring we could give them a canter in a passage way.

Prince Hal was obviously in great form, and settled down to his jumping with sureness and enjoyment. Tosca was not so happy in the soft sand of the arena. Her feet sank into the sand, making it more difficult to jump, and she was ready for her winter's rest. Of the competitions, Prince Hal has never given me such a feeling of confidence as at this show. I had jumped at the show two years before, when Prince Hal and Tosca had won between them the Grand Prix de la Ville de Bruxelles. This had been a competition with the rider jumping the course with each of his two horses in turn, the winner having the least faults in the shortest time. Tosca and Hal rather specialize in this partnership type of competition, having won the President of Mexico Trophy in New York, run on similar lines—so the horses had many friends in Brussels and people remembered them. One finds that any horse with a lot of character can make its personality felt with the crowd, sometimes even to the extent of getting fan mail and parcels of sugar!

It is always encouraging to a horse and the rider to have the crowd's enthusiasm. People are usually very fair, giving the greatest credit to the best performance, even if a foreign horse has beaten one of their own team. There are exceptions of course, just as the public at a bull-fight can turn against a matador. Then they force him into attempting the impossible, turning bravery into certain death. Too late, the people mourn the hero they have killed.

There was no hint of favouritism from the crowd when Prince Hal had his duel with Hicamboy—a Belgian horse. It was in the

Puissance competition, when a reduced number of fences are greatly increased in size for each jump-off, until the winner is found. After the second jump-off, these were the only two horses clear, both good-looking chestnut geldings determined not to touch a fence. Hicamboy is a bigger horse than Prince Hal, but that was not to affect the issue. For the fourth round there were only two fences: first a straight red wall on the left-hand side of the arena, and then down the centre to an enormous spread fence, made of white bars either side of an imitation bank.

The Belgian horse ridden by M Poffé went first. To the joy of the crowd he cleared both fences. Prince Hal came in. There was a hush from the crowd. He was pulling and fighting a little, as he still was not sure whether this round might be on speed—the possibility of a timed jump-off excited him terribly. I soon dispelled these thoughts of his by firmly keeping him in control at a slow canter before jumping the wall. In fact I had him almost too slow on the take-off, but in the last stride he crouched like a dog about to jump on to a high chair, and sprang over the wall with inches to spare. Turning for the spread fence, this control I had gained was more than necessary. There was the distraction of the 'way out' after the big jump; the gates into the collecting ring opened in a direct line after the fence. All horses are keener on the home-ward journey, and these gates were an enticement. However, we were under control as we cantered down and jumped the fence to qualify for the next jump-off. Up went the two fences, the spread was widened, and men were running about getting new layers to put on the wall. Into the ring went Hicamboy. He scraped over the wall, but it did not fall, and when he cleared the spread, in grand style, the crowd went mad. Prince Hal stumbled in the soft sand churned up at the corner of the ring, as I turned him for the wall, but as we approached he had settled, and was well balanced. After jumping it I turned for the last fence, and had the luck to sense the correct stride for the take-off as we turned. It could not have been easier. For the sixth round, it did not look so easy. The wall was up to 6 ft 6 in and so was the last fence, which also added the problem of a 6 ft 6 in spread. The jumps were high, the hour was late, and the horses were hot.

The battle was on, and Hicamboy faced the wall yet again. He cleared it, and there was a 'shush' from some people to stop the crowd clapping in jubilation before he jumped the last fence. Alas, he could not manage the huge spread and he hit it badly. Hal was keen to get going, and there was a murmur from the crowd as if they were speculating on his chances. He jumped the wall, and turned nearly too quickly. For a moment he seemed too excited to be obedient, and it would be a very nasty moment for the rider if he arrived inaccurately at a fence of this size. Hal's courage was superb, and he used all his ability to gather himself, and easily cleared the spread. I felt as though we were diving down from the stars as we landed on the sand as winners of the Puissance.

The final competition was a high jump in place of the usual Grand Prix. Prince Hal was entered for this although he had never before competed in a competition of this type. Each horse is allowed three tries to clear the high jump before qualifying for the next height. The first time, with the fence at about 5 ft 6 in, Hal was surprised to find that he only had one obstacle to tackle. He soon got the idea, and each time the fence went up he jumped it on his first try. By the time we reached 6 ft 6 in we were getting a little anxious as to whether the poles would last out for a further height. The poles are specially made of padded bamboo, so that the horses will not damage themselves. So many poles had been broken by horses that could not quite make the height, that the carpenters had to start a running repair service.

There were only three horses left to face 2 m 10 (6 ft 10$\frac{7}{8}$ in) and when Prince Hal jumped it I was thrilled. Col Llewellyn's great horse Kilgeddin had cleared that height with me in Paris. It was the first time since that night in 1950 that I had competed in another high jump.

At 2 m 20 (7 ft 3 in) Prince Hal again jumped it on his first attempt. He had won the competition, so there was no need to ask more of him. He also now held the official Ladies' European

High Jump record. He was the leading horse of the show, and with the points also gained by Tosca, he made me the leading rider of the show. Prince Hal deserved a crown. The greatest credit was also due to Pauline for keeping the horses so well through the strenuous shows, long journeys and hours of waiting in winter weather.

When the horses arrived back at Miserden they found the flags out and 'Welcome' over their stable door. The rain was dripping off the Union Jack outside, but there was a good feed in the manger inside the stable. They were worn out after their journey home, and retired to bed soon after they had eaten their supper.

During the winter the horses are rested. On fine days they are allowed out in the paddock, where they give a rodeo display of bucking, to show the joy of living. They look so bonny and feel so naughty that I always fear that their sense of humour will be worked off on me when we start work again.

After the high lights of the shows, the star performers become bored with their temporary retirement: but this is the time when their legs can be rested, and they can forget the strain of the big competitions. They then come back to their work with renewed zest at the beginning of the next season.

The rider has no such rest. I can use this time to concentrate on finding and training young horses ready to start in novice jumping events in the spring. One cannot produce a top-class horse in a moment, and it is the hours of background work put in at home that count in the long run. Years later, one hopes to get the thrill and satisfaction from having the horse that has been trained at home, winning and jumping consistently. On the other hand, after all this work, one may find that the horse lacks some quality to make him a top-class performer. Then with patience, one must start training another, with faith that the result will prove more satisfactory. Life is never dull, for the more horses I ride, the more I learn how little I know. Success in any walk of life is never easily won, but in show jumping, the work behind the scenes is always interesting and worth while.

MR WINKLE'S EQUESTRIAN ADVENTURE

Charles Dickens

The Pickwick Club has four members—Mr Samuel Pickwick, Mr Tracy Tupman, the poetic Mr Snodgrass and the sporting Mr Winkle. Here the four Pickwickians are going to visit some friends at Manor Farm, Dingley Dell.

Bright and pleasant was the sky, balmy the air, and beautiful the appearance of every object around, as Mr Pickwick leant over the balustrades of Rochester Bridge, contemplating nature, and waiting for breakfast. The scene was indeed one which might well have charmed a far less reflective mind, than that to which it was presented.

On the left of the spectator lay the ruined wall, broken in many places, and in some, overhanging the narrow beach below in rude and heavy masses. Huge knots of seaweed hung upon the jagged and pointed stones, trembling in every breath of wind; and the green ivy clung mournfully round the dark and ruined battlements.

Behind it rose the ancient castle, its towers roofless, and it massive walls crumbling away, but telling us proudly of its own might and strength, as when, seven hundred years ago, it rang with the clash of arms, or resounded with the noise of feasting and revelry. On either side, the banks of the Medway, covered with cornfields and pastures, with here and there a windmill, or a distant church, stretched away as far as the eye could see, presenting a rich and varied landscape, rendered more beautiful by the changing shadows which passed swiftly across it, as the thin and half-formed clouds skimmed away in the light of the morning sun. The river, reflecting the clear blue of the sky, glistened and sparkled as it flowed noiseless on; and the oars of the fishermen dipped into the water with a clear and liquid sound, as the heavy but picturesque boats glided slowly down the stream.

Mr Pickwick was roused from the agreeable reverie into which he had been led by the objects before him, by a deep sigh, and a touch on his shoulder. He turned. The dismal man was at his side.

'Contemplating the scene?' inquired the dismal man.

'I was,' said Mr Pickwick.

'And congratulating yourself on being up so soon?' Mr Pickwick nodded assent.

'Ah! people need to rise early, to see the sun in all his splendour, for his brightness seldom lasts the day through. The morning of day and the morning of life are but too much alike.'

'You speak truly, sir,' said Mr Pickwick.

'How common the saying,' continued the dismal man, '"The morning's too fine to last." How well might it be applied to our everyday existence. God! what would I forfeit to have the days of my childhood restored, or to be able to forget them for ever!'

'You have seen much trouble, sir,' said Mr Pickwick.

'I have,' said the dismal man, hurriedly; 'I have. More than those who see me now would believe possible.' He paused for an instant, and then said, abruptly:

'Did it ever strike you, on such a morning as this, that drowning would be happiness and peace?'

'God bless me, no!' replied Mr Pickwick, edging a little from the balustrade, as the possibility of the dismal man's tipping him over, by way of experiment, occurred to him rather forcibly.

'*I* have thought so, often,' said the dismal man, without noticing the action. 'The calm, cool water seems to me to murmur an invitation to repose and rest. A bound, a splash, a brief struggle; there is an eddy for an instant, it gradually subsides into a gentle ripple; the waters have closed above your head, and the world has closed upon your miseries and misfortunes for ever.' The sunken eye of the dismal man flashed brightly as he spoke, but the momentary excitement quickly subsided; and he turned calmly away, as he said:

'There—enough of that. I wish to see you on another subject. You invited me to read that paper, the night before last, and listened attentively while I did so.'

'I did,' replied Mr Pickwick; 'and I certainly thought...'

'I asked for no opinion,' said the dismal man, interrupting him, 'and I want none. You are travelling for amusement and instruction. Suppose I forwarded you a curious manuscript—observe, not curious because wild or improbable, but curious as a leaf from the romance of real life. Would you communicate it to the club, of which you have spoken so frequently?'

'Certainly,' replied Mr Pickwick, 'if you wished it; and it would be entered on their transactions.'

'You shall have it,' replied the dismal man. 'Your address'; and, Mr Pickwick having communicated their probable route, the dismal man carefully noted it down in a greasy pocket-book, and, resisting Mr Pickwick's pressing invitation to breakfast, left that gentleman at his inn, and walked slowly away.

Mr Pickwick found that his three companions had risen, and were waiting his arrival to commence breakfast, which was ready laid in tempting display. They sat down to the meal; and broiled ham, eggs, tea, coffee, and sundries, began to disappear with a rapidity which at once bore testimony to the excellence of the fare, and the appetites of its consumers.

'Now, about Manor Farm,' said Mr Pickwick. 'How shall we go?'

'We had better consult the waiter, perhaps,' said Mr Tupman, and the waiter was summoned accordingly.

'Dingley Dell, gentlemen—fifteen miles, gentlemen—cross road—post-chaise, sir?'

'Post-chaise won't hold more than two,' said Mr Pickwick.

'True, sir—beg your pardon, sir. Very nice four-wheeled chaise, sir—seat for two behind—one in front for the gentleman that drives—oh! beg your pardon, sir—that'll only hold three.'

'What's to be done?' said Mr Snodgrass.

'Perhaps one of the gentlemen would like to ride, sir?' suggested the waiter, looking towards Mr Winkle; 'very good saddle-horses, sir—any of Mr Wardle's men coming to Rochester bring 'em back, sir.'

'The very thing,' said Mr Pickwick. 'Winkle, will you go on horseback?'

Mr Winkle did entertain considerable misgivings in the very lowest recesses of his own heart, relative to his equestrian skill; but, as he would not have them even suspected on any account, he at once replied with great hardihood, 'Certainly. I should enjoy it, of all things.'

Mr Winkle had rushed upon his fate; there was no resource. 'Let them be at the door by eleven,' said Mr Pickwick.

'Very well, sir,' replied the waiter.

The waiter retired; the breakfast concluded; and the travellers ascended to their respective bedrooms, to prepare a change of clothing, to take with them on their approaching expedition.

Mr Pickwick had made his preliminary arrangements, and was looking over the coffee-room blinds at the passengers in the street, when the waiter entered, and announced that the chaise was ready —an announcement which the vehicle itself confirmed, by forth-with appearing before the coffee-room blinds aforesaid.

It was a curious little green box on four wheels, with a low place like a wine-bin for two behind, and an elevated perch for one in front, drawn by an immense brown horse, displaying great symmetry of bone. An hostler stood near, holding by the bridle another immense horse—apparently a near relative of the animal in the chaise—ready saddled for Mr Winkle.

'Bless my soul!' said Mr Pickwick, as they stood upon the pavement while the coats were being put in. 'Bless my soul! who's to drive? I never thought of that.'

'Oh! you, of course,' said Mr Tupman.

'Of course,' said Mr Snodgrass.

'I!' exclaimed Mr Pickwick.

'Not the slightest fear, sir,' interposed the hostler. 'Warrant him quiet, sir; a hinfant in arms might drive him.'

'He don't shy, does he?' inquired Mr Pickwick.

'Shy, sir?—He wouldn't shy if he was to meet a vaggin-load of monkeys with their tails burnt off.'

The last recommendation was indisputable. Mr Tupman and Mr Snodgrass got into the bin; Mr Pickwick ascended to his perch, and deposited his feet on a floor-clothed shelf, erected beneath it for that purpose.

'Now, shiny Villiam,' said the hostler to the deputy hostler, 'give the gen'lm'n the ribbins.' 'Shiny Villiam'—so called, probably, from his sleek hair and oily countenance—placed the reins in Mr Pickwick's left hand; and the upper hostler thrust a whip into his right.

'Wo—o!' cried Mr Pickwick, as the tall quadruped evinced a decided inclination to back into the coffee-room window.

'Wo—o!' echoed Mr Tupman and Mr Snodgrass, from the bin.

'Only his playfulness, gen'lm'n,' said the head hostler encouragingly; 'jist kitch hold on him, Villiam.' The deputy restrained the animal's impetuosity, and the principal ran to assist Mr Winkle in mounting.

'T'other side, sir, if you please.'

'Blowed if the gen'lm'n worn't a gettin' up on the wrong side,' whispered a grinning post-boy to the inexpressibly gratified waiter.

Mr Winkle, thus instructed, climbed into his saddle, with about as much difficulty as he would have experienced in getting up the side of a first-rate man-of-war.

'All right?' inquired Mr Pickwick, with an inward presentiment that it was all wrong.

'All right,' replied Mr Winkle faintly.

'Let 'em go,' cried the hostler—'Hold him in, sir,' and away went the chaise, and the saddle-horse, with Mr Pickwick on the box of the one, and Mr Winkle on the back of the other, to the delight and gratification of the whole inn yard.

'What makes him go sideways?' said Mr Snodgrass in the bin, to Mr Winkle in the saddle.

'I can't imagine,' replied Mr Winkle. His horse was drifting up the street in the most mysterious manner—side first, with his head towards one side of the way, and his tail towards the other.

Mr Pickwick had no leisure to observe either this or any other particular, the whole of his faculties being concentrated in the management of the animal attached to the chaise, who displayed various peculiarities, highly interesting to a bystander, but by no means equally amusing to anyone seated behind him. Besides constantly jerking his head up, in a very unpleasant and uncomfortable manner, and tugging at the reins to an extent which rendered it a matter of great difficulty for Mr Pickwick to hold them, he had a singular propensity for darting suddenly every now and then to the side of the road, then stopping short, and then rushing forward for some minutes, at a speed which it was wholly impossible to control.

'What *can* he mean by this?' said Mr Snodgrass, when the horse had executed this manoeuvre for the twentieth time.

'I don't know,' replied Mr Tupman; 'it *looks* very like shying, don't it?' Mr Snodgrass was about to reply, when he was interrupted by a shout from Mr Pickwick.

'Woo!' said that gentleman; 'I have dropped my whip.'

'Winkle,' said Mr Snodgrass, as the equestrian came trotting up on the tall horse, with his hat over his ears, and shaking all over, as if he would shake to pieces, with the violence of the exercise, 'pick up the whip, there's a good fellow.' Mr Winkle pulled at the bridle of the tall horse till he was black in the face; and having at length succeeded in stopping him, dismounted, handed the whip to Mr Pickwick, and grasping the reins, prepared to remount.

Now whether the tall horse, in the natural playfulness of his disposition, was desirous of having a little innocent recreation with Mr Winkle, or whether it occurred to him that he could perform the journey as much to his own satisfaction without a rider as with one, are points upon which, of course, we can arrive at no definite and distinct conclusion. By whatever motives the animal was actuated, certain it is that Mr Winkle had no sooner touched the reins, than he slipped them over his head, and darted backwards to their full length.

'Poor fellow,' said Mr Winkle, soothingly—'poor fellow—good old horse.' The 'poor fellow' was proof against flattery: the more Mr Winkle tried to get nearer him, the more he sidled away; and, notwithstanding all kinds of coaxing and wheedling, there were Mr Winkle and the horse going round and round each other for ten minutes, at the end of which time each was at precisely the same distance from the other as when they first commenced—an unsatisfactory sort of thing under any circumstances, but particularly so in a lonely road, where no assistance can be procured.

'What am I to do?' shouted Mr Winkle, after the dodging had been prolonged for a considerable time. 'What am I to do? I can't get on him.'

'You had better lead him till we come to a turnpike,' replied Mr Pickwick from the chaise.

'But he won't come!' roared Mr Winkle. 'Do come, and hold him.'

Mr Pickwick was the very personation of kindness and humanity: he threw the reins on the horse's back, and having descended from his seat, carefully drew the chaise into the hedge, lest anything should come along the road, and stepped back to the assistance of his distressed companion, leaving Mr Tupman and Mr Snodgrass in the vehicle.

The horse no sooner beheld Mr Pickwick advancing towards him with the chaise whip in his hand, than he exchanged the rotary motion in which he had previously indulged, for a retrograde movement of so very determined a character, that it at once drew Mr Winkle, who was still at the end of the bridle, at a rather quicker rate, than fast walking, in the direction from which they had just come. Mr Pickwick ran to his assistance; but the faster Mr Pickwick ran forward, the faster the horse ran backward. There was a great scraping of feet, and kicking up of the dust; and at last Mr Winkle, his arms being nearly pulled out of their sockets, fairly let go his hold. The horse paused, stared, shook his head, turned round, and quietly trotted home to Rochester, leaving Mr Winkle and Mr Pickwick gazing on each other with countenances of blank dismay. A rattling noise at a little distance attracted their attention. They looked up.

'Bless my soul!' exclaimed the agonized Mr Pickwick, 'there's the other horse running away!'

It was but too true. The animal was startled by the noise, and the reins were on his back. The result may be guessed. He tore off with the four-wheeled chaise behind him, and Mr Tupman and Mr Snodgrass in the four-wheeled chaise. The heat was a short one. Mr Tupman threw himself into the hedge, Mr Snodgrass followed his example, the horse dashed the four-wheeled chaise against a wooden bridge, separated the wheels from the body, and the bin from the perch: and finally stood stock still to gaze upon the ruin he had made.

The first care of the two unspilt friends was to extricate their unfortunate companions from their bed of quickset—a process which gave them the unspeakable satisfaction of discovering that they had sustained no injury, beyond sundry rents in their garments, and various lacerations from the brambles. The next thing to be done was, to unharness the horse. This complicated process having been effected, the party walked slowly forward, leading the horse among them, and abandoning the chaise to its fate.

An hour's walking brought the travellers to a little roadside

Mr Tupman threw himself into the hedge, and Mr Snodgrass followed his example.

public house, with two elm-trees, a horse-trough, and a signpost, in front; one or two deformed hay-ricks behind, a kitchen garden at the side, and rotten sheds and mouldering outhouses jumbled in strange confusion all about it. A red-headed man was working in the garden; and to him Mr Pickwick called lustily—'Hallo there!'

The red-headed man raised his body, shaded his eyes with his hand, and stared, long and coolly, at Mr Pickwick and his companions.

'Hallo there!' repeated Mr Pickwick.

'Hallo!' was the red-headed man's reply.

'How far is it to Dingley Dell?'

'Better er seven mile.'

'Is it a good road?'

'No t'ant.' Having uttered this brief reply, and apparently satisfied himself with another scrutiny, the red-headed man resumed his work.

'We want to put this horse up here,' said Mr Pickwick; 'I suppose we can, can't we?'

'Want to put that 'ere horse up, do ee?' repeated the red-headed man, leaning on his spade.

'Of course,' replied Mr Pickwick, who had by this time advanced, horse in hand, to the garden rails.

'Missus'—roared the man with the red head, emerging from the garden, and looking very hard at the horse—'Missus!'

A tall bony woman—straight all the way down—in a coarse blue pelisse, with the waist an inch or two below her arm-pits, responded to the call.

'Can we put this horse up here, my good woman?' said Mr Tupman, advancing, and speaking in his most seductive tones. The woman looked very hard at the whole party; and the red-headed man whispered something in her ear.

'No,' replied the woman, after a little consideration, 'I'm afeerd on it.'

'Afraid!' exclaimed Mr Pickwick, 'what's the woman afraid of?'

'It got us in trouble last time,' said the woman, turning into the house; 'I woant have nothin' to say to 'un.'

'Most extraordinary thing I ever met with in my life,' said the astonished Mr Pickwick.

'I—I—really believe,' whispered Mr Winkle, as his friends gathered round him, 'that they think we have come by this horse in some dishonest manner.'

'What!' exclaimed Mr Pickwick, in a storm of indignation. Mr Winkle modestly repeated his suggestion.

'Hallo, you fellow!' said the angry Mr Pickwick, 'do you think we stole this horse?'

'I'm sure ye did,' replied the red-headed man, with a grin which agitated his countenance from one auricular organ to the other. He turned into the house, and banged the door after him.

'It's like a dream,' ejaculated Mr Pickwick, 'a hideous dream. The idea of a man's walking about, all day, with a dreadful horse that he can't get rid of!' The depressed Pickwickians turned moodily away, with the tall quadruped, for which they all felt the most unmitigated disgust, following slowly at their heels.

It was late in the afternoon when the four friends and their four-footed companion turned into the lane leading to Manor Farm: and even when they were so near their place of destination, the pleasure they would otherwise have experienced was materially damped as they reflected on the singularity of their appearance, and the absurdity of their situation. Torn clothes, lacerated faces, dusty shoes, exhausted looks, and, above all, the horse. Oh, how Mr Pickwick cursed that horse: he had eyed the noble animal from time to time with looks expressive of hatred and revenge; more than once he had calculated the probable amount of the expense he would incur by cutting his throat; and now the temptation to destroy him, or to cast him loose upon the world, rushed upon his mind with tenfold force. He was roused from a meditation on these dire imaginings, by the sudden appearance of two figures at a turn of the lane. It was Mr Wardle, and his faithful attendant, the fat boy.

'Why, where *have* you been?' said the hospitable old gentleman; 'I've been waiting for you all day. Well, you *do* look tired. What! Scratches! Not hurt, I hope—eh? Well, I *am* glad to hear that— very. So you've been spilt, eh? Never mind. Common accident in these parts. Joe—he's asleep again!—Joe, take that horse from the gentleman, and lead it into the stable.'

The fat boy sauntered heavily behind them with the animal; and the old gentleman, condoling with his guests in homely phrase on so much of the day's adventures as they thought proper to communicate, led the way to the kitchen.

'We'll have you put to rights here,' said the old gentleman, 'and then I'll introduce you to the people in the parlour. Emma, bring out the cherry-brandy; now, Jane, a needle and thread here; towels and water, Mary. Come, girls, bustle about.'

Three or four buxom girls speedily dispersed in search of the different articles in requisition, while a couple of large-headed, circular visaged males rose from their seats in the chimney-corner (for although it was a May evening, their attachment to the wood-fire appeared as cordial as if it were Christmas), and dived into some obscure recesses, from which they speedily produced a bottle of blacking, and some half-dozen brushes.

'Bustle!' said the old gentleman again, but the admonition was quite unnecessary, for one of the girls poured out the cherry-brandy, and another brought in the towels, and one of the men suddenly seizing Mr Pickwick by the leg, at imminent hazard of throwing him off his balance, brushed away at his boot, till his corns were red-hot; while the other shampoo'd Mr Winkle with a heavy clothes-brush, indulging, during the operation, in that hissing sound which hostlers are wont to produce when engaged in rubbing down a horse.

Mr Snodgrass, having concluded his ablutions, took a survey of the room, while standing with his back to the fire, sipping his cherry-brandy with heartfelt satisfaction. He describes it as a large apartment, with a red brick floor and a capacious chimney; the ceiling garnished with hams, sides of bacon, and ropes of onions. The walls were decorated with several hunting-whips, two or three bridles, a saddle and an old rusty blunderbuss, with an inscription below it, intimating that it was 'Loaded'—as it had been, on the same authority, for half a century at least. An old eight-day clock, of solemn and sedate demeanour, ticked gravely in one corner; and a silver watch, of equal antiquity, dangled from one of the many hooks which ornamented the dresser.

'Ready?' said the old gentleman inquiringly, when his guests had been washed, mended, brushed, and brandied.

'Quite,' replied Mr Pickwick.

'Come along, then,' and the party having traversed several dark passages, and being joined by Mr Tupman, who had lingered behind to snatch a kiss from Emma, for which he had been duly rewarded with sundry pushings and scratchings, arrived at the parlour door.

'Welcome,' said their hospitable host, throwing it open and stepping forward to announce them, 'Welcome, gentlemen, to Manor Farm.'

THE COUNTRY OF THE HOUYHNHNMS

Jonathan Swift

Gulliver's Travels **was first published in 1726. It was written as a satire on human beings by the argumentative Irishman, Dean Jonathan Swift. The tale is told by a ship's surgeon, Lemuel Gulliver, who is shipwrecked in a strange, far-off land.**

I continued at home with my wife and children about five months in a very happy condition, if I could have learned the lesson of knowing when I was well. I left my poor wife big with child, and accepted an advantageous offer made me to be Captain of the *Adventure*, a stout merchantman of 350 tons: for I understood navigation well, and being grown weary of a surgeon's employment at sea, which however I could exercise upon occasion, I took a skilful young man of that calling, one Robert Purefoy, into my ship. We set sail from Portsmouth upon the seventh day of August, 1710; on the fourteenth we met with Captain Pocock of Bristol, at Teneriffe, who was going to the bay of Campechy, to cut logwood. On the sixteenth he was parted from us by a storm; I heard since my return that his ship foundered, and none escaped but one cabin boy. He was an honest man, and a good sailor, but a little too positive in his own opinions, which was the cause of his destruction. For if he had followed my advice, he might have been safe at home with his family at this time, as well as myself.

I had several men died in my ship of calentures, so that I was forced to get recruits out of Barbadoes, and the Leeward Islands, where I touched by the direction of the merchants who employed me, which I had soon too much cause to repent: for I found afterwards that most of them had been buccaneers. I had fifty hands on board, and my orders were that I should trade with the Indians in the South Sea, and make what discoveries I could. These rogues whom I had picked up debauched my other men, and they all formed a conspiracy to seize the ship and secure me; which they did one morning, rushing into my cabin, and binding me hand and foot, threatening to throw me overboard, if I offered to stir. I told them I was their prisoner and would submit. This they made me swear to do, and then they unbound me, only fastening one of my legs with a chain near my bed, and placed a sentry at my door with his piece charged, who was commanded to shoot me dead, if I attempted my liberty. They sent me down victuals and drink, and took the government of the ship to themselves. Their design was to turn pirates, and plunder the Spaniards, which they could not do, till they got more men. But first they resolved to sell the goods in the ship, and then go to Madagascar for recruits, several among them having died since my confinement. They sailed many weeks, and traded with the Indians, but I knew not what course they took, being kept a close prisoner in my cabin, and expecting nothing less than to be murdered, as they often threatened me.

Upon the ninth day of May 1711, one James Welch came down to my cabin; and said he had orders from the Captain to set me ashore. I expostulated with him but in vain; neither would he so much as tell me who their new Captain was. They forced me into the longboat, letting me put on my best suite of clothes, which were as good as new, and a small bundle of linen, but no arms except my hanger; and they were so civil as not to search my pockets, into which I conveyed what money I had, with some other little necessaries. They rowed about a league, and then set me down on a strand. I desired them to tell me what country it was. They all swore they knew no more than myself, but said that the Captain (as they called him) was resolved, after they had sold the lading, to get rid of me in the first place where they could discover land. They pushed off immediately, advising me to make haste, for fear of being overtaken by the tide, and so bade me farewell.

In this desolate condition I advanced forward, and soon got upon firm ground, where I sat down on a bank to rest myself, and consider what I had best to do. When I was a little refreshed I went up into the country, resolving to deliver myself to the first savages I should meet, and purchase my life from them by some bracelets, glass rings, and other toys which sailors usually provide themselves with in those voyages, and whereof I had some about me. The land was divided by long rows of trees, not regularly planted, but naturally growing; there was great plenty of grass, and several fields of oats. I walked very circumspectly for fear of being surprised, or suddenly shot with an arrow from behind or on either side. I fell into a beaten road, where I saw many tracks of human feet, and some of cows, but most of horses. At last I beheld several animals in a field, and one or two of the same kind sitting in trees. Their shape was very singular and deformed, which a little discomposed me, so that I lay down behind a thicket to observe them better. Some of them coming forward near the place where I lay, gave me an opportunity of distinctly marking their form. Their heads and breasts were covered with a thick hair, some frizzled and others lank; they had beards like goats, and a long ridge of hair down their backs and the fore-parts of their legs and feet, but the rest of their bodies were bare, so that I might see their skins, which were of a brown buff colour. They had no tails, nor any hair at all on their buttocks, except about the anus; which, I presume, nature had placed there to defend them as they sat on the ground; for this posture they used, as well as lying down, and often stood on their hind feet. They climbed high trees, as nimbly as a squirrel, for they had strong extended claws before and behind, terminating in sharp points, and hooked. They would often spring and bound and leap with prodigious agility. The females were not so large as the males; they had long lank hair on their heads, but none on their faces, nor any thing more than a sort of down on the rest of their bodies, except about the anus, and pudenda. Their dugs hung between their fore-feet, and often reached almost to the ground as they walked. The hair of both sexes was of several colours, brown, red, black, and yellow. Upon the whole, I never beheld in all my travels so disagreeable an animal, nor one against which I naturally conceived so strong an antipathy. So that thinking I had seen enough, full of contempt and aversion, I got up and pursued the beaten road, hoping it might direct me to the cabin of some Indian. I had not got far when I met one of these creatures full in my way, and coming up directly to me. The ugly monster, when he saw me, distorted several ways every feature of his visage, and stared as at an object he had never seen before; then approaching nearer, lifted up his fore-paw, whether out of curiosity or mischief, I could not tell. But I drew my hanger, and gave him a good blow with the flat side of it, for I durst not strike him with the edge, fearing the inhabitants might be provoked against me, if they should come to know that I had killed or maimed any of their cattle. When the beast felt the smart, he drew back, and roared so loud that a herd of at least forty came flocking about me from the next field, howling and making odious faces; but I ran to the body of a tree, and leaning my back against it, kept them off by waving my hanger. Several of this cursed brood getting hold of the branches behind, leapt up into the tree, from whence they began to discharge their excrements on my head; however, I escaped pretty well, by sticking close to the stem of the tree, but was almost stifled with the filth, which fell about me on every side.

In the midst of this distress, I observed them all to run away on a sudden as fast as they could, at which I ventured to leave the tree, and pursue the road, wondering what it was that could put them into this fright. But looking on my left hand, I saw a horse walking softly in the field; which my persecutors having sooner discovered, was the cause of their flight. The horse started a little when he came near me, but soon recovering himself, looked full in my face with manifest tokens of wonder; he viewed hands and feet, walking round me several times. I would have pursued my journey, but he placed himself directly in the way, yet looking with a very mild aspect, never offering the least violence. We stood gazing at each other for some time; at last I took the boldness to reach my hand towards his neck, with a design to stroke it, using the common style and whistle of jockeys when they are going to handle a strange horse. But this animal seeming to receive my civilities with disdain, shook his head, and bent his brows, softly raising up his right fore-foot to remove my hand. Then he neighed three or four times, but in so different a cadence, that I almost began to think he was speaking to himself in some language of his own.

While he and I were thus employed, another horse came up; who applying himself to the first in a very formal manner, they gently struck each other's right hoof before, neighing several times by turns, and varying the sound, which seemed to be almost articulate. They went some paces off, as if it were to confer together, walking side by side, backward and forward, like persons deliberating upon some affair of weight, but often turning their eyes towards me, as it were to watch that I might not escape. I was amazed to see such actions and behaviour in brute beasts, and concluded with myself, that if the inhabitants of this country were endued with a proportionable degree of reason, they must needs be the wisest people upon earth. This thought gave me so much comfort, that I resolved to go forward until I could discover some house or village, or meet with any of the natives, leaving the two horses to discourse together as they pleased. But the first, who was a dapple grey, observing me to steal off, neighed after me in so expressive a tone, that I fancied myself to understand what he meant; whereupon I turned back, and came near him, to expect his farther commands, but concealing my fear as much as I could, for I began to be in some pain, how this adventure might terminate; and the reader will easily believe I did not much like my present situation.

The two horses came up close to me, looking with great earnestness upon my face and hands. The grey steed rubbed my hat all round with his right fore-hoof, and discomposed it so much that I was forced to adjust it better, by taking it off, and settling it again; whereat both he and his companion (who was a brown bay) appeared to be much surprised; the latter felt the lappet of my coat, and finding it to hang loose about me, they both looked with new signs of wonder. He stroked my right hand, seeming to admire the softness and colour; but he squeezed it so hard between his hoof and his pastern, that I was forced to roar; after which they both touched me with all possible tenderness. They were under great perplexity about my shoes and stockings, which they felt very often, neighing to each other, and using various gestures, not unlike those of a philosopher, when he would attempt to solve some new and difficult phenomenon.

Upon the whole, the behaviour of these animals was so orderly and rational, so acute and judicious, that I at last concluded they must needs be magicians, who had thus metamorphosed themselves upon some design, and seeing a stranger in the way, were resolved to divert themselves with him; or perhaps were really amazed at the sight of a man so very different in habit, feature, and complexion from those who might probably live in so remote a climate. Upon the strength of this reasoning, I ventured to address them in the following manner: Gentlemen, if you be conjurers, as I have good cause to believe, you can understand any language; therefore I make bold to let your worships know that I am a poor distressed Englishman, driven by his misfortunes upon your coast, and I entreat one of you, to let me ride upon his back, as if he were a real horse, to some house or village where I can be relieved. In return of which favour I will make you a present of this knife and bracelet (taking them out of my pocket). The two creatures stood silent while I spoke, seeming to listen with great attention; and when I had ended, they neighed frequently towards each other, as if they were engaged in serious conversation. I plainly observed, that their language expressed the passions very well, and the words might with little pains be resolved into an alphabet more easily than the Chinese.

I could frequently distinguish the word *Yahoo*, which was repeated by each of them several times; and although it was impossible for me to conjecture what it meant, yet while the two horses were busy in conversation, I endeavoured to practise this word upon my tongue; and as soon as they were silent, I boldly pronounced *Yahoo* in a loud voice, imitating, at the same time, as near as I could, the neighing of a horse; at which they were both visibly surprised, and the grey repeated the same word twice, as if he meant to teach me the right accent, wherein I spoke after him as well as I could, and found myself perceivably to improve every time, though very far from any degree of perfection. Then the bay tried me with a second word, much harder to be pronounced; but reducing it to the English orthography, may be spelt thus, *Houyhnhnm*. I did not succeed in this so well as the former, but after two or three farther trials, I had better fortune; and they both appeared amazed at my capacity.

After some further discourse, which I then conjectured might relate to me, the two friends took their leaves, with the same compliment of striking each other's hoof; and the grey made me signs that I should walk before him, wherein I thought it prudent to comply, till I could find a better director. When I offered to slacken my pace, he would cry *Hhuun, Hhuun*; I guessed his meaning, and gave him to understand as well as I could, that I was weary, and not able to walk faster; upon which he would stand a while to let me rest.

Having travelled about three miles, we came to a long kind of building, made of timber stuck in the ground, and wattled across; the roof was low, and covered with straw. I now began to be a little comforted, and took out some toys, which travellers usually carry for presents to the savage Indians of America and other parts, in hopes the people of the house would be thereby encouraged to receive me kindly. The horse made me a sign to go in first; it was a large room with a smooth clay floor, and a rack and manger extending the whole length on one side. There were three nags, and two mares, not eating, but some of them sitting down upon their hams, which I very much wondered at; but wondered more to see the rest employed in domestic business. These seemed but ordinary cattle; however, this confirmed my first opinion, that a people who could so far civilize brute animals, must needs excel in wisdom all the nations of the world. The grey came in just after, and thereby prevented any ill treatment which the others might have given me. He neighed to them several times in a style of authority, and received answers.

Beyond this room there were three others, reaching the length of the house, to which you passed through three doors, opposite to each other, in the manner of a vista; we went through the second room towards the third; here the grey walked in first, beckoning me to attend: I waited in the second room, and got ready my presents for the master and mistress of the house: they were two knives, three bracelets of false pearl, a small looking-glass, and a bead necklace. The horse neighed three or four times, and I waited to hear some answers in a human voice, but I heard no other returns than in the same dialect, only one or two a little shriller than his. I began to think that this house must belong to some person of great note among them, because there appeared so much ceremony before I could gain admittance. But, that a man of quality should be served all by horses, was beyond my comprehension. I feared my brain was disturbed by my sufferings and misfortunes: I roused myself, and looked about me in the room where I was left alone; this was furnished like the first, only after a more elegant manner. I rubbed my eyes often, but the same objects still occurred. I pinched my arms and sides to awake myself, hoping I might be in a dream. I then absolutely concluded, that all these appearances could be nothing else but necromancy and magic. But I had no time to pursue these reflections; for the grey horse came to the door, and made me a sign to follow him into the third room, where I saw a very comely mare, together with a colt and foal, sitting on their haunches, upon mats of straw, not unartfully made, and perfectly neat and clean.

The mare soon after my entrance, rose from her mat, and coming up close, after having nicely observed my hands and face, gave me a most contemptuous look; then turning to the horse, I heard the word *Yahoo* often repeated betwixt them; the meaning of which word I could not then comprehend, although it were the first I had learned to pronounce; but I was soon better informed, to my everlasting mortification: for the horse beckoning to me with his head, and repeating the word *Hhuun, Hhuun*, as he did upon the road, which I understood was to attend him, led me out into a kind of court, where was another building at some distance from the house. Here we entered, and I saw three of those detestable creatures, whom I first met after my landing, feeding upon roots, and the flesh of some animals, which I afterwards found to be that of asses and dogs, and now and then a cow dead by accident or disease. They were all tied by the neck with strong withes, fastened to a beam; they held their food between the claws of their forefeet, and tore it with their teeth.

The master horse ordered a sorrel nag, one of his servants, to untie the largest of these animals, and take him into the yard. The beast and I were brought close together, and our countenances diligently compared, both by master and servant, who thereupon repeated several times the word *Yahoo*. My horror and astonishment are not to be described, when I observed in this abominable animal a perfect human figure: the face of it indeed was flat and broad, the nose depressed, the lips large, and the mouth wide. But these differences are common to all savage nations, where the lineaments of the countenance are distorted by the natives suffering their infants to lie grovelling on the earth, or by carrying them on their backs, nuzzling with their face against the mother's shoulders.

The beast and I were diligently compared by master and servant.

The fore-feet of the Yahoo differed from my hands in nothing else but the length of the nails, the coarseness and brownness of the palms, and the hairiness on the backs. There was the same resemblance between our feet, with the same differences, which I knew very well, though the horses did not, because of my shoes and stockings; the same in every part of our bodies, except as to hairiness and colour, which I have already described.

The great difficulty that seemed to stick with the two horses, was to see the rest of my body so very different from that of a Yahoo, for which I was obliged to my clothes, whereof they had no conception. The sorrel nag offered me a root, which he held (after their manner, as we shall describe in its proper place) between his hoof and pastern; I took it in my hand, and having smelt it, returned it to him again as civilly as I could. He brought out of the Yahoo's kennel a piece of ass's flesh, but it smelt so offensively that I turned from it with loathing: he then threw it to the Yahoo, by whom it was greedily devoured. He afterwards showed me a wisp of hay, and a fetlock full of oats; but I shook my head, to signify that neither of these were food for me. And indeed, I now apprehended that I must absolutely starve, if I did not get to some of my own species; for as to those filthy Yahoos, although there were few greater lovers of mankind, at that time, than myself, yet I confess I never saw any sensitive being so detestable on all accounts; and the more I came near them, the more hateful they grew, while I stayed in that country. This the master horse observed by my behaviour, and therefore sent the Yahoo back to his kennel. He then put his fore-hoof to his mouth, at which I was much surprised, although he did it with ease, and with a motion that appeared perfectly natural, and made other signs to know what I would eat; but I could not return him such an answer as he was able to apprehend; and if he had understood me, I did not see how it was possible to contrive any way for finding myself nourishment. While we were thus engaged, I observed a cow passing by, whereupon I pointed to her, and expressed a desire to let me go and milk her. This had its effect; for he led me back into the house, and ordered a mare-servant to open a room, where a good store of milk lay in earthen and wooden vessels, after a very orderly and cleanly manner. She gave me a large bowl full, of which I drank very heartily, and found myself well refreshed.

About noon I saw coming towards the house a kind of vehicle, drawn like a sledge by four Yahoos. There was in it an old steed, who seemed to be of quality; he alighted with his hind-feet forward, having by accident got a hurt in his left fore-foot. He came to dine with our horse, who received him with great civility. They dined in the best room, and had oats boiled in milk for the second course, which the old horse ate warm, but the rest cold. Their mangers were placed circular in the middle of the room, and divided into several partitions, round which they sat on their haunches upon bosses of straw. In the middle was a large rack with angles answering to every partition of the manger; so that each horse and mare ate their own hay, and their own mash of oats and milk, with much decency and regularity. The behaviour of the young colt and foal appeared very modest, and that of the master and mistress extremely cheerful and complaisant to their guest. The grey ordered me to stand by him, and much discourse passed between him and his friend concerning me, as I found by the stranger's often looking on me, and the frequent repetition of the word *Yahoo*.

I happened to wear my gloves, which the master grey observing, seemed perplexed, discovering signs of wonder what I had done to my fore-feet; he put his hoof three or four times to them, as if he would signify that I should reduce them to their former shape, which I presently did, pulling off both my gloves, and putting them into my pocket. This occasioned farther talk, and I saw the company was pleased with my behaviour, whereof I soon found the good effects. I was ordered to speak the few words I understood, and while they were at dinner the master taught me the names for oats, milk, fire, water, and some others; which I could readily pronounce after him, having from my youth a great facility in learning languages.

When dinner was done the master horse took me aside, and by signs and words made me understand the concern that he was in, that I had nothing to eat. Oats in their tongue are called *hlunnh*. This word I pronounced two or three times; for although I had refused them at first, yet upon second thoughts I considered that I could contrive to make of them a kind of bread, which might be sufficient with milk to keep me alive, till I could make my escape to some other country and to creatures of my own species. The horse immediately ordered a white mare-servant of his family to bring me a good quantity of oats in a sort of wooden tray. These I heated before the fire as well as I could, and rubbed them till the husks came off, which I made a shift to winnow from the grain; I ground and beat them between two stones, then took water, and made them into a paste or cake, which I toasted at the fire, and ate warm with milk. It was at first a very insipid diet, though common enough in many parts of Europe, but grew tolerable by time; and having been often reduced to hard fare in my life, this was not the first experiment I had made how easily nature is satisfied. And I cannot but observe, that I never had one hour's sickness while I stayed in this island. 'Tis true, I sometimes made a shift to catch a rabbit or bird by springes made of Yahoos' hairs, and I often gathered wholesome herbs, which I boiled, or ate as salads with my bread, and now and then, for a rarity, I made a little butter, and drank the whey. I was at first at a great loss for salt; but custom soon reconciled the want of it; and I am confident that the frequent use of salt among us is an effect of luxury, and was first introduced only as a provocative to drink; except where it is necessary for preserving of flesh in long voyages, or in places remote from great markets. For we observe no animal to be fond of it but man: and as to myself, when I left this country, it was a great while before I could endure the taste of it in anything that I ate.

This is enough to say upon the subject of my diet, wherewith other travellers fill their books, as if the readers were personally concerned whether we fared well or ill. However, it was necessary to mention this matter, lest the world should think it impossible that I could find sustenance for three years in such a country, and among such inhabitants.

When it grew towards evening, the master horse ordered a place for me to lodge in; it was but six yards from the house, and separated from the stable of the Yahoos. Here I got some straw, and covering myself with my own clothes, slept very sound. But I was in a short time better accommodated, as the reader shall know hereafter, when I come to treat more particularly about my way of living.

OPERATION SIPPACIK

Rumer Godden

Rifat saw the group of men from the schoolhouse window, and guessed why Hasan Dincer had left his boys and girls in charge of the assistant teacher; the schoolmaster was acting as an interpreter, for there, in Arif Ali's field, were three British soldiers. Then, as Rifat watched, he saw his grandfather come limping across the field, leading an unmistakable small donkey, black with a white nose. For a moment Rifat stared, then he slid down from his seat, crawled along the floor under the desks to the back of the room and slipped out of the door. Nazihar, who was on a bench among the infants at the back, slid down and ran after him. They ran across the field to where the men stood, all looking at Sippacik.

Sippacik was now five years old and at five a donkey is full size—
'If you can call it a size,' Arif used to tease Rifat. 'She's far too
small,' and Rifat always rose, like a fish to a fly.

'Small? Dede!' each time Rifat flashed back. 'She's the sturdiest,
prettiest, cleverest donkey in Cyprus.'

Rifat was twelve now, tall for his age, strong and sturdy with
bright brown eyes and close-cropped dark hair. Nazihar had the
frizzy auburn curls of many Turkish women and their dark grey
eyes, but both children had olive-brown skins, their cheeks tinged
with rosiness and both wore tiny gold rings in their ears, rings
handed down by their grandparents' great-grandmothers.

Now Rifat and Nazihar came and stood beside their grandfather Arif where he held Sippacik.

'She's small,' said Bombardier Garnett.

'Small?' cried Arif when the schoolmaster had interpreted.
'Small! She's the sturdiest, prettiest, cleverest donkey in Cyprus.'
Rifat could not help smiling and, 'She's mine,' he said proudly.
The schoolmaster swung round. 'Rifat Ali, Nazihar, go back to
the schoolhouse *at once*,' but Rifat only hid himself behind Arif
and Nazihar went to her friend the Sergeant Major and put her
hand in his.

'She's small,' said Garnett of Sippacik again.

'She's gorgeous,' said Kip, full of admiration.

'What other donkey is there?' The schoolmaster seemed to be
asking it of the sky. 'We are gathering the carobs, the harvest is at
its height; every other donkey is being used.

'Except this dud,' said Garnett.

Rifat did not know what a 'dud' was, but he did not like the
sound of it, and he glared at Garnett. Kip glared too. 'Dud! She's
a little smasher.'

'She is young, well-trained,' said the schoolmaster. 'Arif Ali
trains well.'

'But can she carry weight?' asked the Sergeant Major doubtfully,
as Kip fondled Sippacik's ears.

Rifat still did not understand what was happening; from his

post behind Arif he watched while the Sergeant Major and Garnett examined Sippacik from head to tail, picking up her hooves to look at her feet, feeling her backbone, leading her up and down. Rifat thought they were admiring her and swelled with pride; then he saw the Sergeant Major and Garnett nod in agreement; the next moment the Sergeant Major was counting out money. 'Better to buy outright,' he had advised Bluebell.

'Yes, HQ have agreed,' said Bluebell. 'We don't know how long we shall want the donkey and we can sell when we're finished. There's always a sale for a good donkey.' Now the Sergeant Major counted twenty-five pounds in notes into Arif's hand; the Paymaster had brought up the money that day.

'Twenty-five pounds to include the pad, the wooden saddle, halter, rope and panniers,' said Garnett.

'To include the pad, the wooden saddle, halter, rope and panniers,' repeated the schoolmaster.

'Better include the stick,' said Garnett.

Rifat's eyes had looked puzzled from one man to another, but now he understood. Arif was selling Sippacik. His Sippacik! 'But she's mine!' Rifat had forgotten all about the schoolmaster and was shouting. 'Dede! Grandfather. You can't sell her. She's mine,' but Arif was counting out the notes, his tongue licking his lips. He had not dreamed he could ever get a full donkey's price for a donkey as small as Sippacik. These days things were even worse with the Ali household; Arif had not been able to gather his carobs in time to get a good price—he had not finished reaping his mustard though Suzan had helped him. Arif knew he spent far too much time sitting in the café with the other men but, 'An old man should be able to take a little ease,' he said. 'Not if he hasn't a son,' said Suzan who, with field work and housework, felt as if her back would break. 'If only Osman Ali would come back,' moaned Grandmother and, 'United Nations are here beside us,' she argued again. 'He would be safe in Yalova, once he gets here,' and again Arif answered, 'And how would he get here? Do you want your son to be *shot*?'

No one would risk that, though life on the farm was difficult without a strong man. To sell Sippacik was a golden chance, but now Arif became aware of Rifat's frantic cries. 'You can't sell her, she's mine. Mine!' cried Rifat in a storm of tears.

'Grandson, I have to sell her,' said Arif. 'We must eat,' and he gave the rope into Kip's hand. 'Take her,' he said.

Rifat caught Arif's arm. 'Dede! Grandfather. At least let me go with her.'

Arif looked down into Rifat's pleading face, at his swollen tearfilled eyes. 'Would you take the boy to look after her?' he asked. 'Ask them,' he said to the schoolmaster. 'Would they take the boy?'

'We have plenty of boys,' said Garnett, looking scornfully at Kip.

'Please! Please!' cried Rifat, using the English word they had learned at school, only he said, 'Pleess. Pleess, Sir.'

Rifat and Nazihar were dressed no better or worse than other Turkish Cyriot children; Rifat wore thin, patched drill trousers, a ragged sweater and a man's old waistcoat; Nazihar had a dress over what looked like a pair of cotton flowered pyjama trousers; their feet were bare and though their hair was combed it had never been brushed so that it looked dusty; they did not wash often because there was no running water in their home, it had to be fetched from the village tap. Arif, Grandmother, Suzan and the schoolmaster saw nothing wrong with them, but to Bombardier Garnett they were dirty shabby ragamuffins, and he did not want to be bothered with them; nor was he moved by Rifat's tears—Nazihar too was crying in sympathy—nor by the desperation in Rifat's voice. 'Let's get on back,' he said to Kip and, as Kip swung Sippacik round, Garnett turned on Rifat. 'Out of the way,' he said. 'Git. Vamoose.'

Rifat gave a shout of rage and tried to run at Kip, to get Sippacik's rope out of his hand, but Hasan Dincer caught him by the back of his waistcoat, like a kitten by the scruff of its neck, and lifted him out of the way. Rifat shouted again but the schoolmaster gave him a cuff that silenced him. 'Be quiet. Get back to the school at once,' said Hasan Dincer in a terrible voice. 'This is men's business.'

In a few minutes Sippacik was gone.

The whole Camp turned out to greet the new member of the Battery. 'A moke like any other,' Garnett had said, introducing her, but, 'She's dandy,' the men said when they saw Sippacik and, 'That's something like a donkey!' or, 'When I was a kid I always wanted a donkey,' and, 'Seems a little bit of a thing to carry loads up that mountain to the OPs.'

Arif had shown Kip how to hobble Sippacik to let her graze but the men decided that was cruel, and she was tethered by a long rope from her halter to a tree, the rope to prevent her from straying. Not that Sippacik had any intention of straying; there was grazing all round her, quite enough to feed one small donkey, but the Sergeant Major had bought a bag of chaff and a feed was put into a wash-basin. Sippacik did not eat the feed because the men brought her so many titbits of apples and carrots, sugar and slices of bread, and their ration of chocolate. Spud even sacrificed a potato. 'I'll teach her to like potatoes,' said Spud.

'She won't do a stroke of work if you feed her like that,' Garnett cautioned them.

'Piffle! She needs feeding,' crooned Kip.

'Far too thin!' said Spud.

Kip commandeered a stiff brush and brushed the dust out of Sippacik's coat; Spud painted her hooves with gun-oil to prevent them cracking. Straw was spread to make her a bed, and then one or two of the men got knives and cut her a pile of fresh grass. 'Yes, let's hand-feed her,' said Garnett.

They were all so interested and pleased that Bluebell felt he must warn them. 'The donkey's here just for this Operation, remember. When it's over we shall re-sell her,' but the men were already making plans. 'The Paras have a pony for a mascot; the Irish Guards have a wolfhound. Why shouldn't we have a mascot?' they asked.

'A donkey's just right as a mascot for this Battery,' said Garnett.

Sippacik stood stock still and refused to move.

Sippacik stopped her munching and looked at Garnett. He said it was a coincidence but, 'She looked at him terrible straight,' said Kip.

'You didn't hear or pick up anything in Yalova about a man called Osman Ali?' Bluebell asked the Sergeant Major when they were alone. 'The Cypriot Turk, Osman Ali?'

'Arif, not Osman,' said the Sergeant Major. 'Arif Ali was the old farmer who sold the donkey to us.'

'Arif. An old man.' Bluebell was thoughtful. 'This Osman Ali might be his son.'

'Rather a coincidence, wouldn't it be, Sir?' asked the Sergeant Major but, 'Coincidences happen,' said Bluebell. He went on. 'Osman Ali was a Turkish leader in the last troubles, and was concerned in the killings. The police arrested him but he escaped to the mainland. Now the story is that he's back—just landed.'

'Landed where, Sir?'

'Somewhere along the coast, and of course he's being hunted. Did you notice when we drove to Headquarters there were Greek Cypriot soldiers at every crossing, posted outside every village? As you know, we mustn't interfere,' said Bluebell. 'Next week probably the Turks will be chasing a Greek. No, we can't take sides, but if Osman Ali could reach Yalova he would be safe. It would save us a mint of trouble if he could get there without an incident.'

'Yes,' said the Sergeant Major and sighed. 'Incidents! Incidents!'

'This could be a bad one,' said Bluebell. 'If the Greek Cypriots catch Osman Ali he will be brought to trial and probably be hung and that will start a real fight.'

Kip saddled Sippacik next morning with the wooden saddle. Arif had shown him how to fit it. Hung from it were two sealed Army-cans of water, one on each side. 'Seem heavy, don't they, for such a little 'un,' said Kip anxiously; 'Fifty pounds or thereabouts, each.'

'I know. I've carried 'em!' said Spud.

'It's too much,' said Kip.

'Go on!' said Garnett. 'A donkey can carry a hundred and fifty pounds,' and he quoted the official figures: 'A mule, two hundred pounds: a goat, forty: a sheep, thirty.'

'She's not much bigger than a goat,' said Kip.

'A flipping big goat,' said Garnett.

Kip had found a floppy old military hat in which he cut two slits for Sippacik's ears and crowned her head with it. 'S'ignorant you are,' he told Garnett when Garnett laughed. 'Donkeys wear hats in Italy against the sun; the sun's far hotter here.'

Kip was to lead Sippacik; Spud and Garnett, carrying the rations, were going up to the OP as reliefs; the Sergeant Major had come to superintend and Bluebell was making an inspection. 'Quite a procession,' said Garnett. The whole Camp turned out to see them start: Sippacik followed Kip, her hat shading her eyes, the black water-cans hanging like panniers: Spud, Garnett and the Sergeant Major came behind her and Bluebell brought up the rear. Sippacik trotted nicely along the road until they branched off into a defile where she jerked the rope from Kip and snatched a thistle. Then, slowly, in single file they began the climb up the hill. High on the mountain above them fluttered the blue flag of the OP. Sippacik was a little finicky now, picking her way through the stones of the narrow track, but Kip was patient. Bit by bit the thistle disappeared into her mouth; she looked round for another but the mountain yielded nothing. Sippacik flicked her tail.

The air was clear, the sun warm; the men had nothing to carry but their rations and their packs—'Sippacik can come down and go up again, with the batteries,' said the Sergeant Major—and everyone was in good spirits. Bluebell had begun his clear whistle that was as good as a march tune, when he saw that the men were beginning to tread on one another, he to tread on the Sergeant Major who was in front of him as they crowded up. They were going more and more slowly. 'Hurry along,' Bluebell shouted ahead to Kip. 'There's no need to take it as slowly as this.'

'Sorry, Sir,' Kip called back. 'But she won't go no faster.'

'Give her a tug,' said Spud.

'Whack her!' said Garnett.

Kip tugged but Sippacik hung back on the rope; he used the stick Garnett had taken from Arif, giving Sippacik a light tap. 'Ar! C'mon!' said Garnett; he seized the stick from Kip and gave Sippacik two smart thwacks. For a moment she trotted, then slowed, tucking her tail in pathetically as if she feared more blows. 'That's enough, Garnett,' said the Sergeant Major and, in his turn, seized the stick from Garnett and gave it to Spud. 'Give her enough to keep her going,' he said. 'No need to be brutal.' Spud thwacked, but gently. Sippacik looked back out of the corner of her eye to see who held the stick and, at once, slowed down.

'We'll be here all day, at this rate,' said Bluebell and again to Kip, '*Can't* you bring her along, man?' but neither Kip, who was scarlet in the face now from tugging and chiding, nor Spud who was steadily thwacking, could bring Sippacik along, except by one or two unwilling steps at a time. Then, when the 'fhunda' ended and they came to the rocks where the track showed bare as it went up and up, winding among the rocks, Sippacik stopped altogether. 'Go on!' shouted Garnett. 'Git on, you lazy little basket!'

Sippacik looked at him with eyes that Kip swore were swimming in tears, her head drooped, and suddenly, her legs began to tremble. 'You see,' cried Kip. 'I told you. Them tins are far too heavy.'

'Garn!' said Garnett. 'A wily, four-legged hussy, a minx, that's what she is. Having you all on,' said Garnett.

'We'll have her on,' said Bluebell, coming up from the back, and to Kip, 'Turn her round. Lead her downhill; then, when she's really going, swing back in a circle and she may not realize she's going uphill.'

But Sippacik knew. As soon as her head was pointed downhill, towards the Camp—and grass, carrots, bread, sugar—she went with alacrity, her small hooves treading neatly, her tail alert; when Kip led her round, she came, but as soon as she recognized the track going uphill she stopped, 'Instantly!' said Bluebell, vexed. Kip tried again and this time, when they faced uphill, Spud gave her a cut with the stick below her hind quarters. Sippacik only tucked her tail in further and trembled. 'C'm on girl,' Kip besought. The sun was hot now and sweat was pouring off him. 'C'm on!' Sippacik stood stock still. Spud and Kip and the Sergeant Major looked at one another in despair and, 'This is ridiculous,' said Bluebell. 'We're lower down than we were. We should have been at the top by now.'

'Left to ourselves,' said Garnett who had come up behind.

Suddenly Sippacik gave a start, as if she had been taken off guard; with a shrill whinny she trotted up the track with Garnett behind her. Then she stopped and her hind hooves lashed out, catching Garnett just under the knee. Garnett bent double with the pain and swore; while Sippacik stood and trembled, not only her legs but her whole body. 'Here, w'ot did you do?' cried Kip. 'W'ot did he do, Sir?' and Bluebell repeated the question. 'Garnett, what did you do?'

'Gave her a prick, Sir, the . . .' Garnett was still swearing.

Garnett showed the tip of his penknife.

'You jabbed her with *that*!' If Kip had not been red with heat he would have turned white with indignation; his eyes were not dreamy now, they glared. 'Jabbed a knife into a dumb animal?'

'That animal's not dumb,' said Garnett and, 'It's not a knife, it's a penknife, and I didn't jab, I pricked.' Garnett was sullen. 'It's what she's used to,' but an angry chorus broke out.

'Ought to have the RSPCA put on to you, you did.'

'Jab a knife into a little donkey!'

'Well, I got her going, didn't I?' asked Garnett.

'You will not get her going like that,' said the Sergeant Major curtly. 'Put your knife away.'

'Yes, Sir. What are you going to do, Sir?' hissed Garnett.

Sippacik's head drooped further, she still trembled. 'The load's too heavy, Sir,' said Kip again.

'Very well,' said Bluebell. 'Take off one of the cans and see if you can balance the other, and we'll try like that.'

One can came off. Spud took it on his back—'Exactly as before,' said Garnett—the Sergeant Major and Kip managed to lash the other can flat on the struts of the saddle and the procession started again—if it could be called a procession. 'We've been two hours!' said Bluebell.

Though there was only one can now, Sippacik barely moved. Kip pulled, the Sergeant Major pushed. It grew hotter and hotter; tempers were getting short. By the time they had rounded the next outcrop of rock they were exhausted. It seemed Sippacik was too; she suddenly lay down, rolled on her side and, before their horrified eyes, rolled over and over down the outcrop and hill to a ledge where she lay motionless, the water-can still tied and intact on top of her. Kip gave a cry and dashed down; all of them, except Garnett, followed him. 'She's dead!' cried Kip. 'We've killed her! Her heart's bust!'

Even Bluebell was perturbed by the stillness but when they reached her Sippacik was simply lying as if waiting for them to come, her eyes accusing.

'If she's broken her leg . . . her leg or her back,' Kip was incoherent. 'She was too small for that great load! I knew it. I knew it,' but when the water-can was lifted off, then the saddle, and Bluebell's gentle hands went over her, nothing could be found wrong with Sippacik except a small cut on one hind leg.

'Did she do it a'purpose?' asked Spud.

Sippacik was helped upright, and though she trembled she could stand. The Sergeant Major and Kip moved her a foot or so on the track; 'She can walk,' said Kip, relieved, but Sippacik tottered on the path, obviously a very ill and shaken little donkey and again she looked at them with those great accusing eyes.

'Stay with her until she has recovered,' Bluebell said to Kip. 'Then head her back to Camp. We'll go on up. Garnett, you carry the second can.'

'Are you sure, Sir,' asked Garnett, 'you don't want me to carry the donkey?'

As soon as Kip turned Sippacik campwards she trotted quite blithely but when she came in sight of the tents she slowed down. Whether the cut hurt her more on the level, Kip never knew, but she started to limp and in the Camp once more she did 'her trembling act,' as Garnett called it later when he heard. 'Been an accident?' asked the men, running out and, 'Poor little critter! Poor old moke!'

Sippacik was rubbed down—'As if she were a flipping race horse,' said Garnett afterwards—her cut was dressed from the First Aid kit. She was given water and, as they had no grain, the Quartermaster Sergeant issued some Quaker oats which the cooks made into porridge, sweetening it with sugar. 'Sugar's good for shock.' Sippacik liked it very much.

For six days Sippacik stayed in the camp while the men carried the water, the stores and heavy batteries up and down to the OPs. 'Well, Sir, her leg's swelled,' the Sergeant Major reported. 'It's swelled.'

'By an infinitesimal amount,' said Bluebell.

'Better wait till it's healed, Sir.'

'I'm not going up the mountain with that animal again,' said Spud but he still gave her potatoes. The porridge had become a daily feed; the men saved all their sugar lumps. Sippacik grew plumper and plumper. Bluebell, sitting in his canvas chair outside the Officers' Mess, eyed her thoughtfully. Then he sent for the Sergeant Major.

'Is the donkey better?' The Sergeant Major noticed Bluebell did not call her Sippacik.

'Better? In what way, Sir!' The Sergeant Major was hedging and Bluebell knew it.

'Her leg,' he said.

'Yes, Sir. It's healed.'

'Will she go up the mountain?'

'I couldn't say, Sir,' The Sergeant Major's face was bland. 'I couldn't say.'

'You could,' said Bluebell's expression. 'You know she won't go up for us,' and he said aloud, 'That donkey is here for transport. If she's not transport she must be changed.'

'Changed?' the Sergeant Major hedged again. 'Did you say changed, Sir?'

'Yes,' said Bluebell.

The two men exchanged glances, then, 'It's the way the men have taken to her,' the Sergeant Major explained. 'It's made all the difference out here where they are bored. She's something for them to think about, Sir, a pet.'

'She's transport,' said Bluebell. 'Go to the village and bring that farmer here.'

'And Sergeant Major,' he said as the Sergeant Major was going. 'Keep your ears and eyes pricked for any sign of that man.'

Bluebell had lowered his voice and the Sergeant Major did too as he asked, 'Osman Ali?'

Bluebell nodded. 'They say he has been shot.'

'Then perhaps he's dead, Sir.'

'It would be hard to kill Osman Ali. No, I think he's somewhere near, making for home and the Greek Cypriots know it. A party of them were found, setting up a check point near Yalova. We managed to get them to dismantle it. They are onto something though they said it was only routine.'

'Odd time and place to choose if it's just routine,' said the Sergeant Major.

'Yes,' said Bluebell and he added, 'I'm pretty sure Osman Ali is somewhere near.'

When the landrover drove into the village, Arif Ali was not at home. At long last, with Suzan's help, he had finished picking his carobs and had loaded them on to Siyergar and two borrowed donkeys to take them into the carob depot in the town, nine miles away. He would not be back until nightfall and Suzan fell into a panic when she saw the Sergeant Major, Spud and the schoolmaster in the courtyard. Grandmother was no help; she quickly veiled herself with her black head-veil and kept up her perpetual moan, 'If only our son were here.'

'Please,' Suzan begged Hasan Dincer, when he had told the story of Sippacik on the mountain, 'Please, please don't let them send the donkey back.' If Sippacik were returned, all the lovely money would be taken away—there was no disputing with a United Nations Sergeant Major—and, 'Please,' begged Suzan frantically.

'But how can they keep her if she won't work?' said the schoolmaster.

'Let them take Rifat,' begged Suzan. 'She'll work for him. Rifat can stay in the Camp—he won't eat much. Sir,' she said to the Sergeant Major, 'Rifat will make the donkey go. She always goes best for him. It won't be for long,' she said, turning to Hasan Dincer, 'and when he gets back he will work twice as hard.'

The schoolmaster gave a disbelieving snort.

'I swear he will,' cried Suzan, wringing her hands. 'If not, Arif will beat him, but of your kindness let Rifat go with the soldiers' We have so little, little money. Of your kindness . . .'

At last Hasan Dincer consented.

There was no need to make up a bundle for Rifat because he had nothing to bring; he had no pyjamas because he slept in his clothes and he did not own a toothbrush or a wash-cloth or a comb. 'We'll fix him up,' said the Sergeant Major.

Rifat could not believe it when he was ordered out of school and told to get up into the landrover. 'A landrover!' cried the other children. He was to go with the soldiers. 'To the Camp!' he cried. 'The Camp!' 'Aie! Aie! Aie!' said all the other boys in envy. 'Be a man now,' the schoolmaster told him. 'Give no trouble and make the donkey go. Be strong.' Rifat threw out his chest as he stood in the landrover; his eyes glowed. 'She'll go for me,' he said exultantly.

He did not feel quite so confident when he stood before Bluebell in the tent. Had Sippacik been up to real mischief? Was there something really wrong? Rifat could not keep his eyes from straying to the wonders of the Camp: the trucks and tents with their neat beds: the big radio-truck: the smell of cooking that came out from under the awning: the guns: but Bluebell's deep blue gaze was stern and penetrating and Rifat felt himself quail. Yet when he was taken to Sippacik he could not see anything wrong. Sippacik, tethered to her tree, seemed fat and well, fatter and sleeker than he had ever seen her before. A fresh green cabbage leaf hung out of her mouth; she did not give Rifat so much as a whinny.

'Load her up,' said Bluebell to Kip. 'Two water cans, exactly as before.' Sippacik rolled an eye at Rifat and dropped the cabbage leaf.

The wooden saddle came out, two cans of water were hung; Rifat watched; it all seemed perfectly normal to him. Then Bluebell took the rope and gave it to Rifat. 'Donkey go up there,' said Bluebell, pointing up, up to the first OP. 'Up there.' Rifat looked up too and was puzzled. Why was the Captain making such a to-do about it? 'Donkey go.' Why not? thought Rifat, puzzled.

He took the stick from Kip, led Sippacik out on the road and down the defile. Kip, Spud, Bombadier Garnett, the Sergeant Major and Bluebell followed. At the end of the defile Sippacik stopped, looking up the steep track. Rifat wound the rope round her neck; it was better to let her go up herself, and when she did not move he gave her a thwack. She went on slowly, too slowly for Rifat; he took a nail out of his pocket and fitted it into a notch in the stick.

'See!' cried Garnett. 'See?'

One prick was enough; Sippacik knew Rifat when he had that nail; she bounced away and next minute she was trotting merrily upwards; not only that; Rifat ran after her and jumped on her back, 'On top of the water tins!' cried Kip. 'It's too much. It's crool,' but Sippacik's legs were not trembling, they went on steadily up. It was true that her trot slowed to a walk when they came to the steep rocks and Rifat slid to the ground but up and up she went with never a falter. The men had all the work they could do to keep up. It was only when they came out on the flat rock under the pine marking the OP that Rifat and Sippacik stopped. Sippacik's sides were heaving—she had put on far too much weight—she blew a little through her white nose but otherwise she was perfectly composed and Rifat's dark eyes, looking up at Bluebell, said plainly, 'What was the trouble?'

'Well, I'll be blowed,' said Kip.

'Yes, we're made to look proper silly by one small boy,' said Garnett.

'Not silly; brought back to our senses,' said Bluebell.

THE COWBOY

Vincent Paul Rennert

The cowboy had a style of dress uniquely suited to his way of life. Though his outward appearance might seem flamboyant to the stranger, every article of clothing was essential in his work. The extent to which he decorated his clothes and the money he chose to spend on them reflected his personal idiosyncracies and individual pride.

The cowboy usually spent a considerable amount of money on his clothes and saddle gear. This was one of the few pleasures allowed him. His work was hard, dirty, tiring, and seemingly endless. There were no days off on the roundups and trail drives, and no regular hours. His relaxation came at the end of the trail in the cow towns or between duties on the home ranch.

The cowboy coming in from the trail after a long, hard ride, and with several months pay in his shirt pocket, wanted to show off a little. One of the first things he did was to buy himself a new outfit. If the man was an old-time cowhand, he wanted an outfit that would set him off from those with less time in the saddle. And no one wanted to look like a beginner, new to the range.

The 'tenderfoot' could be spotted easily. Knowing the range only from dime novels or romanticized newspaper accounts, he would arrive ready for work with laced boots and a silk shirt. Naturally, the old hands would make fun of him until he exchanged his fancy duds for something more practical and modest. The young man, now dressed for work and not show, could buy a pony and saddle in the early days for twenty-five dollars. Another fifteen would go for leather chaps, a hat, and saddle blankets. A pistol could be bought for about twelve dollars.

The cowboy 'code' did, however, allow the experienced hand to splurge his hard-earned cash on a fancy outfit if he wanted to, without fear of ridicule. It was possible to spend as much as five hundred dollars on a rig, which would include inlaid silver on his saddle, a silver-mounted bridle for his horse, and silver-mounted spurs for his custom-made boots. He could have gold trim on his hat, goat's wool on his chaps, and a pearl handle on his Colt ·45.

But, as a rule, even the most weather-beaten, saddle-wedded puncher was seldom this lavish. Fancy shirts or gaudy accessories were out of place and impractical on the range. A reasonably fine yet serviceable outfit could be had for under two hundred and fifty dollars, including a sixty dollar saddle.

The basic cowboy outfit did not change much with time. Styles changed, of course, as they do today, largely due to 'fads'. Changes came also as a result of differences in climate or the nature of the country, as well as the cowboy's desire to be identified with a part of the range country by the clothes that he wore. It's been said that one could tell a man's home base—whether he worked on the southwestern or northwestern range—by looking at his hat.

Three types of hats were popular at various times: the Mexican sombrero, the Stetson, and the broad-brimmed soft felt hat. The sombrero was a high-crowned hat with an embroidered, up-turned brim. Its cost, depending on the trim, might run as high as fifty dollars.

The Stetsons had crowns, or tops, that were up to eight inches high and brims wide enough to give good shade at high noon. The brims were often decorated with silk braid or with holes punched around the edges so that a piece of leather could be wound through to provide both stiffness and decoration. Generally the crown was dented around the sides if worn by a Texas cowboy, but left smooth sided, with the top pleated or folded down low, if the wearer came from the Northwest. A band of leather circled the base of the crown. Sometimes this leather band would be studded with silver. The cowboys of Arizona and New Mexico were known to substitute the skin of a rattlesnake for the regular band. If the wearer was a Texan, the band would often be of gold or silver wire.

Brim widths, too, were different, depending upon where the cowboy was from. Wide brims were favoured in the Southwest, where protection from the sun was more important, while the Northwest cowboy kept his brim narrow to present less of a sail to the wind.

Whatever the variety, hats performed important jobs. With the brims turned up they served as drinking cups if nothing else was around. They could be used to fan campfires into life and chase mosquitoes. Wide brims could be pulled way down and tied over the ears as protection against the cold. They also protected the rider against the wind, rain, blazing hot sun, and clouds of sand.

The cowboy was never without his neckerchief or bandanna. This was a large piece of cloth folded over several times to form a triangle and tied around his neck. The drag riders—cowboys who rode behind the cattle in a trail drive—protected themselves from the dust by pulling their bandannas up over the lower half of their faces.

The 'wipes', as the puncher called his neckerchief, was usually

The cowboy's horse was small, tough, and fast.

worn with the knot at the back and the fold hanging down over his chest. On a hot day, with the sun slanting from behind, it would be reversed so that the cloth would protect his neck.

The neckerchief was usually made of cotton, although silk was not unknown. Some neckerchiefs were black or blue in colour, but red was the favourite. White was never worn, simply because it showed the dirt too fast.

The cowboy wore a loose-fitting flannel shirt, open at the neck, and in the early days, woollen pants. Later, Levis became popular, but never denim coveralls, which were considered the outfit of a farmer.

Chaps, or 'leggins', were worn by all cowboys when on the range. They were usually made of leather and were open at the seat. They extended down the front and side of each leg to provide full protection when riding through brush and cactus country. In the Southwest chaps were generally smooth and without much adornment. A calfskin pair sold for about nine dollars. In the Northwest they were usually made from animal skins with the hair left on for added protection against the cold, and a pair of good ones would run up to twenty dollars.

The cowboy's boots were a source of great pride to him. They were made of the finest leather and handsomely decorated around the tops. The boots came up to just below the knee, with heels about two inches high, and thin, narrow soles. The thin sole gave the rider the 'feel' of the stirrup, and the high heel kept his foot from slipping. Vanity takes different forms at different times, but the cowboy's weak spot was the size of his feet. For his own reasons, he wanted people to think his feet were small, and he squeezed himself into the smallest boot size he could stand.

Spurs, or 'grappling irons', were worn most of the time. They were most useful in roundup work. The rider did not use them to hurt or punish the horse, but to make him move quickly, whether this be turning, stopping, or starting.

Most spurs were ornate in design, and the cowboy took great pride in owning a beautiful pair. Among the many different types were big rowelled spurs with bells, and hand-forged, silver-inlaid types with droop shanks and small rowels. Sizes and designs varied with individual preference, but all made quite a noise when the cowboy walked along a wooden sidewalk or entered a room.

Gloves were standard throughout the year. The most commonly worn were of fine buckskin. Gloves offered warmth in the winter and protection from rope burn in the summer.

Deep cuffed or gauntleted gloves were the most popular, as they gave protection to the wrists. The gauntlet, which was part of the glove, was about five inches deep and usually embroidered. Cuffs were separate from the gloves themselves and were fastened about the wrist with snaps or buckles.

The cowboy also had a raincoat—a yellow slicker similar to the type fishermen wear. He always wore a vest, mostly because of the extra pockets it gave him. Nearly every man owned an extra fancy and colourful vest for special trips into town for celebrations or dances. It was made of wool and dyed a bright, solid colour.

The saddle was the most valuable piece of gear that the cowboy owned, and he paid a great deal of money to get the very best. Not only did saddles have to be comfortable, they had to be ruggedly built as well. They weighed as much as forty pounds and were made of leather-covered wood. The pommel, or 'horn', was of forged steel covered with leather. Costs ran as high as a hundred and fifty dollars for a fine silver-buckled saddle with intricate designs tooled into the leather. An ordinary one could, however, be bought for about forty dollars.

The saddle was fastened to the horse with 'cinches', or leather straps running under the horse's belly from one side of the saddle to the other. A saddle with one cinch was called a 'centre-fire'; a two-cinch saddle was called a 'double-fire', or 'double-barrelled', saddle.

In the early days on the range, a cowboy was never without his gun. Later, as the threat of Indian raids and other hazards disappeared, the gun went out of fashion, except for show.

The Colt revolver, using a ·45 calibre metallic cartridge, was the favourite, but before this came into regular use many men carried 'horse pistols'—single-shot weapons. The drawbacks to this gun were many, but the chief difficulty was the necessity of reloading after every shot.

In 1836, Samuel Colt developed a repeating gun, or revolver, for men serving in the Texas Navy. Later, some of these guns found their way into the hands of the Texas Rangers. In 1844, a party of fifteen Rangers came upon a war party of eighty mounted Comanches spoiling for a fight. The warriors, confident of victory against a small party of men armed with single-shot guns, taunted the Rangers to come and fight. The Indians had never seen 'repeating' guns, and in the battle that followed, half of the startled Indians were killed, and the rest fled. From then on, the Colt revolver fast became the standard gun of the West.

The early Colt, like the Remington-Beals Army revolver, held self-consuming combustible cartridges and was muzzle loaded. To load it, one had to remove the cylinder and load the cartridges in the front, then ram them home with a lever attached to the bottom of the barrel. While these revolvers were a revolutionary advance over previous weapons, they were not trouble free. Sometimes when they were fired, the flash from one cylinder would ignite the powder in the next, so that all five or six cartridges exploded at once, demolishing the weapon.

The cowboy never wore two six-shooters. The most he ever carried was one pistol and one rifle. The 'two-gun' men were the outlaws and the marshals.

The cowboy's horse was small, tough, and fast. Like the longhorn cattle, it was of Spanish origin and had evolved into an animal suited to the range. In *The Story of the Cowboy*, written in 1897, Emerson Hough commented on the Spanish pony: 'For generation after generation it lost flesh and gained angles, lost beauty and gained 'wind' and stomach and bottom and speed, until at the time of the first American cowboy's meeting with it, it was a small, hardy, wiry, untamed brute, as wild as a hawk, as fleet as a deer, as strong as an ox.'

These horses turned quickly and easily, good qualities for roundup work. They weighed no more than 600 pounds as a rule, and could travel fast and far. They were remarkably strong and could withstand great punishment. Sometimes the cowboy would have to ride his horse until the animal was exhausted, but the very next morning the horse would be full of spirit, and would show it by trying to throw his rider off as the first act of the day.

Some of the horses were never really tamed. Theodore Roosevelt, in his book *Ranch Life and the Hunting Trail*, notes that many of his horses 'have to this day [1888] traits not likely to set a timid or a clumsy rider at his ease. One or two run away and cannot be held by even the strongest bit; others can hardly be bridled or saddled until they have been thrown; two or three have a tendency to fall overbackward; and half of them buck more or less, some so hard that only an expert can sit them; several I never ride myself, save from dire necessity'.

The cowboy rode only male horses or geldings; never a mare. In the Southwest, the horse was called a cow horse or cow pony; on the northern ranges it was a 'cayuse'. Broncos were wild, or 'bad', horses, and as Theodore Roosevelt suggested, they caused a great deal of trouble.

As time went on, many ranchmen began to hire men to break the broncs. These men became quite skilled—some of them became famous for their work—and the profession known as bronco busting came into being.

Generally, the cowboy did not provide his own horse when doing roundup or trail work. He was given use of from seven to ten horses by the man who hired him. The only things the cowboy carried with him were his saddle and personal gear. He took good care of his string of horses, however, and these mounts were his to ride until the work was over.

THE
STORM BREAKS

Gerald Raftery

While staying at his Uncle Ira and Aunt Martha's farm in Vermont, Ken finds a runaway white stallion. He tracks it down and gradually manages to tame the wild creature.

The hot dry weather continued. The haying was finished, and every night Uncle Ira watched the western sky for a hint of changing weather. There was no sign of rain.

Aunt Martha had been feeling the heat very much, and finally Uncle Ira and Ken drove her into town to see Dr Smathers. The doctor nodded knowingly over his stethoscope and reached into the big glass cabinet behind his desk.

'Now, Martha, this is heart medicine,' he said gravely. 'And it won't do you a bit of good'—he paused solemnly—'it won't do you any good at all unless you take a little rest along with it.'

Aunt Martha frowned; she talked about canning and jelly

making and all the other things she had to do.

The doctor waved her excuses aside. 'You go right ahead and do as you please, Martha,' he said sternly. 'But I tell you it'll be the last summer you will. If you take this medicine—and rest—you'll be pretty near as good as new in a month. Otherwise, I won't guarantee anything.'

Uncle Ira promised to see that she rested. They drove back through the little village and stopped to do some shopping. Uncle Ira always called it trading.

Ken greeted a man in a grey uniform outside the store.

'Hello there, young fellow,' the State trooper responded heartily. 'How's that big grey horse these days?'

'First-rate,' said Ken. 'How did that cattle thief make out?'

'Why, he told us everything we wanted to know.' The trooper took off his wide-brimmed hat and mopped his brow. 'That is, everything but the name of his pal. We found that out ourselves.'

'You really did!'

'Yes, sir,' said the trooper proudly. 'He was a York State man, and the troopers over there picked him up two days later.'

Ken congratulated him. The officer went on, 'A fellow down the road a couple of miles got a postcard from young Sam Bushey last week.'

Ken's heart skipped a beat. Young Sam Bushey!

'He trained that horse of yours, didn't he?' asked the trooper.

Ken nodded nervously. 'What did Sam have to say?' There was a tremor in his voice that he could not control.

'He's doing fine! Just a-doing fine!' The officer did not seem to notice Ken's worried expression. 'He's working. Out West somewhere, I think.'

'Is he coming home soon?'

The trooper turned his hat slowly in his big hands. 'Well, now, it seems to me he did say something about seeing this friend of his soon. I don't remember for sure.'

Uncle Ira beckoned from the store window, and Ken was glad to hurry in and help with the packages. His head was whirling at the unexpected news. Young Sam Bushey was Snow's owner; there was no doubt about that. If he came back tomorrow, he would have a perfect right to demand the return of his horse. Mr Bushey had made that very clear.

On the drive back to the farm Ken was silent and thoughtful. As soon as the purchases had been unloaded, he rushed out to the pasture to see Snow. The big horse came to his whistle and stared down in surprise as Ken patted his smooth neck. He seemed to sense his master's worries and lowered his proud head to rub a caressing nose against the boy's chest. When Ken walked slowly away the stallion followed him. He nickered questioningly when Ken started to leave him at the gate, and that was enough for Ken. He decided to saddle up and take a ride.

Snow was anxious to go and he danced with enthusiasm at the sight of the bridle and gear. It was too warm to climb the hills, so they travelled through the flat lower fields. Snow seemed to be trying to cheer up his young master by the smoothness and speed of his pace. The exhilaration of the ride helpèd to raise Ken's spirits.

Later, while he was grooming Snow in the cool stable, Uncle Ira came in.

Ken told him what he had learned from the State trooper, and the old man shook his head in sympathy.

'It sure would be hard after all your work to have young Sam come back and take Snow,' he said. 'But look at it this way. You've had a lot of fun along with your work. And you know what the Turks and the Arabs say? I think it's in the Koran; that's a sort of a Bible of theirs. They say the Lord writes down in a book of good deeds every grain of barley you give to a horse. And I don't know, but I guess that goes for corn and oats and carrots and lumps of sugar, too.'

Ken listened quietly, but he didn't take much comfort from his uncle's words. He felt angry that young Sam had a right to claim a horse which he had abandoned. For all he cared, his father might have shot the horse in anger. Or Snow might have broken a leg and died out in the woods. Uncle Ira watched his face for a moment. 'I know how you feel,' he said. 'The best way to forget your worries is to do a little work. Let's get going on these chores. I like to work slowly in this hot weather.'

They brought the cows in and started the milking. Talking back and forth as they hooked up the stanchions, they decided they would have to take some of the work off Aunt Martha's shoulders. They would get their own breakfast in the morning, and perhaps they might be able to induce her to sleep late for a while.

When they finished the chores, Uncle Ira paused in the middle of the barnyard and pointed to the declining sun. 'It's going to be a grey sunset. We're about due for a break in this hot spell.'

After supper they sat on the porch for a while. The air was still and breathless; they could hear a dog barking a mile away at the Johnson place. Heat lightning played far off on the horizon, and the usual evening breeze did not spring up.

'When we get that storm, it's going to be a corker. It might even be tonight,' said Uncle Ira.

Ken slept fitfully, his rest disturbed as much by the worry over Snow as by the heat. The hoped-for rain did not arrive, and in the morning it was still hot and sticky. As they went out to do the chores, the sunrise was red and angry. High threads of clouds were stretched across the sky.

'It's coming, all right,' said Uncle Ira, shaking his head. 'We won't get much work done today.'

They got their own breakfast, and later Aunt Martha came down looking fresh and rested in spite of the heat.

'I guess Dr Smathers knew what was wrong,' said Uncle Ira, smiling his satisfaction. 'You do what he says and you'll be all right in a hurry.'

'That was good medicine,' said Aunt Martha. 'I think I'll bake a batch of pies this morning.'

'Now, you'll do nothing of the kind,' began Uncle Ira, before he saw that she was laughing at him.

Ken felt a little more cheerful as they went out to work. Aunt

Martha's improvement almost counterbalanced his worries about Snow. The day was still hot and sunny, but huge castle-like clouds were piling up on the horizon. There was not a breath of wind stirring the heavy air.

'We'll take the team down to that lower field and spread fertilizer,' said Uncle Ira, casting a practised glance at the sky. 'We might get a morning's work in before the storm.'

He took turns with Ken, one driving while the other shovelled at the tail gate of the wagon. It was hot work and they looked longingly at the sky every few minutes. The clouds were moving in on the valley now. They could see the billowing peaks of the great piles as the tremendous air currents inside sent the tops boiling and reaching up towards the sun. Stopping to breathe the horses, they saw that the oncoming storm had topped the rim of the valley, half a dozen miles away. The summit of the mountain ridge vanished behind a veil of rain.

'There's going to be plenty of wind in that when it gets here,' said Uncle Ira. 'We'd better finish this up and get the team under cover.'

They hurried down the length of the field, flinging shovelfuls of fertilizer after them. The flying clouds had reached high enough to cover the sun, and the still air was cool and electric. Every time they looked up, the rushing veils of rain had slipped nearer down the sloping side of the valley. Lightning flickered through the black clouds above the rain.

The horses, sensing the coming storm, tossed their heads and stared around. Off in the distance could be heard the soft roar of the rain and the occasional rolling of thunder.

At last they turned towards the stable, the lightened wagon jouncing and jolting over the ground as Butch and Babe threw all their weight into the collars. A chilly gust of wind caught up with them and sent the horses' tails whipping against their flanks. A cold spatter of rain flickered across them.

Ken looked back. A flying scud of broken clouds was overhead, and the white curtain of the rain had reached the highway through the valley. He could see the tops of the trees lashing wildly in the wind and hear a steady roar from the storm. As he watched, a forked flash of lightning halted for an instant over a tree at the edge of the open meadow, and a splitting crash of thunder made him flinch. A huge leafy section toppled slowly out of the side of the tree and then hurtled to the ground, blocking the road that led down to the highway. Ken gripped Uncle Ira's shoulder and shouted to him.

The full force of the rain was upon them as they pounded into the barnyard. Ken leaped over the side of the wagon and ran to the horses' heads, holding them steady while Uncle Ira unhooked the traces. Together, with arms crooked over their faces, they led the horses through sheets of blinding rain to the stable door.

Inside, it seemed strangely quiet by comparison with the wild outdoors. There was a steady drumming of rain upon the roof, but the whistling of the wind seemed far away. Snow had come into the stable and he whinnied inquiringly as Butch and Babe tramped, dripping, into the stalls.

Uncle Ira picked up a grain sack to hold over his head. 'I'm going to run up to the house and help Martha close the windows. I'll be back in a minute and lend you a hand with the horses.'

As he opened the door, the wind snatched it out of his hand and banged it against the wall of the stable. He ducked out into the slashing rain and slammed it behind him.

Ken began rubbing the horses dry with a piece of sacking. They had quieted down now that they were out of the rain and they seemed content to rest in the dimness of the stable. The rain drummed on the roof far overhead, and there was an occasional squealing of wind around the eaves.

Suddenly Ken stopped working. He listened hard. Was that a voice? Or was it the gurgling of the flooded rainspout? He walked out of the stall and stood listening at the closed door. Someone was calling him. He eased the door open against the wind and peered out. Uncle Ira stood on the porch, beckoning wildly. Ken ducked out and ran splashing through the puddles to the house.

Uncle Ira was white-faced and frightened. 'Come on in!' he gasped. 'Martha's had a heart attack.'

Ken followed him into the house and closed the door to shut out the sound of wind and rain. 'Did you call Dr Smathers?'

'I couldn't get an answer.' He picked up the phone again and jiggled the hook, talking over his shoulder. 'She was running around closing windows when she felt the pains. She got the medicine out, but her hands shook so she dropped the bottle. Right in the sink. It's smashed.'

He broke off suddenly and spoke into the phone. 'Dr Smathers —and hurry!' He said to Ken, 'She's in bed now, but she looks awful peaked.'

'Hello, Doc,' he began, as the connection was made, and poured out his story.

Ken listened to him while the wind howled outside and rattled the windows of the darkened house. It was clear to him from one side of the conversation that the doctor could not come.

Uncle Ira protested for a moment, and then listened. 'Yes, I did that, Doc!' He listened again. 'Well, if we have to, I guess . . .'.

A flash of lightning glared across the room and a sudden blast of thunder drowned out his words.

'Hello, hello! Doc!' Uncle Ira jiggled the hook again and then slowly replaced the receiver. 'The line's dead; that last stroke must have brought a tree down on it.'

They faced each other in silence for a moment across the quiet room.

'The doctor can't come!' Uncle Ira seemed suddenly very old and tired. 'Trees are down across the road in the village and there's been a bad car accident south of town. He was just starting out for that on foot. He says if we can get in to his place his wife has the medicine there.'

'We'd never get the car past that fallen tree on our road,' said Ken.

Uncle Ira sat down and buried his face in his hands. The windows rattled as another blast of wind swept around the house like a hurricane. Torrents of rain slashed against the windows and drummed at the walls.

Ken paced the floor. The eight miles to town and back would take hours on foot in weather like this. Suddenly he reached a decision. He strode across the room and put a hand on his uncle's shoulder. 'I'll saddle Snow and make a try for it. It's better than doing nothing.'

Uncle Ira lifted a haggard face. 'It's an awful chance. Snow'll run wild in a storm like this. You know how lightning scares a horse.'

Ken was already in the kitchen, hauling a poncho out of the piled clothes rack. He pulled an oilskin cap down tight on his head.

His uncle followed him. 'Watch out for falling branches. I remember how it was when the hurricane hit us up here in '44. Stick to the open fields where you can, no matter how heavy the rain is.'

Ken nodded, and tightened his belt. With his hand on the knob of the door, he said, 'I'll be back as quick as I can.'

Outside, the wind came in gusts that took his breath away. He dashed for the stable through puddles that had swelled tremendously in the last few minutes. After he had closed the stable door, he paused for a moment to calm himself and catch his breath. Snow would sense any nervousness or excitement; he would have to act as naturally as possible. He walked into the stall, forcing himself to move as slowly as he could. He patted the big stallion for a moment and then brought out the bridle from behind his back. Snow tossed his head happily and blew a soft snort of eagerness.

When Ken finally led the horse out of the stall, he paused for a moment before opening the door. He waited until Snow stirred restlessly and nickered before he swung the door wide into the storm. Then he stepped out quickly and slammed the door shut as soon as Snow sidestepped clear of it. He gave him no time to worry about the wind and rain. Putting his foot in the stirrup, he swung quickly up into the saddle.

Snow shied and jibbed a little at facing into the wind. He pranced nervously through the splashing puddles until they gained a little shelter from the bushes along the side of the yard. Ken waved an arm automatically to the empty windows as they passed the farmhouse and swung out into the road. Snow moved more surely now, and for a hundred yards or so he galloped easily and freely. Then the fallen tree loomed ahead, a huge leafy barrier. He flung up his head and slowed his pace, turning half away to look it over warily.

Ken leaned forward and talked to him, patting his neck and murmuring reassuringly. He let him slow down to a walk and approach the strange sight at his own speed. When he was reassured, Ken guided him off the road to circle the ruin of the shattered elm.

Out in the open field they felt the full force of the wind, and the driven rain pelted and stung like sand. Snow broke into a gallop and, with a clear open stretch before them, Ken let him have his head and run as he liked. Half a mile farther on they came to the belt of trees that bordered the little river into which Johnsons' brook flowed. The trees sheltered them from the wind for a minute, and Snow quieted down as they pounded across the wooden bridge.

Before them was the concrete highway. Ken turned left and kept Snow to the soft level footing on the shoulder of the road. There was no sign of traffic; the smooth surface was speckled with leaves and broken twigs. The horse had the wind at his side now and he went more willingly.

Ken relaxed for a moment and stared around. Suddenly, like the explosion of a giant flash bulb, came a dazzling flare of lightning and a simultaneous crash of thunder. Snow leaped forward in alarm. Ken was almost as frightened himself, and it was only the instinctive ducking forward of his head and the sudden tightening of his knees that kept him from losing his seat. Snow shot ahead like an arrow, running unrestrained in a mad panic for a hundred yards. Only the flood of rain, pouring down even more heavily than before, slowed him to a steadier pace.

The oncoming storm had topped the rim of the valley.

A quarter of a mile farther on they encountered a new difficulty. Rounding a sharp curve on a sloping hillside, they came suddenly upon another fallen tree blocking the road. Beyond it, a truck had been halted. There was no room to pass, even for Snow.

Ken swung to the ground and passed the slippery reins forward over the horse's head. Snow shivered and stared about him with white-rimmed eyes, but he followed as Ken plunged downhill through dripping bushes below the upflung roots of the great tree. When they regained the road on the other side, Snow seemed a little less nervous. Ken stood in the rain for a moment to pat him before he swung into the saddle again.

As they passed the truck, he noticed that it was empty. Up on the hill-side he saw that the two men who had been riding in it had taken shelter in an open shed. They waved to him and he tossed up an arm in reply.

For a mile the road was open and empty and there was only the steady pelting of the rain to worry about. The wind was still fierce and strong, however, and ahead of them beyond the clear stretch there was a place where the road was lined on both sides with a heavy growth of trees. Ken slowed to a walk. He saw now how good Uncle Ira's advice had been. The treetops tossed and clashed in the wild gusts of wind, and the dark road under the trees was littered with leaves and twigs and whole branches.

Snow seemed to sense the danger. For the first time since they had started, he came to a full stop of his own accord. Ken stared around. There was no way to circle the wooded stretch. On one side the trees extended a quarter of a mile down to the river and on the other far up the mountain-side. He patted Snow's neck and murmured an encouragement that he did not feel. They would have to go straight through the dim tree-shadowed stretch of road. The darkness of the storm made it seem even more murky and ominous.

Ken urged Snow forward under the trees. It was hard to resist the temptation to dash through at full speed. He reined the horse firmly down to a steady trot and watched sharply for dangling limbs and falling branches overhead. Underneath the stormy canopy the rain and wind ceased to bother them, but there was a steady roaring through the storm-lashed treetops high above. Ken wiped the trickling rain from his face with a wet hand and stared at the leaky roof that stretched before him.

Once Snow shied and reared at a split branch hanging from a tree that shook and quivered alarmingly as the tree swayed in the wind. Ken soothed him with hand and voice and coaxed him past it.

The end of the grove was visible as a brightness on the road ahead when suddenly there was a fierce cracking and splintering sound almost directly above them. Ken did not pause to look. Almost by instinct he urged the stallion forward and slapped the rains loose on his neck. Snow quivered at the sound and sprang forward instantly into a full gallop. Ken sensed rather than saw the huge bulk of a broken branch bearing down almost on his back. An instant later the crash of its fall sent Snow forward in uncontrolled flight.

The boy made no effort to restrain him, but leaned forward and murmured words of praise in a voice that he tried to keep calm. Running out his fright was the best thing for Snow under the circumstances. They flashed forward and in a few moments they were out in the storm again.

As they broke into the open, the rain and wind were upon them. The first gust caught Ken with his face raised to the sky; it tore the sou'wester cap from his head and sent it flying off into a field. He stared at it over his shoulder as it went spinning and rolling away before the wind. It would be more trouble than it was worth to go after it now.

In half a minute he missed it. There was rain in his eyes, and his soaked hair straggled down on his forehead. A steady trickle of water began running down the back of his neck. He lowered his head against the wind and peered ahead as Snow slowed to a trot. There was only a little more than a mile to go, and he might be able to cut that down a bit. The highway took a long sweeping curve into the village. He could leave it and cut across the open fields without too much trouble. He ran over the route in his mind. There were only two fences and both had gates, but there was a narrow little brook. It might be swollen by the rain, but it would hardly be too deep for Snow to wade.

There was an open barway ahead. Ken tapped Snow's neck with the near rein and guided him into it. He could have sworn that the big horse gave a sigh of relief as he felt the soft ground under his hoofs and saw the clear fields ahead of him. Snow broke into a long easy canter without any signal from his rider.

Now that there was no immediate danger, Ken found his mind turning to the purpose of his hazardous journey. Aunt Martha's illness had been a nagging worry at the back of his mind through the whole ride and, now that he faced it, he felt a stirring of real fear. Automatically, he urged Snow into a full gallop.

They topped a little hill and saw the brook in the fold of the field before them. It had widened unbelievably, but it was still shallow. Snow swept down the slope and splashed through it with no distaste at all. He laboured up the farther hill and swung without any guiding rein towards the wide gate. He stood breathing hard while Ken climbed stiffly to the ground and threw the gate open. After they had walked through and Ken was in the saddle again, having closed the gate behind him, Snow set off at a trot, as though he realized the need to hurry.

At the top of the next rise they caught their first glimpse of the village houses. Snow moved up into a canter at the sight and did not slow his pace until he reached the last fence before the outskirts of the little settlement. When that was behind them, Ken felt that his journey was half completed. He headed across the field and in a couple of minutes was out once more upon the highway. Before him lay the main street. It was a battered shambles. Two huge trees had been felled by the storm and now lay across the pavement.

One had been completely torn up, and a wall of tangled roots and muddy earth rose twenty feet in the air at the end of the fallen trunk. The other had been broken off by the force of the wind at a point where it separated into two branches, and each of the huge limbs had fallen a different way. One had smashed the porch of a house and the other lay angled across the road.

Snow was uneasy in these strange surroundings. Although there was no human being in sight along the rain-swept street, he sensed that this was a closed-in place. He was tired, but he managed to dance and fling his head nervously around as they moved into town between the two rows of houses. Realizing that he was afraid, Ken swung to the ground at once and took him by the bridle. He talked soothingly over his shoulder to the big stallion as he led him down the street to the doctor's house. Snow went more willingly when he could see his master walking calmly before him.

Ken was stiff and sore from the effort of controlling the horse and tense from the strain of worry. He was glad to use his legs for a change and get a little circulation in his cramped muscles. He realized, too, how wet he was when he could feel the water squishing in his sodden shoes.

He turned into the doctor's driveway and looked for a place where he could keep Snow out of the rain while he went in for the medicine. There was an open shed that had been used for carriages once. He led the horse in and looped his reins loosely on a nail. With a pat on the neck and a word of praise, he turned and hurried towards the house.

Ken rapped on the door of the doctor's waiting-room and then turned the knob impatiently and strode in. The door to the kitchen was open and there was a bustle of movement in there.

'Just a minute,' called a calm voice. 'I'll be right out.'

Ken stepped back with a momentary start as he looked around the room. A young man with a bloodstained bandage around his forearm slumped in a chair. His face was pale and the corners of his mouth drooped with the obvious signs of shock.

'Hurt bad?' murmured Ken sympathetically.

The man closed his eyes and shook his head slightly, as though it ached. 'A tree branch out there scraped me.'

'A big one nearly hit me down the road,' said Ken.

'This one darn' near missed me.' He managed a sickly smile and Ken grinned back at him.

The doctor's motherly wife came bustling in with a steaming cup in her hand for the injured man. 'Now drink this right down and you'll feel a lot better. That's a nasty cut, but you're pretty lucky all around. And what can I do for you?' She looked at Ken and then answered her own question. 'Oh, you're Martha Benton's nephew. This is the medicine—right here in this bottle. And give her double the usual dose, the doctor says.'

'Can you wrap it in a cloth or something so it won't break if I fall?'

She stepped to the kitchen door and rolled the bottle deftly in a dish towel she snatched from a rack.

'Stick it inside your shirt and button it up,' she said as she handed it to him. 'And don't you let Martha stir until the doctor sees her.' She turned briskly away as a boy came in the door to report that the doctor wanted more bandages.

Ken mumbled his thanks to her departing back and went out into the rain. Snow was watching him from the shed and, as he ran forward to him, the big horse tossed his head and nickered a welcome. In a moment Ken was in the saddle and cantering down the empty street. He heaved a sigh of relief; since he had gotten into town, he certainly should be able to get back.

When he was clear of the houses, he turned into the open fields again. He ran over the route in his mind as Snow splashed through the spongy grass. If they could only avoid that stretch of woods, the trip back should be quick and easy. The worst of the wind was over, but there were still gusts that might bring down a weakened branch or tree.

There was only one other way to do it. He could stick to the open fields, as Uncle Ira had advised, and cross the little river at the bridge that led to Johnsons' wood lot. There were a few fences that way and he would have to open and close the gates, but there were no stretches of woods that he could not go around.

He made up his mind at once and swung off at an angle to the right, leaving the road farther behind him. The gusty wind was almost at his back now, and Snow went as willingly as he could across the soggy fields. The big horse no longer had the spring to his legs that had made the first part of the trip so swift. Ken, too, was beginning to tire. He shivered as the rain worked down his neck and across his chest and shoulders. He was soaked to the skin, for the poncho was not much help without the hat.

All about them were signs of the storm. They passed a field of corn that had been beaten almost flat by the force of wind and rain. Farther on they skirted the edges of a maple grove. Several trees were down in tangled ruins and the sugar house had been unroofed. In the low places among the fields the water lay in wide grey lakes, their surfaces dotted by the threshing rain.

The lightning was no longer close, but far ahead they could see the bright flashes on the slopes of Green Mountain and hear the peals of thunder rolling and rumbling like a distant artillery battle.

Snow toiled valiantly up the last slope before the river. Almost at the summit of the little rise was a straggling fence. Ken wearily dismounted, opened the gate, and walked through beside Snow. It was no longer necessary to hold his reins; he was far too tired to be skittish. After Ken had swung into the saddle again, a dozen strides brought them to the top of the hill. Now the narrow plank bridge across the river was in plain sight. Ken saw, to his dismay, that it was blocked by a stalled truck. Hastily he urged Snow forward. As they cantered down the gentle slope to the river, he could see at a glance what had happened, although there was no one there to tell him. The truck's hood had been propped open to cool the labouring motor as it hauled the heavy load of chained logs up from the wood lot. Then the storm had struck suddenly and literally drowned the engine.

Ken did not have to stop Snow. He halted of his own accord at the bridge. There was no way of passing. Ken could have got over on foot, clinging to the sides of the wide truck, but there was no room for a horse.

Underneath the span the little river ran swift and dark. Half a mile downstream there was a shallow riffle, but it was bordered by thick, high brush and scrub growth. Upstream there was no crossing nearer than the bridge they had used on the way to the village, and that would mean a wide detour.

Ken slumped in the saddle, discouraged. He should have risked the dangers of the tree-lined road; it would have been quicker in the long run. He surveyed the river, about fifty feet wide at this point. It wasn't deep—only eight or ten feet at the most—but they were both tired. He was afraid, too, that the shock of cold water on the steaming horse might harm him seriously.

The sky darkened again as a heavier downpour drummed loudly on the cab of the abandoned truck. Snow stiffened and rolled his eyes. He seemed to sense the danger ahead.

Ken made up his mind. To turn back might be as dangerous as to try the crossing, and going ahead would be much quicker. The medicine had to reach Aunt Martha as soon as possible; that was all that really mattered.

He slid out of the saddle, looped the reins over his arm, and trudged along the bank with Snow plodding warily behind him. A dozen yards downstream he found a place where he could see bottom through the turbid water. He considered for a moment and then shrugged the poncho off over his head and tossed it to the ground. It would be better not to have anything that would hamper the swing of his arms.

'Let's go, boy!' He patted Snow's wet shoulder, gave a gentle tug on the reins, and stepped boldly into the water. It was much colder than he had expected. He was glad to stop for a moment to coax Snow to follow him. The horse stared gravely at him for a moment and then moved clumsily down the bank, setting his hoofs before him with care. He splashed in, sliding a little on the round stones of the stream bed.

Ken waded forward into deeper water and at once he felt the power of the current as it tugged strongly at his knees. Then the reins tightened around his arm and he looked back. Snow had braced his feet obstinately and was rolling his eyes. He laid back his ears uneasily and refused to move. Ken waded back to the bank and patted the big fellow. He would have to ride him in; he should have remembered that before. He swung himself heavily into the saddle, shivering as the wind struck his wet legs.

'Come on, boy!' he urged. 'This is the last lap.'

Snow moved forward more confidently. He waded far out into the swirling water before he began to swim. Through his clothes Ken felt the water lap coldly at his stomach. Deciding that he could take some of the work off Snow, he slipped his feet free of the stirrups, dropped the reins, and pushed himself clear of the horse on the upstream side. He buried his face in the cold water and struck out strongly.

Suddenly he felt something clutch at his foot, dragging him strongly down. After a split second of unthinking panic he realized that it must be a sunken bough drifting downstream. He kicked out strongly to clear himself, flailing at the water. The bough was bigger than he thought. Before he knew it, a tough branch struck across the back of his knees and he was pulled underwater by the force of his own kicking. He gulped a hasty mouthful of air as he went down, but he knew he couldn't hold it long. He tried to turn upstream; if he were carried down under Snow's threshing hoofs he might never come up at all.

It was an impossible task. The heavy bough dragged him steadily with it. His head was singing and his chest burning, when one groping hand touched metal. A stirrup! He clutched it with both hands and felt Snow surge powerfully forward. The sunken bough had struck against him, too, but his magnificent strength was more than a match for it. In half a dozen strides he reached shallow water, dragging Ken with him. Gasping and choking, the boy stood waist-deep in the water and gratefully filled his lungs with air. Snow plunged onward and slipped and scrambled up the muddy bank. He stood there, shivering and miserable, as Ken slowly waded ashore behind him.

Ken checked the safety of the medicine bottle inside his dripping shirt and then stroked the big horse affectionately before mounting. He felt that he owed him some special expression of thanks for that last half-minute in the chilly waters of the stream. Then he pulled himself into the wet saddle and turned Snow's head towards the farm. His spirits began to rise now; this really was the last lap.

Snow was a very tired horse as he plodded up the little rise beyond the river. Ken hated to do it, but he urged him into a stiff trot to warm him up a little. There was a clear half-mile of open fields ahead and the big stallion realized the nearness of home. When the ground levelled out, he moved into a canter, heading eagerly towards the distant plume of wind-flattened chimney smoke that marked the farm. The rain was still falling steadily, but it seemed lighter overhead.

Ken realized suddenly that he was very hungry. It had been nearly dinner-time when the storm struck, and he had put in a good morning's work before that. When they reached a gate, he leaped down to open it and remounted at once. He could close it later.

As they raced on over the last meadow, Ken felt almost cheerful in spite of his chattering teeth and sodden clothes. Taking a straight line for the stable, Snow swerved wilfully away from the direction of the gate and faced the fence boldly. Ken leaned forward with a loose rein and urged him forward with his voice alone, gripping hard with his knees as the horse rose to the jump. They landed cleanly, but Snow skidded and staggered on the wet footing, and the stretched girth gave just a few inches. Ken went sailing over his head and sprawled in a puddle, his shoulder ploughing the mud.

He got up on his hands and knees and shook his head to clear it. His first thought was for the medicine; it was safe inside the sodden towel. He got to his feet and managed a mud-streaked grin at Snow, who stood with bowed head, staring at him. Together they trudged across the puddle-dotted barnyard to the house.

Uncle Ira met them half-way, his face worried. 'You hurt?' he demanded.

At the same instant Ken asked, 'How's Aunt Martha?'

'She's a lot better. She's been asking for you. Called me down for letting you go out in this weather.'

Ken smiled contentedly as he handed over the medicine and repeated the doctor's instructions. If Aunt Martha was talking like that, she was probably out of danger.

Uncle Ira trotted back to the house through the rain, and Ken went to the stable. He rubbed Snow down with a blanket, pausing only occasionally to rest his aching shoulder. Butch and Babe watched curiously, as though they wondered why their stablemate was receiving such careful attention and such floods of praise.

He was almost finished when the stable door opened. Uncle Ira stepped in with a steaming kettle in his hand.

'Your aunt says I'm to give Snow a hot mash and send you right in to get some dry clothes on.' He set the kettle carefully on the floor. 'There's some hot soup on the stove and if you're not in there eating it in five minutes, she says she's coming out after you.'

'I've got to finish taking care of Snow,' insisted Ken wearily.

Uncle Ira gently took the blanket out of his hands. 'If Aunt Martha says she's coming after you, she means it. Now you go in there and get some dry clothes on. I left them on a chair in the kitchen.'

Ken didn't feel like disagreeing. He had the light-headed feeling that comes with hunger and semi-exhaustion.

Half an hour later Uncle Ira found him seated beside the kitchen stove finishing his third bowl of soup. His wet clothes and a soggy towel lay in a heap on the floor. He looked dry and comfortable and his face was clean.

'How about taking a little ride after the rain lets up?' joked his uncle.

Ken grinned cheerfully. 'I believe I'll have another bowl of that soup first.' He started to ladle it out and then stopped. 'You know, Uncle Ira, when I came in Aunt Martha called out that she was just getting up to come after me. Do you think she'd have done that?'

'Well, I'll tell you,' answered his uncle. 'When she had

pneumonia one winter, she got up out of bed to clean the windows in her room while she was waiting for the doctor. She said they were a disgrace.' Uncle Ira shook his head dubiously. 'Your aunt's a very determined woman.'

Acknowledgments

The publishers would like to extend their grateful thanks to the following authors, publishers and others for kindly granting them permission to reproduce the extracts and stories included in this anthology.

THE FORTY POUND PONY from *Fly-By-Night* by K. M. Peyton, published by Oxford University Press. © 1968 K. M. Peyton. Reprinted by permission of Oxford University Press.

THE OLD GREY MARE from *The Mustangs* by J. Frank Dobie. © 1952 J. Frank Dobie. Reprinted by permission of Little, Brown & Co.

MY FRIEND FLICKA by Mary O'Hara. © 1941 *Story Magazine*. Reprinted by permission of Paul R. Reynolds, Inc.

THE GIPSIES' PONY from *All Creatures Great and Small* by James Herriot, published by Michael Joseph. Reprinted by permission of David Higham Associates Ltd.

HOLLYWOOD HORSES from *Movie Horses* by Anthony Amaral, published by The Bobbs-Merrill Co. Inc. © 1967 Anthony Amaral. Reprinted by permission of The Bobbs-Merrill Co. Inc and J. M. Dent & Sons Ltd.

THE HAUNTED HUNT by R. J. Richardson, from *Strange Stories of The Chase* edited by the Countess of Feversham. Reprinted by permission of the Countess of Feversham and Geoffrey Bless Ltd.

MARENGO AND COPENHAGEN from *Horses of Renown* by Stella A. Walker, Country Life Books Ltd. Reprinted by permission of the Hamlyn Publishing Group Ltd.

CARROT FOR A CHESTNUT by Dick Francis. Reprinted by permission of the author.

THE PONY'S SIXTH SENSE from *Pit Pony Heroes* by Eric Squires, published by David and Charles. Reprinted by permission of Mrs Sylvia Ball.

THE LITTLE HORSES by Shirley Marler from *The Horseman's Year, 1968* edited by Dorian Williams. Reprinted by permission of Collins Publishers.

THE GYMKHANA from *National Velvet* by Enid Bagnold. © 1935 Enid Bagnold Jones. Copyright renewed Enid Bagnold Jones. Reprinted by permission of Brandt & Brandt, Inc. and William Heinemann Ltd.

A EUROPEAN TITLE from *Princess Anne and Mark Phillips – Talking About Horses* with Genevieve Murphy, published by Hutchinson/Stanley Paul & Co. Ltd. Reprinted by permission of the Hutchinson Publishing Group.

THE CONNEMARA DONKEY from *The Little Bookroom* by Eleanor Farjeon, published by Oxford University Press, 1955. Reprinted by permission of David Higham Associates Ltd.

THE COOP from *Educated Evans* by Edgar Wallace. Reprinted by permission of Miss Penelope Wallace.

BAREBACK from *A Horse Came Running* by Meindert DeJong. © 1970 Meindert DeJong. Reprinted by permission of Lutterworth Press and Macmillan Publishers, Inc.

EBONY JOINS THE CIRCUS from *Black Ebony* by Josephine Pullein-Thompson, from the volume *Black Ebony's Clan*, published by Hodder & Stoughton Children's Books. Reprinted by permission of the author and publisher.

THE QUEEN MEETS THE LIPIZZANERS from *My Dancing White Horses* by Alois Podhajsky. Reprinted by permission of George G. Harrap & Co. Ltd.

SILVER BLAZE from *The Memoirs of Sherlock Holmes* by Sir Arthur Conan Doyle. Reprinted by permission of John Murray Ltd. and André Milos.

A HORRIBLY HORSEY DAUGHTER by Josephine Pullein-Thompson. Reprinted by permission of the author with acknowledgments to the *Pony Club Annual*.

JUMPER from the book *Jumper* by Nicholas Kalashnikoff, published by Oxford University Press and Charles Scribner's Sons. Reprinted by permission of Oxford University Press, Laurence Pollinger and Joan Daves.

FOLLYFOOT FARM from the book *Follyfoot Farm* by Monica Dickens, published by William Heinemann Ltd. © Monica Dickens. Reprinted by permission of the author and publisher.

RED RUM'S FIRST NATIONAL from *Red Rum* by Ivor Herbert, published by William Luscombe. Reprinted by permission of David Higham Associates Ltd.

SWEETBRIAR TURNS A SOMERSAULT from *Flambards* by K. M. Peyton, published by Oxford University Press. © 1967 K. M. Peyton. Reprinted by permission of Oxford University Press.

SHASTA SETS OUT ON HIS TRAVELS from *The Horse And His Boy* by C. S. Lewis. Reprinted by permission of Collins Publishers and Macmillan Publishing Co. Inc.

INTERNATIONAL SHOW JUMPING from *Jump For Joy* by Pat Smythe. Reprinted by permission of the author and John Farquharson Ltd.

OPERATION SIPPACIK from the book *Operation Sippacik* by Rumer Godden. Reprinted by permission of Macmillan Publishing Group and Viking Penguin Inc.

THE COWBOY, an extract originally entitled 'Clothes, Guns and Horses' from *The Cowboy* by Vincent Paul Rennert. © 1966 the Macmillan Publishing Co. Inc. Reprinted by permission of the Macmillan Publishing Co. Inc.

THE STORM BREAKS from *Snow Cloud, Stallion* by Gerald Raftery. © 1951 Gerald Raftery. Reprinted by permission of The Bodley Head and William Morrow & Co. Inc.

Designed by Astrid Publishing Consultants

Illustrations by Reginald Gray